PENGUIN MODERN CLASSICS

A FAMILY AND A FORTUNE

Ivy Compton-Burnett once wrote: 'I have had such an uneventful life that there is little information to give. I was educated with my brothers in the country as a child, and later went to Holloway College, and took a degree in Classics. I lived with my family when I was quite young but for most of my life have had my own flat in London. I see a good deal of a good many friends, not all of them writing people. And there is really no more to say.'

Ivy Compton-Burnett died in 1969 and in her obituary *The Times* wrote: 'Her work, from the first appreciated by a few discerning admirers, was for many years dismissed by the critics and by the general public as the object of a modish cult. The bare, stylized dialogue needs a closer attention than most novel-readers are prepared to give. But the fine comedy and the deep humanity of her books in later years achieved a wider recognition', and Pamela Hansford-Johnson said of her: 'Writing of a dying age she stands apart from the mainstream of English fiction. She is not an easy writer nor a consoling one. Her work is an arras of embroidered concealments beneath which the cat's sharp claws flash out and are withdrawn, behind which the bitter quarrels of the soul are conducted "tiffishly", as if cruelty and revenge and desire, the very heart itself, were all trivial compared with the great going clock of society, ticking on implacably for ever behind the clotted veilings.'

In 1925 she published *Pastors and Masters*, which began the series of novels in which she created a chilling world of late Victorian upper-class people; other titles include, *Daughters and Sons*, *Brothers and Sisters*, *Elders and Betters*, *Manservant and Maidservant*, *Two Worlds and their Ways*, *Darkness and Day*, *Parents and Children*, *Mother and Son*, *A House and its Head*, *A Father and His Fate*, *A Heritage and its History*, *The Present and the Past* and *A God and his Gifts*.

Ivy Compton-Burnett

A Family and a Fortune

PENGUIN BOOKS

Penguin Books Ltd, Harmondsworth, Middlesex, England
Penguin Books, 625 Madison Avenue, New York, New York 10022, U.S.A.
Penguin Books Australia Ltd, Ringwood, Victoria, Australia
Penguin Books Canada Ltd, 2801 John Street, Markham, Ontario, Canada L3R 1B4
Penguin Books (N.Z.) Ltd, 182–190 Wairau Road, Auckland 10, New Zealand

First published by Victor Gollancz Ltd 1939
Published in Penguin Books 1962
Reprinted in Penguin Modern Classics 1983

Made and printed in Great Britain by
Richard Clay (The Chaucer Press) Ltd,
Bungay, Suffolk

CHAPTER I

"JUSTINE, I HAVE told you that I do not like the coffee touched until I come down. How can I remember who has had it, and manage about the second cups, if it is taken out of my hands? I don't know how many times I have asked you to leave it alone."

"A good many, Mother dear, but you tend to be rather a laggard. When the poor boys sit in thirsty patience it quite goes to my heart."

"It would not hurt them to wait a few minutes. Your father and your uncle are not down yet. There is no such hurry."

Mrs. Gaveston dealt with the coffee with small, pale, stiff hands, looking with querulous affection at her children and signing in a somewhat strained manner to the servant to take the cups. She had rather uncertain movements and made one or two mistakes, which she rectified with a sort of distracted precision. She lifted her face for her children's greetings with an air of forgetting the observance as each one passed, and of being reminded of it by the next. She was a rather tall, very pale woman of about sixty, who somehow gave the impression of being small, and whose spareness of build was without the wiriness supposed to accompany it. She had wavy, grey hair, a long, narrow chin, long, narrow, dark eyes in a stiff, narrow, handsome face, and a permanent air of being held from her normal interest by some passing strain or distraction.

Her only daughter and eldest child was shorter and stronger in build, with clear, light eyes, a fuller face, pleasant features which seemed to be without a plan, and a likeness to her mother which was seen at once to overlie a great difference. She looked as much less than her thirty years as her mother looked more than her double number. Strangers often took Blanche for her children's grandmother, a fact which she had not suspected and would not have believed. She considered that she looked young for her age, or rather assumed that she did so, as she also took it for granted that she was successful, intelligent and admired, an attitude which came from a sort of natural buoyancy and had little meaning. She really gave little thought to herself and could almost be said to live for others. Her children had for her a lively, if not the deepest affection, and she was more than satisfied with it. She would hardly have recognised the deepest feeling, as she had never experienced or inspired it.

The three sons kissed their mother and returned to their seats. The eldest was a short, solid young man of twenty-eight, with large, grey eyes, the dark, curly hair his mother had had in her youth, a broader, blunter but perhaps more attractive face, and an air of being reasonably at peace with himself and his world. The second, Clement, was taller and thinner, with straight hair and darker skin, and looked the same age as Mark, although two years younger. He had cold, dark eyes, a cold, aloof expression, and a definite resemblance in feature to his mother. He seemed to look what he was, and neither to require nor repay observation. Aubrey, the youngest by eleven years, was a boy of fifteen, small and plain to the point of being odd and undersized, with a one-sided smile which often called for the abused term of grin, an indefinable lack of balance in movement, and a reputed backwardness which did not actually extend beyond his books. They had all been named after god-parents from whom their mother had vague expectations for them. The expectations had not materialised, but Blanche had been too indefinite about them to resent it, or even actually to imagine their doing so, and felt less disappointment than vague appreciation that they had been possible.

Justine and Mark conversed with goodwill and ate with an ordinary appetite; Clement did not converse and showed an excellent one; Blanche watched her children's plates and made as good a meal as she could without giving her attention to it; and Aubrey sat and swung his feet and did not speak or eat.

"Are you not enjoying your breakfast, my dear?" said Blanche, in a faintly outraged and incredulous manner, which was possibly due to surprise that this should happen again after so many times.

Aubrey gave her a smile, or gave a smile in her direction. The smile seemed to relate to his own thoughts, and did so.

"Wake up, little boy," said Justine, leaning across to tap his shoulder.

Her brother gave a smile of another kind, intended to show that he was at ease under this treatment.

"If I have some toast, perhaps I shall grow tall enough to go to school."

Aubrey's life at home with a tutor was a source of mingled embarrassment and content, and the hope that he would eventually go to Eton like his brothers, was held by everyone but himself. Everyone knew his age of fifteen, but he alone realised it, and knew that the likelihood of a normal school life was getting less. Blanche regarded him as a young child, Justine as a slightly older one, Mark as an innocently ludicrous exception to a normal family, and Clement as a natural object of uneasiness and distaste. Aubrey saw his family as they were, having had full opportunity to know them, and made his own use of it.

"This omelette is surely a breach with tradition," said Clement.

"It is not," said Blanche, instantly and without looking at it or following the words beyond recognising a criticism. "It is very good and very wholesome."

"Clement speaks from experience," said Aubrey, glancing at his brother's plate.

"Why do you eat it, if you don't like it?" said Mark, with no sting in his tone.

"I am hungry; I must eat something."

"There is ham," said Justine.

"Clement will eat the flesh of the pig," said Aubrey.

"It is certainly odd that civilised people should have it on their tables," said his brother.

"Do uncivilised people have things on tables?"

"Now, little boy, don't try to be clever," said Justine, in automatic reproof, beginning to cut the ham.

"Justine understands Clement," said Aubrey.

"Well, I know you all in and out. After all, I ought, having practically brought you all up."

"Well, hardly that, dear," said Blanche, looking at her daughter with the contraction of her eyes which marked her disagreement. "You were only two when Mark was born. It is I who have brought up the four of you, as is natural."

"Well, well, have it your own way, little Mother."

"It is not only Mother's way. It is the way of the world," said Mark.

"Would some ham make me grow?" said Aubrey. "I am afraid my size is really worrying for Clement."

"What does it matter on what scale Aubrey is?" said the latter.

"I should always be your little brother. So you do not mind."

"Always Mother's little boy," said Blanche, taking Aubrey's hand.

"Mother's hand looks lily-white in my brown, boyish one."

"Don't let us sit bickering all through breakfast," said Justine, in an absent tone.

"We are surely not doing that, dear," said Blanche, her eyes again contracting. "We are only having some conversation. We can't all think alike about everything."

"But you do all agree that I am hardly up to my age," said Aubrey. "Not that there is anything to take hold of."

"I thought the conversation was tending to a bickering note."

"I don't think it was, dear. I do not know what you mean."

"Well, then, neither do I, little Mother. I was only talking at random."

"Suppose Justine's voice was to be stilled!" said Aubrey. "What should we feel about it then?"

"Don't say such things," said his mother, turning on him sharply.

"I am not so very late," said a voice at the door. "You will be able to feel that you had me in the first hour of your day."

"Well, Uncle dear," said Justine, accepting the normal entrance of a member of the house.

"Good-morning, good-morning," said another voice. "Good-morning, Blanche; good-morning, Justine; good-morning, my sons. Good-morning."

"Good-morning, Father dear," said Justine, leaning forward to adjust the cups for her mother.

The two brothers who entered were tall, lean men in the earlier fifties, the elder being the squire of the neighbourhood, or rather the descendant of men who had held this title together with a larger estate. He had thick, straight, speckled hair, speckled, hazel eyes, vaguely speckled clothes, a long, solid nose and chin, a look of having more bone and less flesh than other men, a face and hands which would have been called bronzed, if there had been anything in the English climate of his home to have this effect on them, and a suggestion of utter honesty which he had transmitted to his daughter. The younger brother, Dudley, was of the same height and lighter build, and was said to be a caricature of the elder, and was so in the sense that his face was cast in a similar mould and had its own deviations from it. His nose was less straight; his eyes were not entirely on a line, and had a hint of his youngest nephew's; and his skin was rather pale than bronzed, though the pair had lived in the same place, even in the same house all their lives. It was a question in the neighbourhood which brother looked the more distinguished, and it was thought a subtle judgement to decide for Dudley. The truth was that Dudley looked the more distinguished when he was seen with his brother, and Edgar by himself, Dudley being dependent on Edgar's setting of the type, and Edgar affording the less reward to a real comparison. The butler who followed them into the room, bearing a dish to replace the cold one, was a round-featured, high-coloured man about thirty, of the same height as his masters but in other respects very different.

"Good-morning, sir; good-morning, sir," he said with a slight, separate bow to each.

"Good-morning," said Dudley.

"Good-morning, good-morning," said Edgar, taking no longer over the words.

Blanche looked up in a daily disapproval of Jellamy's initiative in speech, which had never been definite enough to be expressed.

"It is a very unsettled day, sir."

"Yes, it appears to be," said Edgar; "yes, it is unsettled."

"The atmosphere is humid, sir."

"Yes, humid; yes, it seems to be damp."

Edgar seldom made a definite statement. It was as if he feared to commit himself to something that was not the utter truth.

"I love a conversation between Father and Jellamy," said Justine, in an undertone.

Blanche looked up with an expression which merely said that she did not share the feeling.

"The plaster is peeling off the walls in the hall, sir."

"I will come some time and see. I will try to remember to come and look at it."

"I meant the servants' hall, sir," said Jellamy, as if his master would hardly penetrate to this point.

"That room you all use to sit in? The one that used to have a sink in it?"

"The sink has been removed, sir. It is now put to the individual purpose."

"That will do, Jellamy, thank you," said Blanche, who disliked the presence of servants at meals. "If we want you again we will ring."

"It would be a good plan to remove all sinks and make all rooms into halls," said Dudley. "It would send up the standard of things."

"In this poor old world," said Aubrey.

"How did you sleep, Father?" said Justine.

"Very well, my dear; I think I can say well. I slept for some hours. I hope you have a good account to give."

"Oh, don't ask about the sleep of a healthy young woman, Father. Trust you to worry about the sleep of your only daughter!" Edgar flinched in proportion to his doubt how far this confidence was justified. "It is your sleep that matters, and I am not half satisfied about it."

"The young need sleep, my dear."

"Oh, I am not as young as all that. A ripe thirty, and all my years lived to the full! I would not have missed out one of them. I don't rank myself with the callow young any longer."

"Always Father's little girl," murmured Aubrey.

"What, my son?" said Edgar.

"I still rank myself with the young," said Aubrey, as if repeating what he had said. "I think I had better until I go to school. Anything else would make me look silly, and Clement would not like me to look that."

"Get on with your breakfast, little boy," said Justine. "Straight on and not another word until you have finished."

"I was making my little effort to keep the ball of conversation rolling. Every little counts."

"So it does, dear, and with all our hearts we acknowledge it."

Blanche smiled from her eldest to her youngest child in appreciation of their feeling.

"Aubrey meets with continual success," said Mark. "He is indeed a kind of success in himself."

"What kind?" said Clement.

"Too simple, Clement," said Justine, shaking her head. "How did you sleep, Uncle?"

"Very well until I was awakened by the rain. Then I went to the window and stood looking out into the night. I see now that people really do that."

"They really shut out the air," said Clement.

"Is Clement a soured young man?" said Aubrey.

"I had a very bad night," said Blanche, in a mild, conversational tone, without complaint that no enquiry had been made of her. "I have almost forgotten what it is to have a good one."

"Poor little Mother! But you sleep in the afternoon," said Justine.

"I never do. I have my rest, of course; I could not get on without it. But I never sleep. I may close my eyes to ease them, but I am always awake."

"You were snoring yesterday, Mother," said Justine, with the insistence upon people's sleeping and giving this sign, which seems to be a human characteristic.

"No, I was not," said Blanche, with the annoyance at the course, which is unfortunately another. "I never snore even at night, so I certainly do not when I am just resting in the day."

"Mother, I tiptoed in and you did not give a sign."

"If you made no sound, and I was resting my eyes, I may not have heard you, of course."

"Anyhow a few minutes in the day do not make up for a bad night," said Mark.

"But I do not sleep in the day, even for a few minutes," said his mother in a shriller tone. "I don't know what to say to make you all understand."

"I don't know why people mind admitting to a few

minutes' sleep in the day," said Dudley, "when we all acknowledge hours at night and indeed require compassion if we do not have them."

"Who has acknowledged them?" said Clement. "It will appear that as a family we do without sleep."

"But I do not mind admitting to them," said Blanche. "What I mean is that it is not the truth. There is no point in not speaking the truth even about a trivial matter."

"I do not describe insomnia in that way," said Mark.

"Dear boy, you do understand," said Blanche, holding out her hand with an almost wild air. "You do prevent my feeling quite alone."

"Come, come, Mother, I was tactless, I admit," said Justine. "I know people hate confessing that they sleep in the day. I ought to have remembered it."

"Justine now shows tact," murmured Aubrey.

"It is possible—it seems to be possible," said Edgar, "to be resting with closed eyes and give the impression of sleep."

"You forget the snoring, Father," said Justine, in a voice so low and light as to escape her mother's ears.

"If you don't forget it too, I don't know what we are to do," said Mark, in the same manner.

"Snoring is not a proof of being asleep," said Dudley.

"But I was not snoring," said Blanche, in the easier tone of one losing grasp of a situation. "I should have known it myself. It would not be possible to be awake and make a noise and not hear it."

Justine gave an arch look at anyone who would receive it. Edgar did so as a duty and rapidly withdrew his eyes as another.

"Why do we not learn that no one ever snores under any circumstances?" said Clement.

"I wonder how the idea of snoring arose," said Mark.

"Mother, are you going to eat no more than that?" said Justine. "You are not ashamed of eating as well as of sleeping, I hope."

"There has been no question of sleeping. And I am not ashamed of either. I always eat very well and I always sleep very badly. There is no connection between them."

"You seem to be making an exception in the first matter to-day," said her husband.

"Well, it upsets me to be contradicted, Edgar, and told that I do things when I don't do them, and when I know quite well what I do, myself," said Blanche, almost flouncing in her chair.

"It certainly does, Mother dear. So we will leave it at that; that you know quite well what you do yourself."

"It seems a reasonable conclusion," said Mark.

"I believe people always know that best," said Dudley. "If we could see ourselves as others see us, we should be much more misled, though people always talk as if we ought to try to do it."

"They want us to be misled and cruelly," said his nephew.

"I don't know," said Justine. "We might often meet a good, sound, impartial judgement."

"And we know, when we have one described like that, what a dreadful judgement it is," said her uncle.

"Half the truth, the blackest of lies," said Mark.

"The whitest of lies really," said Clement. "Or there is no such thing as a white lie."

"Well, there is not," said his sister. "Truth is truth and a lie is a lie."

"What is Truth?" said Aubrey. "Has Justine told us?"

"Truth is whatever happens to be true under the circumstances," said his sister, doing so at the moment. "We ought not to mind a searchlight being turned on our inner selves, if we are honest about them."

"That is our reason," said Mark. "'Know thyself' is a most superfluous direction. We can't avoid it."

"We can only hope that no one else knows," said Dudley.

"Uncle, what nonsense!" said Justine. "You are the most transparent and genuine person, the very last to say that."

"What do you all really mean?" said Edgar, speaking rather hurriedly, as if to check any further personal description.

"I think I only mean," said his brother, "that human beings ought always to be judged very tenderly, and that no one will be as tender as themselves. 'Remember what you owe to yourself' is another piece of superfluous advice."

"But better than most advice," said Aubrey, lowering his voice as he ended. "More tender."

"Now, little boy, hurry up with your breakfast," said Justine. "Mr. Penrose will be here in a few minutes."

"To pursue his life work of improving Aubrey," said Clement.

"Clement ought to have ended with a sigh," said Aubrey. "But I daresay the work has its own unexpected rewards."

"I forget what I learned at Eton," said his uncle.

"Yes, so do I; yes, so to a great extent do I," said Edgar. "Yes, I believe I forgot the greater part of it."

"You can't really have lost it, Father," said Justine. "An education in the greatest school in the world must have left its trace. It must have contributed to your forming."

"It does not seem to matter that I can't go to school," said Aubrey. "It will be a shorter cut to the same end."

"Now, little boy, don't take that obvious line. And remember that self-education is the greatest school of all."

"And education by Penrose? What is that?"

"Say Mr. Penrose. And get on with your breakfast."

"He has only had one piece of toast," said Blanche, in a tone which suggested that it would be one of despair if the situation were not familiar. "And he is a growing boy."

"I should not describe him in those terms," said Mark.

"I should be at a loss to describe him," said Clement.

"Don't be silly," said their mother at once. "You are both of you just as difficult to describe."

"Some people defy description," said Aubrey. "Uncle and I are among them."

"There is something in it," said Justine, looking round.

"Perhaps we should not—it may be as well not to discuss people who are present," said Edgar.

"Right as usual, Father. I wish the boys would emulate you."

"Oh, I think they do, dear," said Blanche, in an automatic tone. "I see a great likeness in them both to their father. It gets more striking."

"And does no one think poor Uncle a worthy object of emulation? He is as experienced and polished a person as Father."

Edgar looked up at this swift disregard of accepted advice.

"I am a changeling," said Dudley. "Aubrey and I are very hard to get hold of."

"And you can't send a person you can't put your finger on to school," said his nephew.

"You can see that he does the next best thing," said Justine. "Off with you at once. There is Mr. Penrose on the steps. Don't keep the poor little man waiting."

"Justine refers to every other person as poor," said Clement.

"Well, I am not quite without the bowels of human compassion. The ups and downs of the world do strike me, I confess."

"Chiefly the downs."

"Well, there are more of them."

"Poor little man," murmured Aubrey, leaving his seat. "Whose little man is he? I am Justine's little boy."

"It seems—is it not rather soon after breakfast to work?" said Edgar.

"They go for a walk first, as you know, Father. It is good for Aubrey to have a little adult conversation apart from his family. I asked Mr. Penrose to make the talk educational"

"Did you, dear?" said Blanche, contracting her eyes. "I think you should leave that kind of thing to Father or me."

"Indeed I should not, Mother. And not have it done at all? That would be a nice alternative. I should do all I can for you all, as it comes into my head, as I always have and always shall. Don't try to prevent what is useful and right."

Blanche subsided under this reasonable direction.

"Now off with you both! Off to your occupations," said Justine, waving her hand towards her brothers. "I hope you have some. I have, and they will not wait."

"I am glad I have none," said Dudley. "I could not bear to have regular employment."

"Do you know what I have discovered?" said his niece. "I have discovered a likeness between our little boy and you, Uncle. A real, incontrovertible and bona fide likeness. It is no good for you all to open your eyes. I have made my discovery and will stick to it."

"I have always thought they were alike," said Blanche.

"Oh, now, Mother, that is not at all on the line. You know it has only occurred to you at this moment."

"No, I am bound to say," said Edgar, definite in the interests of justice, "that I have heard your mother point out a resemblance."

"Then dear little Mother, she has got in first, and I am the last person to grudge her the credit. So you see it, Mother? Because I am certain of it, certain. I should almost have thought that Uncle would see it himself."

"We can hardly expect him to call attention to it," said Clement.

"I am aware of it," said Dudley, "and I invite the attention of you all."

"Then I am a laggard and see things last instead of first. But I am none the less interested in them. My interest does not depend upon personal triumph. It is a much more genuine and independent thing."

"Mine is feebler, I admit," said Mark.

"Now, Mother, you will have a rest this morning to make up for your poor night. And I will drive the house on its course. You can be quite at ease."

Justine put her hand against her mother's cheek, and Blanche lifted her own hand and held it for a moment, smiling at her daughter.

"What a dear, good girl she is!" she said, as the latter left them. "What should we do without her?"

"What we do now," said Clement.

"Indeed we should not," said his mother, rounding on him at once. "We should find everything entirely different, as you know quite well."

"Indeed, indeed," said Edgar in a deliberate voice. "Indeed."

Edgar and Blanche had fallen in love thirty-one years before, in the year eighteen hundred and seventy, when Edgar was twenty-four and Blanche thirty; and now that the feeling was a memory, and a rare and even embarrassing one, Blanche regarded her husband with trust and pride and Edgar his wife with compassionate affection. It meant little that neither was ever disloyal to the other, for neither was capable of disloyalty. They had come to be rather shy of each other and were little together by day or night. It was hard to imagine how their shyness had ever been enough in abeyance to allow of their courtship and marriage, and they found it especially the case. They could only remember, and this they did as seldom as they could. Blanche seemed to wander aloof through her life, finding enough to live for in the members of her family and in her sense of pride and possession in each. It was typical of her that she regarded Dudley as a brother, and had no jealousy of her husband's relation with him.

Edgar's life was largely in his brother and the friendship which dated from their infancy. Mark helped his father in his halting and efficient management of the estate, and as the eldest son had been given no profession. Clement had gained a fellowship at Cambridge with a view to being a scholar and a don. Each brother had a faint compassion and contempt for the other's employment and prospect.

"Mother, dear," said Justine, returning to the room. "here is a letter which came for you last night and which you have not opened. There is a way to discharge your duties! I suggest that you remedy the omission."

Blanche held the letter at arm's length to read the address, while she felt for her glasses.

"It is from your grandfather," she said, adjusting the glasses and looking at her daughter over them. "It is from my father, Edgar. It is so seldom that he writes himself. Of course, he is getting an old man. He must soon begin to feel his age."

"Probably fairly soon, as he is eighty-seven," said Clement.

"Too obvious once again, Clement," said Justine. "Open the letter, Mother. You should have read it last night."

Blanche proceeded to do so at the reminder, and Edgar gave a glance of disapproval at his son, which seemed to be late as the result of his weighing its justice.

His wife's voice came suddenly and with unusual expression.

"Oh, he wants to know if the lodge is still to let. And if it is, he thinks of taking it! He would come with Matty to live here. Oh, it would be nice to have them. What a difference it would make! They want to know the lowest rent we can take, and we could not charge much to my family. I wish we could let them have it for nothing, but I suppose we must not afford that?"

There was a pause.

"We certainly should not do so," said Mark. "Things are paying badly as it is."

"It opens up quite a different life," said Justine.

"Are we qualified for it?" said her brother.

"I don't see why we should not ask a normal rent," said Clement. "They would not expect help from us in any other way, and they do not need it."

"They are not well off, dear," said Blanche, again looking over her glasses. "They have lost a good deal of their money and will have to take great care. And it would be such an advantage to have them. We must think of that."

"They think of it evidently, and intend to charge us for it. I wonder at what they value themselves."

"They ought to pay us for our presence too," said Mark. "I suppose it is worth an equal price."

"I believe I am more companionable than either of them," said Dudley.

"Oh, we ought not to talk like that even in joke," said Blanche, taking the most hopeful view of the conversation. "We ought to think what we can do to help them. They have had to give up their home, and this seems such a good solution. With my father getting old and my sister so lame, they ought to be near their relations."

"Do you consider, Mother dear, how you and Aunt Matty are likely to conduct yourselves when you are within a stone's throw?" said Justine, with deliberate dryness. "On the occasions when you have stayed with each other, rumours have come from her house, which have been confirmed in ours. Do remember that discretion is the better part of many another quality."

"Whatever do you mean? We have our own ways with each other, of course, just as all of you have, and your uncle and your father; as brothers and sisters must. But it has been nothing more."

"Edgar and I have not any," said Dudley. "I don't know how you can say so. I have a great dislike for ways; I think few things are worse. And I don't think you and your sister ought to live near to each other, if you have them."

"What an absurd way to talk! Matty and I have never disagreed. There is no need for us to treat each other as if we were strangers."

"Now, remember, Mother dear," said Justine, lifting a finger, "that there is need for just that. Treat each other as strangers and I will ask no more. I shall be utterly satisfied."

"What a way to talk!" repeated Blanche, her tone showing her really rancourless nature. "Do let us stop talking like this and think of the pleasure they will be to us."

"If they bring any happiness to you, little Mother, we welcome them from our hearts. But we are afraid that it will not be without alloy."

"I think—I have been considering," said Edgar, "I think we might suggest the rent which we should ask from a stranger, and then see what their not being strangers must cost us." He gave his deliberate smile, which did not alter his face, while his brother's, which followed it, seemed to irradiate light. "We must hope it will not be much, as we have not much to spare."

"I suppose the sums involved are small,"said Justine.

"We are running things close," said Mark. "And why should they put a price on themselves when other people do not?"

"Oh, my old father and my invalid sister!" said Blanche. "And the house has been empty for such a long time, and the rents in this county are so low."

"We shall take all that into account," said Edgar, in the tone he used to his wife, gentler and slower than to other people, as if he wished to make things clear and easy for her. "And it will tend to lower the rent."

"Then why not just ask them very little and think no more about it? I don't know why we have this kind of talk. It will be so nice to have them, and now we have made it into a subject which will always bring argument and acrimoniousness. It is a great shame." Blanche shook her shoulders and looked down with tears in her eyes.

"They want us to write at once, if Mother does not mind my looking at the letter," said Justine, assuming that this was the case. "Dear Grandpa! His writing begins to quaver. They have their plans to make."

"If his writing quavers, his rent must be low, of course," said Mark. "We are not brutes and oppressors."

Blanche looked up with a clearing face, as reason and feeling asserted themselves in her son.

"Yes, yes, we must let them know," said Edgar. "And of course it will be an advantage to have them—any benefit which comes from them will be ours. We cannot dispute it."

"We do not want to," said his daughter, "or to dispute anything else. This foretaste of such things is enough. Let us make our little sacrifice, if it must be made. We ought not to jib at it so much."

"Let us leave this aspect of the matter and turn to the others," said Mark, keeping his face grave. "Do you suppose they really know about Aubrey?"

"I don't see how they can," said Clement. "He was too young the last time they were here, for it to be recognised."

"I don't know what you mean," said Blanche, who fell into every trap. "They will be devoted to him, as people always are."

"Yes, Aubrey will be a great success, I will wager," said Justine. "We shall all of us pale beside him. You wait and see."

"I shall have the same sort of triumph," said Dudley. "They will begin by noticing my brother and find their attention gradually drawn to me."

"And then it will be all up with everyone else," said Justine, sighing. "Oh, dreadful Uncle, we all know how it can be."

"And then they will think—I will not say what. It will be for them to say it."

"Well, poor Uncle, you can't always play second fiddle."

"Yes, I can," said Dudley, his eyes on Edgar. "It is a great art and I have mastered it."

Edgar rose as though hearing a signal and went to the door, resting his arm in his brother's, and a minute later the pair appeared on the path outside the house.

"Those two tall figures!" said Justine. "It is a sight of which I can never tire. If I live to be a hundred I do not wish to see one more satisfying."

Blanche looked up and followed her daughter's eyes in proper support of her.

Mark took Clement's arm and walked up and down before his sister.

"No, away with you!" she said with a gesture. "I don't want an imitation; I don't want anything spurious. I have the real thing before my eyes."

"I like to see them walking together like that," said Blanche.

"Well, I do not, Mother. It is a mockery of something better and I see nothing about it to like."

"I am sure they are very good friends. We need not call it a mockery. It illustrates a genuine feeling, even if the action itself was a joke."

"Genuine feeling, yes, Mother, but nothing like the feeling between Father and Uncle. We must face it. You have not produced that in your family. It has skipped that generation."

Blanche looked on in an impotent way, as her daughter left the room, but appreciation replaced any other feeling on her face. She had the unusual quality of loving all her children equally, or of believing that she did. If Mark and Aubrey held the chief place in her heart, the place was available for the others when they needed it, so that she was justified in feeling that she gave it to them all. Neither she nor Clement suspected that she cared for Clement the least, and if Dudley and Aubrey knew it, it was part of that knowledge in them which was their own. Edgar would not have been surprised to hear that her second son was her favourite.

Jellamy came into the room as his mistress left it, and carried some silver to the sideboard.

"So we are to have Mr. Seaton and Miss Seaton at the lodge, sir?"

"How did you know?" said Mark. "We have only just heard."

"The same applies to me, sir," said Jellamy, speaking with truth, as he had heard at the same moment. "Miss Seaton will be a companion for the mistress, sir. The master and Mr. Dudley being so much together leaves the mistress rather by herself." Jellamy's eyes protruded over a subject which was rife in the kitchen, and had never presented itself to Blanche.

"She is never by herself," said Clement. "We all live in a chattering crowd, each of us waiting for a chance to be heard."

Luncheon found the family rather as Clement described it. Edgar sat at the head of the table, Blanche at the foot; Dudley and Justine sat on either side of the former, Mark and Clement of the latter; and Aubrey and his tutor faced each other in the middle of the board. Mr. Penrose was treated with friendliness and supplied with the best of fare, and found the family luncheon the trial of his day. He sat in a conscious rigour, which he hardly helped by starting when he was addressed, and gazing at various objects in the room with deep concentration. He was a blue-eyed, bearded, little man of forty-five, of the order known as self-made, who spoke of himself to his wife as at the top of the tree, and accepted her support when she added that he was in this position in the truest sense. He had a sharp nose, supporting misty spectacles, and neat clothes which had a good deal of black about them. He was pleasant and patient with Aubrey, and made as much progress with him as was possible in view of this circumstance, and had a great admiration for Edgar, whom he occasionally addressed.

Edgar and Dudley treated him with ordinary simplicity and never referred to him in any other spirit. Justine spoke of him with compassion, Mark with humour, Blanche with respect for his learning. Clement did not speak of him, and Aubrey saw him with the adult dryness of boys towards their teachers.

"Well, Mr. Penrose, a good morning's work?" said Justine.

"Probably on Mr. Penrose's part," said Clement.

"Yes, I am glad to say it was on the whole satisfactory, Miss Gaveston. I have no complaint to make."

"I wish we could sometimes hear some positive praise of our little boy."

"He is before you," said Mark. "Consider what you ask."

"Don't talk nonsense," said Blanche. "None of you was perfect at his age. If you tease him, I shall be very much annoyed. Have you done well yourself this morning, Clement?"

"Well enough, thank you, Mother."

"We hear some positive praise of Clement," said Aubrey.

"Clement ought to have a mediocre future before him," said Dudley, "and Aubrey a great one."

"I don't agree with this theory that early failure tends to ultimate success," said Justine. "Do you, Mr. Penrose?"

"Well, Miss Gaveston, that has undoubtedly been the sequence in some cases. But the one may not lead to the other. There may be no connection and I think it is probable that there is not."

"Dear little Aubrey!" said Blanche, looking into space. "What will he become in time?"

Mr. Penrose rested his eyes on her, and then dropped them as if to cover an answer to this question.

"That is the best of an early lack of bent," said Clement. "It leaves an open future."

"The child is father of the man," said Mark. "It is no good to shut our eyes to it."

"I cannot grow into anything," said Aubrey, "until I begin to grow. I am not big enough to be my own son yet."

Edgar laughed, and Blanche glanced from him to his son with a mild glow in her face.

"We were talking of the growth of the mind, little boy," said Justine.

"I am sure he is much taller," said Blanche.

"Mother dear, his head comes to exactly the same place on the wall. We have not moved it for a year."

"I moved it yesterday," said Aubrey, looking aside. "I have grown an inch."

"I knew he had!" said Blanche, with a triumph which did not strike anyone as disproportionate.

"If we indicate Aubrey on the wall," said Clement, "have we not dealt sufficiently with him?"

"Why do you talk about him like that? Why are you any better than he is?"

"We must now hear some more positive praise of Clement," said Aubrey.

"It need not amount to that," said his brother.

"I don't want to have him just like everyone else," said Blanche, causing Aubrey's face to change at the inexplicable attitude. "I like a little individuality. It is a definite advantage."

"A good mother likes the ugly duckling best," said Justine, coming to her mother's aid in her support of her son, and with apparent success, as the latter smiled to himself. "How do you really think he is getting along, Mr. Penrose?"

"Mr. Penrose has given us one account of him," said Edgar. "I think we will not—perhaps we will not ask him for another."

"But I think we will, Father. The account was not very definite. Unless you really want to leave the subject, in which case your only daughter will not go against you. That would not be at all to your mind. Well, have you heard, Mr. Penrose, that we are to have a family of relations at the lodge?"

"No, I have not, Miss Gaveston. I have hardly had the opportunity."

"Grandpa and Aunt Matty and Miss Griffin," said Aubrey.

"How did you know, little boy? We had the news when you had gone."

"Jellamy told me when he was setting the luncheon."

"Father, do you like Aubrey to make a companion of Jellamy?"

"Well, my dear, I think so; I do not think—I see no objection."

"Then there is none. Your word on such a matter is enough. I shall like to see poor Miss Griffin again. I wonder how she is getting on."

"Do I understand, Mr. Gaveston, that it is Mrs. Gaveston's family who is coming to the vicinity?" said Mr. Penrose.

"Yes, Mr. Penrose," said Justine, clearly. "My mother's father and sister, and the sister's companion, who has become a friend."

"My father is an old man now," said Blanche.

"Well, Mother dear, he can hardly be anything else with you—well, I will leave you the option in the matter of your own age—with a granddaughter thirty. Mr. Penrose hardly needed that information."

"And my sister is a little older than I am," continued Blanche, not looking at her daughter, though with no thought of venting annoyance. "She is an invalid from an accident, but very well in herself. I am so much looking forward to having her."

"Poor little Mother! It sounds as if you suffered from a lack of companionship. But we can't skip a generation and become your contemporaries."

"I do not want you to. I like to have my children at their stage and my sister at hers. I shall be a very rich woman."

"Well, you will, Mother dear. What a good thing you realise it! So many people do not until it is too late."

"Then they are not rich," said Clement.

"People seem very good at so many things," said Dudley, "except for not being quite in time. It seems hard that that should count so much."

"Mother will be rich in Aunt Matty," said Aubrey.

"I shall," said Blanche.

"Really, you boys contribute very tame little speeches," said Justine. "You are indifferent conversationalists."

"If you wish us to be anything else," said Clement, "you must allow us some practice."

"Do you mean that I am always talking myself? What a very ungallant speech! I will put it to the vote. Father, do you think that I talk too much?"

"No, my dear—well, it is natural for young people to talk."

"So you do. Well, I must sit down under it. But I know who will cure me; Aunt Matty. She is the person to prevent anyone from indulging in excess of talk. And I don't mean to say anything against her; I love her flow of words. But she does pour them out; there is no doubt of that."

"We all have our little idiosyncrasies," said Blanche. "We should not be human without them."

"It is a pity we have to be human," said Dudley. "Human failings, human vanity, human weakness! We don't hear the word applied to anything good. Even human nature seems a derogatory term. It is simply an excuse for everything."

"Human charity, human kindness," said Justine. "I think that gives us to think, Uncle."

"There are great examples of human nobility and sacrifice," said Blanche. "Mr. Penrose must know many of them."

"People are always so pleased about people's sacrifice," said Dudley; "I mean other people's. It is not very nice of them. I suppose it is only human."

"They are not. They can admire it without being pleased."

"So I am to write—you wish me to write to your father, my dear," said Edgar, "and say that he is welcome as a tenant at a sacrifice to be determined?"

"Yes, of course. But you need not mention the sacrifice. And I am sure we do not feel it to be that. Just say how much we want to have them."

"Father dear, I don't think we need bring out our little family problems before Mr. Penrose," said Justine. "They concern us but they do not—can hardly interest him."

"Oh, I don't think that mattered, dear," said Blanche. "Mr. Penrose will forgive us. He was kind enough to be interested."

"Yes, indeed, Mrs. Gaveston. It is a most interesting piece of news," said Mr. Penrose, relinquishing a spoon he was examining, as if to liberate his attention, which had certainly been occupied. "I must remember to tell Mrs. Penrose. She is always interested in any little piece of information about the family—in the neighbourhood. Not that this particular piece merits the term, little. From your point of view quite the contrary."

"We shall have to do up the lodge," said Blanche to her husband. "It is fortunate that it is such a good size. Matty must have remembered it. The back room will make a library for my father, and Matty will have the front one as a drawing-room. And the third room on that floor can be her bedroom, to save her the stairs. I can quite see it in my mind's eye."

"Drawing-room and library are rather gandiloquent terms for those little rooms," said Justine.

"Well, call them anything you like, dear. Sitting-room and study. It makes no difference."

"No, it makes none, Mother, but that is what we will call them."

"We need not decide," said Clement. "Aunt Matty will do that."

"Aunt Matty would never use exaggerated terms for anything to do with herself."

"There are other ways of exaggerating," said Mark.

"Mrs. Gaveston," said Mr. Penrose, balancing the spoon on his finger, to show that his words were not very serious to him, "it may interest you to hear how Mrs. Penrose and I arranged rooms on a somewhat similar scale, as I gather, as those you mention."

"Yes, we should like to hear indeed."

"Thank you very much, Mr. Penrose," said Justine, warmly, sitting forward with her eyes on Mr. Penrose's face.

"We selected large patterns for the carpets, to give an impression of space, though it might hardly be thought that the choice would have that result. And we kept the walls plain with the same purpose."

"We can have the walls plain," said Justine, "but we must use the carpets at our disposal, Mr. Penrose. We are not as fortunate as you were."

"We shall not be able to write in time for them to hear by the first post," said Blanche. "I hope it won't seem that we are in any doubt about it."

"About the sacrifice," said Dudley. "I hope not. I said that people were pleased by other people's sacrifice. They would not like them to have any hesitation in making it."

"It would be an unwilling sacrifice," said Aubrey.

"Another point to be made," continued Mr. Penrose—

"Yes, Mr. Penrose, one moment," said Justine, leaning to her father and laying a hand on his arm, while glancing back at the tutor. "It is very kind and we are so interested, but one moment. Would it not be better, Father, to send the letter into the town to catch the afternoon post? Things always get to Grandpa in the morning if we do that."

"It might be—it probably would be better. I will write directly after luncheon, or as soon as we have decided what to say. What is Mr. Penrose telling us?"

"It does not matter, Mr. Gaveston. I was only mentioning that in the experience of Mrs. Penrose and myself—it is of no consequence," said Mr. Penrose, observing that Justine had turned to her mother, and resuming the spoon.

"Indeed it is of consequence," almost called Justine, leaning towards Blanche over Aubrey and giving another backward glance.

"You have one of our seventeenth-century spoons?" said Edgar.

"Yes, Mr. Gaveston, I was wondering if it was one of them. I see it is not," said Mr. Penrose, laying down a spoon which his scrutiny had enabled him to assign to his own day. "You have some very beautiful ones, have you not?"

"They are all put away, Mr. Penrose," called Justine, in a voice which seemed to encourage Mr. Penrose with the admission of economy. "We are not allowed to use them any more. They only come out on special occasions."

"Do go and write the letter, Edgar," said Blanche.

"Poor Father, let him have his luncheon in peace."

"He has finished, dear. He is only playing with that fruit and wasting it."

"Waste not, want not, Father," said Justine, in a warning tone which seemed to be directed to Mr. Penrose's ears.

Edgar rose and left the room with his brother, and Justine's eyes followed them.

"Are they not a perfect pair, Mr. Penrose?"

"Yes, indeed, Miss Gaveston. It appears to be a most conspicuous friendship."

"What are you doing?" said Blanche, suddenly, as she perceived her elder sons amusedly regarding the youngest, whose expression of set jauntiness told her that he was nearly in tears. "You are teasing him again! I will not have it. It is mean and unmanly to torment your little brother. I am thoroughly ashamed of you both. Justine, I wonder you allow it."

"I merely did not observe it, Mother. I was talking to

you and Father. Now I certainly will not countenance it. Boys, I have a word to say."

"It is unworthy to torment someone who cannot retaliate," said Blanche, giving her daughter the basis of her homily.

"I have managed to get my own back," said Aubrey, in an easy drawl, depriving her of it.

"We were only wondering how to keep Aubrey out of Grandpa's sight and Aunt Matty's," said Mark. "A shock is bad for old and invalid people."

"You are silly boys. Why do you not keep out of their sight yourselves?" said his mother.

"That might be the best way to cover up the truth," said Mark, looking at his brother as if weighing this idea. "It would avoid any normal comparison."

"Suppose either should come upon him unawares! They have not seen him since we could hope it was a passing phase."

"A phase of what?" said Blanche. "I do not know what you mean and neither do you."

"We thought a postcript might be added to the letter," said Mark. "So that they might be a little prepared."

"Prepared for what?"

"Just something such as: 'If you see Aubrey, you will understand.' "

"Understand what?" almost screamed his mother. "You don't understand, yourselves, so naturally they would not."

"Mother, Mother dear," said Justine, laughing gently, "you are pandering to them by falling into their hands like that. Take no notice of them and they will desist. They are only trying to attract attention to themselves."

"Well, that is natural at their stage," said Aubrey.

"We did take no notice and they had reduced poor Aubrey nearly to tears," said Blanche, too lost in her partisanship of her son to observe its effect upon him.

"They are naughty boys, or, what is worse, they are

malicious young men, and I am very much annoyed with them. I did not mean that I was not."

"Then speak to them about it," said Blanche, standing back and looking with expectance born of experience from her daughter to her sons.

"Boys, boys," said Justine gravely, "this will not do, you know. Take example from that." She pointed to the garden, where Edgar and Dudley were walking arm-in-arm. "There is a spectacle of brotherhood. Look at it and take a lesson."

"So your father has not written the letter!" said Blanche.

"If you will excuse us, Mrs. Gaveston, Aubrey and I should be thinking of our walk," said Mr. Penrose, who had been uncertain whether the family had forgotten his presence.

"Yes, of course, Mr. Penrose, please do as you like," said Blanche, who had forgotten it, and even now did not completely recall it. "If he does not write it soon, it will have no chance of the post."

Aubrey went up to his brothers and linked their arms, and taking a step backwards with a jeering face, took his tutor's arm himself and walked from the room.

"Dear, dear, what a little boy!" said Justine. "I think Mr. Penrose carried that off very well."

"Edgar!" called Blanche from the window. "You are not writing that letter! And it has to go in an hour."

"We are deciding upon the terms—we are discussing the wording, my dear," said her husband, pausing and maintaining the courtesy of his voice, though he had to open his mouth to raise it. "It needs to be expressed with a certain care."

"Indeed," said Mark. "There is no need to employ any crudeness in telling Grandpa that we can't do him too much charity."

"Oh, that is all right then," said Blanche, turning from the window. "There is no question of charity. That is not the way to speak of your grandfather. It is the coachman's day out. Who had better drive the trap into the town? I have seen Jellamy drive. Would your father mind his driving the mare? I wish you would some of you listen to me, and not leave me to settle everything by myself."

"Mother, come and have your rest," said Justine, taking Blanche's arm. "I will take the trap myself. You need have no fear. I also have seen Jellamy drive, and if Father does not grudge him the particular indulgence, I do."

Blanche walked compliantly out of the room, relaxing her face and her thoughts together, and her husband and his brother passed to the library.

"I think that will express it," said Dudley. "You are to drop a sum every year and not refer to it, and feel guilty that you take money from your wife's relations for giving them a bare roof."

"I think it should be good for Blanche to have them. I hope we may think it should. I fear there may be—I fear—"

"I fear all sorts of things; I am sick with fear. But we must think what Blanche is facing. I always think that women's courage is hard on men. It seems absurd for men and women to share the same life. I simply don't know how we are to share Blanche's life in future."

"I am never sure how to address my father-in-law."

"When we speak to him, we say 'sir'. I like saying 'sir' to people. It makes me feel young and well-behaved, and I can't think of two better things, or more in tune with my personality. What a good thing that Blanche will not ask to see the letter! I have a great respect for her lack of curiosity. It is a thing I could never attain."

Dudley drafted and dictated the letter, and Edgar wrote it and submitted it for his inspection, and then suggested a game of chess. When Justine came for the letter, the brothers were sitting silent over the board. They played chess often, Dudley playing the better, but Edgar playing for the sake of the game, careless and almost unconscious of success. Justine tiptoed from the room, mutely kissing her hand towards the table.

CHAPTER II

"Is this a house or a hutch? It is meant, I suppose, for human habitation," said Blanche's father, walking about his new home. "It is well that I shall soon be gone and leave you alone in it. For it is better for one than for two, as I cannot but see."

"Come, Father, pluck up heart. You are an able-bodied man and not a crippled woman. I must not be given any more to bear. You must remember your poor invalid, though I never remind you that I am that."

"If that was not a reminder, I need not take it as one. I grant that that fall made a poor thing of you, but you want a chair to sit upon, all the more. And I don't see where we are to put one, on a first sight."

"There are plenty of chairs, Father. Let us sit down in two of them. Come, I think they have done their best. It only needed a little best for such a little home, but such as it had to be, I think it is done. And we must be as grateful as they will expect us to be." Blanche's sister put back her head and went into mirth. "This room is quite a pretty little place. So we must try to feel at home in it. We are not people to fail in courage."

Matilda Seaton was two years older than Blanche, of the same height as her sister, but of the suppler, stronger build of her niece, Justine. She had hair less grey than her sister's, a darker skin less lined, and the same narrow, dark eyes looking out with a sharper, deeper gaze. A fall from a horse had rendered her an invalid, or rather obliged her to walk with a stick, but her energy seemed to accumulate, and to work itself out at the cost of some havoc within her. Her voice was deeper than her sister's and had some sweeter tones. She appeared handsomer, though she also looked her age and her features were of the same mould. Her father admired her the more, and believed her maidenhood to be due to her invalid state, though her accident had not happened until she was middle-aged. It had done him a service in a way, as he had been at a loss to account for the position. The truth was that Matty had had many chances to marry and had not accepted them. She had never met a man whom she saw as her equal, as her conception of herself was above any human standard. She may also have had some feeling that a family would take her attention and that of others from herself. The idea that anyone could pity her found no place in her mind; there was no place there for such a feeling. Even her lameness she saw as giving a touch of tragic interest to an already remarkable impression. Oliver knew of her offers, or rather had been told of them, as his daughter kept nothing which seemed to exalt her, to herself, but he thought it normal self-respect in a woman to invent proposals if they were not forthcoming. Matty did not guess that she had not justice from her father, as he thought it wise to keep his doubt to himself, indeed knew it was. The father and daughter were less alike than they had been, for Oliver's face, once the original type, was fallen and shrunk from age. His figure was of the same size for a man as his elder daughter's for a woman, and had a touch of the awkwardness of the younger's, which was something apart from the stiffness of the old. When he was seen with Blanche and her youngest son, this lack of balance became a family trait. His wife had been some years his senior and had herself lived to an advanced age, and at her death he had been old enough to accept his daughter in her place.

"Yes, I am sure they have done what they can," said Matty, still looking round. "It is a funny little pattern on the paper. Suitable for the funny little room, I suppose. We are not to forget how we are placed. They thought it was better for us to take the plunge at once. Well, I daresay they are right. We will try to think they are. That is a lesson we shall have to learn."

"You seem to be failing at the moment," said Oliver, as Matty wiped her eyes. "I can't see that the scrawl on the paper makes much odds. And the room seems to hold two people, which is what we want of it. What are you crying about? Aren't you thankful to have a home?"

"I am not so very at the moment. I can't help thinking of the one we have left. Perhaps it shows the feeling I had for that," said Matty, putting her handkerchief away with a courageously final movement. "I shall soon be able to be myself, but it is rather a sudden difference, the little paper and all." She put her hand to her mouth in her sudden laughter. "Well, shall we say that we appreciated our old home so much? I think we may say that without being unthankful."

Oliver was silent. He had suffered from leaving his home as well as his daughter, almost feeling that he left his youth and his prime and his married life behind in it, but the lessening grasp of his age had saved him the worst. He had lived all his life on private means, and his capital had dwindled, partly in the natural course—his investments suffering from age like himself, and even in some cases succumbing like his wife—and partly because he had annually spent a portion of it. The eventual result struck him as a sudden misfortune, and he and his daughter faced their retrenchment in this spirit.

"Is that commotion to continue?" he said, as sounds of adjusting furniture came from the hall. "No one would guess that we left our possessions behind. I should not have thought that the place was large enough to allow of it."

"We must have a few necessities even in a little home. But there is less to be done than if we were to have what we have always had. That is one bright side to it."

"And you see it, do you? When did you get your glimpse?"

"Things will soon be done, and you can have your dinner," said Matty, retaliating on her father by explaining his mood. "Miss Griffin will come and tell us."

"You will eat as well as I, I suppose, and so will she. Will she be able to put up with the corner in which she finds herself?"

"It is the only home we can give her. We have to be content with it."

"I meant what I said, her corner of it," said Oliver, with a grin which recalled his youngest grandson. "I still mean what I say."

"We cannot help having had to leave our house for this one. It is not a pleasure for us."

"No, my dear, you give no sign that it is. I grant it to you. Well, Miss Griffin is a good woman not to leave us. She has indeed been a remarkable person not to do that. I cannot say what she gets out of serving us."

"Of course you can. It is quite clear. We give her a home when she has no other."

"Sell it to her for herself, I should say. I would not congratulate her on her bargain."

"It is better to stay with people who are fond of her, than to start again with strangers."

"Strangers would treat her as a stranger. That was rather in my mind. And fond of her! You may be that; I am myself. But I shouldn't be proud of your way of showing it. Indeed I am not proud of it."

"It would take her a long time to get to the same stage with another family."

"Why, that is what I meant; this stage could not come at once. But I suppose women understand each other. I can only hope it. I don't see what I can do more. But it doesn't seem enough to keep a human being at my beck and call."

"They have not come down to see us," said Matty, glancing at the time. "They have not run across from their big house to see how we are faring on our first evening in our small one. Well, I suppose they have many other claims: we must think they have." She looked again at the clock and tapped her knee with her hand, making a simultaneous movement with her foot, as if she would have tapped the ground if she had been able.

"Well, I cannot tell. But we have not been in the house above two hours."

"They are long hours when you have to sit still and hear other people about and doing, and feel how much better you could do it all, if you were as they are. They have been long ones."

"Why, so they have, child, for me as well as for you."

"Well, we must be still and go on a little longer."

"Why, so we must, and for how much longer we cannot say. But it will not help us for you to cry about it. And what is your reason? You have a home and a bed and women to wait on you, haven't you?"

"Yes, I have, and I am going to feel it. I have more than many people. But it did seem to me for a moment that people who have more still—and we must say much more—might spare a thought to us in our first isolation. It was just for the moment."

"Then it doesn't seem to you so any longer."

"No, it must not," said Matty, again concealing her handkerchief. "There shall be nothing in our minds but bright and thankful thoughts."

"Well, that will make a difference. And here is someone in the hall. So if you want to hide your handkerchief, find a place that serves your purpose. It is well that you are what you say in time."

"Well, Matty dear, well, Father dear!" said Blanche's voice, the unconscious order of the names telling its tale. "Well, here is a red letter day for us all!"

"Red letter day, when we have left our home and all we have, behind!" said Matty in a rapid aside to her father, pressing her handkerchief to her face in another spirit.

Blanche entered with outstretched arms and stumbled slightly over nothing apparent, as she hurried forward.

"Well, how do you like coming here amongst us? We like to have you so much. How are you both after your journey? I could not wait another minute to come and see."

Blanche gave her father and sister a long embrace, stooping to the latter, as she remained in her seat, and then stood back to receive her response.

"Well, how do you feel about coming to share our life?" she said, as something more was needed to produce it.

"We shall be happy in it, dear. We shall," promised Matty, rapidly using her handkerchief and hiding it. "We see that now. We did not feel quite amongst you until this moment. But we do now indeed." She took her sister's hand and lifted it to her face, as Blanche often did her daughter's.

"Sit down, my dear, sit down," said Oliver. "You give us a welcome and we do the same for you. I think there is a chair; I think there is room for three."

"Of course there is. It is a very nice little room," said Blanche, sitting down and looking round. "How do you like the little paper? Don't you think it is just the thing? It is the one the boys have in their study."

"Yes, dear, is it? Yes, it would be nice for that," said Matty, following her sister's eyes. "Just the thing, as you say. For this room in my house, and for a little, odd room in yours. It is the suitable choice."

"Don't you like it in this room, dear?" said Blanche, evidently accustomed to answering her sister's meaning rather than her words.

"Yes, yes, I do. It is best to realise that we are in a little room, and not in a big one any longer. Best to leap the gulf and have a paper like the one in the boys' study." Matty began to laugh but checked herself at once. "Far better not to try to make it like the room at home, as we might have done by ourselves. We might have tried and failed, and it is so much wiser not to do that. Yes, it was best for people to deal with it, who saw it from outside and not from within. And it was so good of you to do it for us, and it is kindly and wisely done."

"I thought you would like it so much; I did not know that you would want it like the drawing-room at home. That was so much larger that I thought it would be better to start afresh."

"So it was, dear; that is what I said."

"No, you said other things, child," said Oliver.

"That is what we are doing, starting afresh, and finding rather a task at the moment," said Matty, not looking at her father. "But we shall manage it. It is only hard at first, and we can't help it that you find us in the first stage." She touched her eyes and this time retained the handkerchief.

"Keep it, my dear," said Oliver, offering her another. "It is more convenient to you at hand."

Matty held up the handkerchief to her sister with a smile for its size, and went on as if she had not paused.

"We shall make a success of it, as you have done with the room."

"The room serves its purpose, my dear," said Oliver to Blanche. "The paper covers the walls and the plaster would not look as well without it, and what more should be done? You have managed well for us, and so we should tell you, and I do so for us both."

"Yes, if we have seemed ungrateful, we are not," said Matty, not explaining the impression. "We both thank you from our hearts. So Edgar did not come with you to see us?"

"He came with me to the door and left me. He thought we should like our first meeting by ourselves."

"He is always so thoughtful, and we have liked it indeed. And we shall like one with him as well the next time he is at our door. We have come to a place where we hope there will be so many meetings."

"Blanche is enough for us," said Oliver. "We do not want her man. Why not say that you want the whole family? You almost did say it."

"Well, I did have a thought that they might all come running down to greet the old aunt on her first night. I had almost imagined myself the centre of a family circle."

"You imagined yourself the centre! So that is what is wrong. No wonder you wanted a room like the one at home. I don't know where you would have put them."

"They could have got in quite well," said Blanche. "No doubt they will often do so. But to-night we thought you would want to be spared." She paused and seemed to yield to another impulse. "I am glad that you are so little depressed by the good-bye to the old home. We thought you might be rather upset by it." Her way of speaking with a sting seemed an echo of her sister's in a lighter medium.

"We are too affected by that to show it on the surface," said Matty. "That is not where the feeling would appear. Is that where you would look for it?"

"Then what can we see there?" said Oliver. "Your sister can find something, and does so. If that isn't where it ought to be, put it in its place."

"Edgar is coming to fetch me in an hour," said Blanche, resuming her normal manner. "You will see him then and he will see you. He is looking forward to it."

"You are only staying an hour, dear? I thought that you might have dinner with us, or we with you, on our first night."

"Why pack so much into it?" said Oliver. "There are other nights and others after those. And your sister is right that we are not fit for it. You were certainly not when you were crying into a rag. And why did you order dinner here, if you wanted to eat it somewhere else?"

"We had to have it somewhere, Father, and we did not hear."

"Oh, we thought you would be tired," said Blanche. "And there are so many of us. It would not be restful for you. And we are not prepared for you to-night. We shall be so delighted to see you when it is arranged, and we hope that will be very often."

"I did not make anything of extra guests, when I ran a large house," said Matty, with a simple wonder which was not entirely assumed, as her housekeeping had played its part in her father's debts.

"And that may be partly why you are now running a small one," said the latter, with a guess rather than a glimpse at the truth.

"We are hoping to see you constantly," said Blanche. "We can't quite manage our home so that people can come without notice, but we hope to plan so many things and to carry them out."

"We can't run in and out, as if we were of the same family? We felt we were that when we came. That indeed is why we are here. You can do so in this little house. You will remember and tell the children?"

"I hope she will not retain any of this talk," said Oliver, looking at his elder daughter, nevertheless, with his own admiration. "I will ask her to forget it. Well, Miss Griffin, have you done enough of putting away what we have, in a space that cannot hold it?"

"We shall have to get rid of some furniture, dear," said Matty to her sister, with a vague note of reproach.

"My dear, you have not brought all the furniture of that big house?"

"No, no, we remembered the size of this one, and only brought the things we knew and loved. I daresay you would not remember some of them. But we did not realise that it was quite such a cot. I expect our thoughts of it were tinged with memories of you and your large one, as that is how we have seen the life here. Never mind, we shall call it our cottage home, and be quite happy in it."

"Then pray begin to be so," said Oliver. "Happiness is too good a thing to put off. And I am not at the age for doing that with anything."

"How do you do, Miss Griffin?" said Blanche, shaking hands with her sister's attendant and companion. "I hope you are not too tired with all your efforts?"

"How do you do, Mrs. Gaveston? No, I am not so very tired," said Miss Griffin, a short, thin woman of fifty, with a long, sallow face, large, hazel eyes, features which might have been anyone's except for their lines of sufferance and kindness, hands which were more developed than her body, and a look of being very tired indeed. "It is very good of you to come to welcome us."

"Mrs. Gaveston came in to see her father and sister, of course," said Matty, in a tone which said so much more than her words, that it brought a silence.

"Yes, indeed, dear," said her sister. "And when you want me to go and leave you to your dinner, you must tell me."

"The dinner is not—the dinner will not be ready yet," said Miss Griffin, in a stumbling tone, glancing at Matty and away. "The maid does not know where anything is yet. She is quite new."

"Of course she is, as we did not bring her with us," said Matty, with her little laugh. "Couldn't you show her where the things are, as you have just unpacked them?"

"She put everything together—I put it all together—we have not sorted them yet. She is just finding what she can."

"I should have put all the things in their places as I took them out. I should not have thought of any other way."

"We couldn't do that. The men were waiting to take the cases. We had to put them all down anywhere."

"I should have known where anywhere was. I often wish I were able-bodied, for everyone's sake."

"We wish you were, child, but for your own," said Oliver.

"I think Miss Griffin has managed wonders from the look of the house," said Blanche.

"We have all done that to-day," said her sister. "I almost think I have managed the most, in keeping still through all the stir and turmoil. I hope we shall never have such a day again. I can't help hoping it."

"I know I shall not," said her father.

"I remember so well the day when you came to us, Miss Griffin," said Blanche. "It was thirty-one years ago, a few days before my wedding. And you were so kind in helping me to pack and put the last touches to my clothes. I wished I was taking you with me."

"I remember thinking that you were using my companion as your own," said Matty, smiling from one to the other.

Miss Griffin turned her face aside, finding it unsteadied by ordinary kindness.

"Sit down, Miss Griffin, and rest until dinner," said Matty. "There is no need to stand more than you must, though I often wish I could do a little of it. That may make me think other people more fortunate than they are."

Miss Griffin sat down in the sudden, limp way of someone who would soon have had to do so.

"There is Edgar," said Blanche. "He will come in and say a word, and then we will leave you all to rest."

"Why, Edgar, this is nice," said Matty, rising from her seat as she had not done for her sister, and showing that she stood tall and straight, in spite of disabled lower limbs. "I did not think you would forget us on our first night. We had not forgotten you. No, you have been in our minds and on our lips. Now what do you say to our settling at your very gates?"

"That it is—that I hope it is the best place for you to be," said Edgar, putting out all his effort and accordingly unable to say more.

"And your brother! I am never quite sure what to call him," said Matty, putting round her head to look at Dudley. "Come in and let us hear your voice. We have been cheered by it so many times."

"I am glad you have. I have always meant you to be. I am in my element in a chat. My strong point is those little things which are more important than big ones, because they make up life. It seems that big ones do not do that, and I daresay it is fortunate."

"Yes, it is indeed. We have been involved in the lattter to-day, and we see that we could not manage too many. Now it is so good to hear you talk again. We see we have not given up our home for nothing."

"Indeed you have not. You have left it to make a new one with all of us," said Blanche, relieved by the turn of the talk and not disturbed that she had been unable to produce it.

"Such a lot of happiness, such a lot of affection and kindness," said Matty, in a tone charged with sweetness and excitement. "It is so good to know that we are welcome."

"It is indeed," said Oliver; "for a moment since I should have thought that we could not be."

"How are you, sir?" said Edgar and Dudley, speaking at one moment but obliged to shake hands in turn.

"I am well, I thank you, and I hope that both of you are better by thirty odd years, as you should be."

Oliver put a chair for his son-in-law and settled down to talk. He gave his feeling to his daughters but he liked to talk with men.

"How are you, Miss Griffin?" said Dudley, turning from the pair. "I hope you are not hiding feelings of your own on the occasion."

"No, I am not; it all makes a change," said Miss Griffin, admitting more feeling than she knew into the last word. "And we did not want that large house for so few people. It is better to be in a little one, where there is less work and more comfort. And I don't mind the small rooms. I rather like to be snug and compact."

"Now I would not claim that that is just my taste. I confess to a certain disposition towards the opposite," said Matty, in a clear tone. "It is not of my own will that I have changed my scale of life. I admit that I felt more at home with the other. It is all a matter of what fits our different personalities, I suppose."

"I hope I do not make cosy corners wherever I go," said Dudley. "I don't want too many merely lovable qualities. They are better for other people than for oneself."

"Well, there will always be such a corner for you here. I shall be grateful if you will help me to make one, as it is rather outside my experience and scope. But once made, it will be always hospitable and always ready. If we can't have one thing we will have another, or anyhow I will. I am not a person to give up because I can't have just what I should choose, just what fits me, shall we say?"

"I don't know why we should say it, child," said Oliver. "And anyhow you should not."

"I wish my parents were not dead," said Dudley. "I should like to be called 'child' by someone. It would prove that there were people about who were a generation older than me, and it will soon want proof."

"Welcome, welcome to your new home!" said Justine's voice. "Welcome to your new life. I know I am one too many; I know you are tired out; I know your room is full. I know it all. But I simply had to come to wish you happiness, and to say to you, Welcome, well come."

"So you had, dear, and it gives us such pleasure to hear it," said Matty, raising her face from her chair. "I did hope that some of you would feel that and come to tell us so. It seemed to me that you would, and I see I was not wrong. One, two, three, four dear faces! Only three left at home. It is such a help to us in starting again, and it is a thing which does need help. You don't know that yet, and may it be long before you do."

"Well, I judged it, Aunt Matty, and that is why I am here. Of course, you must need courage. You can't start again without a good deal of looking back. That must be part of it. And I did feel a wish to say a word to help you to look forward."

Blanche looked at her daughter in simple appreciation; Edgar threw her a glance and withdrew it; and Oliver surveyed the scene as if it were not his concern.

"You help us, dear, indeed," said Matty. "It was a kind and loving wish, and as such we accept it and will try to let it do its work."

"I know you will, Aunt Matty dear; I know your inexhaustible fund of courage. You know, I am of those who remember you of old, straight and tall and proud, as you appeared to my childish eyes. My feeling for you has its ineradicable root in the past."

The words brought a silence, and Justine, fair in all her dealings, broke it herself.

"How are you, Miss Griffin?" she said, shaking hands with great cordiality, and then sitting down and seeming to render the room at once completely full. "Now this is a snug, little, cottage parlour. Now, how do you take to it, Aunt Matty?"

"We shall be content in it, dear. We mean to be. And where there is a will there is a way. And it should not be difficult to come to like it, our little cottage parlour. Those are good and pretty words for it. They give the idea without any adding to it or taking away."

"It is not a cottage, dear," said Blanche, looking at her daughter.

"Isn't it, Mother? Well, no, we know it strictly is not. But it gives all the idea of one somehow. And I mean nothing disparaging; I like a roomy cottage. When I am a middle-aged woman and Mark is supreme in the home, I shall like nothing better than to have perhaps this very little place, and reign in it, and do all I can for people outside. Now does not that strike you all as an alluring prospect?"

"Yes, it sounds very nice," said Miss Griffin, who thought that it did, and who was perhaps the natural person to reply, as the arrangement involved the death of most of the other people present.

"I don't think it gives the idea of a cottage at all," said Blanche, looking round with contracting eyes. "The rooms are so high and the windows so broad. One could almost imagine oneself anywhere."

"But not quite," said her sister, bending her head and looking up at the men from under it. "We can't, for example, imagine ourselves where we used to be."

"Well, no, not there, dear. We must both of us leave that. It was my old home too, as you seem to forget."

"No, dear. You do at times, I think. That is natural. You have put too much over it. Other things have overlaid the memory. I chose to keep it clear and by itself. There is the difference."

"Well, it *is* natural, Aunt Matty," said Justine. "I don't think Mother must be blamed for it. There *is* a difference."

"Yes, dear, and so you will not blame her. I have said that I do not. And is the old aunt already making herself tiresome? She must be so bright and easy as an invalid in a strange place?"

"Come, Aunt Matty, invalid is not the word. You are disabled, we know, and we do not underrate the handicap, but your invalidism begins and ends there. Now I am not going to countenance any repining. You are in your virtual prime; you have health and looks and brains; and we are going to expect a good deal from you."

"My dear, did Aunt Matty ask you to sum up her position?" said Blanche, a faint note of triumphant pride underlying her reproof.

"No, Mother, you know she did not, so why put the

question? I did not wait to be asked; it is rather my way not to. You need not put on a disapproving face. I have to be taken as I am. I do not regret what I said, and Aunt Matty will not when she thinks it over."

"Or forgets it," said her aunt. "Yes, I think that is what Aunt Matty had better do. She has not the will or the energy to think it over at this juncture of her life. And forgetting it will be better, so that is the effort she must make."

"Now I am in disgrace, but I do not regard it. I have had my say and I always find that enough," said Justine, who was wise in this attitude, as she would seldom have been advised to go further.

"How very unlike Edgar and Justine are, dear!" said Matty to her sister. "They have not a touch of each other, and they say that daughters are like their fathers. They are both indeed themselves."

"Well, that is as well," said Justine. "Father would not like me to be a copy of him. He would not feel the attraction of opposites."

"Opposite. Yes, that is almost the word," said her aunt.

Miss Griffin gave the sudden, sharp breath of someone awaking from a minute's sleep, and looked about with bewildered eyes.

"Poor Miss Griffin, you are tired out," said Blanche.

"I am so glad you got off for a minute, Miss Griffin," said Justine.

"I did not know where I was; I must have dropped off with all the voices round me," said Miss Griffin, with a view of the talk which she would hardly have taken if she had heard it. "I don't know why I did, I am sure."

"Being overtired is quite enough reason," said Justine.

"So Miss Griffin is the first of us to make it one," said Matty, in an easy tone.

"It is a stronger reason in her case."

"Is it, dear?" said Matty, so lightly that she hardly seemed to enunciate the words.

"Why, Aunt Matty, she must have done twice as much as you—as anyone else. You know that."

"Twice as much as I have, dear? Many times as much, I daresay; I have been able to do hardly anything. And of course I know it." Matty gave her little laugh. "But what we have mostly done to-day, is sitting in the train, and we have done it together."

"Yes, but the preparations before and the unpacking afterwards! It must have been overwhelming. The time in the train must have been quite a respite."

"Yes, that is what I meant, dear."

"But it was only one day, only part of one. The work must have begun directly you reached this house. I can see how much has been achieved. You can't possibly grasp it, sitting in a chair."

"So sitting in a chair has become an advantage, has it?"

"Poor, dear Aunt Matty!" said Justine, sitting on the arm of the chair, as if to share for the moment her aunt's lot. "But it cannot contribute to the actual weariness, you know. That is a thing by itself."

"So there is only one kind of weariness," said Matty, putting her hand on her niece's and speaking in a tone of gentle tolerance towards her unknowing youth.

"Dear Aunt Matty! There must be times when to be hustled and driven seems the most enviable thing in the world. You are more unfortunate than anyone," said Justine, indicating and accepting her aunt's lot and Miss Griffin's.

Miss Griffin rose and went to the door with an explanatory look at Matty. Dudley opened it and followed her.

"How do people feel on a first night in a new place? I have never had the experience. I have lived in the same house all my life."

Miss Griffin lifted her eyes with a look he had not expected, almost of consternation.

"It does make you feel uncertain about things. But I expect you soon get used to it. I was in the last house thirty-one years. Miss Seaton had never lived in any other."

"And are you sorry to come away from it?"

"No, not very. It makes a change. We shall see different people. And it will be nice for Miss Seaton to have her sister and her family. It was the wisest plan."

"The best plan, not the wisest. It was very unwise. But a great many of the best things are that."

Miss Griffin looked at him with a hint of a smile.

"You agree with me, do you not?"

Miss Griffin checked her smile and looked aside.

"You and I must be very much alike. We both live in other people's houses; we are both very kind; and I am very good at playing second fiddle, and I believe you are too."

"Oh, I never mind doing that," said Miss Griffin in a full tone.

"I have minded in my weaker moments, but I have conquered my worse self. You have no worse self, have you?"

"No," said Miss Griffin, speaking the truth before she thought. "Well, I don't know. Perhaps everyone has."

"You have to think of other people's. So I see that you have not. And as I have suppressed mine, it is another point we have in common."

Miss Griffin stood with a cheered expression.

"Has Miss Seaton a better self?" said Dudley.

Miss Griffin gave him a half smile which turned to a look of reproach.

"Yes, of course she has. Everyone has."

"So it was her worse self we saw this evening?"

"I did not mean that she had a worse self. You know I did not. She was very tired. It must be so dreadful not to be able to get about." Miss Griffin's voice died away on a note of pure pity.

"Well, good night, Miss Griffin; we shall often meet."

"Good-night, Mr. Dudley," said Miss Griffin, turning towards the kitchen with a lighter step.

Dudley returned to the parlour to find the family dispersing. Matty was on her feet, talking with the lively affection which followed her difficult moods, and which she believed to efface their memory.

"Goodbye, dearest; goodbye, my Justine; you will often come in to see the cross old aunt who loves you. Good-bye, Dudley; where have you been wandering? It was clever to find enough space to lose yourself. Good-bye, Edgar; my father has so enjoyed his masculine talk. It is a thing that does him so much good."

"And how have you enjoyed your feminine one?" said Oliver, who had caught snatches of this dialogue. "Upon my word, I daresay a good deal. You look the better for it."

"Good-bye, Aunt Matty dear," said Justine. "I have seemed a brute, but I have meant it for your good, and you are large enough to take it as it was meant."

"Good-bye," said Edgar at once. "We shall often meet; I hope we shall meet very often."

"Well, of course, people are only human," said Dudley to his brother, as they walked to the house behind the women. "But it really does not seem much for them to be."

"Yes, we must do what we can in our new life," said Edgar, as if in reply. "I think we may call it that. It may be a better life for Blanche. I think—I trust it may."

"Is her present life so bad?"

"She may be lonely without knowing it. I fear it may have been the case. I feel—I fear I have little to be proud of in my family life."

"It is I who have the cause for pride. It is wonderful, the way in which I have put myself aside and kept your affection and won your wife's. But I think the things we suffer without knowing are the best, as we are born to suffer. It is not as if Blanche had suspected her loneliness. And she can't be with her sister and be unconscious of it."

"Neither can any of us," said Edgar, with the short, broken laugh which was chiefly heard by his brother. "I could see—I saw that she realised it to-day."

"I saw that Justine did too. The sight became too much for me and I had to escape."

"What were you doing all that time?"

"Why do people say that they do not like having to account for their every action? I do like it. I like telling everything about myself and feeling that people take an interest. I was saying a kind word to Miss Griffin. They say that a kind word may work wonders; and I saw that something had to work wonders for her; and so I said the word and it did."

"Poor Miss Griffin! I mean that we cannot judge of other people's lives."

"Of course we can. We all have lives and know about them. No one will have it said that he has no knowledge of life; and it could not be true."

"She has been with Matty and her father for a long time. I am not sure how long."

"I am. She told me. But there are things which cannot pass my lips."

"It must be over thirty years."

"You are a tougher creature than I am. I wonder if people know that you are."

"It is difficult to form a picture of all those years."

"Edgar, you do sometimes say the most dreadful things. You should remember my shrinking nature. I shall have to see a great deal of Miss Griffin. Will seeing her take away that picture before my eyes?"

"Come along, you two," called Justine, turning with beckoning hand. "If you wait every minute to argue, we shall never get up the drive. Mother does not like to keep stopping."

This was true of Blanche, and therefore she had not

stopped, but was proceeding towards the house, with her short, unequal steps carrying her rapidly over the ground. When she came to the porch she paused, as if waiting there affected her differently.

"There is that little brick house beyond the trees," said Justine, turning to look back as they all met.

"Your eyes do not deceive you," said her father, with a smile.

"Now don't try to snub me, Father; that is not like your dealings. There it is, and it is good to think of Grandpa and Aunt Matty snugly sheltered in it. I shall call up the picture to-night when I am in bed."

"At night," murmured Dudley, "and in bed! In those hours when things rise up before us out of their true proportion!"

"What are you murmuring about to yourself, Uncle?"

"About the picture which you will call up in the night."

"You like to share it with me? It is a pretty picture, isn't it? Dear Grandpa, with his white hair and fine old face; and Aunt Matty, handsome in the firelight, vivacious and fluent, and no more querulous than one can forgive in her helpless state; and dear, patient Miss Griffin, thinking of everyone but herself. It is a satisfying sight."

"Perhaps it is healthier to bring it out into the light."

"You were the one who did not forgive your aunt," said Edgar, smiling again at his daughter.

"Now, Father, don't think that your naughty little thrusts are atoned for by your especial smile for me, dear to me though it is." Edgar's expression wavered as he heard it defined. "Aunt Matty and I are the firmest friends and very good for one another. We never mind looking at ourselves through each other's eyes and getting useful light on our personalities. I do not believe in putting disabled people on one side and denying them their share in healthy human life. It seems to me a wrong thing to do, and in the end bad for everyone. So I sound my bracing note and snap my fingers at the consequences." Justine illustrated what she said.

The scene in the lodge was as she saw it, except that Matty's querulousness was missing. The latter was sitting at dinner, talking with a great liveliness, as if her audience were larger than it was, almost as if in practice for greater occasions. She often threw herself into the entertainment of her father and her companion, with or without thought of imaginary listeners.

"And then those funny, little, country shoes! Dear Blanche, still full of her quaint, little, old touches! I had to laugh to myself when I saw her coming tripping and stumbling in, such a dear, familiar figure!"

"No one would have known you had," said Oliver. "It might have been better to give some sign. It seemed the last thing to expect of you."

Matty was indifferent to her father's criticism and knew that her talk diverted him.

"And then her own little, charitable ways, a mixture of daughter and sister and lady bountiful! So full of affection and kindness and yet with her own little sharpness, just our old Blanche! And her dear Justine"—Matty put her hand to her lips and fell into mirth—"so sure of her right to improve us all and so satisfied with it! So pleased with her effort to influence her aunt, who has faced so much more than she could conceive! Dear child, may she never even have to attempt it. Well, we are not all alike and perhaps it is as well. Perhaps it is good that we are all on our different steps in the human scale. And there are good things on each level. In some ways we might take a leaf out of her book."

"We might, but I do not think of it, and I do not ask it of you."

"It is naughty to say it, but does she remind you of that church worker at home? Someone so good and useful that everyone loved her and no one admired her? Now how unkind and malicious! I am quite ashamed."

"Have I met a person of that kind?"

"You must remember poor Miss Dunn at home."

"Why should I single her out of all that I remember? And how could I guess her employment?"

"The coat and the collar and the shoes," said Matty, again in mirth.

"They both wear such things, I grant you. I do the same and shall do it still for a short time."

"Poor Miss Griffin, you were the target. You might have been a little dark slave or a wee beastie in a trap, from the way she spoke. We do not move every day, do we? It has only been once in thirty years."

Miss Griffin felt that there was some reproach in the rareness of the step, though she would willingly have taken it oftener.

"She meant to be very kind, I am sure."

"She meant to be a little stern with me, just a tiny bit severe. But I did not mind. She is my dear, good niece and wants to improve the world and the people in it, Aunt Matty into the bargain."

"They might be the better for it," said Oliver, "but it is not her business."

"She feels it is, and so we must let her do it. We must take it up as a funny little cross and carry it with us."

"Why do that? Why not close her mouth upon things which are not her concern? That is a thing you can do. I have observed it."

"Edgar is a handsome man," said Matty in another tone. "He was very tall and distinguished in this little room. Oh, wasn't it funny, the way they kept talking about it? Calling it snug and cosy. We might be cottagers."

"That is what we are, though your sister did not allow it."

"And Justine said that she was glad we were safe in it. We had no other refuge, had we?"

"I cannot tell you of one. So we have our cause for

thankfulness. But it is not for her to point it out. She seems to me to have greater cause."

"Mr. Gaveston and Mr. Dudley are not so much alike when you get to know them," said Miss Griffin.

"They are of the same type, but Mr. Gaveston is the better example," said Matty, who maintained the full formal distance between herself and her companion, in spite of her habit of frankness before her.

"I like Mr. Dudley's face better."

"Do you? It is not the better face. It has not the line or the symmetry. It is a thought out of drawing. But they are a fine pair of brothers."

"There is something in Mr. Dudley's face that makes it quite different from Mr. Gaveston's. I hardly know how to say what I mean."

"That might be said of any two people. They are not just alike, of course."

"Mr. Dudley's face has a different kind of attraction."

"There is only one kind, of the one we were talking of," said Matty in a tone which closed the subject.

"Miss Griffin has found another," said Oliver, "or has fancied it. But why talk of the fellows' looks? They are not women. And both of you are, so it is wise to leave the matter."

"Was Mr. Dudley talking to you outside?" said Matty in a sudden, different tone to Miss Griffin.

"No—yes—he just said a word, and then went out to look at the night, into the porch," said Miss Griffin, who told a falsehood when she could see no other course.

Oliver had heard the voices in the hall, but he did not speak. He never crossed the barrier into the women's world. If he had done so, he would have had to protect Miss Griffin and anger his daughter; and he felt unequal to either of these things, which would have tried the strength of a younger man.

"Did you notice the way they set off home?" said Matty, with a return of mirth. "I saw them from the window. My eyes are still alert for what they can see, though I am tied to my chair. Blanche leading the way, and Justine trying to keep up and to keep step, and failing in both in spite of her youth and her strength! And the two men walking behind, as tranquil as if they were unconscious of the feminine creatures in front! Blanche leading a group is one of my earliest memories. Her stiff, little legs marching on, how they come back to me! And they are so little different, the active, determined, little legs. How much of her height is in her body! Well, my legs are not so much to boast of now. I have not my old advantage. Dear, dear, it is a funny thing, a family. I can't help feeling glad sometimes that I have had no part in making one."

"Why try to help it? It is well to be glad of anything, and you do not too often seem so. Though some people might not choose just that reason."

"Well, mine is not a lot which calls for much gladness. It needs some courage to find any cause for it."

"So courage is the word for your talk of your sister. We could find others."

"Blanche and I are the closest friends. I am going to rejoice in being the elder sister again. You and she are the only people who see me as I was, and not as I am, the poor, baffled, helpless creature who has to get her outlet somehow. Yes, I was bright and young once. Even Miss Griffin remembers part of that time."

"Yes, indeed I do; indeed you were," said Miss Griffin.

"Miss Griffin was even younger," said Oliver, bringing a new idea to both his hearers as he rose to leave them.

"Yes, I was a naughty, sprightly person," continued Matty after a moment's pause, during which the idea left her. "Always looking for something on which to work my wits. Something or someone; I fear it did not matter as long as my penetration had its exercise. Well, we can't choose the pattern on which we are made. And perhaps I would not alter mine. Perhaps there is no need to meddle with it, eh, Miss Griffin?"

Miss Griffin was standing with her hand on her chair, thinking of the next step in her day. She gave a faint start as she realised her plight and saw the look on Matty's face. The next moment she heard her voice.

"Don't go dragging away from the table like that. Either move about and get something done, or don't pretend to do anything. Just posing as being a weary drudge will not get us anywhere."

"Perhaps the things which have made me that, have got us somewhere," said Miss Griffin, in an even, oddly hopeless tone, with little idea that the words on her lips marked a turning point in her life.

"You need not answer like that. That is not going to begin, so you need not think it is. I do not expect to have my words taken up as if I were a woman on the common line. I am a very exceptional person and in a tragic position, and you will have to grasp it, or you are no good to me. And going off in that way, pretending not to hear, taking advantage of my helplessness! That is a thing of such a dreadful meanness that no one would speak to you if he knew it; no one would go near you; you would be shunned and spat upon!"

Matty's voice rose to a scream, as her words did nothing and Miss Griffin passed out of hearing. She rocked herself to and fro and muttered to herself, with her hands clenched and her jaw thrust forward in a manner which would have made a piece of acting and really had something of this in it, as she did not lose sight of herself.

Miss Griffin went along the passage and paused at the end where the wall made a support, and looked to see that Matty had not followed.

"It is all I have. Just this. I have nothing else. I have no home, no friends. I go on, year after year, never have any pleasure, never have any change. She feels nothing for me after I have been with her for thirty years. All the best years of my life. And it gets worse with every year. I thought this move might make a change, but it is going to be the same. And my life is going; I may never have anything else; and no one ought to have only that." She shed some tears, scanty through fear and furtiveness, and lightening her face and throwing off a part of her burden, went into the kitchen to the maid, glad of this degree of human fellowship.

Matty, left to herself, relaxed her body and her mind and hoped that her father had not heard her voice, or rather recalled that he would behave as if he had not done so. When Oliver came from his study to bid her a good night, she rose to meet him, hiding what she could of her lameness, and led him to a chair, amending both his and her own conception of herself.

"I come to take my leave of you, my dear, in case I do not see you again. My end may come at any time and why not to-night? The strength ebbs after dark and I have used too much of mine to-day. So good-night and more, if that is to be."

"Come, Father, you are overtired and depressed by being in this funny little place. Cosy we are to call it, and we will do our best. We have to try to do so many things and in time we shall succeed. We are not people who fail. We will not be."

"I am almost glad that your mother is not here to-night, Matty. This would not have been a home for her. It will do for you and me."

"I don't know why we should be so easily satisfied," said Matty, unable to accept this view of herself in any mood. "But we shall have another outlook to-morrow and it will seem a different place, and we shall wish Mother back with us, as I have wished her many times to-day." Her father must pay for using such words of his daughter. "But we can't do anything more to-night. We have striven to our limit and beyond. It is no wonder if we fail a little. I daresay we have all had our lapses from our level."

Oliver, who was in no doubt of it, left her and mounted the stairs, bringing his feet together on each. In his room above the step became stronger, and Matty listened and put him from her mind. She understood her father. A good deal of him had come down to her.

Miss Griffin came in later with a tray, to find Matty in an attitude of drooping weariness, with a pallor which was real after her stress of feeling.

"Will you have something hot to drink?" she said in a tone which seemed to beseech something besides what it said. "It will do you good before you go to bed."

"It will do us both good. It was a sensible thought. If you will bring up that little table and move that chair" —Matty indicated with vivacious hand this further effort for Miss Griffin—"we will have a cosy time together and feel that we are doing what we should, as cosy is what we are supposed to be."

"It really is rather cosy in here," said Miss Griffin, looking round with a faint air of surprise.

"Yes, it is foolish to fret for the might-have-beens. Or for the have-beens in this case."

Miss Griffin did not fret for these.

"Now do not shirk drinking your share," said Matty, replenishing the cups. "You need it as much as I do. Being up and doing is as tiring as sitting still, however much one may envy it. Mr. Seaton has gone to bed. He was overtired and sorry for himself, but I did not take much notice. It was wiser not to sympathise."

"Oh, I expect he was very tired," said Miss Griffin, sitting up as if to put her full energy into her compassion.

"He begins to feel his age, but he is very well and strong. And we are all tired."

"Yes," said Miss Griffin, speaking in a mechanical tone and suddenly enlivening it. "But it is a healthy tiredness." She had been so often told of the beneficial effects of weariness on the human frame, that she felt she should know them.

"It has gone a little beyond that to-day. But it is only once in a lifetime. We must not complain."

Miss Griffin was not going to do this, but her nod had something besides agreement.

"Come, come now, we must go to bed," said Matty, keeping her eyes from the other as if in fear of what might meet them. "We shall be a couple of sleepy old maids in the morning, if we do not take care."

Miss Griffin's eyes opened wide and held themselves on Matty's face.

"We owe it to ourselves and to other people not to sink to that. We must not quite lose our self-respect. This is a matter in which considering ourselves is best for everyone. Has Emma gone to bed?"

"Yes, hours ago," said Miss Griffin, only realising her implication when she had spoken.

Matty did not comment on it, possibly for the reason that Emma had only been half a day in her service and had not yet learned the benefits of exhaustion.

"Well, then she can be up bright and early to wait upon us," she said with an effort which did not say nothing for her will. "We will not be down until ten o'clock. We have had a nice little chat. Good-night, and mind you sleep."

Matty went to her room, feeling that she had made her companion ample amends, and the latter, waiting to turn out the lamps, wondered that she did not feel the same, as she had felt it so many times. This was the reason for her not feeling it again.

CHAPTER III

"I AM READY for Aunt Matty," said Aubrey.

"Are you, little boy? And very nice and trim you look. I wish I could feel the same. I am done with village dressmakers. I am not much of a woman for personal adornment, but there are stages beyond even me. I ought to think of my family; it was selfish and lazy of me. I certainly can't expect to rejoice their eyes." Justine sighed over her conclusion.

"Won't smoothing it make it better?"

"No, it will not, impertinent child. It will leave it as it is." Justine aimed a blow in her brother's direction without moving towards him.

"Mark, are you ready for your aunt?" said Aubrey.

"As far as the outward man can count. But her eyes may pierce the surface and pounce on what is beneath."

"Now I won't have Aunt Matty laughed at for her penetration," said Justine. "It is a valuable quality and one which deserves to be reckoned with."

"And is more than any other."

"She has none," said Clement. "She attributes motives to people, whether they are there or not. That gets us further from the truth than anything. Mother has really a sounder penetration."

"Dear little Mother," said Justine, giving a pitying tenderness to the same quality in Blanche.

"Clement, are you ready for your aunt?"

"Nothing would prepare me for the manners, the morals and the methods of such a woman. She is at once super and sub-human. I always wonder if she is goddess or beast."

"Clement, Clement, that is neither gallant nor kind,"

said Justine. "A man does not speak of a woman like that, you know. And can't you brush the collar of your coat? Not that I have any right to speak."

"But I think both the boys look very nice Justine," said Aubrey.

"How does Justine appear?" said Clement. "I will hear the accepted view before I express my own."

"Oh, you are right; it is hopeless. It deserves anything you like to say. You need not be afraid that I shall rise up in its defence like a mother with her young."

"You might help to smooth it, Clement," said Aubrey. "It is all that can be done now."

"Why don't you change it?" said Mark. "What about that one you generally wear?"

"No, I will stick to it now. I will remain in it and face the music. Mother is expecting to see me in something different, and I daresay she will like it. I won't take refuge in some old one which does not catch the eye. It will teach me a lesson that I deserve."

"It is not a matter of such mighty import," said Clement.

"Indeed it is! It should be a point of great interest to you all, how your only sister looks. I will not have it in any other way. I have no patience with that kind of high-and-mightiness. It is the last thing that exalts anyone."

"Clement, are you listening to Justine?" said Aubrey.

"He does not know how true quality is shown," said Mark. "That is a thing which cannot be taught."

"All Clement's learning will stand him in but poor stead."

"Here are the guests! And Father and Mother are not down!" said Justine, in a tone of consternation.

"They are remedying the position," said Clement, showing that he did not recommend the feeling.

Blanche led the way into the room, in an old-fashioned gown of heavy material and indifferent cut, which had been altered to show successfully how it should have been made, and which in its countrified quality and stiffness became her well.

"Well, dear ones, how nice you look! Justine, it is a very pretty colour. I do want Aunt Matty to see you all at your best. And dear Grandpa has seen so little of you for so long." Blanche spoke to her children of their relations either from their point of view or her own.

"Mr. and Mrs. Middleton," said Jellamy.

"How are you, Mrs. Middleton? It is kind of you to adapt yourselves to our early hours," said Blanche, who observed the formalities with guests with sincerity and goodwill. "My father and sister will be here in a moment. It is a long time since you have met."

"Whose idea was it that they should come to live here?"

"It was their own. But we welcomed it with great delight. My sister and I have missed each other for so many years."

"Isn't the lodge rather small after their old home?"

Sarah Middleton's questions seemed to come in spite of herself, as if her curiosity were stronger than her will.

"Yes, it has to be that. They have lost money lately and are obliged to live on a small scale. And it is a nice little house."

"Very nice indeed," said Sarah, with the full cordiality of relief from pain, which was the state produced in her by a satisfied urge to know.

Sarah Middleton was a tall, upright woman of seventy, strong and young for her age, with a fair, rather empty face and an expression at once eager and soured and kind. Her grey hair was done in some way which seemed to belong to a world where men and women were more different, and her cap had been assumed in her prime in tribute to matronhood, though to Justine and her brothers it was a simple emblem of age. She looked about as she talked, as if she feared to miss enlightenment on any matter, a thing which tried her beyond her strength and which happily seldom occurred. Her husband, who was ten years younger and in the same physical stage, was a tall, spare, stooping man, with a good head, pale, weak eyes, a surprisingly classic nose, and an air of depression and an excellence of deportment which seemed to depend on each other, as though he felt that the sadness of life entitled people to courtesy and consideration. He had wanted to write, and had been a schoolmaster because of the periods of leisure, but had found that the demands of the other periods exhausted his energy. After his marriage to a woman of means he was still prevented, though he did not give the reason, indeed did not know it. Neither did he state what he wished to write, and this was natural, as he had not yet decided. Sarah felt that the desire gave him enough occupation, and he almost seemed to feel the same.

"Yes, say what you like, Uncle," said Justine, standing before Dudley and holding out her skirts. "It merits it all and more. I have not a word to say. This will teach me not to waste my time and energy on going backwards and forwards to poor Miss Spurr. She has not an ounce of skill in her composition."

Blanche looked at the dress with mild, and Sarah with eager attention.

"It could be made into a dressing gown," said Dudley, taking a sudden step forward. "I see just how it could be done."

"My dear, that beautiful material!" said Sarah, holding up her hands and turning her eyes on Justine to indicate the direction of her address.

"I am sure it is a very pretty colour," said Blanche, implying and indeed feeling that this was a great part of the matter.

"I knew I could count on a word of encouragement from you, little Mother."

"Dressing gowns are always the best colours," said Aubrey. "I go in and look at them sometimes."

"You little scamp," said Justine. "You are happy in being young enough for that sort of thing."

"Dear boy!" said Sarah.

"What is the matter with the dress?" said Edgar, with careful interest. "Do you mean that it ought to be better made?"

"Yes, Father, I do mean that. Everyone means it. We all mean it. Don't go unerringly to the point like that, as if it were almost too obvious to call for comment."

"I don't think it calls for so much comment," said Clement.

"Well, I daresay it does not. Let us leave it now. After all, we all look ourselves in whatever we wear," said Justine, deriving open satisfaction from this conclusion, and taking Aubrey's chin in her hand. "What are you meditating upon, little boy?"

"I was expecting Aunt Matty," said Aubrey, reluctant to explain that he had been imagining future daughters for himself and deciding the colours of their dressing gowns.

"Well, dear ones all," said Matty, almost standing still on the threshold, partly in her natural slowness and partly to be seen. "Well, here is a happy, handsome"—she rapidly substituted another word—"healthy family. So much health and happiness is so good to see. It is just what I want, isn't it?"

Blanche looked up with narrowing eyes at the change of word, though she knew that it was prompted by the sight of more and not less handsomeness than her sister had expected.

"Is not Father coming?" she said in a cool tone, putting down her embroidery before she rose.

Sarah looked from sister to sister with full comprehension and the urbanity which accompanied it.

"Yes, dear, he will not be a moment. He is only rather slow. I came on to get a start of him, as I am even slower." Matty kissed Blanche with more than her usual affection in tacit atonement for what had passed, but seemed to feel rather soon that atonement had been made. "It seems that I know him better in these days and have to tell you about him. Perhaps he has always belonged to me a little the most. Why, Mrs. Middleton, how are you both? So we are to be neighbours as well as friends."

"It did not take you long to make up your mind to the change," said Sarah, her tone leading up to further information.

"No, I am a person of rapid decision. Fleet of foot, fleet of thought and fleet of action I used to be called in the old days." Blanche looked up as if in an effort of memory. "And I have retained as much of my fleetness as I can. So I made my resolve and straightway acted upon it."

"My dear, you have retained so much of what you had," said Sarah, shaking her head.

"Mr. Seaton," said Jellamy.

"Now I can barely walk forward to greet you," said Oliver, pushing his feet along the ground, "but I am glad to find myself welcome as I am. There have come moments when I thought that we might not meet again. So, Middleton, I am pleased to see you once more on this side of the grave."

Thomas shook hands with an air which accepted and rejected these words in the right measure.

"Why are people proud of expecting to die soon?" said Dudley to Mark. "I think it is humiliating to have so little life left."

"They are triumphant at having made sure of more life than other people. And they don't really think they will die."

"No, of course, they have got into the way of living. I see it is a lifelong habit."

"Have we no relations who can enter a room in the usual way?" said Clement.

"None in the neighbourhood," said his brother.

"Now, Grandpa, that is naughty talk," said Justine,

leading Oliver forward by the arm as if no one else would think of the office. "Now which chair would you like?"

"Any one will serve my purpose; I ask but to sit in it."

"Dear Grandpa!" said Justine, keeping her hands on his arms as he sat down, as if she were lowering him into it.

"That is a fine gown, my dear," he said, as he let go the chair and sank back.

"It is the most fearful thing, Grandpa; I forbid you to look at it. It will be my shame all the evening."

"You know why you put it on, I suppose. I should have thought it was intended to catch the eye, as it has caught mine."

"I think it is such a nice colour," said Blanche.

"Beautiful," said Sarah, shaking her head again.

"Why, so it is, my dear," said Oliver, relaxing his limbs. "Your girl looks well in it, and what more would you have?"

"But the shape of it, Grandpa!" said Justine, withdrawing her strictures upon his looking, to the extent of disposing herself that he might the better do so. "The cut, the hang, the balance, the fit!"

"Well, I do not see any of those, my dear; I do not know if you are trying to show them to me."

"I am trying to show you the lack of them."

"Then you do so, child; I see it," said Oliver, lifting one leg over the other.

"Well, if anyone received a snub!" said Justine, looking about her at the success of her effort.

"What is the colour?" said Matty, her easy tone revealing her opinion that enough had been said on the matter. "Magenta?"

"No, dear," said Blanche. "It is a kind of old rose."

"Is it, dear?" said Matty, contracting her eyes on the dress and looking almost exactly like her sister for the moment. "A new sort of old rose then." She smiled at her niece, taking her disparagement of the dress at its literal value.

"Oh, come, Aunt Matty, there is nothing wrong with the colour. It is the one redeeming point."

"Yes, dear?" said Matty, in questioning agreement, her eyes again on the dress.

"Oh dear, this garment! Is it destined to be a bone of contention in addition to its other disadvantages?"

"I tremble to think about its destiny," said Clement, "as its history up to date is what it is."

"Why is magenta an offensive term?" said Mark. "It seems to be."

"It is odd how colours seem to owe their names to some quality in them," said his aunt.

"Their names come about in quite a different way."

"Now we don't want a philological lecture," said Matty, showing her awareness of this.

"Magenta can be a beautiful colour," said Sarah, in a tone of considerable feeling. "I remember a dress I once had of a kind of brocade which we do not see now. Oh, it would have suited you, Mrs. Gaveston."

"Those old, thick brocades were very becoming," said Matty.

"Aunt Matty does not restrict the application of her words," said Aubrey, seeming to speak to himself, as he often did when he adopted adult phrase.

"I can imagine you looking regal in one of them, Aunt Matty," said Justine, in a tone of saying something that was expected.

"Dinner is ready, ma'am," said Jellamy.

"And not too soon," said Clement. "I hope that food will be a better subject for our attention than clothes."

Edgar gave his arm to Sarah and led the way in conventional talk, which he maintained at whatever happened to be the cost to himself. Dudley adapted his step to Matty's with an exactness which involved his almost standing still, and kept up a flow of conversation at no personal expense at all. Matty was known to prefer Dudley to a son of the house, and her nephews supported her choice. Blanche and her father walked together, as the result of his suggestion that it might be their last opportunity, which was proffered to Thomas as an excuse and duly repudiated and accepted. They were assisted by Justine to link their arms and take their first steps—and indeed there might have been a less perilous association—and checked by her serious hand from a too precipitate advance. Justine herself went with Thomas, placing her free arm in Mark's.

"Now I do not require four partners, but I may as well use up one superfluous young man. Follow on, you other two. Aubrey can be the lady."

"I place my delicate hand on Clement's arm and lean on his strength."

Thomas gave a laugh and Clement shook off the hand and walked on alone.

"What a really beautiful room, dear!" said Matty to her sister, with appreciation brought to birth by the lights and wine and the presence of Dudley and Edgar. "It is like a little glimpse of home, or if I may not say that, it is like itself and satisfying indeed to my fastidious eye. And my own little room seems to gain, not lose by the comparison. This one seems to show how beauty is everywhere itself. I quite feel that I have taken a lesson from it."

"And one which was needed, from what I hear," said Mark.

"Is that how happiness does not depend on surroundings?" said Aubrey.

Mark and Aubrey often talked aside to each other. Clement would join them when inclined to talk, Justine when inclined to talk aside. Aubrey also talked aside to himself.

"Naughty boys, making fun of the poor old aunt!" said Matty, shaking her finger at them without interest in what they said.

"What was it, Mark?" said Edgar, with a hint in his tone that his eldest son should speak for the ears of the table.

"I was agreeing with Aunt Matty, Sir."

"Yes, yes, we may praise our own home, may we not, when it is as good as this?" said his aunt.

"I was doing the same, Father—the same, sir," said Aubrey, who had lately followed his brothers in this mode of address.

"Dear boy!" said Sarah, moved by the step towards maturity.

Edgar had come as near the reproof as he ever did. His hints were always heeded, and if it was not true that they were followed more than if he had raised his voice or resorted to violence, it was as true as it ever is. To Justine he never hinted a reproof, partly because of her sex and partly because he might have had to hint too much. Edgar did not love his children, though he believed or rather assumed that he did, and meted out kindness and interest in fair measure. He had a concerned affection for his wife, a great love for his brother and less than the usual feeling for himself. Dudley spent his emotion on his brother, and gave any feeling which arose in him to anyone else. Justine believed that she was her father's darling, and Edgar, viewing the belief with an outsider's eye, welcomed it, feeling that it ought to be a true one, and made intermittent effort to give it support. Other people accordingly accepted it, with the exception of Dudley and Aubrey, who saw the truth. Clement would have seen it if he had regarded the matter, and Blanche liked the belief and accordingly cherished it.

"Does Jellamy manage by himself in this room now?" said Matty to her sister. "It seems rather much for one person."

"Yes, he has to, dear. It makes us slower, of course, but it cannot be helped. We have to be very economical."

Matty glanced about the room with a faintly derisive smile.

"No, indeed, Aunt Matty," said Justine, answering the look, "you are quite wrong. Mother is speaking the simple truth. Strict economy is necessary. There is no pose about it."

Matty lifted her brows in light enquiry.

"Now, Aunt Matty, you made the comment in all good faith, as clearly as you could have made it in words, intending it to be so taken. And that being the case, it must be so answered. And my answer is that economy is essential, and that Jellamy works single-handed for that reason."

"Is it, dear? Such a lot of answer for such a little question."

"It was not the question. It was the comment upon the reply."

"No one is to make a comment but you, dear?"

"Justine does make them," murmured Aubrey.

"Now, little boy, how much did you follow of it?"

"Upon my word, I do not follow any of it," said Oliver.

Sarah leaned back almost in exhaustion, having followed it all. Her husband had kept his eyes down in order not to do so.

"Well, we mustn't get too subtle," said Justine. "They say that that is a woman's fault, so I must beware."

Aubrey gave a crow of laughter, checked it and suffered a choke which exceeded the bounds of convention.

"Aubrey, darling!" said Blanche, as if to a little child.

"Now, little boy, now, little boy," said Aubrey, looking at his sister with inflamed cheeks and starting eyes.

"Now, little boy, indeed," she said in a grave tone.

"Poor child!" said Sarah.

"What shall I do when there is no one to call me little boy?" said Aubrey, looking round to meet the general eye, but discovering that it was not on him, and returning to his dinner.

"Aubrey has a look of Father, Blanche," said Matty.

"I believe you are right, Aunt Matty," said Justine, with more than the usual expression. "I often see different likenesses going across his face. It has a more elusive quality than any of our faces."

"I meant something quite definite, dear. It was unmistakable for the moment."

"Yes, for the moment. But the moment after there is nothing there. It is a face which one has to watch for its fleeting moods and expressions. Would not you say so, Father?"

Edgar raised his eyes.

"Father has to watch," said Aubrey, awaiting the proceeding with a grin.

"What a gallant smile!" said Clement, unaware that this was the truth.

"There, Uncle's smile!" said Justine.

The quality of the grin changed.

"And now Grandpa's! Don't you see it, Aunt Matty?"

"I spoke of it, dear. Yes."

"And don't you, Father? You have to look for a moment."

Edgar again fixed his eyes on his son.

"There, it has gone! The moment has passed. I knew it would."

Aubrey had not shared the knowledge, the moment having seemed to him interminable.

"Father need not watch any longer," he said, and would have grinned, if he had dared to grin.

"The process does not seem to be attended by adequate reward," said Mark.

Clement raised his eyes and drew a breath and dropped his eyes again.

"Clement need not watch any longer either," said Aubrey.

"Now, little boy, you pass out of the common eye." Oliver turned his eyes on his grandson.

"The lad is getting older," he said.

"Now that is indubitably true, Grandpa," said Justine. "It might be said of all of us. And it is true of him in another sense; he has developed a lot lately. But do take your eyes off him and let him forget himself. This is all so bad for him."

"He could not help it, dear," said Blanche, expressing the thought of her son.

"Now are our little affairs of any interest to you?" said Matty, who had been waiting to interpose and at once arrested Sarah's eyes. "If they are, we have our own little piece of news. We are to have a guest, who is to spend quite a while with us. I am looking forward to it, as I have a good deal of time to myself in my new life. There are many people whom I miss from the old one, though I have others to do their part indeed. And this is one of the first, and one whose place it would be difficult to fill."

"We have found a corner for her," said Oliver "though you might not think it."

"She will have the spare room, of course, Father," said Blanche. "It is quite a good little room."

"Yes, Mother, of course it is," said Justine, in a low, suddenly exasperated tone. "But it is to be like that. The house is to be a hut and the room a corner, and there is an end of it. Let us leave it as they prefer it. People can't do more than have what they would choose."

Matty looked at the two heads inclined to each other, but did not strain her ears to catch the words. Sarah did so and controlled a smile as she caught them.

"Well, are you going to let me share this advantage with you?" went on Matty. "It is to be a great pleasure in my life, and I hope it will count in yours. There is no great change of companionship round about."

"Well, no, I suppose there is not," said Justine. "We are in the country after all."

"So I am not a host in myself," said Dudley.

"It is known to be better for the country to be like itself," said Sarah, who found this to be the case, as it was the reason of her acquaintanceship with the Gavestons.

Thomas looked up with a faintly troubled face.

"This is a very charming person, who has been a great deal with me," continued Matty, as if these interpositions did not signify. "Her parents have lately died and left her at a loose end; and if I can help her to gather up the threads of her life, I feel it is for me to do it. It may be a thing I am equal to, in spite of my—what shall I call them?—disadvantages."

"I always tell you that your disadvantages do not count, Aunt Matty," said Justine.

"I feel that they do, dear. They must to me, you see. But I try not to let them affect other people, and I am glad of any assurance that they do not."

"Do you mean Maria Sloane?" said Blanche. "I remember her when we had just grown up and she was a child. She grew up very pretty, and we saw her sometimes when we stayed with you and Father."

"She grew up very pretty; she has remained very pretty; and she will always be pretty to me, though she is so to everyone as yet, and I think will be so until she is something more."

"It is odd to see Aunt Matty giving her wholehearted admiration to anyone," said Justine to Mark. "It shows that we have not a complete picture of her."

"It also suggests that she has one of us."

"It is pleasant to see it in a way."

"We may feel it to be salutary."

"She has only seen one or two of my many sides," said Dudley.

"Miss Sloane has not married, has she?" said Blanche.

"No, she is still my lovely Maria Sloane. I don't think I could think of her as anything else. A rose by any other name would smell as sweet, but it seems that marriage might be a sort of desecration of Maria, a sort of plucking of the rose." Matty ended on an easy note and did not look into anyone's face.

Sarah regarded her with several expressions, and Blanche with an easy and almost acquiescent one.

"Mrs. Middleton has been plucked," murmured Aubrey. "Mr. Middleton has plucked her."

Thomas gave a kindly smile which seemed to try to reach the point of amusement.

"Is she well provided for, Aunt Matty?" said Justine in a clear tone.

Sarah nodded towards Justine at the pertinence of the question.

"I think so, dear; I have not heard anything else. Money seems somehow not to touch her. She seems to live apart from it like a flower, having all she needs and wanting nothing more."

"Flowers are plucked," said Aubrey.

"They look better when they are not, dear."

"Money must touch her if she has all she needs," said Clement. "There must be continual contact."

"Well, I suppose she has some, dear, but I think it is not much, and that she does not want any more. When you see her you will know what I mean."

"We have all met people of that kind, and very charming they are," said Justine.

"No, not anyone quite like this. I shall be able to show you something outside your experience."

"Come, Aunt Matty, think of Uncle Dudley."

"I could not say it of myself," said her uncle.

"Yes, I see that you follow me, dear. But there is no one else who is quite as my Maria. Still you will meet her soon, and I shall be glad to do for you something you have not had done. I take a great deal from you, and I must not only take."

"Is she so different from other people?" said Blanche, with simple question. "I do not remember her very well, but I don't quite know what you mean."

"No, dear? Well, we shall see, when you meet, if you do know. We can't all recognise everything."

"Would it be better if Mother and Aunt Matty did not address each other in terms of affection?" said Mark.

"Is it supposed to excuse everything else? It seems that something is."

"Well, perhaps in a way it does," said Justine, with a sigh. "Affection should be able to stand a little buffeting, or there would be nothing in it."

"There might be more if it did not occasion such a thing," said Clement.

"Oh, come, Clement, people can't pick their way with their intimates as if they were strangers."

"It is only with the latter that they attempt it."

"Father and Uncle behave like friends," said Aubrey, "Mother and Aunt Matty like sisters, Clement and I like brothers. I am not sure how Mark and Clement behave. I think like strangers."

"No, I can't quite subscribe to it," said Justine. "It is putting too much stress on little, chance, wordy encounters. Our mild disagreement now does not alter our feeling for each other."

"It may rather indicate it," said Clement.

"We should find the differences interesting and stimulating."

"They often seem to be stimulating," said Mark. "But I doubt if people take much interest in them. They always seem to want to exterminate them."

"I suppose I spend my life on the surface," said Dudley. "But it does seem to avoid a good deal."

"Now that is not true, Uncle," said Justine. "You and Father get away together and give each other of the best and deepest in you. Well we know it and so do you. Oh, we know what goes on when you are shut in the library together. So don't make any mistake about it, because we do not."

Edgar's eyes rested on his daughter as if uncertain of their own expression.

"Do you live on the surface, Aunt Matty?" said Aubrey.

"No, dear. I? No, I am a person who lives rather in the deeps, I am afraid. Though I don't know why I should say 'afraid', except that the deeps are rather formidable places sometimes. But I have a surface self to show to my niece and nephews, so that I need not take them down too far with me. I have a deal to tell them of the time when I was as young as they, and things were different and yet the same, in that strange way things have. Yes, there are stories waiting for you of Aunt Matty in her heyday, when the world was young, or seemed to keep itself young for her, as things did somehow adapt themselves to her in those days. Now there is quite a lot for Aunt Matty to talk about herself. But you asked her, didn't you?" Matty looked about in a bright, conscious way and tapped her knee.

"It was a lot, child, as you say," said Oliver.

"Aubrey knew not what he did," said Clement.

"He knew what he meant to do," said Mark. "Happily Aunt Matty did not."

"We both used to be such rebels, your aunt and I," said Blanche, looking round on her children. "We didn't find the world large enough or the time long enough for all our pranks and experiments. I must tell you all about it some time. Hearing about it brings it all back to me."

"Being together makes Mother and Aunt Matty more alike," said Mark.

"Suppose Mother should become a second Aunt Matty!" said Aubrey.

"Or Aunt Matty become a second little Mother," said Justine. "Let us look on the bright side—on that side of things. Grandpa, what did you think of the two of them in those days?"

"I, my dear? Well, they were young then, as you are now. There was nothing to think of it and I thought nothing."

"We were such a complement to each other," continued Blanche. "People used to say that what the one did not think of, the other did, and vice versa. I remember what Miss Griffin thought of us when she came. She said she had never met such a pair."

"Miss Griffin!" said Justine. "I meant to ask her to come in to-night and forgot. Never mind, the matter can be mended. I will send a message."

"Is it worth while, dear? It is getting late and she will not be ready. There is not much left for her to come for. We will ask her to dinner one night and give her proper notice."

"We will do that indeed, Mother, but there is still the evening. And she is just sitting at home alone, isn't she, Aunt Matty?"

"Why, yes, dear, she is," said Matty with a laugh. "When two out of three people are out, there must be one left. But I think she enjoys an evening to herself."

"I see it myself as a change for the better," said Oliver.

"Now I rather doubt that," said Justine. "It is so easy, when people are unselfish and adaptable, to assume that they are enjoying things which really offer very little. Now what is there, after all, in sitting alone in that little room?"

"Cosiness, dear, perhaps," said Matty, with a change in her eyes. "I have asked that same question and have had an answer."

"The size of the room is well enough for one person," said Oliver. "That is indeed its scope."

"Mother dear, I have your permission to send for her?" said Justine, as if the words of others could only be passed over.

"Well, dear, if you have your aunt's. But I don't know whom we are to send. The servants are busy."

"There is no problem there; I will go myself. I have eaten enough and I will be back before the rest of you have finished."

"One of the boys could go," said Edgar.

"No, Father, I will leave them to satisfy their manly appetites. No one else will understand the exigencies of Miss Griffin's toilet, and be able by a touch and a word to put things right, as I shall."

"Certainly no one else will undertake that," said Mark.

"Should I come to help with the toilet?" said Aubrey.

"One of you should walk with your sister," said Edgar, without a smile.

Aubrey rose with a flush, stood aside for Justine to pass and followed her out of the room.

"Oh, my baby boy has gone," said Blanche, not referring to the actual exit.

"He has developed very much, dear," said Matty. "We shall have him like his brothers after all."

"Why should he not be like them?"

"Well, he will be. We see that now."

"He has always seemed to me as promising as either of them. A little less forward for his age, but that is often a good sign."

"It must be difficult to judge of children," said Mark, "when their progress must count against them."

"I can't think of a childhood with less of the success that spells failure," said Clement.

"Slow and steady wins the race," said Oliver, without actually following.

"He is not particularly slow. He is only different from other people, as all individual people are," said Blanche. "No one with anything in him is just like everyone else."

"That cannot be said of anyone here, can it?" said her sister. "We are an individual company."

"Yes, but no one quite so much so as Aubrey. He is without exception the most individual person I have ever met."

"Without exception, dear?" said Matty, bending her head and looking up from under it. "Have you forgotten the two young rebels we were talking about just now?"

"No, but even you and I did not quite come up to him in originality. He is something in himself which none of the rest has been."

"I think that is true," said Mark.

"Now what do you mean by that? If you mean anything disparaging, it is very petty and absurd. I wish Justine were here to take my part. I can only repeat that there is something in Aubrey which is to me peculiarly satisfying. Edgar, why do you not support me?"

"You do not seem—you hardly seem to need my help."

"But what do you think yourself of the boy? I know you always speak the truth."

Edgar, who had lately hoped that his son might after all attain the average, broke this record.

"I see there is much—that there may be much in what you say."

"Aubrey is the one with a touch of me in him," said Dudley. "I wish Justine were here too."

"Hark! Hush! Listen," said Matty. "Do not make so much noise. Is it Maria's voice in the hall? Blanche, do ask your boys to stop talking. Yes, it is my Maria; Justine must have brought her. She must have arrived this evening. It is a full moment for me, and I am glad for you all to share it." Matty broke off and sat with a listening expression and set lips.

"What a pity for her to come like this," said Blanche, "with dinner nearly over! I hope she has had something to eat, but Miss Griffin will have seen to that."

"Yes, Miss Griffin will have cared for her, but I am here to give her welcome. And I cannot get my chair away from the table; I cannot manage it; I am dependent upon others; I must sit and wait for help. Yes, it is her voice. Sometimes patience is very hard. Thank you, Dudley; thank you, Edgar; I knew I should not wait long. No one else, Jellamy; too many cooks spoil the broth. I am on my feet now, and I can arrange my lace and touch my hair and make myself look my best, vain person that I am; make myself look like myself, I should rather say, for that is all my aim."

"What relation is this friend to you all?" said Sarah, leaning towards Blanche.

"No relation, only an old friend. She lived near to our old home and my sister saw a good deal of her."

Sarah gave a grateful nod and leaned back, ready for the scene.

Justine spoke in the doorway.

"Now, I am simply the herald. I claim no other part. I found Miss Sloane already in the lodge and Miss Griffin at a loss how to manage the situation. So I took it into my own hands. And I feel a thought triumphant. I induced Miss Sloane, tired as she was, travel stained and unwilling as she was, harassed and moithered by crossing letters and inconsistent trains, to come and join us to-night. Now do you not call that a success? Because it was a hardly earned one. And now you can all share the results."

A tall, dark woman of fifty entered the room, came towards Matty with a swift but quiet step, exchanged a natural embrace and looked round for her hosts. Blanche came forward in the character; Matty introduced the pair with an air of possession in each; Miss Griffin watched with the open and almost avid interest of one starved of interest and accordingly unversed in its occasions, and Justine took her stand at her side with an air of easy friendship.

"I do not need an introduction," said Blanche. "I remember you so well, Miss Sloane. I am afraid that my daughter has asked rather much of you, but we do appreciate your giving it to us."

"Miss Sloane has made a gallant capitulation, Mother, and does not want credit for it any more than any other generous giver."

"It is more than we had a right to expect," said Edgar.

"It is certainly that, Father. So we will take it in a spirit of simple gratitude."

"Well, stolen waters are sweet."

"Bravo, Father!" said Justine, smiling at Miss Griffin. "He comes up to scratch when there is a demand on him."

"I have less right to expect what I am having," said

the guest, in a voice which did not hurry or stumble, shaking hands with several people without hastening or scamping the observance. "I am a travel-worn person to appear as a stranger."

"It is only a family gathering, Miss Sloane," said Justine. "We honestly welcome a little outside leavening."

"We are glad indeed to see you, my dear," said Oliver, who had got himself out of his chair. "You are a good person to set eyes on. I do not know a better."

"For heaven's sake sit down, Miss Sloane," said Justine, when they reached the drawing-room. "I shall feel so guilty if you continue to stand."

"Now I am dependent upon help to get into a place by my guest," said Matty, in a clear tone. "I cannot join in a scramble."

"Poor, dear Aunt Matty, the help is indeed forthcoming. And, boys, you must see that Miss Griffin has no chair. Thank you, Uncle; I knew you would not countenance that."

Maria Sloane was a person who seemed to have no faults within her own sphere. She had a tall, light figure, large, grey eyes, features which were good and delicate in their own way rather than of any recognised type, and an air of finished and rather formal ease, which was too natural ever to falter. Matty had said that money seemed not to touch her, and that when they saw her they would understand; and Edgar and Dudley and Mark saw her and understood. Justine and Sarah thought that her clothes were of the kind of simplicity which costs more than elaboration, but she herself knew that when these two qualities are on the same level, simplicity costs much less. Blanche simply admired her and Miss Griffin welcomed her coming with fervid relief. She had lost a lover by death in her youth, and since then had lived in her loss, or gradually in the memory of it. Her parents had lately died, and she had left the home of her youth with the indifferent ease which had come to mark her. She believed that nothing could touch her deeply again, and losing her parents at the natural age had not done so. Her brothers and sisters were married and away, and she now took her share of the money and went forth by herself, seeing that it would suffice for her needs, rather surprised at herself for regretting that they must be modified, and welcoming a shelter in the Seatons' house while she adapted herself to the change. She had rather felt of herself what Matty said of her, that she lived apart from money like a flower, but she had lately realised that not even the extreme example of human adornment was arrayed as one of these.

"Confess now, Miss Sloane," said Justine. "You would rather be in this simple family party than alone in that little house. Now isn't it the lesser of two evils? I think that nothing is so hopeless as arriving after a long journey and finding the house empty and a cheerless grate, and everything conspiring to mental and moral discomfort."

"Has Justine had that experience?" said Mark. "If so, we are much to blame."

"That could hardly have been the case, dear," said Matty, "with Miss Griffin and Emma in the house."

"I meant metaphorically empty and cheerless. We all know what that means."

"We are even more to blame," said Mark.

"Make up the fire, Aubrey dear," said Blanche, following the train of thought.

"It is metaphorically full," said her son from a chair.

There was laughter, which Aubrey met by kicking his feet and surveying their movement.

"Get up and make up the fire," said Clement, who found these signs distasteful.

His brother appeared not to hear.

"Get up and make up the fire."

"Now that is not the way to ask him, Clement," said Justine. "You will only make him obstinate. Aubrey darling, get up and make up the fire."

"Yes, do it, darling," said Blanche.

"Now I have been called darling twice, I will. Why should I be obliging to people who do not call me darling or little boy or some other name of endearment?"

There was further laughter, and Aubrey bent over the fire with his face hidden. This seemed a safe attitude, but Clement observed the flush on his neck.

"Don't go back to the best chair in the room."

Aubrey strolled back to the chair; Clement intercepted him and put a leg across his path; Justine came forward with a swift rustling and a movement of her arms as of separating two combatants.

"Come, come, this will not do: I have nothing to say for either of you. Both go back to your seats."

"Will one of you help me to move the chair for your mother?" said Edgar, who did not need any aid.

"Yes, sir," said Aubrey, with almost military precision.

"Now I think that Aubrey came out of that the better, Clement," said Justine.

"The other fellow doesn't seem to be out of it yet," said Oliver, glancing at his second grandson. "I am at a loss to see why he put himself into it."

"Miss Sloane, what must you think of our family?"

"I have belonged to a family myself."

"And do you not now belong to one?"

"Well, we are all scattered."

"I do not dare to think of the time when we shall be apart. It seems the whole of life to be here together."

Thomas lifted his eyes at this view of a situation which he had just seen illustrated.

"Do you belong to a family, Miss Griffin?" said Dudley.

"I did, of course, but we have been scattered for a long time."

"I have lived in the same house all my life, and so has my brother," said Edgar.

"I have lived in two houses," said Blanche.

"I am just in my second," said Matty, "and very

strange I am finding it, or should be if it were not for this dear family at my gates. The family at whose gates I am, I should say."

"Why should you say it, Aunt Matty?" said Justine. "What difference does it make?"

"I too have just entered my second," said Oliver, "though it hardly seemed worth while for me to do so. I had better have laid myself down on the way."

"And you, Miss Sloane?" said Edgar.

"I am on my way to my second, which must be a very tiny one. It will be the first I have had to myself."

"And you have not had your road made easier," said Oliver. "You have been dragged out of it in the dead of night, when you thought that one of your days was done. The way you suffer it speaks well for you."

"I have an idea that a good many things do that for Miss Sloane," said Justine. "But you make me feel rather a culprit, Grandpa."

"You have done a sorry thing, child, and I propose to undo it. Good-night, Blanche, my dear, and good-bye I hope until to-morrow. If it is to be for ever, I am the more glad to have been with you again."

"Father is tired," said Blanche, who would never admit that Oliver at eighty-seven might be near the end of his days.

"I am tired too," said Matty, "but after such a happy evening with such a satisfying end. I thank you all so much, and I am sure you thank me."

"We do indeed," said Justine. "You are tired too, Miss Griffin, and I am afraid after a very brief taste of happiness. But we will make up for it another time."

"Oh, I am not tired," said Miss Griffin, standing up and looking at Matty.

"Be careful, both of you, on this slippery floor," said Blanche. "I always think that Jellamy puts too much polish on it. Do not hurry."

"We shall neither of us be able to do that again," said Oliver.

Blanche followed her father and sister with her eyes on their steps, and perhaps gave too little attention to her own, for she slipped herself and had to be saved. Justine moved impulsively to Maria.

"Miss Sloane, I do hope that you are going to spend some time with them? It comes to me somehow that you are just what they need. Can you give me a word of assurance?"

"I hope they will let me stay for a while. It is what I need anyhow, a home and old friends at this time of my life."

"And there are new friends here for you. I do trust that you realise that."

"I have been made to feel it. And they do not seem to me quite new, as they are relations of such old ones."

"Dear Aunt Matty, she does attach people to her in her own way."

"We have enjoyed it so much, Mrs. Gaveston. We shall have a great deal to think and talk of," said Sarah, able to express her own view of the occasion.

"We need not thank you," said Thomas, uttering the words with a sincere note and acting upon them.

"You did not mind the inclusion of Aubrey?" said Justine. "It is so difficult to keep one member of the family apart, and we know Mr. Middleton is used to boys."

"Can that give him only one view of them?" said Mark.

"Oh, come, he would not have given his best years to them, if they had not meant something to him. I daresay he often finds his thoughts harking back to the old days."

"His best years!" said Sarah, laughing at youth's view of a man in his prime.

"Mr. Middleton, what do you think of the little boy?" said Justine in a lowered tone. "Don't look at him; he is enough in the general eye; but would you in the light of your long experience put him above or below the level?"

Thomas was hampered in his answer by being forbidden to look at the subject of it, a thing he had hardly done.

"He seems to strike his own note in his talk," he said in a serious tone, trying to recall what he had heard.

"Yes, that is what I think," said Justine, as if the words had considerable import, "I am privately quite with you. But quiet; keep it in the dark; tell it not in Gath. Little pitchers have long ears. You see I feel quite maternally towards my youngest brother."

Thomas was able to give a smile of agreement, and he added one of understanding.

"Do you think that we are alike as a family, Miss Sloane?" said Blanche, willing for comment upon her children.

"Really, Mother, poor Miss Sloane! We have surely had enough from her to-night."

Maria regarded the faces round her, causing Aubrey to drop his eyes with a smile as of some private reminiscence.

"I think I see a likeness between your brother-in-law and your youngest son."

"A triumph, Miss Sloane!" said Justine. "That is a great test, and you are through it at a step. Now you can turn to the rest of us with confidence."

"But perhaps with other feelings," said Mark. "Miss Sloane will think that we have one resemblance, an undue interest in ourselves."

"In each other, let us say. She will not mind that."

"I think there are several other family likenesses," said Maria.

"And they are obvious, Miss Sloane. Quite unworthy of a discerning eye. You have had the one great success and you will rest on that. Well, I think that there is nothing more fascinating than pouncing on the affinities in a family and tracing them to their source. I do not pity anyone for being asked to do it, because I like so much to do it myself."

"Must it be a safe method of judging?" said Clement.

"Now, young man, I have noticed that this is not one of

your successful days. I can only assure Miss Sloane that you have another side."

It now emerged that Matty and her father had reached the carriage, and the party moved on with the surge of a crowd released. Justine withheld her brothers from the hall with an air of serious admonishment, and assisted Edgar and Blanche and Dudley to speed the guests.

"Good-bye, Miss Griffin," she called at the last moment. "That is right, Uncle; hand Miss Griffin into the carriage. Good-night all."

The family reassembled in the drawing-room.

"Now there is an addition to our circle," said Justine.

"Indeed, yes, she is a charming woman," said Blanche. "I had not remembered how charming. It is so nice to see anyone gain with the years, as she has."

"I believe I have been silent and unlike myself," said Dudley. "Perhaps Justine will explain to her about me, as she has about Clement."

"Indeed I will, Uncle, and with all my heart."

"I find that I want her good opinion. I do not agree that we should not mind what other people think of us. Consider what would happen if we did not."

"Miss Sloane behaved with a quiet heroism," said Mark.

"Under a consistent persecution," said his brother.

"Oh, things were not as bad as that," said Justine. "She did not mind being asked to look at the family. Why should she?"

"She could hardly give her reasons."

"And she was not actually asked to look at Aubrey," said Mark. "If her eyes were drawn to him by some morbid attraction, it was not our fault."

"Don't be so silly," said his mother at once.

"I really wonder that she was not struck by the likeness between you and Uncle, Father," said Justine.

"We may perhaps accept an indifference to any further likeness," said Edgar with a smile.

"We have to make conversation with our guests," said his wife.

"I am glad that my look of Uncle flitted across my face," said Aubrey.

"Little boy," said Justine, pointing to the clock, "what about Mr. Penrose to-morrow? He does not want to be confronted by a sleepy-head."

"Good-night, darling," said Blanche, kissing her son without looking at him and addressing her husband. "I do hope Matty enjoyed the evening. I could see that my father did. I am sure that everything was done for her. And Miss Sloane's arrival was quite a little personal triumph."

"I could see it was," said Mark, "but I did not quite know why. It seemed that it had happened rather unfortunately."

"Yes, dear Grandpa was quite content," said Justine. "He does like to be a man among men. We cannot expect him not to get older."

"We can and do," said Mark, "but it is foolish of us."

"I was sincerely glad of Aunt Matty's little success. It was something for her, herself, apart from what she was taking from us, something for her to give of her own. It seemed to be just what she wanted."

"I think Miss Griffin will enjoy having Miss Sloane," said Blanche, guarding her tone from too much expression.

"And I am glad of that from my soul," said Justine, stretching her arms. "I would rather have Miss Griffin's pleasure than my own any day. And now I am going to bed. I have enjoyed every minute of the evening, but there is nothing more exhausting than a thorough-going family function."

"You need not work so hard at it," said Clement.

"Clement has a right to speak," said Mark. "He has followed his line."

"Yes, anyhow I have done my best. I could spare myself a good deal if I had some support."

"Yes, that is true, Clement dear," said Blanche. "You ought to come out of yourself a little and try to support the talk."

"Is it worthy of any effort?"

"If it is worthy of Justine's, it is worthy of yours. That goes without saying."

"Then why not let it do so?"

"I had not realised that we were indebted to Clement for any regard of us," said Edgar.

"I believe I had without knowing it," said Dudley. "I believe I felt some influence at work, which checked my spirits and rendered me less than myself."

"Really, Clement, you should not do it," said Blanche, turning to her son with a scolding note as she learned his course.

Clement walked towards the door.

"We will follow—perhaps we will follow our custom of parting for the night," said his father.

"Good-night, Mother," said Clement, slouching to Blanche as if he hardly knew what he did.

"Good-night, dear," said the latter, caressing his shoulder to atone for her rebuke. "You will remember what I say."

"Father is sometimes nothing short of magnificent," said Justine. "The least said and the most done. I envy his touch with the boys. Good-night, Father, and thanks from your admiring daughter."

Edgar stooped and held himself still, while Justine threw her arms about his neck and kissed him on both cheeks, a proceeding which always seemed to him to take some time.

"I was so proud of them all," said Blanche, when her children had gone. "I do see that Matty has much less than I have. I ought to remember it."

"You ought not," said Dudley. "You ought to assume that she has quite as much. I am always annoyed when people think that I have less than Edgar, because he has a wife and family and an income and a place, and I have not. I like them to see that all that makes no difference."

"Neither does it to you, because you share it all."

"That is not the same. I like it to be thought that there is no need for me to share it, that that is just something extra. I hope Miss Sloane thinks so."

"Has Miss Sloane as much as Blanche?" said Edgar, smiling.

"Yes, she has," said his wife, with sudden emphasis. "She is such a finished, satisfying person that anything she lacks is more than balanced by what she has and what she gives. I am not at all a woman to feel that everyone must have the same. I am prepared to yield her the place in some things, as she must yield it to me in others. And I think she will be such a good example for Justine." Blanche put her needle into her work without alluding to her intention of going to bed, and observing Dudley retrieving her glasses and putting them into their case, seemed about to speak of it, but let the image fade. "I mean in superficial ways. It is the last thing we should wish, that the dear girl's fundamental lines should be changed. We are to have breakfast half an hour later: did I remember to tell Jellamy? I must go and see if Aubrey is asleep. Good-night, Edgar; good-night, Dudley. I hope my father has got to bed. He seemed to be feeling his age to-night. If you are going to talk, don't sit up too long. And if you smoke in the library, mind the sparks."

"We must be a little later than Blanche means," said Dudley, as he brought the cigars to his brother and sat down out of reach of them himself. "I want to talk about how Matty behaved. Better than usual, but so badly. And about how Miss Sloane behaved. Beautifully. I do admire behaviour; I love it more than anything. Blanche has the behaviour of a person who has no evil in her; and that is the rarest kind, and I have a different admiration for it."

"I fear we cannot say much for Clement on the point."

"We will not say anything. The less said about it, the better, and it is silly to say that and then talk about it."

"Do you think he is developing on the right lines?"

"People don't alter at his age as much as older people think."

"How old is he?" said Clement's father, wishing to know at this stage.

"Twenty-six the month before last. The change now must be slow. Perhaps the lad ought to be a grief to me, but I don't suffer a great deal; I hardly even think of him as the lad. To tell you the truth, I feel so young myself that I hardly feel I am any older than he is; but you will not tell anyone that. And now I have made one confession, the ice is broken and I should be able to make another. But do not look at me or I could not make it. You are looking at me, and for the first time in my life I cannot meet your eyes. Why don't you tell me to sit down quietly on that little stool and tell you everything?"

"Well, do that."

"You know my old godfather?"

"The one who is ninety-six?"

"Yes, that one; I have no other. At least, of course people have two godfathers, but the other is dead. And now this one is dead too. I hope he was not feeling his age, but I expect he felt as young as Clement. You know he had no children?"

"Yes, I had heard it, or I think I had. Has he left you any money?"

"Edgar, is it possible that your thoughts have run on sordid lines?"

"I had not thought of it until this moment."

"I am glad of that. I should not like to feel that I had lost my brother. It would be quite different from losing a godfather."

"It would in the matter of money," said Edgar, with

his short laugh. "Is it surprising that a childless man should leave money to his godson?"

"Yes, very. People have not any money. And they always have a family. It is very rare to have the first and not the second. I can't think of another case, only of the opposite one. We see that Matty has relations."

"I did not know that he had much money."

"I see you will feel the shock as well. I am not alone in my distress."

"Why is it distress? Why not the opposite feeling?"

"Edgar, you must know that money is the cause of all evil. It is the root of it."

"How did he get so much?"

"He speculated and made it. I knew he speculated, but I thought that people always lost every farthing. And it is wrong to speculate, and he has left the fruits of his sin to me."

"The sins of the father are visited upon the children. And in default of them there is a godson."

"Unto the third and fourth generation. But I expect they have generally lost it all by then."

"Can you bring yourself to tell me how much it is?"

"No. You have only brought yourself to ask."

"Is it very much?"

"Yes."

"How can I help you?"

"I must leave it to you. You have never failed me yet."

"Shall we wait and look at *The Times*?"

"No, that would imply a lack of confidence. There have never been secrets between us."

"Is it as much as a thousand a year?"

"Yes."

"As much as fifteen hundred?"

"Yes."

"As much as three thousand?"

"No. How easy it is after all! It is about two. I am glad you have not failed me. Now our danger point is past, and we know that we can never fail each other."

"Those letters you have had in these last days? That one you went away to answer?"

"I see there has been no secret between us."

"It will make a great deal of difference, Dudley."

"Yes, it will. I am not going to pretend that I don't think much of it. I think too much, as is natural. And I am not going to refer to it as a nice little fortune. I think it is a large one, though I am rather ashamed of thinking it. I don't know why people do such aggravating things. It must be because money brings out the worst in them. I shall never even say that I am a comparatively poor man. I have actually begun to push the thought from me."

The door opened and Blanche appeared with a lamp, pale and different in the half light, her loose, grey hair and straight garments giving her the look of a woman from another age.

"What are you talking about all this time? I had no idea that you had not come up. I went to get something from Edgar's room and thought he must be asleep. I can never get to sleep myself while I know that other people are about. I am so afraid of fire. You know that."

"Indeed I did not, Blanche," said Dudley. "At least, I thought that you slept in spite of your fear, like everyone else."

"I thought the same, assumed it," said Edgar.

"I cannot sleep when I feel that people are doing their best to set the house in a blaze every moment. How could I?"

"I don't see how you could. I did not know that Edgar did that when he sat up. It seems sly somehow, when he never does it in the day. And it does show that he ought to be in bed. But I do my best with quite different things. You can sleep in peace when you know that I am about."

"You will accept our excuse when you hear it, Blanche. Dudley has been left a fortune—a sum of money by his godfather."

"He hasn't," said Blanche in a petulant tone. "Not large enough to make all that talk and keep you up half the night. I know he was quite a poor man; I did not know why anyone had him for a godfather. Now come upstairs, both of you, and put out the lamps and push back the coals, as Dudley implies that he does it, and let us hear about it in the morning."

The brothers occupied themselves with these measures.

"How much is it?" said Blanche, shading her lamp with her hand and speaking as if she might as well hear while she waited.

"It is a large sum, my dear, really very large. You must be prepared."

"How much is it? It is very nice if it is large. I saw his death in the papers, and meant to speak about it and forgot. He was over a hundred, wasn't he?"

"He was ninety-six," said Dudley, "but that is old enough to make it excusable to forget his death."

"How much is it? Why do you not tell me? Is there some mystery?"

"No, there is not; I wish there were; I hate having to manage without one. Edgar, you are failing me at last."

"It is two thousand a year," said Edgar, "or probably about that sum."

"Two thousand pounds a year?"

"Yes, yes. About that, about two thousand pounds."

"Two thousand pounds a year or two thousand pounds?"

"Two thousand pounds a year."

"Why, how very nice!" said Blanche, turning to lead the way from the room, with her hand still over her lamp. "When did you hear? Dear Dudley, I do congratulate you. It is just what you deserve. I never was so glad about anything. And you were wise not to talk about it before Matty. It sometimes upsets her to hear that people have much more than she has. We might be the same in her place. Well, no wonder you stayed up to talk about that. We must talk it all over in the morning; I shall quite look forward to it. Well I shall sleep very soundly after hearing this."

Blanche, meaning what she said and about to act upon it, went upstairs, guarding her lamp, and the brothers followed, pausing to whisper outside their doors.

"We have seen things out of their true proportion," said Dudley. "How is it that our outlook is so material? I was prepared to toss on my bed, and really we ought to sleep particularly well. I thought when I saw Miss Sloane, that she and I lived apart from tangible things. And really we have only been kept apart from them. Well, you can't separate yourself from me on the occasion. All that I have is yours."

A flash from Blanche's door sent Edgar into his room and Dudley on tiptoe to her side.

"Blanche, I am only waiting for the morrow, to come and pour it all into your lap. And I am sure the house is not in a blaze."

"Good-night, dear Dudley," said Blanchc, smiling and closing her door.

CHAPTER IV

"WELL, HAS YOUR uncle told you his news?" said Blanche at breakfast, as she moved her hands uncertainly amongst the cups. "I heard it last night and I found it quite a tonic. I was feeling so very tired and it quite pulled me up. I slept so well and I still feel quite stimulated. I have been looking forward to talking about it."

"What is it?" said Mark. "Is Uncle going to be married?"

"No, of course he is not. What a thing to ask! There are other kinds of news."

"Well, I must say, Mother, it occurred to me," said Justine. "What interpretation do you want put upon your words? That would be quite a natural one. I was already feeling a mingled sense of excitement and coming blank. And people were springing to my mind as likely candidates. As you have created the void, you owe it to us to fill it."

"Perhaps your uncle would like to tell you himself."

"No, I should not; I do not talk about my own affairs. I have come down early on purpose to hear you do it."

"Or perhaps they would like to guess?"

"Really, Mother, we are not so young. And there is nothing to put us on the track. If Uncle has neither become engaged nor been left a fortune, we clearly cannot guess."

"I think you can," said Edgar. "Indeed you have almost done so."

"Have I? Oh, dear Uncle!" said Justine, springing up and hurrying round the table to Dudley. "Dear, dear Uncle, who have given all your mind and your life to other people, to think that you have something for yourself at last! I would rather it were you than anyone else in the world. Far, far rather than that it were me."

"I would rather it were me too."

"I know you wouldn't. You would rather it were anyone and everyone. But it isn't this time. You are the hero of this occasion. And utterly rejoiced we all are that it is so."

Blanche glanced from her daughter to Dudley with eyes of modest but irrepressible pride.

"We should like to know just at what we are to rejoice," said Clement.

"I should not; I am quite indifferent. I just like to know that a piece of luck has crossed Uncle's path; and what it is and how much it is can stand over while I savour the main truth. It is what I have always waited for."

"I suppose we all wait in case we shall be left a fortune," said Dudley. "But I never heard of anyone's waiting for other people to be left one. Because why should they be? They have no claim. And we should spend part of ours on them, and what can they want more?"

"Yes, that is what you want it for," said Justine, sighing. "To spend it on other people. And we shall all share in it evenly and equally. It was idle to hope that you would have anything for yourself. It hardly becomes us to ask how much it is. Oh, what am I saying? What a pass your dealings with us have brought us to! Somebody say something quickly to cover my confusion."

"Perhaps someone who does not assume that it is his as much as Uncle's, may put the question," said Clement. "Our interest in Uncle may lead us to that."

"Well, who will do it?" said Mark.

"I cannot," said Justine, leaning back. "Leave me out of it."

"You were hardly anticipating that fate."

"They all feel sensitive about it," said Blanche, smiling at Dudley. "This is something outside their experience."

"But why should they feel like that? I do, of course, because I have something which I have done nothing to earn, and which makes me one of those people who have too much, when some people have not enough to live on;

and anyone would be sensitive about that. I expect that is partly why rich people say they are poor. But only partly: they really think they are poor. I begin to understand it and to think I am poor myself, really to see that I am. So no one need feel sensitive for my sake. There is no reason."

"I need not say how I feel for my own," said Justine. "Oh yes, Father, you may look as if your only daughter could do and say no wrong. I crossed the bound that time."

"I don't see how we are to hear the main thing," said Clement.

"Can we ask who has left the money?" said Mark.

"My godfather," said his uncle.

"The man who was nearly a hundred?"

"Well, he was ninety-six."

"Well, we need feel no sorrow; that is one thing," said Justine, as if further complication of feeling would be too much.

"Is it a million pounds?" said Aubrey.

"Now, little boy, you are not as young as that."

Aubrey fell into silence as he found what he did by words.

"What proportion of a million is it?" said Clement.

"A terribly small one," said Dudley. "About a twentieth, I should think. It is really very small. I have quite got over my sensitiveness and am afraid that people will think I am better off than I am. I see now how that happens. I am sorry I have so often said that people can surely afford things, when they are so well off. I feel so much remorse. I really don't like inheriting so little, except that now I suppose I should starve without it."

"Oh, we shall not find it so very little. Make no doubt about that," said Justine, meeting the general laughter with her own. "Well, why should we not speak the truth after all?"

"You have seen no reason why you should not speak

it," said Clement. "I mean, as you see it. Don't sit grinning at me, Aubrey. It makes you look more vacant than usual."

"It is an immense family event," said Mark. "I mean a great event for Uncle. It seems that we cannot speak without tripping, that all words mean the same thing."

"I hope you are not all forgetting your breakfast," said Blanche.

"I am so ashamed of being excited and toying with my food," said Dudley. "And all about my own little affairs! I have explained how little they are. I am grateful to Justine for taking the matter as concerning us all. It makes me feel less egotistic, sitting here chasing morsels round my plate."

"Would you like something fresh and hot, sir?" said Jellamy, who had stood behind the table with prominent eyes, and now spoke as if any luxury would be suitable for Dudley in his new situation. "Shall I give the word to Cook, ma'am?"

"No, you may go now. We have not really needed you all this time. We will ring if we want anything."

"No, ma'am; yes, ma'am," said Jellamy, going to the door with a suggestion of coat-tails flying.

"Jellamy has had a good half-hour," said Mark, "and will now have another."

"Well, we have all had that," said his sister.

"You have had the best," said Clement. "No one has been left anything but you and Uncle, and he has had his hour already."

"That is unworthy, Clement. And there is something I do not like in the tone of the speech. Father, are you not going to say a word on the great occasion? We know it is greater to you in that it concerns Uncle and not yourself. And we seem to want your note."

"Father said all that he felt last night," said Blanche, unsure of her husband under the demand.

"What did the godfather die of?" said Clement, with

a retaliatory note, as if to add a touch of trouble and reproach.

"Of old age and in his sleep," said Dudley.

"He has shown us every consideration," said Mark, "except by living to be ninety-six."

"I have been kept out of my inheritance too long, I might have saved by now, and then I should not have had so little. But I must conquer any bitterness."

"There is little Mr. Penrose," said Justine. "Aubrey, you can put all this excitement out of your head."

"Perhaps I can have a full-sized tutor now."

"Now, now, none of that. This makes no difference to you, except that you rejoice with Uncle. Apart from that you can just forget it."

"He can indeed," said Blanche, looking up. "Are you paying attention, Aubrey?"

"Good-morning, Mrs. Gaveston; good-morning, Mr. Gaveston. May I offer you my congratulations upon the piece of news which has just come to my ears? Good-morning, Mr. Dudley; I feel that I should have addressed you first on this occasion."

"So you meet an occasion when you do not find me second to my brother."

"Oh, I do not know that, Mr. Dudley," said Mr. Penrose, laughing. "I have never had any feeling of that kind. One naturally comes to the elder brother first. That has been all the distinction in my mind."

"So good news runs apace," said Edgar.

"How did you hear, Mr. Penrose?" said Justine.

"From your manservant at the door. I do not generally talk to the man, but to-day he addressed me and volunteered the information. And if I may say so, he was full of the most pleasant and spontaneous goodwill towards the family."

"I think we could not expect him to be silent upon such a piece of news."

"Indeed no, Miss Gaveston," said Mr. Penrose,

laughing. "Not upon the accession of a quarter of a million to the family. It would indeed be much to expect."

"It is about a twentieth of a million," said Dudley.

"Well, well, Mr. Dudley, putting it in round numbers."

"But surely numbers are not as round as that. What is the good of numbers? I thought they were an exact science."

"Well, taking the bearing of the sum upon ordinary life, shall we say?"

"No, we will not say it. We will say a twentieth."

"Well, we may as well be numerically accurate," said Mr. Penrose, not pretending to appreciate any further difference. "Come, Aubrey, we must be setting out. I suppose, Mr. Gaveston—I suppose this modification of your affairs will not affect your plans for Aubrey's education?"

"No, no, not at all. As far as I can see, not at all."

"Oh, no, Mr. Penrose, not in the least," said Justine. "There is no difference in Aubrey's prospects."

"Thank you, Miss Gaveston, thank you. You do not mind my asking? It is best to be clear on such a matter."

"Poor, little Mr. Penrose, he went quite pale," said Justine. "It would be sad if our rise in fortune should spell disadvantage for him."

"Let us talk of something else," said Dudley. "We have had enough of me and my affairs. Of course I don't mean that. I am so worried about the confusion in people's minds. Mr. Penrose has thoroughly upset me. You don't think he has any influence on Aubrey?"

"None," said Mark.

"Oh, I am sure he has," said Blanche, who had half heard.

"Well, that would be rather much to expect," said Justine, "that a tutor should be accepted as an influence by a pupil. But dear Uncle! I don't think I have seen you so much engaged with your own experience in all my life."

"There, wealth has already ruined me. And I have not

got wealth. I must be in the stage where I only have its disadvantages. I have heard of that. Do you think that people will think more of me or less?"

"More of you," said Clement.

"Yes, well, I think we can hardly expect them not to do that in a way," said Blanche.

"So they have not thought as much of me as they could?"

"I am sure they have in one sense, in any sense that matters."

"Little Mother, you are coming out very nicely on this occasion," said Justine. "We could not have a better lead. And the occasion is something of a test."

Blanche gave her daughter a rather absent smile, put her needle into her work and rose and went to the window.

"Father and Matty, Edgar! I thought I caught a glimpse of them. Coming up the drive! Both of them and on foot! It must have taken them half an hour. What can it be?"

"I will go out and help them to come in," said Justine.

"What can Justine do?" said Clement. "Carry them in, in her strong young arms?"

"It would be a useful piece of work," said Mark. "They can hardly be fit to take another step."

"Oh, I am not at all ashamed of being strong!" called his sister. "I have no wish to be the other thing. It would seem to me a very odd ambition. I like to be a good specimen physically, as well as in every other way."

"I think we might all like that," said Edgar, smiling and at once changing his tone. "If arms are needed we all have them."

"I will go," said Dudley. "I must keep my simple ways. I must not let myself become different. That sounds as if I have admired myself, and in a way I have."

"Now, Grandpa dear, come in," said Justine, keeping her eyes on Oliver as if to see that he followed her direction.

"We will have you established in a minute. Don't have any misgiving."

"Thank you, my dear, you take it all off me; I have none."

"Well, dear ones all," said Matty, pausing in the door as if she could go no further, "so here is a great occasion. I am come to share it with you, to rejoice in your joy. I could not remain in my little house and feel that so much had come—so much more had come to you in your big one, without coming to add my sympathy to all you have. For your happiness is mine. It shall be. And I shall have plenty if I can find it like that. And it is a lesson I have learnt, one that has come my way. And it isn't a hard lesson, to rejoice in the good of those so dear."

"My dear, nothing has come to us. It is to Dudley," said Blanche, emerging from her sister's embrace.

"Yes, and there is a difference, isn't there?" said Matty in an arch manner. "And we are all to see it? Well, we can't, and that is flat, as the boys would say. And that is a great compliment to him and to you."

"When do we say it?" said Mark.

"You can take that view too readily, Aunt Matty. Of course there is a difference," said Justine.

"But Justine ought to sympathise with Aunt Matty in the idea," said Aubrey.

"Of course, yes, of course," said Matty, looking at Dudley. "And you will let them say so? Well, I will not, I promise you. I will guard your reputation, I who know you almost as a brother. My sister's brother must be partly mine, as Blanche and I have always shared our good things. Now let me get to a chair and have my share of the news."

"How did you hear?" said Clement.

"Well, well, little birds flit about the chairs of people who are tied to them. And it would be rather a sad thing if they did not, as they would be the last to hear so much, when it seems that they ought to be the first. So the news came, I won't say how."

"I will do so," said her father. "It came through a tradesman's lad, who comes to our house after yours, or who comes to it on the way to yours and to-day chose to come again on his way back."

"So Jellamy was the bird," said Mark.

"Well, anyhow we heard," said his aunt. "But I should have liked to hear it from one of you, coming running down to tell me."

"We should have been down in a few minutes," said Justine.

"Would you, dear? But the minutes passed and nobody came. And so we came up to hear for ourselves."

"A bold step for anyone tied to a chair," muttered Clement.

"And came on foot!" said Blanche. "Whatever made you do that?"

"Well, dear, what were we to do?" said her sister, laughing and glancing at Edgar.

"You could have waited a little while."

"Well, it is true that that occupation palled," said Oliver.

"I expect Miss Griffin was very interested," said Justine.

"Well, now, let us settle down to hear the story," said Matty, in a tone of leaving a just annoyance, smoothing her dress in preparation for listening. "The full news of this happy quarter of a million. Let us hear it all from the first."

"My dear, it is not as much as that. It is not a quarter as much; it is about a fifth as much," said Blanche. "It is barely a fifth. It is about a twentieth of a million."

"Is it, dear? I am afraid they do not convey much to me, these differences between these very large sums. They have no bearing upon life as I know it."

"But it is just as well to be accurate."

"Well, you have been so, dear. So now tell me all about it. The exact sum makes no difference."

"Of course it does. The one is precisely four times the other."

"Well, but we don't have to think of proportions, after people have everything that they can have," said Matty, giving a glance round the room as if this appeared to her to be already the case.

"But you can't have everything you can have, from a moderate fortune belonging to somebody else."

"Oh well, dear, moderate. Your life has altered you more than I thought. Altered your attitude: of course you yourself are always my old Blanche. But a quarter of a million or some other proportion of one! We were not brought up to differentiate between such things. And belonging to somebody else! Dudley and I know better."

"It is not a quarter of a million or some proportion of one. I said it was barely a twentieth," said Blanche, her voice unsteady.

"You might say that fifty pounds is a proportion of one," said Mark.

"I had better go and lie down," said Dudley. "I may feel better when I get my head on the pillow."

"I don't care which it is," said Justine. "A simple life for me."

"Yes, and for me too, dear," said her aunt. "I always feel that in my heart."

"And keep it in your heart then," said her father.

"Well, let me hear all about it," said Matty, tapping her knee. "I have asked more times than I can count."

"Calculation does not seem to be Aunt Matty's point," said Mark.

"I want to hear the beginning, the middle and the end. Not the exact sum; I won't press that; but the romance of it from the first. That would be a small thing to deny your invalid, who is dependent on you for the interest of her life."

"Oh, how is Miss Sloane this morning?" said Justine, reminded of her aunt's other interests.

"That is another question, dear. Thank you, she is well and rested. And now for my own answer."

"My godfather died and left no heir. That is the romance," said Dudley.

"Left no heir!" said Matty, with a roguish look. "He has left an heir indeed, and very much we all rejoice with him. There is the romance in truth."

"That very old fellow," said Oliver, "who lived not far from us?"

"Yes, dear Grandpa, he was ninety-six," said Justine smoothing Oliver's sleeve in tender recognition of an age that was approaching this.

"He must have seen a lot," said Oliver, making his own comparison.

"I remember him," said Matty. "Edgar and Dudley were staying at his house when Edgar and Blanche first met. I don't know why you object to the word, romance. It all seems to me to fit together in quite a romantic way. So now tell me all about it. When you heard, what you heard, how you heard. How you felt and what you said. You must know all the things that I want to be told."

"They must by now," said Oliver. "I agree."

"We heard at breakfast this morning. Mother and Father had heard from Uncle last night," said Justine, in a running tone with a faint sigh in it. "It is only an hour or two ago. And what did we feel? I declare it already eludes me."

"That is really not fair on Aunt Matty," said Mark.

"Then I heard nearly as soon as you," said Matty, turning her eyes from her niece and nephew. "But my feelings do not play such tricks on me; no, they were too strong and eager for you for that. But I want to know how Dudley felt when the truth broke upon him. That is the main issue of the story."

"We heard last night, Edgar and I," said Blanche. "Edgar and Dudley sat up late, and when I came down to scold them, I was met by this piece of news. I told them it was quite a tonic. I slept so well after hearing it."

Matty looked at her sister and simply turned to other people.

"But what did you feel, Dudley? That is the main point."

"Uncle, gratify Aunt Matty's curiosity," said Justine. "She has every right to feel it."

"Well, dear, more than a right, I think, and curiosity is an odd word. It is natural and sympathetic to feel an interest in an important change for a friend. It would not even be quite affectionate not to feel it."

"No, no, Aunt Matty, you are all on the safe side. So now, Uncle."

"I heard a few days ago and kept the matter in my heart."

"Ah, that shows how deep it went."

"Oh no, does it? If I had known that, I would have brought it out. I thought it showed that I did not attach enough importance to it, even to mention it. I meant it to be showing that."

"Ah, we know what that kind of indifference means. Keeping the matter in your heart, indeed! And at last it got too big even for your big heart"—Matty gave Dudley a smile—"and you revealed it to your second self, to Edgar. And didn't you have the tiniest feeling of interest? Not the least spark of excitement?"

"I had all the natural feelings. Shock, delight, excitement; compunction at having so much; worry lest I should be thought to have more than I had, though I did not know then how much reason there would be. Pleasure in what I could do for people; fear lest they should take it all for granted, or think I was conferring favours, and it does seem unlikely that they should avoid both. And then I told it all to Edgar, and the matter assumed its just proportions—you will remember that the sum is a twentieth of a million—and I went to bed feeling that my little affairs had a small place in the general scheme, and that it would all be the same a hundred years hence; which is not true, but it was right for me to feel it. And now I ought to say that that is the longest speech I have ever made, but I never know how people can be sure of that."

"There, Aunt Matty, there is a proper effort," said Justine.

Matty's swift frown crossed her face.

"You don't any of you seem to feel quite what I should have expected."

"Well, no, child, I am rather of your mind," said Oliver.

"We have not inherited anything," said Blanche. "It is Dudley who has had the good fortune."

"A good fortune in two senses. And what do the two young men feel, whose prospects are now so different?"

"They are nothing of the kind," said Blanche, with both her voice and her needle rising into the air. "This had nothing to do with them, and they are not giving a thought to it, except to rejoice in their uncle's happiness."

"I am not as bad as that," said Dudley. "Happiness depends on deeper things. Love in a cottage is the most important kind of love; no other kind is talked about so much. I can only hope to be allowed to share what I have with other people, and of course I shall feel that the generosity is theirs."

"I am sure you will," said Matty. "And now what about the unchanged prospects of the two young men? Was I right or wrong in saying what I did?"

"You were wrong in saying it," said her father. "It was not a thing to say."

"Well, was I wrong—incorrect in thinking it?"

"Your sister says that you were, her brother-in-law that you were not. You must decide."

"Well, I decide that it was a true and natural thing to

think, and therefore to say. And most heartily do I rejoice with them in the truth of it."

"Clement and I have all we need," said Mark. "We should have no right or reason to ask for more."

"And the people who do not ask for things, are the people who have them, I have heard. You would not ask, I am sure. Yes, I must not be denied my little bit of excitement for you. It is the one kind I have left, to let my spirits soar for other people, and I must be allowed to make the most of it. It is the best kind."

"I suppose it is, Aunt Matty. Anyhow it is nice of you to feel it," said Justine, "but there doesn't really seem to be much need. I am with the boys there. We have our home and our happiness and each other, and the simple tastes and pleasures which are the most satisfying. We do not ask or need anything more. I am quite sorry for Uncle that it is so, because he would like nothing better than to pour out his all upon us. But our simple lot suffices us, and there it is."

"They are all so self-reliant," said Blanche, with mingled apology and pride. "They have been brought up to be independent of things outside themselves."

Matty gave her glance about the room, this time with an open smile.

"Yes, I see what you are thinking," said her niece at once. "We have been brought up in a beautiful and dignified home; that is the truth. I should be the last person to deny it. But it has become our background, and that means that we are independent of it in a way. Not that we do not love it; I do from the bottom of my heart. And that brings it to my mind that I should be glad for something to be done for the dear old house, to prevent its falling into decay. I have long wished that its faithful service could be repaid. It would be a relief to Father, who sees it as a life trust and not as his own in any personal sense, so that he would not really be taking anything for himself. And Mark feels about it in the same way. Yes, I think I may say that we should all be grateful for succour for the fine old walls which have sheltered us and our forebears."

"Well, there is one bright spot in the darkness," said Matty to Dudley, changing her tone as she spoke. "I cannot but support my niece, though I must admit that my gratitude would have a personal quality."

"But the house has sheltered me and my forebears too," said Dudley. "Perhaps it does not count."

"Well, well, it may count a little. And anyhow it will cost a little. That must be your comfort."

"What do you say, Father?" said Justine.

"I must say what you do, my dear; I cannot but say it. It is a thing that your uncle and I could do together."

"Ah, that strikes the right note. That clinches the matter. You and Uncle can do it together. It stands that it will be done."

"Better and better," said Matty to Dudley with a smile.

"We can scarcely say that Father and Mark—that as a family we take nothing," said Clement. "The house hardly belongs to Father the less, that it will go to his descendants."

"No, I do not feel that I can say it," said Mark.

"No, you will not shirk your part as a benefited and grateful person," said Matty, in a tone of approval and sympathy.

"That is hardly straight, Aunt Matty," said Justine. "I wish you would not let these touches of unfairness creep into your talk. It gives to all our response that little undercurrent of defensiveness. We are not ungrateful because we want something beautiful preserved, which will be of advantage to future generations as well as ourselves, and because we realise that that is the case. You have admitted to the same feeling."

"I have it indeed, dear, but then I feel definitely grateful. It is a great thing in my life, this lovely background that I see behind you all, and feel behind myself at stated intervals.

I should feel unthankful indeed if I did not appreciate it. And I ask your uncle to accept my gratitude for any service that he does to it."

"The east walls are crying for attention," said Edgar, as if his thought broke out in spite of himself. "I have hardly dared to look at them, but they must be sinking. I can almost feel it; I know it must be the case. You and I might go round, Dudley, and sketch out a plan for the work. This—I find this one of the days of my life."

Blanche looked up at her husband as if uncertain what she should feel.

"There, Uncle!" said Justine. "I congratulate you. That is what you want. You have what you would ask."

"Better still," said Matty to Dudley. "There is progress. I don't think you need fear."

"Justine dear, will you fetch my silks from my room?"

"No, Mother, I can't be sent out of the room like that, even if I have been a little frank and definite and may be so again. You must know me by now, and if you want me you must take me as I am."

"And as we cannot do without her, she has us in a tight place," said Matty, retrieving her position.

"It is half past eleven," said Blanche, relinquishing her work as if her thoughts had not returned to it. "Matty dear, would you like anything? Or would Father? It is surprising how the time goes."

"Well, I really don't think it is to-day," said Justine. "I should not have been surprised to find ourselves at the last stroke."

"Well, dear, some coffee for me, and for Father a glass of wine and a sandwich," said Matty, somehow implying that in the risen fortunes of the house such requirements would hardly count. "I hope you are going to join us."

"Yes, we will all have something; I think our nerves need it," said Justine.

"Are you feeling guilty?" said Matty, in a low, mischievous tone to Dudley.

"Will Miss Seaton and Mr. Seaton be staying to luncheon, ma'am?" said Jellamy.

"Yes. You will be staying, won't you, Matty? Father won't find it too much? He can have his rest."

"We will quarter ourselves upon you," said Oliver. "You will put up with what comes to you to-day. I take it that you wouldn't alter it."

"Yes, they will both be here for luncheon, Jellamy."

"And Miss Sloane and Miss Griffin, Jellamy," said Justine, throwing a glance from her chair.

"My dear, have you heard that?"

"No, Mother, I have just decided it. I think we need the effect of their presence."

"But are they free, dear child?"

"Well, we can soon find out. If they are not, they cannot come, of course. But I fail to see what engagements they can have in a place where neither knows anyone."

"But Miss Sloane may not care to come. What does Aunt Matty say? Miss Sloane is her guest."

"Well, for that reason I should like to have her with me. It is a kind thought of Justine's. I was wondering if I could leave her alone, and how to send a message. But Miss Griffin finds it a change to be without us." Matty's tone quickened and her eyes changed. "And I find a certain relief in being only with my relations. So I will say what I mean in my family circle and feel it is said."

"You will be better apart, if I may still depend on my eyes and ears," said her father. "I do not know what Maria makes of it all. I do not ask. She could not give a true answer and a false one would be no help. You forget the size of the house, though you talk of it."

"Well, I am not used to it yet."

"You would do well to become so."

"Let me have my own way, Aunt Matty," said Justine, sitting on the arm of her aunt's chair. "Don't deny it to me because we have got a little across. Give it to me all the more for that."

"Well, well, take it, dear. You know how I like you to have it."

"You have your own way a good deal, Justine," said Blanche.

"Oh, well, Mother, a mature woman, the only sister amongst three brothers, Father's only daughter! What can you expect?"

Edgar looked up as if to see how his own name had become involved.

"Everyone must rejoice with me to-day," said Dudley. "That always seems to me an absurd demand, but I am going to make it."

"And if there is anyone for selfless rejoicing for other people, Miss Griffin is that person, if I know her," said his niece. "And I shouldn't be surprised if Miss Sloane has a touch of the same quality."

"Suppose we keep people apart, dear," said Matty in a light tone.

"Oh, Aunt Matty, Miss Sloane has not a touch of that feeling. She would not mind being coupled with Miss Griffin. Even being with her once told me that. I should think it is not in her."

"But keep her apart, nevertheless, dear," said Blanche, in a low voice that was at once reproving and confidential. "She has nothing to do with anyone else."

"I am not sure that she would say that," said Justine audibly. "She has the connection with Miss Griffin of a long friendship. I should say that she would be the first to recognise it."

"Well, well, dear, are you going to run down and ask them?"

"No, no, not I this time," said Justine, shaking her head. "I am not always going to present myself as the bearer of such messages. It would mean that we thought too much of them altogether."

"Clement and I will go," said Mark. "That will give a trivial air to the errand. And we can imply that we think little of it."

"That should be easy," said his brother. "We have only to be natural."

"Ah, that is not always so easy as you seem to think," said Justine.

"Perhaps you find it too much so."

"Well, run along, dears," said Blanche, in a neutra manner. "You can wait and bring them back."

"If they consent to come, Mother," said Justine, witl a note of reproof.

"Well, you thought they had no other engagements dear. Let the boys go now. It will be a breath of fresh ai for them after their exciting morning. We can't have nothing but excitement."

"Do you know where to look?" said Matty to Dudley, in a mischievous aside.

"Mother talks as if we were guilty of some excess," said Clement to his brother as they left the house. "Our excitement has been for Uncle. Nothing has come to most of us."

"A good deal has come to Father, and in a certain sense to me."

"A good deal to you both. A house handed on intact is different indeed from one gaping at every seam, and sucking up an income to keep it over our heads. You are full of a great and solemn joy."

"And my happiness is not yours?"

"Any satisfaction of mine must come out of my own life, not out of other people's. But I ought to have some of my own. Father's money will be set free and Uncle has no one to spend on but us."

"What are your personal hopes?"

"Much as yours, except that they are on a smaller scale and yours are already fulfilled. I don't want a place or could not have one. But I do want a little house of my own in Cambridge. I hate the college and I am obliged to live in the town. And a little income to add to what I earn. Then I should not need to spend my spare time at home. I cannot suffer much more of Aubrey and Justine."

"And I can?"

"Your prospects are safe. You have no right to speak."

"I shall have nothing until Father dies, but the life which you must escape."

"Your future is bound up in the place. Mine has nothing to do with it. The house is a halting place for me."

"And for Justine and Aubrey what is it?"

"Aubrey is a child and Justine is a woman. There is no comparison."

"Aubrey will not always be a child and Justine not always a young and dependent woman. I can imagine her in her own house as well as you."

"Mine is the need of the moment."

"So is mine. I could do with many things. But I don't know if we can make the suggestions to Uncle."

"They may occur to him."

"Images will have to come crowding on his mind."

"I don't see why they should not. He must have seen our straitened life."

"He must have lived it," said Mark.

"You can make a joke of other people's needs, when your own are satsified. He can hardly go on for ever, spending all he has on the house. All sorts of demands must arise. We have been held very tight and insensibly the bonds will be loosened."

"When Father dies, you will have your share of what there is. Both he and Uncle must leave what they have to us."

"And how long will that be to wait?"

"Clement, what manner of man are you?"

"The same as you, though you pretend not to know it. You can go in here and offer this invitation. Explain that we observe a piece of good fortune for one of us as a general festival."

"I am in command of such a situation. You are right to imply that you are not."

"There is Miss Griffin at the window. She is there whenever we come."

"She sees the shadows of coming events. Such a gift would develop in her life."

In due course the four emerged from the lodge and set off towards the house. Mark was ready to discuss the event; Clement was inclined to glance at Maria to judge of her view of it, and to try to talk of other things; Maria was lively and interested and Miss Griffin was alternately reflective and disposed to put sudden questions.

"Here is a fairy-tale piece of news!" said Maria, as she met the family. "I shall always be glad to have heard it at first hand. We must thank you for our experience as well as congratulate you on yours."

"Thank you, Miss Sloane. That is a pleasant congratulation indeed," said Justine, turning to her brothers to continue. "What a contrast to poor Aunt Matty's! What a difference our little inner differences make!"

"A quarter of a million pounds!" said Miss Griffin, standing in the middle of the floor. "I have never heard anything like it."

"Neither have I," said Dudley. "It is about a twentieth of a million."

"A twentieth of a million!" said Miss Griffin, in exactly the same tone

"About fifty thousand pounds."

"Fifty thousand pounds!" said Miss Griffin, with the fuller feeling of complete grasp.

"We ought not to keep talking about the amount," said Blanche. "We value the thought and the remembrance."

"But if we leave it out," said Dudley, "people will think it is so much more than it is."

"I think it is better than that," said Maria. "It will not eliminate planning and contrivance from your life, and it will keep you in the world you know."

"Sound wisdom," said Justine. "How it falls from unexpected lips!"

"I feel very comforted," said Dudley. "People may realise my true position after all."

"It was deep sagacity, Miss Sloane," said Justine. "I daresay you hardly realise how deep. Words of wisdom seem to fall from your lips like raindrops off a flower."

"Justine dear, was that a little frank?" said Blanche, lowering her voice.

"Well, Mother, pretty speeches always are," said Justine, not doing this with hers. "But I don't think that a genuine impulse towards a compliment is such a bad thing. It might really come to us oftener. And Miss Sloane is not in the least embarrassed. It is not a feeling possible to her. I had discerned that, or I had not taken the risk."

"The impulse has come to Justine again," said Mark to his brother.

"And embarrassment is a feeling possible to the rest of us."

"Well, I have not been saying words of wisdom, perhaps," said Matty, in a tone that drew general attention. "But I have done my best to show my joy in others' good fortune. Though others is hardly the word for people with whom I feel myself identified. Contrivance had not struck me as one of the likely results, but if they like to enjoy the poverty of the rich, we will not say them nay. It is only the poverty of the poor which we should not welcome for them. We have that enough in our thoughts." Matty's voice died away on a sigh which was somehow a thrust.

"I shall have to give to the poor," said Dudley. "It is a thing I have never done. It shows how nearly I have been one of them. I have only just escaped being always in Matty's mind."

"A dangerous place to be," said Mark.

"I suppose I shall subscribe to hospitals. That is how people seem to give to the poor. I suppose the poor are always sick. They would be, if you think. I once went round the cottages with Edgar, and I was too sensitive to go a second time. Yes, I was too sensitive even to set my eyes on the things which other people actually suffered, and I maintain that that was very sensitive. Now I shall improve things out of recognition, and then I can go again and not recognise anything, and feel no guilt about my inheritance."

"No one can help being left money," said Miss Griffin.

"That is not on any point," said Matty lightly.

"I don't know, Aunt Matty; I don't think I agree with you," said Justine. "But I have disagreed with you enough; I will not say it."

"Well, it may be as well not to let it become a habit, dear."

"Justine dear, come and sit by me," said Blanche.

"Oh, you mean to be repressive, Mother. But I feel quite irrepressible this morning. Uncle's good fortune sets my heart singing even more than yours or Father's would. Because he has been the one rather to miss things himself and to see them pass to other people, and to see it in all goodwill. And that is so rare that it merits a rare compensation. And that the compensation should come, is the rarest thing of all. 'My heart is like a singing bird, whose nest is in a water'd shoot.' "

"Are we all going to stay in the whole morning?" said Blanche. "Justine, it is not like you to be without energy."

"Surely an unjust implication," said Mark.

"Well, we can hardly bring Miss Sloane and Miss Griffin up here, Mother, and then escort them out again at once."

"They might like to join us in a walk round the park. I sleep so much better if I get some exercise, and I expect we shall sit and talk after luncheon."

"An indulgence which can be expiated in advance by half an hour in a drizzle," said Clement.

"Well, what do you feel, Miss Sloane?" said Justine.

"I should like to go with your mother."

"And you, Miss Griffin?"

Miss Griffin opened her mouth and glanced at the fire and at Matty.

"Miss Griffin prefers the hearth. And I don't wonder considering the short intervals which she probably spends at it. So you set off with Miss Sloane, Mother, and the rest of us will remain in contented sloth. I believe that is how you see the matter."

Blanche began to roll up her silks without making much progress. Justine took them from her, wound them rapidly round her hand, thrust them into the basket and propelled her mother to the door with a hand on her waist. Maria followed without assistance, and Blanche shook herself free without any change of expression and also proceeded alone. Matty at once addressed the group as if to forestall any other speaker.

"Now I must tell you of something which happened to me when I was young, something which this occasion in your lives brings back to me. I too might have been left a fortune. When we are young, things are active or would be if we let them, or so it was in my youth. Well, a man was in love with me or said he was; and I could see it for myself, so I cannot leave it out; and I refused him—well, we won't dwell on that; and when we got that behind, he wanted to leave me all he had. And I would not let him, and we came to words, as you would say, and the end of it was that we did not meet again. And a few days afterwards he was thrown from his horse and killed. And the money went to his family, and I was glad that it should be so, as I had given him nothing and I could not take and not give. But what do you say to that, as a narrow escape from a fortune? I came almost as near to it as your uncle."

"Was that a large fortune too?" said Miss Griffin.

"It was large enough to call one. That is all that matters for the story."

"You ran very near the wind, Aunt Matty," said Justine. "And you came out well."

"I shall be obliged to take and not give, if no one will accept anything from me," said Dudley. "Because I am going to take. Indeed I have taken."

"You have not been given the choice," said Miss Griffin.

"Well, well, we all have that," said Matty. "But there is not always reason for using it. There is no obligation to seek out connections when there is no immediate family. This friend of mine had brothers."

"I wish you would not put such thoughts into words," said Dudley.

"I can't help wishing that he had not had them, Aunt Matty," said Justine. "You might have had a happier life or an easier one."

"An easier later chapter, dear, but I do not regret it. We cannot do more than live up to the best that is in us. I feel I did that, and I must find it enough." Matty's tone had a note of truth which no one credited.

"I find it so too," said Dudley. "My best is to accept two thousand a year. It is enough, but I do wish that people would not think it is more."

"Two thousand a year!" said Miss Griffin.

"Well, it is between a good many," said Matty. "It is so good when a family is one with itself. And you are all going to find it so."

"To accept needs the truest generosity," said Dudley. "And I am not sure that they have it. I know that people always underrate their families, but I suspect that they only have the other kind."

"It is that kind which is the first requirement," said Clement.

"Clement, that remark might be misunderstood," said Justine.

"Or understood," said Mark.

"I don't think I should find any difficulty in accepting

something I needed, from someone I loved. But I am such a fortunate person; I always have all I need."

"There, what did I say?" said Dudley. "An utter lack of true generosity."

"I will go further," said his niece. "I will accept an insurance of the future of my little Aubrey. Accept it in my name and in that of Father and Mother. I think I am justified in going so far."

"It is all very well to laugh, Clement," said Dudley, "but how will you look when it appears that your brothers have true generosity, and you have none?"

"I can do as they do and without having it. It seems to me to be the opposite thing that is needed."

"Clement, be careful!" said Justine, in an almost stricken tone.

"People are always ashamed of their best qualities and describe them in the wrong way," said Dudley. "Clement will accept an allowance from me and let me forget that my generosity is less than his."

"Then he is a dear, sensible boy," said Matty.

"Sensible certainly," said her nephew.

"Well, Clement, I don't know what to say," said Justine.

"You can say what you will say to Mark and Aubrey."

"Well, I suppose that is fair in a way, but it does seem that there is a difference. But I will say nothing. The matter is taken out of my hands."

"It was never in them."

"Now don't take that line with your sister. That does not make matters better."

"I have no wish to improve them. I find them well enough."

"I am afraid you do, Clement."

"Now that is not sensible, dear, and perhaps not even quite kind," said Matty.

"It seems fair that all three brothers should have something, if two have," said Miss Griffin.

"Well, it is really a matter for the family."

"Aunt Matty, don't snub Miss Griffin in public like that," said Justine. "That is certainly not quite kind."

"My dear, you may have a way of coming between people, but between Miss Griffin and me there is our own relation."

"I am afraid there is, Aunt Matty."

There was a long silence.

"Dear, dear, money, money, money!" said Justine, leaning back and locking her hands above her head. "Directly it comes in, away fly dignity, decency, everything."

"Everything but true generosity," said Mark.

"Dignity and decency depend up to a point on money," said Clement.

"Indeed that is true," said Dudley. "You have only to go round the cottages. It seems absurd to say that money is sordid, when you see the things that really are."

"And that come from the lack of it."

"Why should it be sordid any more than any other useful thing?" said Matty.

"They say that it is a curse," said Dudley, "but I do not find it so. I like being a person to confer benefits. There, that is the worst."

"Dear Uncle!" said Justine. "Enjoy your money and your generosity and all of it. You have never had a chance before."

"So you don't think that the things I gave, were more valuable than money. I knew that people never really did."

"To talk about money's having no value is a contradiction in terms," said Clement.

"Now I think that is honest, dear," said Matty.

"Aunt Matty, you are going rather far in your implications," said Justine.

"You do not go in for such things, dear, I know."

Justine put back her head in mirth, the action so familiar

in her aunt somehow throwing up her unlikeness to her.

"That may be fair, but we won't start another skirmish. And I don't take it at all as an insult, however it was meant. I am one for the direct and open line. Now here are the other elders, come in the nick of time to prevent our discussion from becoming acrimonious."

"They are running it fine," said Clement.

"Well, have you made up your minds how to spend your uncle's money?" said Oliver.

"Yes, we have," said Clement, pausing a moment to get the plan of his speech. "The house is to be put in repair for Father and Mark; there is to be an allowance for me; and something is to be done for Aubrey's future."

"Oh!" said Blanche. "Oh, it is too quick. I did not think it would all be arranged at once like that."

"Would it be better for being delayed?"

"I don't know what to say. It does not seem right somehow. I really feel almost ashamed."

"To tell you the truth, Mother, so do I," said Justine. "But I could not help it. I plead guilty to the suggestion about Aubrey's future, but otherwise I can hold myself apart."

"As a benefited person, I feel that my tongue is tied," said Edgar. "The mention of me was adroit."

"It was simply true," said Clement.

"Dudley, I don't know what to say," said Blanche. "What can you think of them all?"

"I feel that we are drawn closer. They will not spoil things for me by letting me feel alone. I don't think Clement and I have ever been so close before. And I expect them to share my joy, and people ought not to share a feeling without sharing the cause of it. I should not think it is possible. And I should be ashamed of feeling joy over a thing like money, if no one felt it with me."

"There is something in that, I suppose," said Justine.

"Well, it is nearly time for luncheon," said her mother. "I suppose I must not say any more. We have had such a nice walk. I feel all the better for it and Miss Sloane has quite a colour. It was so kind of her to come with me. Father, did you get your sleep?"

"I slept like a child, my dear, as is well for a person approaching his second childhood."

"That is not the speech of someone doing that, Grandpa," said Mark.

"Father, what a way to talk! Well, I must go and take off my things. Perhaps Miss Sloane would like to come with me. And then we should open these windows. You have all been in here all the morning."

"With all our selfish hopes and desires," said Clement. "But I wonder that Justine has not been like a breath of fresh air in herself."

"I expect she has," said Blanche, patting her daughter's cheek.

"I have certainly been a breath of something, Mother, but I believe it has been felt to be more like a draught. But it may have been fresh and wholesome."

"We did not talk about the good fortune all the time," said Matty. "We had our glimpse of other things. I gave them an early experience of my own, which amused them with its likeness to this one. Its likeness and its difference, shall we say? Well, what do you think of your aunt's varied history? I see you are not to be allowed to dwell on it. Your mother is directing our attention to more material things."

"The luncheon will not improve by waiting, dear, and I like it to be nice for you all. Let the boys help you out of your chair."

"Thank you, dears, Miss Griffin will do it. I am more used to her," said Matty, forgetting that she had objected to Miss Griffin's presence. "But she seems to be having a little nap. Wake up, Miss Griffin; even our pleasure days have their little duties, you know." Matty's tone of rallying reproof changed as she found herself alone with her companion. "You appear to have fallen into a trance.

You can't come out just for enjoyment when you come with me. There is some thought of your being of a little use. You are not quite in the position of Miss Sloane."

"I did not know that you wanted any help."

"Of course I want the help you always give me. I cannot be deprived of the few little things I have, just because other people suddenly have so much. You need not lose yourself in their experience. It will affect no one but themselves. It will anyhow make no difference to you."

"You so often get out of your chair by yourself. I can hardly know when you want help."

"Well, understand that I always want it, when you are standing by doing nothing. It would not be suitable for me to manage alone, when it is easier for me with help, and you are there to give it. I wonder you do not see it. But then I suppose you see nothing."

"Just fancy all that money!" said Miss Griffin, who was used to meeting attacks as if she were unconscious of them. "I can hardly grasp it."

"You won't have to. That is the last thing you will have to do. So that is what you have been doing instead of keeping your eyes open for my convenience. I see that a break from routine does not suit you. I must remember it."

"When a break comes very seldom, it does sometimes upset people," said Miss Griffin, in a lower tone.

"Oh, you are going to be like that! That is to be the result of a little change and pleasure. I must see that you do not have it. I see that it does not work. I must take counsel with myself and arrange for your life to be nothing but duty, as that is what seems to suit you." Matty, as she spoke, was accepting Miss Griffin's ministrations as if they were rendered by a machine, and indeed the latter could only perform them in this spirit. "Well, are we going in to luncheon, or am I going in alone? Perhaps you had better go straight home and be by yourself. That would probably make the best of you."

Miss Griffin followed Matty without reply, and seemed consciously to change her expression to one of anticipation.

"Come in, Miss Griffin," said Justine, as if Miss Griffin needed this encouragement and her aunt did not, an attitude more supported by fact than she knew. "Come in and sit by me. And Aunt Matty, take the seat by Father. And Miss Sloane on his other side, if she will."

"The seats are all arranged, dear," said Blanche.

"Yes, Mother, but a word of help is not amiss. They were all standing about like lost souls. A large family party is the most baffling thing."

"I will sit on the other side of Miss Sloane," said Dudley, "and go over everything from the beginning. She can hardly check me; she does not know me well enough."

"Do not abuse her indulgence, Uncle. Well, Mr. Penrose, what sort of a morning?"

"Well, to be frank, Miss Gaveston, not up to our standard. I am not disposed to make any complaint, as I think the family news is responsible. It is natural and perhaps not wholly undesirable that it should be so. And I hope we shall atone for it to-morrow."

"Now, little boy, what sort of hearing is this? And when Uncle has been thinking of you and your future! What kind of return is this to make?"

"He did not know about that, dear," said Blanche. "He has been excited about his uncle, as you all have. And any difference for him will not be for a long time. We must allow him his share of the pleasure, so I think he might have a holiday this afternoon. We must not expect him to settle down so much sooner than anyone else. You have all been shaken out of yourselves, and no wonder. What do you say, Edgar?"

"What you do, my dear. It is—it seems to me the thing to be said."

"And you, Mr. Penrose?" said Justine. "We should not dream of upsetting the routine without your sanction."

"Well, I should be disposed to be indulgent upon the occasion, Miss Gaveston."

"There, little boy, there is your holiday assured."

"Half holiday," said Aubrey.

"I am afraid it is nearer a whole one than it should be."

"They will be able to go for a long walk," said Blanche, "instead of having to be back by four."

"Well, really, Mother, I think Mr. Penrose might have his share of the celebration. I should guess that he is inclined to shake the dust of this house off his feet. He has his own private life as much as we have."

"Well, Mr. Penrose will do as he likes, dear. Aubrey can play by himself."

"It is very considerate, Mrs. Gaveston."

"Am I big enough to play alone?" said Aubrey.

"No, you are not," said his sister. "You are incapable of managing your time. I will see that we both spend a pleasant and profitable afternoon."

"You have all stopped talking about my inheritance," said Dudley. "Does it mean that you think enough has been said about it? Miss Sloane does not seem to think so. But she may not know how much has been said."

"I have thought of nothing else since I heard of it, Uncle."

"Neither have I," said Aubrey. "I have a witness."

"Neither have I," said Dudley.

"I should like to hear what your uncle is going to do for himself," said Blanche.

"I doubt if we shall have that satisfaction, Mother," said Justine, "great as it would be. Uncle is a man of few and simple desires. Unless he has a house of his own, which heaven forbid as long as we are all in this one, it is hard to see how he is to spend so much on himself. He has his interests and occupations and his brother. More he does not ask of life."

"He has all of us as well," said Mark. "That cannot be left out of account. Anyhow it has not been."

"Our desires have a way of getting bigger with our incomes," said Matty. "Just as they have to get smaller with them. I have had the latter experience, and rejoice the more that all of you are to have the first."

"Miss Sloane shows a great patience with our family drama," said Mark. "I am too enthralled by it myself to wonder."

"I have come on your family at a dramatic moment. Patience is the last thing that is needed."

"That is what I should have thought," said Dudley. "I am wounded by Mark's speech."

"Wait a moment, Miss Sloane, I am going to ask it," said Justine. "It is not a crime, if it is a little unconventional. Which do you consider the better to look at, my father or my uncle? Do not hesitate to say; they will not mind."

"I am afraid I do hesitate," said Maria, laughing. "And I had not thought of making a comparison."

"Oh, come, Miss Sloane, that is not quite ingenuous. People always think of it; it seems inevitable. They can't see the one by the other, without summing up their respective characteristics and ranging them on different sides."

"Dear Justine, Miss Sloane had not thought of it," said Blanche. "She has told us."

"Well, she will think of it now, Mother, as I ask her to. I am sure she has never denied anyone without more reason."

"I have never met two people whom I should see less in terms of each other."

"Ah, now that is subtle, Miss Sloane. And I believe you are right. Now I come to consider, niether have I. It is simply superficial to talk as if one were a feeble copy of the other."

"It is worse than that," said Dudley. "It is too bad."

"They should give more attention to the comparison," said Edgar, smiling at the guest. "My daughter seems only to have grasped the essence of it at this moment."

"Oh, now, Father, you would like me to be perfect, wouldn't you? Well, I am not, so you can make the best of it."

"Father may claim to have done so," said Clement.

"I think we are better when we are greedy than when we are clever," said Mark. "The one quality is natural to us; the other is not."

"And your uncle can satisfy the one, but he can do nothing for the other," said Edgar, with another smile.

"They might all do so much, Miss Sloane, if they would only apply themselves," said Blanche, pursuing the line of her children's ability.

"I suppose—have the arrangements you spoke of taken any form?" said Edgar.

"Not definitely, Father," said Justine, "but they are taking their course. Uncle has opened his purse in the way that I knew he would, as I indeed foretold, though my doing so raised an outcry. Clement is to have an allowance; Aubrey's future is secure; the house benefits in whatever way you have arranged; and what your private and personal benefits are to be, we do not know. They are between you and him and will be left so."

Blanche took something from a dish which Jellamy handed, as if it were no good to interpose.

"And what is my Justine to have from the open purse?"

"Oh, trust you to ask that, Father. My position is safe with you. Well, I am having peace of mind about Aubrey. It is what I asked and what was at once granted to me. I could think of no other need."

"Who was to depend on Father to that extent?" said Clement to his brother.

"Perhaps Justine did. If so, we see that she was right."

"Justine holds herself apart from my easy generosity," said Dudley, "so that to her I am what I have always been, simply her uncle."

"But you shall be more than that!" said his niece.

"I will not stand aside a moment longer. You shall be generous to me. I will take a yearly subscription to my pet charity, to my old men and women in the village. Yes, I think I can ask that, without feeling that I am piling up a life already loaded. And you need not tell me that it is forthcoming, because I know it is. Actually for myself I ask nothing, holding myself already too rich."

"And I have only felt that about myself for a few days. How much better you are than I am! And I already think I am poor."

"You will soon be right," said Mark.

"You know I meant that a twentieth of a million was poor."

"One thing I say!" said Justine, suddenly raising her hand. "One stipulation I make. Uncle shall feel free to break off these undertakings at any time, to stand as fully apart from them as if they had never been made. And this at any hint of demand from his own life. In one moment, at one fell swoop—at one swoop, what is his own is in his hands, to be deflected to his own purposes. It is on this understanding and this alone, that I subscribe to the engagements, and rejoice for other people and accept for myself."

"Well, that goes without saying, dear," said Blanche.

"Oh, no, it does not, Mother. And therefore it shall not on this occasion. I am not quite without knowledge of life, though you probably believe me to be. I know how to safeguard the future or how it should be safeguarded. And as no one else made the move, I did it myself; and I am glad to have done it and glad to have it behind."

"It is well to have it said once," said Edgar. "We will all remember it has been said."

"Thank you, Father. If I could not depend on you, where should I stand?"

"It is wise to say it for another reason. Your uncle can only use the income from his money. The capital is held in trust and cannot be touched."

"I can only will it," said Dudley. "So other people will have the use of it in the end. I am not in at all a selfish position. My godfather must have been afraid that I should rush to ruin. He did not mind if other people did. I do appreciate his special feeling for me. Indeed I approve of all his feeling."

"It may be a wise condition," said Maria. "You would be checked in any headlong course. I daresay you will live to be glad of it."

"I have done that already," said Dudley, lowering his voice. "We began to consider the repairs to the house, and I was checked almost at once. To do them all would take all my income and leave me as I was before, and I could not bear to be that. I think that fifty-three years must have made me tired of it."

"One thing I ask!" said Aubrey, raising his hand in imitation of his sister. "And that is that Mother shall have a new dress to celebrate the event."

"Yes, well, I think I can accept that," said Blanche, "as it is for that reason." She turned to her son with more feeling than she had yet shown. "My little boy does not like his mother to be shabby."

"And so can I," said Justine, "and with all my heart. And rejoice in other people's pleasure in it, which will be greater than my own."

"Justine's advantages will not cost any less, that she gets no personal benefit from them," said Clement to Mark.

"And so can I," said Matty, smiling at Dudley. "And so I will, to show that I rejoice as heartily as anyone in your access to the world's good things. We will all have one good thing for ourselves, to show our wholehearted approval of them."

"Now that is nice of you, Aunt Matty, and nicely put," said Justine.

"They are all too kind," muttered Clement.

"I am so pleased with you all," said Dudley. "No one wants me to feel any misery because I have more than he has. I wish I had never said that anyone had more than was right for any one person. I see now what a revealing thing it is to say."

"It will not be true of you, Uncle," said Mark.

"I will have a new suit," said Aubrey.

"Now, now, little boy, no making a mock of what is serious in itself. There *is* a certain generosity in accepting, as Uncle recognises."

"He has plenty of practice," said Clement.

"Miss Griffin will have a dress too," said Dudley. "She does not grudge me my inheritance any more than anyone else."

"Indeed I do not. Indeed I will, if it is to prove that," said Miss Griffin, flushed and conscious and cordial.

Matty gave her a friendly smile.

"Will Miss Sloane be allowed to escape?" said Mark.

"Shall we have Grandpa decked out for the occasion?" said Clement.

"Miss Sloane, it may be asking too much of you," said Justine. "But if it is not, you will give my uncle the privilege? It will be accepted as such."

"I think I will ask to have my congratulations accepted without any proof of them."

"And being denied does not form a large part of your experience? You will not be in this case. We should not dare to attempt it."

"We must not ask Maria to become one of us quite so soon," said Matty.

"I have seldom felt so much one of a family."

"Never at a loss for a graceful response!" said Justine, turning aside and sighing. "I wonder what it feels like."

"Miss Sloane turned her whole mind on my affairs," said Dudley. "I have never seen anyone do that for anyone else before."

"No, Uncle, you have rather been the one to do it for people yourself. But I daresay it has brought its own reward."

"It has," said Mark.

"Did you hear my mean little speech?" said Dudley to Maria. "I believe I think that I ought to be taken more seriously because I have money. Well, I suppose it had to make me deteriorate in some way."

"You are going to leave us, Blanche, my dear?" said Oliver. "You and the other women. I should like to have my smoke and talk while I have the strength for them."

"Grandpa is a privileged person, you observe, Miss Sloane," said Justine. "Things are permitted in him which would not be in other people."

"You know it is only for a short time, child, and show me that you do."

Aubrey rose with a glance at Clement and passed out of the door as if unconscious what he did. He disliked remaining with the men and facing his brothers' banter more than he disliked the status of a child. He sometimes wondered how he would fill any role but this.

"Now, Mr. Penrose, off with you; out of our house," said Justine. "You do not want to be with us a moment longer, and we do not want you, will not attempt to detain you. So off to keep your holiday in your own way."

"I am more than glad of the cause of it, Miss Gaveston."

"So am I," said Dudley.

The five men settled at the table, Edgar and Dudley to talk to Oliver, and Mark and Clement by themselves. It was at this stage that the latter would have turned their attention to their brother. Dudley presently pointed to Oliver, who had fallen asleep.

"Here is my chance to say something else. Would it be right to give some money to Matty? Would she dislike me more for keeping it or giving it? Both are such disagreeable things, and I must do one of them. No one can carry off either."

"We need not make a suggestion," said Clement. "We have shown the course we prefer."

"You have tried to make me happy. But your aunt

may not really desire my happiness. She may wish me to pay for it."

"Well, you are proposing to do so."

"I mean pay with discomfort."

"She would rather you paid for it with money."

"Such simplicity is seldom the whole truth," said Edgar, without hesitation. "Your aunt has come on evil days, or days which she sees as such, and your uncle on good ones; and if she is struck by the difference it may not mean so much."

"It would make the difference less, if I gave her a little of the money and went without it myself. Or is it true that people want more, the more they have? Of course, she is not my real relation and others have a nearer claim. I am beginning to get the outlook of the rich. Do you hear me talk in their way? You would know how terrible it would be, if she wanted more, the more she had, if you had just inherited money."

"It would have to be a moderate, settled sum. It would be a pleasure to Blanche, Dudley. May I suggest —I will suggest an allowance of about two hundred a year."

"Thank you; that is real help. It is not too much or too little. I think that is the way rich people talk. Fancy saying that two hundred a year is not too little, when you have two thousand a year yourself!"

"That is no longer true," said Mark.

"Yes, you won't have so much more left than you can do with," said Oliver, raising his head. "We shall all be busy relieving you of it. I find I am doing my part, and I do it willingly. Why shouldn't I have my last days made easy? They are my very last. And my daughter has had enough ill fortune to render it worth while to make it less. Thank you, my boy, you are a pleasant person to take it from, and I pay you a compliment."

"Of course the generosity is yours. We have decided that."

"No, it is yours, which pleases me better and serves its purpose. Such a quality in me would serve none."

"What are the other allowances?" said Edgar. "I am still in the dark. It does not do to be shy about these things, if we can take them."

"What dreadful speeches reticent people make!" said Dudley. "I suppose it is want of practice."

"The lads are only like the rest of us," said Oliver.

"We do not know," said Clement, something in his tone showing that he was in suspense.

"I thought three hundred a year for Clement, and two hundred for Mark, as he has an interest in the house. And a hundred for Justine, as she will not spend it on herself and I am mean to a woman and good works. And Aubrey's future to be provided for as it develops. And any bitterness to be at once considered and the cause rectified. Causes of bitterness are always so just. And the rest to be for myself, to dole out as I please and earn gratitude and be able to call the tune. How despicable it sounds, and how I do like it!"

"So do we. Do not worry about our part," said Oliver, rising to his feet. "I will tell my daughter and spare you the scene. And having got what I can get, I will take my leave. Do not come after me. I can walk to the next room, where the women will busy themselves."

"I believe it was too little," said Dudley. "Unless I have reached the stage of expecting extravagant thanks for the least thing. I hope that is what it is. Of course it is a mean sum. Two hundred a year is a tenth of two thousand, and it must be mean to offer anyone a tenth of what you have. It sounds as if I were keeping nine times as much for myself. I hope Matty will not hear before she goes. People don't resent having nothing nearly as much as too little. I have only just found that out. I am getting the knowledge of the rich as well as their ways. And of course anyone would resent being given a tenth."

"I do not," said Mark. "I have the opposite feeling."

"I am overpowered," said Clement.

"I must not forget to thank you for your true generosity. Mine is the other kind and we begin to see what that is. Justine is to have a twentieth and she will appreciate it, which is true generosity indeed. I find myself actually looking forward to it, I am deteriorating so fast. There is her voice. The very sound of it ought to be a reproach."

"Well, so the occasion is at an end," said the voice. "Or the moment has come when it would cease to be a success. We really are seeing something of each other. It is such a good thing when those things don't fail to materialise. There is always the touch of risk. It is a tribute to us all that the risk has not even hinted itself in this case. Miss Griffin and I have had a talk to ourselves. We settled down as two women and made the most of each other."

"So we take our leave after hours so full of happiness," said Matty. "It is a pleasant weariness that follows a long rejoicing for others. I only wish I could call it by some other name, that there was some different word for cramped limbs and aching head. But the happiness outweighs it, and that is all I ask."

"Here is the carriage, dear," said her sister. "You won't have to take the walk a second time."

"Well, I could not do that, dear. We cannot go beyond our strength. Up to it willingly but not beyond. I shall be so glad when you have a second carriage, and it should not be long now. It is a thing I have wanted for you. We get into the way of planning things for other people when we must not imagine them for ourselves. And it is a good and satisfying substitute. We can be grateful for it. The cushion into the carriage, Miss Griffin. It won't walk in by itself."

"Jellamy will take it," said Justine, putting her arm in Miss Griffin's. "It will be safely in its place."

Edgar took the cushion and went to the carriage, and

Miss Griffin stood within Justine's arm as if she would linger in its safety.

"Come, Uncle," said Justine, "tear yourself away from Miss Sloane. She gives no sign of relief in her escape from us, and most heartily do we thank her. But the moment has come for her release."

"Matty cannot know of my meanness," said Dudley, looking after the carriage. "She could not show her view of it as openly as that."

"Does Mother know of all your other meanness?" said Mark.

"Oh, I don't like to think of it," said Blanche, when she had heard the truth. "I cannot bear to feel that you have all taken so much. I ought to blush for my family."

"I don't think you need, Mother," said Justine. "I should be more ashamed if I could not take Uncle's bounty openly and generously, as it is offered. It would show a smaller spirit. It is not for us to hold ourselves above the position of grateful people. We have to be able to accept. Anything else shows an unwillingness to grant someone else the superior place."

"Uncle must feel well established in that," said Mark.

"I have done what I can to help him. I have been able to take more pocket money," said Aubrey, kicking a rug with his eyes upon it.

"Aubrey looks down to get the advantage of the ostrich," said Clement.

"Which is very real," said his brother, instantly raising his eyes.

"Oh, is that what you and Uncle have been talking about?" said Blanche. "I don't know what to think of you all. I feel that I did not know my children. I am glad I am taking nothing for myself."

"Well, it is all for you in a way, Mother," said Justine. "You can't dissociate yourself from the benefits of your family."

"Poor Mother, that is rather hard," said Mark.

"No, that is why I feel it as I do," said Blanche to her daughter in a tone of simple rejoinder. "And Grandpa and Aunt Matty too! Well, I cannot do anything. Here is the carriage coming back. The coachman is bringing a letter."

"For Uncle from Aunt Matty," said Justine, handing it to Dudley. "We should not read the envelopes of letters, but this is an exceptional occasion."

"We can be sure that it will not repeat itself," said Mark.

"It would be very bad for us all," said Blanche.

"I will read it aloud," said Dudley, "and have the general protection. Suppose I have patronised Matty, or presumed on my connection, or thought that money meant something to her. I have taken a foolish risk."

"Read away, Uncle," said his niece. "We are all ranged on your side. But I shouldn't be surprised if Aunt Matty comes out well on this occasion."

"Is it an extreme test?" said Clement.

" 'My dear Dudley,

'I cannot wait to give you my thanks and my father's for your thinking of us as part of my sister's family. We feel that we are related to you, and we can take from you what we would take from a son and a brother. And we thank you as much for being that to us, as for the help that sends us forward lighter of heart. And we rejoice with you in your joy.

'Your affectionate and grateful

'Matilda Seaton'

"I did not know that I was as near to them as that, and I have not given in that measure. I have kept nine times as much for myself. That in a son and a brother does seem dreadful. Riches are a test of character and I am exposed. And Matty still thinks that I have joy in having money, instead of pleasure in giving and other decent feelings. She may know me better than I know myself. People do have a terrible knowledge of sons and brothers."

"Mrs. Middleton is in the carriage," said Aubrey.

"My dears!" said Sarah, emerging on to the gravel with hands upraised. "What you must think of us! Your coachman picked us up as we were coming to hear your news. And I waited while you read your letter: I did not want to interrupt." Sarah spoke the truth; she had wished to hear to the end. "A quarter of a million of money! What a thing for you to face!"

"And to put to other purposes," said Thomas, appearing in his turn and using a tone of kindliness and pleasure.

"It is so good of you to be interested," said Blanche. "It has been a great event for us all. We are still quite excited about it."

Sarah met Blanche's eyes.

"Poor Mrs. Middleton!" said Justine. "Do satisfy her curiosity."

"Yes, I want to hear, dear," said Sarah, almost with pathos. "I want to know how it came about, before we talk of it."

"My godfather's lawyer wrote to say that my godfather had died and left me all he had," said Dudley. "He died a few days ago as a very old man. I am so glad that you would like to hear; I was afraid that people might be getting tired of the subject."

"He had no children, Mrs. Middleton," said Justine, in a benevolent tone. "Indeed he seems to have had no relations."

"Then it was natural that he should leave his money to your uncle?" said Sarah, her face lighting at this clearance of her path.

"Quite," said Dudley. "I have every right to it. But I did not know that he had any. I heard a few days ago and told my brother last night, and to-day we all discussed it at breakfast."

"You did not tell them all at once?"

"No, I waited to get confirmation. It was not needed, but I felt that I wanted to have it."

Sarah bowed her head in full understanding.

"And my father and sister came in to learn all about it," said Blanche, "and have just gone. I found the news such a tonic yesterday I thought I was too tired to sleep, and I had the best night I have had for months."

"That is right, both of you. Tell Mrs. Middleton succinctly all she wants to know," said Justine.

"We are indeed glad to know that," said Thomas, putting a sincere note into his tone.

"How had they heard?" said Sarah, her eyes just crossing Justine's face. "They came quite early, didn't they?"

"They came soon after breakfast," said Justine with indulgent fluency. "They had heard from one of the tradesmen, who had heard from Jellamy. We had discussed it at breakfast in the latter's hearing." She gave a little laugh. "And already it seems quite familiar knowledge. How did you hear?"

"My dear, it is all about everywhere," said Sarah, now able to follow a lead into the drawing room. "And what a sum! A quarter of a million!"

"A twentieth of a million," said Dudley. "No more to do with a million than with any other amount. I do not know why people mention a million. Everything is a fraction of one."

"And this is really a twentieth?" said Sarah, pausing with a world of knowledge in her tone. "Well, I don't know whether to congratulate you or the rest of them. I expect they have already made their wishes known."

Her voice asked for further enlightement, and Mark sat down by her side and gave her as much as he chose.

"A little house in Cambridge for Clement," she said, as she rose at the moment of her satisfaction. "And this house to be put in order for your father. Ah, that will be a joy to you all. This beautiful inheritance! And Aubrey to have what he needs as time goes on. And your dear sister to be helped in her useful work. Well, I will leave you to rejoice with each other. It is pretty to see you doing it together."

"Let us send you in the carriage," said Blanche, who had resumed her work.

"No, we will walk and perhaps drop in on your sister. My husband will like a chat with your father. The men like to talk together."

"The women may not object to it on this occasion," said Thomas, with a smile. "I may say how very pleased I am."

"Now do you feel fully primed, Mrs. Middleton, with all that you want to discuss?" said Justine, as she went to the door with the guests.

"Yes, dear, I know it all, I think," said Sarah, resting her eyes once more on Justine's face. "I don't like things to pass me by, without my hearing about them. We are meant to be interested in what the Almighty ordains."

"Mrs. Middleton gives as much attention to the Almighty's doings as he is supposed to give to hers," said Mark.

"I am glad the Almighty has given half a million to Uncle," said Aubrey.

"Half a million!" said Dudley. "Now I am really upset."

"What did you think of Mrs. Middleton's account of her curiosity, Justine?" said Clement.

"Poor Mrs. Middleton! We can't call it anything else."

"She can and did," said Mark.

Sarah went on to the lodge, desiring to know the Seatons' share in the fortune and hoping that it was enough and not too much. The matter was not mentioned and her compunction at overhearing the letter vanished. She saw that she could not have managed without doing so.

CHAPTER V

"UNCLE IS WALKING with Miss Sloane on the terrace," said Aubrey to his sister.

"Well, that is a normal thing to do, little boy. I notice that Uncle is often with Miss Sloane of late. It may be that it gives Aunt Matty a chance to talk to Father."

"He has been helping her up the steps. She goes up them by herself when she is alone."

"Well, when you are older you will learn that men often do things for women which they can do for themselves. Uncle is a finished and gallant person, and there has been a late development in him along that line. He seems to be more aware of himself since he had this money. I hope it does not mean that we took him too much for granted in the old days. But the dear old days! I can't help regretting them in a way, the days when he gave us more of himself, somehow, though he had less of other things to give. I could find it in me to wish them back. I don't take as much pleasure in my new scope as I did in the old Uncle Dudley, who seems to have taken some course away from us of late. Well, I have taken what I can get, and I am content and grateful. And I hardly know how to put what I mean into words."

Blanche looked up at her daughter as if struck by something in her speech, and rose and went to the window with her work dropping from her hand.

"Mother, what is it? Come back to the fire. Your cough will get worse."

Blanche began automatically to cough, holding her hand to her chest and looking at her daughter over it.

"It is true," she said. "They are walking arm-in-arm. It is true."

"What is true? What do you mean?" said Justine, coming to her side. "What is it? What are we to think?"

"We are spying upon them," said Aubrey, his tone seeming too light for the others' mood.

"Yes, we are," said his sister, drawing back. "No, we are not. I see how it is. Uncle is choosing this method of making known to us the truth. We are to see it and grasp it. Well, we do. We will let it stand revealed. So that is what it has meant, this strange insight I have had into something that was upon us, something new. Well, we accept it in its bearing upon Uncle and ourselves."

"Dear Dudley!" said Blanche, picking up her work.

"Dear Uncle indeed, Mother! And the more he does and has for himself, the dearer. And now go back to the fire. You have grown quite pale. It cannot but be a shock. Aubrey will stay and take care of you, and I will go and do as Uncle wishes and carry the news. For we must take it that that is what his unspoken message meant."

"We must beware how we walk arm-in-arm," said Aubrey.

Blanche extended a hand to her son with a smile which was absent, amused and admonitory, and remained silent until her other sons entered, preceded by their sister.

"Standing at the landing window with their eyes glued to the scene! Standing as if rooted to the spot! Uncle chose his method well. It has gone straight home."

"My Justine's voice is her own again," said Blanche, looking at her sons as if in question of their feeling.

"Well, Mother, I am not going to be knocked down by this. It is a thing to stand up straight under, indeed. I found the boys in a condition of daze. I was obliged to be a little bracing, though I admit that it affected me in that way at first. This is a change for Uncle, not for ourselves. It is his life that is taking a new turn, though ours will take its subordinate turn, of course, and we must remember to see it as subordinate. But dear Uncle! That he should have come to this at his age! It takes away my breath and makes my heart ache at the same time."

"Are we sure of it?" said Mark.

"Let us build no further without a foundation," said his brother.

"Look," said Justine, leading the way to the window. "Look. Oh, look indeed! Here is something else before our eyes. What led me to the window at this moment? It is inspiring, uplifting. I wish we had seen it from the first. We should not have taken our eyes away."

Edgar was standing on the path, his hands on the shoulders of Maria and his brother, his eyes looking into their faces, his smile seeming to reflect theirs.

"Is it not a speaking scene? Dear Father! Giving up his place in his brother's life with generosity and courage. We see the simplicity and completeness of the sacrifice, the full and utter renunciation. It seems that we ought not to look, that the scene should be sacred from human eyes."

"So Justine stands on tiptoe for a last glance," said Aubrey, blinking.

"Yes, let us move away," said his sister, putting his words to her own purpose. "Let us turn our eyes on something fitter for our sight." She accordingly turned hers on her mother, and saw that Blanche was weeping easily and weakly, as if she had no power to stem her tears.

"Why, little Mother, it is not like you to be borne away like this. Where is that stoic strain which has put you at our head, and kept you there in spite of all indication to the contrary? Where should it be now but at Father's service? Where is your place but at his side? Come, let me lead you to the post that will be yours."

Blanche went on weeping almost contentedly, rather as if her resistance had been withdrawn than as if she had any cause for tears. Aubrey looked on with an uneasy expression and Clement kept his eyes aside.

"I am quite with Mother," said Mark. "It is all I can do not to follow her example."

"Has the carriage been sent for Aunt Matty?" said Aubrey.

"Ought it to be?" said Blanche, sitting up and using an easier tone than seemed credible. "We must ask Miss Sloane to stay to luncheon, and I suppose your aunt must come too. It is she who first brought her to the house. We little knew what would come of it. But not Miss Griffin, Justine dear. We had better be just a family gathering. That is what we shall be, of course, now that Miss Sloane is to be one of us."

"We will have it as you say, little Mother. I will send the message. And I commend your taste. It is well to be simply as we are. And in these days there is no risk of the promiscuousness and scantiness which did at intervals mark our board." Justine broke off as she recalled that her uncle's open hand might be withdrawn.

"Are we to take it as certain that Miss Sloane and Uncle are engaged?" said Mark. "The evidence is powerful, but is it conclusive?"

"Conclusive," said Justine, with a hint of a sigh. "Would a woman of Miss Sloane's age and type be seen on the arm of a man to whom she stood in any other relation? Uncle is not her father or her brother, you know."

"Unfortunately not," said Clement. "That should be a certain preventive."

"Come, Clement, it is in Uncle's life that we shall be living in these next days. He has had enough of living in ours."

"It is odd that we are surprised by it," said Mark.

"I suppose we are," said Justine, with another sigh. "But we have had an example of how to meet it. Father has given it to us. Don't remind me of that scene, or I shall be overset like Mother."

"You were unwise to call it up, but I admit the proof."

"Wait one minute," said Justine, going to the door. "I will be back with confirmation or the opposite. I shall not keep you long."

"I must go and make myself fit to be seen," said Blanche in her ordinary tone. "I have been behaving quite unlike myself. I suppose it was thinking of your uncle, and his having lived so much for all of us, and now at last being about to live for himself."

"It is enough to overcome anyone," said Clement, when his mother had gone. "It puts the matter in a nutshell."

"You mean that Uncle may want his own money?" said Mark.

"It seems that he must. Nearly all the balance after the allowances are paid has gone on the house. It seemed to need all but rebuilding. Houses were not meant to last so long. Can things be broken off at this stage?"

"They can at the end of it. I suppose they will have to be. Uncle had very little money of his own. There is so little in the family apart from the place. He was a poor man until he had this money. And he can only use the income; the capital is tied up until his death. And he will want to give his wife the things that go with his means. And she will expect to have them, and why should she not?"

"Because it prevents Uncle from giving them to us," said Aubrey.

"We do not grudge Uncle what is his own."

"We only grudge Miss Sloane what has been ours."

"How about your extra pocket money?" said Clement.

"I grudge it to her. And I thought she liked Father better than Uncle. She always looks at him more."

"I did not think about which she liked better," said Mark. "I thought of her as Aunt Matty's friend."

"Perhaps she did not find Aunty Matty enough for her," said Aubrey. "I can almost understand it. Well, we shall have her for an aunt and she will be obliged to kiss Clement."

"Well, I bring confirmation," said Justine, entering the room in a slightly sobered manner. "Full and free support of what we had gathered for ourselves from the full and frank signs of it. It was not grudged or withheld for a moment. I was met by a simple and open admission such as I respected."

"And did they respect your asking for it?" said Clement.

"I think they did. They saw it as natural and necessary. We could not accept what we could not put upon a definite basis. They could not and did not look for that."

"So you did not have much of a scene?"

"No—well, it was entirely to my taste. It was brief and to the point. There was a natural simplicity and depth about it. I felt that I was confronted by deep experience, by the future in the making. I stood silent before it."

"That was well."

"Are we all ready for Aunt Matty?" said Aubrey.

"Yes, we are not making any change," said Justine. "That would imply some thought of ourselves. We are meeting to-day in simple feeling for Uncle."

"Just wearing our hearts on our sleeves."

"Now, little boy, why are you not at your books?"

"Penrose is not well. He sent a message. And directly his back was turned I betrayed his trust."

"Well, well, it is not an ordinary day. And I suppose that is the carriage. Are we never to have an experience again without Aunt Matty? Now what a mean and illogical speech! When we may owe to her Uncle's happiness! I will be the first down to welcome her as an atonement."

"So you are not too absorbed in the new excitement to remember the old aunt. That is so sweet of all of you. And I do indeed bring you my congratulations. I feel I am rather at the bottom of this. So, Blanche, I have given you something at last. I am not to feel that I do nothing but receive. That is not always to be my lot. I am the giver this time, and I can feel it is a rare and precious gift. And I do not grudge it, even if it may mean yielding up a part of it myself. No, Dudley, it is yours and it is fully given. You and I are both people who can give. That is often true of people who accept. And you find yourself in the second position this time."

"There have to be people there or giving would be no good."

"We are all there together," said Blanche, who looked excited and confused. "Edgar's sister will be a sister to me, as his brother has been my brother."

"We have always valued the relation," said Matty, taking Blanche's hand. "And now we are to be three instead of two, we shall have even more to value. I must feel that I also am accepting. I shall try to feel it and not dwell upon what I relinquish."

"I do not feel that I am losing anything. I know Dudley too well."

"Well, if I feel I am giving up a little, I yield it gladly, feeling that others' gain is more than my loss, or more important. For I have been a dependent person who has had to make demands; and now there has come a demand on me, I am glad to meet it fully. I have had my share of weakness and welcome a position where I have some of the strength."

"I need not talk about what I am accepting," said Maria, "in this house where it is known. I am giving all I have in return."

"Simple and telling, Miss Sloane, as we should have expected," said Justine. "But we did not need you to say it, and hope that it was not at any cost. And we will all give you on our side what is right and meet. And rest assured, Aunt Matty, that we are not unmindful of your sacrifice. If we seem to be a little distant to-day, it is because the march of affairs is carrying us with it. Let us make our little sally and return in course."

"Edgar, we must have a word from you," said Matty. "It may seem hard when you are giving up the most, but you are a person from whom we expect much."

"Surely not in that line," said Clement.

"Well, Aunt Matty, I think it *is* hard," said Justine. "And you have given the reason. Well, just a word, and then we must make a move. We must eat even on the day of Uncle's engagement. Uncle's engagement! Who could know what the words mean to us?"

"I think that will do for my speech," said Edgar.

"Then that is enough," said Justine, taking his arm and setting out for the dining room.

"Dudley must sit by Miss Sloane," said Blanche, "and then that is the whole duty of them both."

"Shall I say my little original word?" said Aubrey.

"Now, little boy, silence is the best kind of word from you."

"I should like to see Clement come out of himself."

"You go back into yourself and stay there."

"Does Miss Sloane know how bad notice is for Clement?"

"You must forgive him, Miss Sloane; he is excited," said Justine, giving an excuse which both satisfied the truth and silenced her brother.

"Blanche, your cough is worse," said Matty. "I believe you ought to be in bed."

"I could not be, dear, on a day like this. What would happen to them all? I am indispensable."

"You are indeed, my dear. That is what I mean."

"Mother was condemned to remaining in one room," said Justine, "but I had not the heart to carry out the sentence. Our little leader shut up alone, with the rest of us observing this celebration! My feelings baulked at it."

"It is a mistake to be all heart and no head," said Clement.

"I am quite well," said his mother. "I am only a little worked up. I cannot sit calmly through a day like this. I was never a phlegmatic person. I feel so keenly what affects other people. I get taken right out of myself. I almost feel that I could rise up and float above you all. I don't know when I have felt so light all through myself.

I don't believe that even your uncle feels as much lifted above his level."

"I see that people really do rejoice in others' joy," said Dudley.

"You have done your share of it, Uncle," said Justine. "And it is well that something else has come in time. A spell of natural selfishness will do you good. Give yourself up to it. We have schooled ourselves for the experience. It will be a salutary one. And a proportion of your thoughts will return to us, supported by someone else's."

"So for the time I have no uncle," said Aubrey.

"You will have a second aunt, dear," said Matty. "Come and sit by your first one. Aunts can be a compensation, and you shall find that they can."

"Perhaps I shall be Miss Sloane's especial nephew."

"You do not deserve it, but I have an idea that you may be," said Justine. "Naughty little boy, to have a way of being people's favourite and knowing it! Confess now, Miss Sloane, that you already look upon him with a partial eye."

Maria smiled at Aubrey but was not in time to check a glance at his brothers.

"Ah, now, you may not be so much the chosen person this time. You can take it to heart and retire into the background," said Justine, as Aubrey did both these things.

"Mother, you don't seem to know what you are doing." said Mark. "You keep on beginning to eat and forgetting and beginning again. You have not accomplished a mouthful in the last ten minutes."

"I am a little wrought up, dear. I can't treat this as an ordinary day. Your uncle has never been engaged before."

"Never and may not be again," said Clement. "He will not spoil Mother's appetite many times."

Blanche began to laugh, pursuing something with her fork and continuing her mirth as she had continued her tears, as if she had not the strength to overcome it.

"Mother, you are over excited," said Justine. "You are on the point of becoming hysterical. Not that that is any great matter. It is pleasant for Uncle in a way to see how you feel yourself involved in his life. It is not your own interest that looms large to you, is it?"

Blanche looked up as if she did not follow the words.

"You are faint from want of food, Blanche," said Edgar. "You ate nothing at breakfast. You must make an effort."

"I can't make an effort," said his wife, in another tone. "I don't feel well enough. And I do not like being told what I am to do. I am used to doing what I choose. I am able to judge for myself." She thrust her plate against her glass, and sat watching the result in a sort of childish relief in having wreaked her feeling.

"Mother is not herself," said Justine, rising to deal with the damage, and speaking for her mother's ears, though not directly to her. "She is at once more and less than herself, shall we say?"

Blanche watched the process of clearing up with vague interest.

"That is one of the best table napkins," she said, reaching towards it. "That wine does not stain, does it? I only put them out last week." Her voice died away and she sat looking before her as if she were alone.

"We must take—it would be well to take her temperature," said Edgar.

"That was in my mind, Father. I was waiting for the end of luncheon."

"Send Jellamy away," said Blanche suddenly. "He keeps on watching me."

"Jellamy can fetch a thermometer," said Mark, giving an explanatory smile to the man. "That will kill two birds with one stone."

Jellamy vanished in complete good-will towards his mistress, and Blanche gave a laugh which passed to a fit of coughing, and sat still and shaken, with her eyes moving about in a motionless head.

"Mother's breathing is very hard and quick," said Clement.

"She must have been feverish all day," said Mark.

"We all see that now," said Justine sharply. "It is no good to wish that someone had seen it before. That will not help. We can only deal with things as they are."

"I thought perhaps no one would notice, if I did not speak," said Blanche, as if to herself. "Sometimes people don't see anything."

Edgar had come to his wife's side. Dudley and Maria had risen and were talking apart. Matty sat with her eyes on her sister, her expression wavering between uneasiness and irritation at the general concern for someone else. Aubrey looked about for reassurance. There was the sudden stir and threat of acknowledged anxiety.

The thermometer told its tale. Blanche lost her patience twice and delayed its action. Matty and Dudley talked to amuse her while she waited. She was interrupted by her cough, and they all realised its nature and its frequency. Her sister's face became anxious and nothing else.

"I heard Mother coughing in the night like that," said Aubrey.

"Then why did you not say so?" said Clement.

"That is no good, Clement," said Justine. "We all wish we had taken earlier alarm. It was not for Aubrey to give us the lead."

Blanche was found to be in high fever, and seemed to take pleasure and even pride in the discovery.

"I never make a fuss about nothing," she said, as she sat by the fire while her room was warmed. "I have always been the last to complain about myself. When I was a child they had to watch me to see if I was ill. I never confessed to it, whatever I felt."

"That was naughty, dearest," said Matty. "And you are not a child now."

"An ignorant and arrogant boast, Mother," said Mark.

"Poor Uncle!" said Justine, in a low tone, touching

Dudley's sleeve. "On your engagement day! We are not forgetting it. You know that."

"I am oblivious of it. I am lost in the general feeling."

"I often kept about when people less ill than I was, were in bed," continued Blanche, her eyes following this divergence of interest from herself. "I remember I once waited on my sister when my temperature was found to be higher than hers. I daresay Miss Sloane remembers hearing of that."

"Don't tell such dreadful stories, dear," said Matty.

"But I often think that not giving in is the best way to get well," said Blanche, putting back her hand to a shawl that was round her shoulders, and glancing back at it as a shiver went through her. "Staying in bed lowers people's resistance and gives the illness a stronger hold. Not that I am really ill this time, though a bad chill is something near to it. I shall not give in for long. I am a person who likes to do everything for herself."

"It is not always the way to do anything for other people, dear."

"You will do it once too often, Mother," said Clement, glad that his words were broken by the opening door.

The room was said to be ready. The doctor was heard to arrive. It seemed incredible that an hour before the household had been taking its usual course, even more incredible that the course had been broken as it had.

Blanche sat still, with her eyes narrower than usual and her hands and face less than their normal size, stooping forward to avoid the full breath which brought the cough.

"I think people know what suits themselves. I have never done myself any harm by keeping about. I shall not stay in bed a moment longer than I must. The very thought of it makes me feel worse. I am worse now just from thinking about it. People's minds do influence their bodies." Her tone showed that she was accounting for her feelings to herself.

The doctor gave his word at a glance. Blanche was

wrapped up and taken to her room. Her sons returned with the chair which had carried her, and glanced at each other as they set it down.

"What a very light chair!" said Clement, giving it a push.

"People who are light are often stronger than heavier ones," said his brother.

Aubrey began to cry.

"Come, come, all of you," said Justine. "Mother can't have got any lighter in the last days. She can never have weighed much. I always feel a clodhopper beside her."

"When is the nurse coming?" said Mark.

"As soon as she can," said Matty, who had returned from seeing the doctor. "That is good news, isn't it? And I have some better news for you. We are sending for Miss Griffin. Your uncle and Maria have gone to fetch her, and she is the best nurse I have ever known. That is why I am yielding her up to you. So Aunt Matty provides the necessary person a second time."

Miss Griffin arrived with her feelings in her face, concern for Blanche and pleasure in the need of herself, and settled at once into the sickroom as her natural place. She had more feeling for helpless people than for whole ones, and it was Matty's lameness rather than the length of their union, which made the bond she could not break. She began to talk to Blanche of Dudley's engagement, feeling it an interest which could not fail, and making the most of the implication that Blanche was bound up with ordinary life.

But Blanche had taken the news more easily than Miss Griffin, and had a lighter hold on the threads of life, though she seemed to have so many more of them. Her lightness of grasp went with her through the next days, working for her in holding her incurious about her state, against her in allowing her less urge to fight for life. With petulance and heroism, childishness and courage she lived her desperate hours, and emerged into peace and weakness with remembrance rather than realisation of what was behind.

Her family was new to such suspense and lived it with a sense of shock and disbelief. After the first relief they accepted her safety and resented that it had been threatened.

When Matty and Maria came to share the rejoicing, they found it took the form of reaction and silence. The first evening after the stress might almost have been one at the height of it.

Justine extended a hand to her uncle as though she had hardly strength to turn her eyes in the same direction. "We must seem selfish and egotistic, Uncle, in that we do not remember your personal happiness."

"Just now we are sharing yours," said Maria.

"And I am afraid we cannot be showing it," said Dudley.

"We can all share each other's," said Matty. "I can give my own illustration. My joy for my sister to-night only gives more foundation to my joy for my friends. Yes, that other happiness which I feel here, is very near to my heart."

"You are fancying it," said Dudley. "Maria and I have laid it aside."

"You have pushed it deeper down. Into a fitter place."

"I am appalled by the threat and danger of life," said Mark.

"It may be good for us to realise that in the midst of life we are in death," said his sister.

"What benefit do we derive from it?" said Clement.

"Oh, don't let us talk like that on this day of all days. It is not suitable or seemly. Our nerves may be on edge, but we must not hold that an excuse for crossing every bound."

"We may have no other excuse," said Edgar, "but our guests will accept that one. We have been tried to the end of our strength and I fear beyond."

"We are not guests, dear Edgar," said Matty. "As a family we have been in darkness, and as a family we emerge into the light. And perhaps it is a tiny bit ungrateful not to see the difference."

"We do not find the light dazzling," said Clement.

"No, so I see, dear. Now I do find it so, but to me the darkness has been so very dark." Matty was easily tried by depression in others, being used to support and cheer herself. "You see, my sister and I are so very near. From our earliest memories our lives have been bound in one. And not even the mother's tie goes back so far."

"Really, Aunt Matty, that is too much," said Justine. "Or I should say it was, if it were not for the occasion."

"It is that which makes it so," said Mark.

"So the occasion does mean something, dears?"

"Aunt Matty, if you do not beware, you will have us turning from you with something like shrinking and contempt," said Justine, allowing her movement to illustrate these feelings.

"Something very like," said Clement.

Edgar looked up as if weariness held him silent.

"Well, well, dear, perhaps I betrayed something of such feelings myself. We are all wrought up and beyond our usual barriers. We must forgive each other."

"I do not see why," said Clement.

"And I am indulging in personal joy all through this," said Dudley. "And Matty said that she shared it. So I suppose this is what joy for others is like. No wonder people rather avoid feeling it."

"Miss Sloane, come to our rescue," said Justine. "We need some sweetness and sanity to save us from ourselves."

"It is the anxiety that is to blame. A happy ending does not alter what has gone before."

"That is what I say," said Clement. "Why should we hold a celebration because Mother's life has been threatened and just saved?"

"Poor little Mother! Are we in danger of losing her experience in our own?"

"Surely not, dear," said Matty. "No, I do not think that you and your brothers would find yourselves coming to that."

Justine gave a laugh which was openly harsh in its acceptance of her aunt's meaning.

Matty raised her brows in perplexed enquiry.

"Come, come," said Edgar.

"No, I shall not come, Father. I shall not rise to that bait any more. I shall not rise to those heights. I will not be forbearing and tolerant through any strain. It is not a fair obligation on anyone. I shall be hard and snappish and full of mean and wounding insinuation like anyone else. Oh, you will find a great difference. You will find that I mean what I say. I feel the strain of temper and malice which is in the family, coming out in me. I am a true daughter of the Seatons, after all."

"Well, you are your mother's daughter, dear," said Matty. "And we will ask nothing better, if you can be that."

"But I cannot. I am not even now saying what I mean. I am not Mother's daughter as much as your niece. That is what I should have said; that is what I did say in my heart. I have nothing of Mother in me. That strain of heroism and disregard of self is wanting in me, as it is in you, as it is in all of us."

Edgar made a sound of appeal to Maria, and she rose and came to his daughter and allowed her to throw her arms round her neck and weep.

"I hope I am not the cause of this," said Matty.

"What is your ground for hope?" said Clement.

Edgar threw his son a look of warning.

"I am not surprised to hear that heroism is not one of my qualities," said Mark, trying to be light. "I have always suspected it."

"Heroism and disregard of self," said Matty, giving

a little laugh. "Has my poor little sister had to show such things?"

"Oh, what will you all think of me?" wept Justine. "What of my poor little boy who is looking at me with such baffled eyes? What is he to do if I fail him?"

"We think you have had more strain than other people, and been of more use," said Maria.

"Indeed, indeed," said Edgar. "The chief demand has fallen on Justine and Miss Griffin. My wife is not happy with strangers, and the actual nursing is a small part of what has been done."

"Father has surpassed himself," said Justine, sitting up and using a voice which became her own as she spoke. "There, I am myself again. I have had my outburst and feel the better for it. And I don't suppose anyone else is much the worse." She wiped her eyes and left Maria and returned to her place.

"I am very shaken," said Aubrey, speaking the truth.

"You have all been very good," said Miss Griffin, who had witnessed the attack on Matty with consternation, pity and exultation struggling through her fatigue, and now lifted eyes that seemed to strive to see.

"You are very tired, Miss Griffin. You had better go home and rest," said Matty, somehow betraying a desire to deprive the family of Miss Griffin's service.

Miss Griffin looked up to speak, assuming that words would come to her and finding her mistake.

"It cannot be good for you or for anyone else, for you to go on in that state."

"It is the best thing for Mother," said Justine. "She will be happier if she knows that Miss Griffin is sleeping in the next room. We shall see to-night that it is real sleep."

"Well, that is a good way of feeling indispensable. Too sound a way to be given up. We shall all be useful like that to-night. I shall be able to sleep for the first time, and I shall be glad to feel that I am doing some good by doing it."

"Well, I think you will be, Aunt Matty," said Justine, who was right in her claim that she was again herself. "Doing what we can for ourselves does make the best of us for other people. And not sleeping is the last thing to achieve either."

"We are certainly more useful—have more chance of being of use when we are not tired out," said Edgar, "though it is only Miss Griffin who seems to be indispensable at the moment of sleep."

"Then she is continually useful," said Matty, glancing at Miss Griffin and using a tone at once light and desperate.

Miss Griffin rose with a feeling that movement would be easier and less perilous than sitting still.

"I will go and take Mrs. Gaveston's temperature. That was the doctor's bell. I will bring it down so that she need not be disturbed again to-night."

"You see us all human again, Dr. Marlowe," said Justine.

"He would hardly have a moment ago," said Clement.

"We could not be more human than we have been in the last week," said Dudley. "We have sounded the deeps of human experience. I am very proud of all we have been through."

"Father, you were going to say some formal words of gratitude to Dr. Marlowe," said Justine. "But there is no need. He is no doubt as skilled in reading people's minds as their bodies."

"Then it is well that he was not here just now," said Aubrey.

"So, little boy, you have found your tongue again," said Justine, stooping and putting her cheek against his.

"Weren't you glad to hear my authentic note?" said Aubrey, glancing at the doctor.

"I meant to sound mine too," said Dudley.

"We heard it, Uncle, and happy we were to do so. But you have had your own support in the last days."

"My feelings have been too deep for words like anyone else's."

"I think we hear our Justine's voice again," said Matty, with an effort to regain a normal footing.

Justine crossed the room and sat down on the arm of her aunt's chair.

"What a thing affection is, as exemplified between Aunt Matty and Justine!" said Mark.

"A thing indeed but not affection," said Clement.

"I think this thermometer must be wrong," said Miss Griffin, in the measured tones of one forcing herself to be coherent in exhaustion. "I used it myself and it has gone up like this. I don't know what can be wrong with it. It has not had a fall."

The doctor took it, read it, shook it, read it again and was suddenly at the door, seeming to be another man.

"Come with me, anyone who should. There may be no time to be lost. The temperature has rushed up suddenly. I hoped the danger was past."

The family followed, at first instinctively, then in grasp of the truth, then with the feelings of the last days rushing back in all their force. The late hour of reaction might have been an imaginary scene, might have been read or written.

They reached the bedroom and Edgar took his daughter's arm. Justine pushed Aubrey back into the passage and then walked forward with her father. Her brothers stood with them, and Dudley a step behind. Maria drew back and waited with Aubrey on the landing.

"You feel hot, Blanche, my dear?" said Edgar.

"Yes—yes, I do feel hot," said his wife, looking at him as if she barely saw him and hardly wished to do more. "What have you all come for?"

"To say good-night to you, Mother dear," said Justine.

"Yes, I am better," said Blanche, as if this accounted for their presence. "I shall soon feel better. Of course it must be slow."

"Yes, you will be better, Mother dear."

"But I don't want Miss Griffin to go," said Blanche, with a sharpness which was her own, though her voice could hardly be heard. "I don't want to have to get well all at once. I am not going to try."

"Of course you are not," said her husband. "You must just lie still and think of nothing."

"I don't often think of nothing. I have a busy brain."

Edgar took her hand and she drew it away with a petulance which was again her own.

"Is Aubrey in bed?"

"He will be soon. He wanted to come and see you, but we thought you were too tired."

"Yes, I am very tired. Not so much tired as sleepy."

"Shut your eyes, Mother, and try to sleep," said Mark.

Blanche simply obeyed but opened her eyes again.

"I want Miss Griffin to be where I can see her. You make her go away."

Miss Griffin drew near and Blanche gave her a smile.

"We are happy together, aren't we? My sister does not know."

"I am very happy with you."

"My bed is right up in the air. Are you all up there too?"

"We are with you, dear," said Edgar. "We are all here."

"It is too many, isn't it?" said Blanche, in a tone of agreement. "Has Matty been here to-day?"

"She is downstairs, waiting to hear how you are."

"She cannot come up here," said his wife, with a note of security.

"No, she will wait downstairs."

"Her brain is not really so much better than mine."

"No, we know it is not."

"Father does not know that I am really a nicer person. But it does not matter, a thing like that."

"We all know it, Mother," said Mark.

"But you must be kind to Aunt Matty," said Blanche, as if speaking to a child.

"Yes, we will be, Mother."

"She wants too much kindness," said Blanche, in a dreamy tone.

"Shut your eyes, dear, and try to sleep," said Edgar.

"Are you that tall man who asked me to marry him?" said Blanche, in a very rapid tone, fixing her eyes on his face.

"Yes, I am. And you married me. And we have been very happy."

"I did not mind leaving Father and Matty. But I don't think that Father will die."

"No, not for a long time."

"Dr. Marlowe is watching me. A doctor has to do that. But I don't like it when Jellamy does it."

"He shall never do it again," said Edgar, stumbling over the words.

The doctor moved out of her sight, and Dudley felt his brother's hand and came to the bed.

"They are not really so alike, when you get to know them," said Blanche to Miss Griffin.

"Mother, try to rest," said Mark.

"Try to rest," echoed his mother, looking before her.

"Perhaps you are a little near to the bed," said the doctor.

They moved away.

"Where have you all gone?" said Blanche at once.

"We are here, dear," said Edgar. "You are not alone."

"Alone? That would be an odd thing, when I have a husband and four children."

"We are all here, Blanche, all with you."

"Matty does not mind not having any children. Some women do not mind."

Justine came closer and her mother saw her face.

"Are you my beautiful daughter?" she said, again in the rapid tone. "The one I knew I should have? Or the other one?"

"I am your Justine, Mother."

"Justine!" said Blanche, and threw up her arms. "Why should we want her different?"

"I am here, dear," said Edgar, bending over her, and saw that his wife was not there.

For another minute they were as silent as she.

Then Miss Griffin spoke.

"I got to love her so much. She was so good. She never made a murmur and it must be dreadful not to be able to breathe. We could hardly wish her to linger like that."

The speech, with its difference of thought, of word, of class, seemed to shock them back into life. Edgar turned from the bed as if forcing himself to return to the daily world. Clement moved towards the door. Dudley turned to speak to the doctor. Mark tried to lead his sister away. Aubrey met them in the passage and stood with the expression of a man before he broke into a child's tears. Maria went down to tell Matty the truth. The day which had been at an end was ending again. Another end had come.

"We must go down and say good-night to Aunt Matty," said Justine, as if feeling that normal speech and action were best. "And then Miss Griffin must go to bed. Uncle, you have Father in your charge. Dr. Marlowe will understand us. We cannot say much to-night."

Matty was sitting in her chair, waiting for them to come. She held out her arms to them, one by one, going through an observance which she had had in her mind, and which seemed to suggest that she offered herself in their mother's place.

"My poor children, your mother's sister is with you. That is the light in my darkness, that I am here to watch over you. It must have been put into my thoughts to come to your gates, that you might not be alone when your sorrow came."

They stood about her, heedless of what she said, and her voice went on on the same note, with another note underneath.

"There is one little comfort I can give you, one poor, sad, little comfort. You have not suffered quite the worst. You have not sat still and felt that you could not go to her side. You were able to obey your hearts."

They did not answer, and as Matty's face fell from its purpose a look of realisation came. Her world would be different without her sister; her place in it would be different. She rose to go and found that she must wait while Dudley and Maria took their leave.

"Come, dear, I must get home to my father. I have more to go through to-night. And if I do not face it now, my strength may fail. I feel I have not too much." She broke off as she remembered that Blanche would not hear and suffer from her words. They would fall on other ears and she must have a care how they fell.

"Well, I must leave you to take care of yourselves, of yourselves and Miss Griffin and each other. I must believe that you will do it. And I will go home and take some thought for myself, as there is no one else to do that."

"There is not, Aunt Matty," said Justine, in a clear, slow, almost ruthless voice. "We cannot tell you that there is. We have all lost her who watched over us. We are all desolate. We cannot tell you that that place will be filled."

CHAPTER VI

"WELL, MY SON," said Oliver, as he entered Edgar's house on the day after his daughter's funeral. "I hope I may always call you that. It is what she has left to me. It is the wrong thing that she is taken and I am left. No one feels it more than I do."

Edgar was silent before the difference made by death. His father-in-law had never used the words before.

"No, Grandpa, you must not feel that," said Justine, walking with her arms about him. "We do not take one person in terms of another. She never did and we do not."

"It is kind of you, my dear, but I cumber the ground in her house."

"If Grandpa had had the choice of sacrificing himself for Mother," said Mark to Clement, "I should have taken it ill if he had not done so."

"I wonder if he would have. There are only records of the opposite feeling."

"Mrs. Middleton, this is kind," said Justine, "and I ought to have greeted you. But I instinctively waited for someone else to do it."

"My dear, if kindness could do anything!"

Thomas stood aside, as if he would suppress a possibly unwelcome presence.

"Well, dear ones," said Matty, looking at her nephews as though uncertain of her new position with them. "Now is anyone good and brave enough to say that he has had a good night?"

"Brave in what sense?" said Clement.

"I am not going to admit that I have no heart and no feeling," said Mark. "I think that is the sense."

"So you slept well, dear?" said Matty.

"They are still in a daze," said Sarah with compassion.

"I wish I could have taken refuge for longer in that first numbness. But it has passed and left me without defence. I have nothing left to me but courage, and I am sure my boys and girl have that. Is it enough for them to tell me that they are better and brighter this morning?"

"We seem to have told her," said Mark.

"Because I have not been able to summon mine as yet," said Matty, lowering herself into a chair with a weakness at once assumed and real. "No, I cannot give a very good account of myself. I am not much of an example."

"We none of us are," said Justine. "It is rather soon to expect it."

"Yes, it is, dear, but I catch a return of spirit in those words, a note of hope and resolve for the future. I fear that I have not got so far. I feel to-day as if I may never do so. There is a confession to make. That is not much of an aunt to boast of."

"We should be out of sympathy with any other feeling."

"That is kind, dear. And I must try to sympathise with your hope and looking forward."

"We must be allowed to live in the moment, Aunt Matty."

"But I must be in sympathy with your moment. I must not feel that it is like my eternity."

Justine gave her aunt a glance and turned away, and Matty sank lower in her chair, in apprehension and remembrance.

"Can't you occupy yourself, little boy?" said Justine.

Aubrey began to cry. Matty looked up and held out her arms, and he faltered towards her and stood within them. Justine did not speak; she would take no more on herself. Sarah sent her eyes from face to face and then put up her hand to steady them.

"What will Father do without either Mother or Uncle?" said Clement to Mark. "I can't imagine his life."

"I shall have to spend more time with him."

"And that will fill the double blank?"

"It will be doing what I can. More than you will do by living your time for yourself."

"If I had it carried on for me, as you have yours, I could be more free with it."

"Boys, boys!" said Justine, with a hand on their arms. "It is a dreadful day, a day which puts more on us than fits our strength, but we shall gain nothing by being conquered by it."

"Will you come into the library?" said Edgar to his father-in-law. "We can do no better than keep to our old ways."

"I will do what you tell me. I have not come here, seeing any good in myself. I must take what is done for me. And who but you will do anything?"

"Whatever is done, is really done by Mother, Grandpa," said Justine, accompanying him to the door.

"I am in no doubt about the bond between us, child."

"Are we to hear your uncle's voice to-day?" said Matty. "Is he to give us anything of himself?"

"He is in the garden with Miss Sloane," said Aubrey. "Perhaps he has given all of it."

"Little boy, I like to see you try to do that with yourself," said Justine in her brother's ear. "We know who would have liked it."

"We do not grudge them to each other," said Matty. "I do not, who gave them. But it seems that they might spare a little of what they have to-day. I might feel now that I went almost too far in giving. I must rise above the feeling, but to-day it seems far to rise."

"They may hesitate to intrude their happiness on our sorrow," said Justine.

"They might give us a little of the one, dear, and share a little of the other. Your uncle lived with your mother for thirty years. It might be that he missed her. If he knew how I envy him those years!"

"Oh, Aunt Matty!" said Justine, shaking her head and

turning away, and then turning impulsively back again. "Poor Aunt Matty, you are old and helpless and alone, and we give ourselves to our own sorrow and forget your greater need. For your need is greater, though your sorrow is less."

"Yes, that is how you would see me, dear. That is how I should seem to you all, now that my sister is gone. I must thank you for trying to feel kindly towards what you see."

Clement gave a faint laugh, and Matty looked at him as if in surprise at such a sound.

"They keep on passing the library window and looking in," said Mark.

"Oh, I know," said Justine. "They are waiting for Grandpa to go, so that Uncle may go in to Father. Their minds are full of us, after all. Miss Sloane is waiting to yield up Uncle to his brother. They say that sorrow makes us sensitive to kindness, but I am touched by that."

Matty sat with her lips compressed and her hands on her chair, as if trying to face the effort of rising. Sarah watched her but did not offer her aid, knowing that it would not be welcome.

"Well, we will go, dear, if they are waiting for that, if that is what we can do to help you. We came to try to give our help."

"Dear Aunt Matty, I believe it would be doing what you can. Grandpa has had his word with Father, and can go, strengthened by it. And Father can have the support of Uncle's companionship. He is hardly in a state to give virtue out himself to-day."

Matty turned and went to the door, hardly looking at her niece.

"Where is Miss Griffin?" she said, in a tone of asking for something that went as a matter of course.

"I don't know. She may not be up yet. We leave her to sleep late. She may not know that you are here."

"Well, no dear, not if she is not awake. If she were,

she would know that I should not have stayed away."

"I will go and see if she can come down."

"She can come down, dear."

"Well, I will go and see."

"Send her down, and then your grandfather can come with me. Until she comes he had better stay with your father."

"She may not be ready, Aunt Matty. Would not Miss Sloane go home with you?"

"We are talking about Miss Griffin, dear," said Matty, with a smile and a sigh.

"We may have to keep you waiting."

Matty turned and went back to her place, loosening her cloak and drawing off her gloves in preparation for this period.

She sat down with her nephews, and began to distract their thoughts with lively accounts of their mother's youth, which neither saddened them nor required them to suppress their feelings, seeming to forget her own trouble in her effort to help them in theirs. When Justine returned she hardly looked up, and maintained her talk as if fully occupied with it.

"Miss Griffin will be ready quite soon. She has only to put her things together."

Matty gave two bright nods in her niece's direction, as if in reference to something that went without saying, and continued to talk.

Miss Griffin came down, a little abashed, a little out of heart, a little the better for her time under another roof. Matty just threw her a glance and gave herself to ending a tale. Then she looked round in faint question, as if expecting something to be taking place.

"Are you ready for Grandpa, Aunt Matty?"

"Yes, dear, I have been ready since we talked about it, since you said that things would be the better for our going. But I don't think my nephews were quite so inclined for me to leave them."

"Shall I fetch him for you?"

"Yes, dear," said Matty, in a tone of full encouragement. "But I see that Aubrey is going for you. He is better and brighter in the last half hour."

"Mrs. Middleton, I feel that we are dismissing you," said Justine. "And it has been so kind of you to come."

"We have had our glimpse of you, dear," said Sarah, in an unconsciously satisfied tone, having had a full sight of the situation.

Thomas departed with a bare handshake, as though he would impose the least demand. He uttered no word as a word would have required an ear.

"Well, it becomes easier for me to leave you all," said Oliver. "I have those who belong to me on both sides. It gets to make less difference to me on which side I am."

His grandsons looked at him with incredulous eyes, startled by the faith of a man who was in other respects a normal being. They had no grasp of the mental background of Oliver's youth.

"I suppose Grandpa is saved," murmured Aubrey.

"People always are," said Clement. "That is the plan. It is specified that sins may be of any dye and make no difference."

"There are arrangements for those who are not," said Mark, "permanent ones. They seem indeed to err on the side of permanency."

"I suppose Aunt Matty is saved," said Aubrey. "Sins being as scarlet——"

"Boys dear," said Justine, "isn't this rather cheap jesting upon subjects which are serious to many people? Do you know, at this moment I could find it in me to envy Grandpa his faith?"

"I see that he has the best of it," said Mark.

"We should like to have some comfort," said Aubrey, his grin extending into the grimace of weeping, as he found himself speaking the truth.

Justine stroked his hair and continued to do so while she addressed her aunt.

"Aunt Matty, as you are taking Miss Griffin and you also have Grandpa, will you leave us Miss Sloane? I feel we need someone to break down the barriers of family grief. And I begin to find it much, this being the only woman in the family."

"Yes, dear, take anything from me; take anything that is mine," said Matty, proceeding on her way. "I am willing to be generous."

Justine ran after her and flung her arms round her neck.

"Dear Aunt Matty, you are generous indeed. And we do value the gift."

Her aunt walked on, perhaps not wishing to go further in this line.

Justine sighed as she looked after her.

"I believe I have put something definitely between Aunt Matty and me. That is what I have done in the first days without Mother. Well, we can't expect to do so well without her."

"Is Miss Sloane remaining with us in simple obedience?" said Mark.

"I should like to stay with you all."

"I will give her to you for a time," said Dudley. "I must learn to talk like a husband."

"And Aunt Matty has given her," said Aubrey.

"Father, she is yours, if you will have it so," said Justine. "No one counts with us as you do."

"Justine has also given Miss Sloane," said Aubrey.

"Then I will talk to your father," said Maria. "And you can have your uncle."

Justine waited for the door to close.

"Uncle, I don't think it is too soon to broach a subject which Mother would wish to be dealt with. This does not seem the wrong day to carry out what may have been her last wish. You know what I would say?"

"Can't you try to say it? Because I cannot. And if your mother would have wished it, you must."

"It goes without saying," said Justine, with a casual gesture. "It is yours, that which you gave us in your generosity when it was yours to give. Now it belongs to another, and we are glad that there is the nearer claim. The lack of it was the shadow over your good fortune. Mother felt it for you and just had time to know that it was lifted. You must have known her feelings."

"What about your old men and women in the village?"

"I shall give them what I gave them before, the work of my heart and head. They like it better, or rather I like it as well for them, as it does not touch their independence. Do not fear, Uncle. There is no sacrifice in rendering to you the things that are yours."

"It seems that there must be sacrifice in rendering things. What does Mark feel about the house?"

"Am I so much worse than Justine?"

"I should think you must be rather worse. Anyone would be. And it is on the weaker person that the greater sacrifice falls."

"Sacrifice? Faugh!" said Justine. "What Father can bear, Mark can, and with as good a grace, I hope, as someone who is less affected and matters less."

"I did not know all that about Mark. And I am still ill at ease. To give a thing and take a thing is so bad that I cannot do it. It must be done for me. And I am glad that a beginning is made."

"We can go on," said Clement, quickly. "Everything is in your hands. Have you anything to tell us of your future home?"

"Do you remember," said Justine, "how I almost foresaw the need of some readjustment like this, and made a stipulation to meet it? Everything was to be as it had been. That is how it is."

"Mark has not told me that he will like to see the house decay. I wish he would."

"I can tell you how glad I am to have parts of it saved, and the parts in most danger. And how glad to feel that you will have a home of your own."

"Here is a little man who is as ready as anyone to make what you will call his sacrifice," said Justine. "He is too shy to say so, but he feels it none the less."

"I am ready indeed," said Aubrey at once, showing his sister's rightness and her error.

"And it is not really a sacrifice," said Dudley. "He will tell me that it is not."

"There is no need to do that, Uncle."

"Haven't you enjoyed the money I gave you? It is dreadful to want you to enjoy it and then to give it back. But am I the only person in the world who really likes money?"

"We have savoured it to the full," said Justine, "but not as much as we shall savour the sense that you are using it for yourself."

"I do not like the sound of that. I want to eat my cake and have it. I had better let Aubrey keep his pocket money. Then I shall feel that I am letting my brother's family have all I can. That is all I can let them have. Five shillings a week."

"Well, the little boy will appreciate it, Uncle. And he will feel that he has shown himself willing to fall into line."

"Aubrey will eat his cake and have it," said Clement.

"So he will," said Dudley. "And I shall keep my cake and give away the smallest morsel of it. I think that is what people do with cakes. I shall have to be like people; I cannot avoid it."

"You cannot," said Justine. "You are caught in the meshes of your own life. It has come at last, though it has been so long delayed."

"You don't think I am old, do you?"

"No, not at all. You are in time to give your full prime to her who has won it. Accepted it, you would like me to say. And I think it may be the truer word."

"And some people always have a touch of youth about them."

"Yes, and you are indeed one of them."

"Thank you, I think that is all. And yet I feel there is something else. Oh, Clement has not told me that he is pleased to give up his allowance."

"It goes without saying, Uncle."

"I see it will have to. And I am taking everything and giving nothing. That is terribly like people. I have so often heard it said of them."

"The tables are turned on you at last," said Justine. "Brace up your courage and meet the truth."

"Of course people never can really part with money. You seem to be the only ones who are different from them. I am getting to know myself better. I knew people before."

"You will have a larger charity."

"Is it larger? It is certainly not the same. Perhaps it is what people have when they give their sympathy and nothing else? I am more and more as they are. I shall have to face it."

"Well, I don't think it does us any harm to look at that straight. I have always regarded it squarely myself."

"But you have never given a thing and taken a thing. You may not really be like people. You can cling to that in your heart."

"I wonder if I do," said Justine, in a musing tone.

"I am going," said her uncle. "I may be told that I am like people and you are not. Saying a thing of yourself does not mean that you like to hear other people say it. And they do say it differently."

"Well, we have come to it quickly," said Clement. "I wonder that Uncle liked to bring another change to our life at once."

"It was Justine who chose the time," said Mark.

"I liked the way he did it," said Justine, still musingly. "It was the way I should have chosen to see him carry it through. My heart ached for him as he tried to keep his own note throughout. And he succeeded as well as anyone can, who attempts the impossible. And I think that I spared both him and us by grasping the rope in both hands."

"You could not have helped him more," said Mark.

"Miss Sloane and I are to share his money," said Aubrey. "It should knit us closer."

"I am glad you are not to make a sacrifice, little boy. You are young to take that sort of part in life."

"I regret that I have to make one," said Clement.

"I would rather that Uncle had the money than I. I am only so glad that he wants it."

"I can't understand his wanting it all at once like this. Our little allowances can't make so much difference."

"He has spent too much on the house," said Mark. "It has taken much more than we foresaw. He has overdrawn his income and the capital he cannot touch. He must actually be in debt. If he did not have this money, he would have nothing for the time. If he had not inherited it, he could not have thought of marrying."

"He would have had to see Miss Sloane quite differently," said Aubrey. "We see the power of wealth."

"He could easily borrow money," said Clement.

"You talk as if you did not know him," said Mark. "He would not do that; he would hardly dare. You must allow for the effect of his life upon him and for his own character. And it may be less easy to borrow when your securities are in trust."

"The income would soon accumulate. He is not going to be married to-morrow."

"Let us face the truth," said Justine suddenly. "Uncle has lost himself heart and soul in Miss Sloane. Nothing counts beside her and his desire to lavish all he has upon her. His old feelings and affections are for the time in abeyance. We must face it, accept it, welcome it. Anything else would be playing a sorry part."

"And he has to take a house and do the part of

an engaged man," said Mark. "He will have expenses."

"We shall have to see that we have none," said Clement.

"And quite time too," said Justine, "if it makes us feel like this. It is a good thing that the change has come before we are quite ruined."

"You are all ruined but me," said Aubrey.

"Make an end to your selfish complacence," said Clement to his sister. "You are giving up nothing."

"Justine has spent what she had on other people," said Mark. "Her old men and women are the sufferers."

"Oh, I have spent on them very wisely, very circumspectly. I have seen to it that they should take no risk. They will feel no sudden change. I have had a care for them."

"Is Aunt Matty to give up her money?" said Clement.

"No. Uncle indicated to me in an aside that there would be no question of that. It is to remain as it is."

"He should have had an aside about Clement," said Aubrey.

"Mother has left her money to Father, hasn't she?" said Clement.

"Yes, most of it. A small legacy to Aunt Matty. She had very little."

"Will Aunt Matty be ruined, Justine?" said Aubrey. "What will she be like then?"

"Poor Aunt Matty!"

"Rich Aunt Matty!"

"Oh, come, she is an invalid woman, living in a small way. It is not for us, in this house and in comparative luxury, to grudge her any extra that she has. And it will make a difference to Grandpa's last years."

"Grandpa is not an old man in the village. Only in the lodge."

"And you are a naughty little boy. We must have Mr. Penrose back. We must make an end of this doing nothing because of our sorrow. We have lost our leader, but we are in no doubt about her lead. We shall get into the way of hiding a good deal of laziness under our grief. I am in her place and I must represent her."

"Your own place entitled you to direct Aubrey," said Mark.

"We must take up our burdens and go forward."

"People say that kind of thing so cheerfully."

"I am at a standstill," said Clement.

"Things go deep with people of Clement's saturnine exterior," said Aubrey, glancing at his brother with a wariness which was not needed, as the latter's demeanour showed that he had not noticed his words and would notice no other words from him.

"I do see his point," said Justine. "But it will not hurt him to show a little grit in his youth."

"Things like that ought to be guaranteed or not given," said Clement. "People can't have credit for giving things just while they do not want them."

"Uncle asked no credit."

"No, but he had it, and we shall have none for giving them up when we are becoming dependent on them. People's outlook alters a great deal in a few months."

"Really, Clement, I don't see that you deserve any praise for your kind of relinquishment. We have not had enough giving up in our lives. We see it as a thing which has to be learnt. I am not quite so pleased with my part in it as I perhaps implied; but in a way I welcome it and look forward to getting my teeth into it and going forward without a sign. We may look back on this early lesson and be grateful."

Aubrey looked at his sister in surprise at the place she gave the lesson in her life.

"What will Father do now?" he said. "There will be no one to be with him."

"Ah," said Justine, shaking her head, "is that ever out of my mind? Does anything matter beside our real problem? We can snap our fingers at any other."

"Yes, we see you can," said Clement.

"We must all do our best," said Mark.

"Mark has confidence in himself as a substitute for Mother and Uncle," said Clement, irritated by this attitude towards problems.

"Now I don't think what he said suggested that, Clement."

"We can't help fate," said Mark.

"We can't help it," said his sister, sighing, "in any sense."

"I suppose all problems solve themselves."

"Why do you think that?" said Clement. "Yours does. My problem and Father's have no solution. We shall have to cut the knots, and the result will be the usual mess and waste."

"Come," said Justine, beckoning with a slow hand and moving to the window. "Come. Perhaps the answer to our question is here."

Maria and the brothers were walking together below.

"Is that our solution? May it be."

"May it," said Clement. "It has served so far for several seconds."

"Come," said his sister, beckoning again. "Is it unfolding itself before our eyes?"

Dudley had left his place in the middle and taken Maria's other arm, leaving the one he relinquished, for his brother.

"There may be the lifting and laying of our fear, the final token of the future."

"You build rather much on it," said Mark.

"I feel it is symbolic, emblematic, whatever you call it. I cannot feel that the future will be left to itself, with Uncle's eyes upon it, with Uncle's hand to steer its way. And by the future I mean Father's future, of course."

"No one else has one," said Clement. "But it is natural that Father should not escape Uncle's thoughts at this time. He has just lost his wife, and his brother is leaving him after fifty years. It is not an average situation."

"Well, I feel that we have had a sign. But you are determined to be contrary until your own little share in the change becomes familiar."

"Why is it little? Because yours is? There is no other reason."

"Look at that and keep it in your heart," said Justine, pulling the curtain further. "Of what do you consider that a sign? What kind of an omen?"

Dudley had gone, and Edgar and Maria were walking together.

"Is not Uncle sharing everything even as Father has shared it?"

"Uncle has his own ways of sharing. He may withdraw it at his pleasure."

"Even their married lives are at the disposal of each other. It is a sobering and cheering thing."

"Boys," said Aubrey, blinking and pointing to the window, "what of the lesson of another pair of brothers?"

"And they are walking in step," pursued Justine, bending over the sill, "Uncle's brother and future wife. Is not that prophetic? I choose to see it so."

Clement came to her side and stood looking down with her.

"May you be able to abide by your choice."

"Away now," said Justine, resuming her ordinary voice. "Away to your daily employment. We must not go on dreamily, self-indulgently, deaf to the normal demands of life. Father has set us the example. He is up and about and turning his eyes on the future. At who knows what cost to himself? We must not be behind him, who has so much more to face. He hears the call of life and obeys it."

Edgar looked up as if feeling eyes upon him.

"They are watching us, those four who are my charge and whom I know so little. My brother has taken too much of my life, and you will not find that hard to understand. I must use the time I shall have to myself, to get to know my children. It may be too late to do anything except for myself."

Maria did not realise the unusual freedom of his words.

"You may find that you know them better than you think. It must be difficult to live with people and not know them, anyhow young people. I think we seem to know them when anything brings them out. Have you often been surprised by these?"

"I think perhaps I have not. I think they are themselves under any test. And if I have not served them much, I have made little demand. I have not much debt to pay. It might speak better for me if I had. I have not set myself apart from the normal relations of life, and I should have done better in them."

"Justine will solve many problems for you and will make none."

"Perhaps that in itself may be a problem."

"You do not often find people good all through as she is."

"You like my Justine?" said Edgar, with what he felt should be his feeling.

"I like good people," said Maria, with the simplicity which in her had its own quality, something which might have been humour if she could have been suspected of it. "I never think people realise how well they compare with the others."

"You have thought about people?"

"I have been a great deal alone and perhaps thought more than I knew. I should have learned more by meeting them."

"You must help me, if Dudley will let you. And I see that he will."

"I will if I can. I have been afraid of coming between you."

"You can hold us together from there. Dudley has put you between us. I do not know what I should do if he had not. It helps me to face the future, to face my double loss. I feel there is something—someone in the place."

Justine turned from the window as her uncle entered.

"Uncle!" she said, extending her hand towards the scene below.

"Perfect. To think that I am the possessor of all that!"

"It is all yours. Your full meed was delayed to come at last. When I look at those two tall figures, walking in step as if they would walk so all their lives, I see you between them, still walking somehow self-effacingly, there to do your part by both. I take it as an augury."

"Perhaps I am marrying for the sake of others. I could not think of myself at such a time. If I could, I might feel that I was doing so, or other people might. I don't suppose we ever feel that we are thinking of ourselves."

"Do you think we do not know you, Uncle?"

"I have been afraid you were getting to know me."

"Go your way, Uncle. Set your heart at rest. Forget yourself and go forward. If there is any little thing on which you do not like to turn your eyes, turn them from it and pass on. Take your life in your own hands. It is yours."

"You are certainly getting to know me."

"I declare this is the first time that I have felt cheerful since Mother left us. But the sight of Father with you and Maria—yes, I will say the name—has helped me to it. I feel I can emulate you and go forward."

"I can't be so very bad, if you are going to be the same."

Justine walked out of the room as if carrying out her words, and passed her brothers on the landing.

"Yes, it is a fascinating spectacle. I don't blame you for standing with your eyes riveted to it. But do not let it be a snare to lure you from righteousness. Life will be rushing by and leaving us in a backwater. Father has embarked upon the stream. We must not be behind him."

"Is that what has happened to Father?" said Clement to his brother. "Or has the stream sucked him in unawares? It has taken him already some distance. I wonder if he knows."

"Knows what?"

"Is it like Father to wander about alone with a strange woman?"

"It is like very few of us, but that is not what he is doing."

There was a pause.

"When is Uncle going to be married?"

"I don't know. I suppose not too soon after Mother's death."

Clement remained at the window after his brother had left him. He was to stand there several times in the next two months. At the end of them he came to the room where his sister was alone.

"Are not Father and Uncle going away in a few days?"

"Yes. Uncle has to see his godfather's lawyer, who manages his money. It may be about settlements or something. I have not asked. It is between him and Miss Sloane."

"Then they are going near Grandpa's old home. It was when he and Father were visiting the godfather, that Father and Mother met."

"Yes, so it was. Yes, they must be going there. It will do Father good to get away alone with Uncle."

"But surely this will not be the suitable change for him. Are we simply passing over Mother's death and expecting him to do the same?"

"Oh, I had not thought. Of course he must not go there. I had forgotten the place. I will speak to Uncle. Poor Father, no wonder he was not very eager over the plan."

"Grandpa and Aunt Matty are more and more anxious to sell their house and the furniture they left in it," said Clement, strolling to the window and twisting the blind cord round his hand, while his eyes went down to what was beneath. "The agent who is supposed to be doing it, seems to need some pressure and supervision. Could not Uncle try to put it through and come home a little later? It would put an end to Aunt Matty's talk."

"Does she talk so much about it? She must talk to you and not to me. It suggests that I am in disgrace. I daresay Uncle could do it. It is a good idea. We will ask him."

"And I believe that Miss Sloane wants something done in her old home."

"Well, he will certainly be glad to do that. She can ask him herself; I will remind her. And I will also remind Aunt Matty. It will make a good approach and help to bridge the rift. What a thoughtful boy you grow!"

Clement still twisted the cord.

"You seem tied to the window in every sense. What is there to be seen from it? If we light upon any uplifting scenes, we are only concerned with them as onlookers. For us there remains the common task."

CHAPTER VII

"I AM JUST the person who should not be going away," said Dudley.

"Courage, Uncle," said his niece. "Absence makes the heart grow fond. And we will all keep an eye on her for you."

"Do you want to give me any instructions as the person in charge?" said Matty.

"I have not had my own yet. I am waiting to be told to take care of myself and to come back as soon as I can. I must take the will for the deed, though that always seems to be giving people too much credit."

"Come away from the hall," said Justine. "Leave the engaged pair to enact their little scene in privacy and peace. They do not want eyes upon them at every moment. Someone give an arm to Aunt Matty."

"I think I may stay here, dear. I am not so able-bodied as to keep running away on any pretext. And I am to take Maria home as soon as your uncle has gone."

"I think it would be better to forget your office for once. Too duenna-like a course is less kind than it sounds."

"It did not sound kind, dear. And the words are not in place. There is nothing duenna-like about me. I have no practice in such things. I have been a person rather to need them from other people."

"Yes, I daresay, Aunt Matty. I did not mean the word to be a barbed one. Well, come along, Father. Leave Aunt Matty to carry out her duty in her own way. It would not be my way, but I must not impose my will on hers."

"You can only do your best," said Mark. "And that you have done."

"Come, let the engaged couple have anyhow only one pair of eyes upon them."

"They are still accustomed to being apart," said Edgar, as he moved from his place. "Their life together is not to begin yet."

"No, but common sense will hardly play much part in their feelings at this time. Whatever they feel, logic will not have much to do with it."

"If they don't want people's eyes they may not want their tongues," said Clement.

"Father, protect me against this unchivalrous brother."

Edgar edged by his daughter and walked down the hall. She misinterpreted his abruptness and followed and put her hand through his arm. He shook it off and went on, giving one backward glance.

"Father's look at Uncle goes to my heart," she said, as she joined her brothers.

Clement looked at her and did not speak. He also had followed his father's eyes.

"Some things are too sacred for our sight," said Aubrey. "They can only bear Aunt Matty's."

"Yes, that is the inconsistence I can't quite get over," said Justine. "It does not seem fair, but we are not allowed to prevent it."

"They have all their lives to be alone with each other," said Mark.

"Oh, why can't people see that the whole of their lives has no bearing on this moment?" said his sister, beating her hands against her sides. "All those moments added together will not make this one. It is one of the high water marks of life, the first parting after an acknowledged engagement. Why must we be so uncomprehending about it all?"

"We need not grasp more than is there," said Edgar, who had returned and now spoke with a smile. "The parting is to be a short one. Your uncle is hardly making so much of it."

"A fortnight or more. You don't know how long a fortnight can be in certain circumstances, Father."

Edgar again turned away, and Justine was after him in a moment, putting her hand in his.

"Oh, Father, what a crass and senseless speech! Why do I talk about people's want of comprehension? Why do I never take a lesson myself? Well, I have had one this time. I hope I shall never again take a fall like that. I hope there is one self left behind."

"It is hard on the people who assist Justine's rise on her dead selves to higher things," said Clement.

Edgar stood with his hand in his daughter's, silent in service to his duty.

"Come, Father, and just wave farewell," she said, as if she thought heroism the best course. "And then we will go and look at the work that was done before the men left. There is one piece of security for the future."

Edgar went with her, without taking the first step, and Mark spoke to his brother.

"Father does not miss Mother more than he will miss Uncle."

"He will miss someone else as much as either."

"Has he fallen in love with Miss Sloane?" said Aubrey.

"Get away," said Clement. "Why do you think we want you here?"

"I don't think so, but why should that make any difference?"

"You should not be always listening to grown up talk."

"I wasn't. Only you two boys were talking."

"That is too childish even for you."

"Well, I am Justine's little boy. And she likes me to be with other boys as I do not go to school."

"Go and hang on to her apron strings. No one else in the house wants you."

Aubrey recoiled, glanced about the room and burst into sudden tears.

"What is the matter?" said Mark.

Neither of his brothers gave the answer they both knew.

"Boys, boys!" said Justine, appearing with a promptness which struck her brothers as natural, but which was caused by her father's wish to be alone. "What is all this? Can I not leave you for a moment without coming back to find disturbance and tears?"

"You have not contrived to this time," said Mark.

"I shall have to learn to be in several places at once."

Aubrey gave a laugh to indicate that his emotion was of an easy nature.

"Tell me what it is."

"It seems to be nothing," said Mark.

"Nothing," Aubrey supported him with a sob.

"Well, I refuse to be left in the dark."

"It appears that you will be," said Clement.

"Clement, what is it?" said Justine, her voice deep with suspicion.

"Nothing at all. We told Aubrey to go out of the room, and he refused and some words resulted."

"You did not touch him?"

Clement raised his shoulders in contempt of her thought, and Aubrey supported him by a derisive laugh at it.

"Am I to conclude that it is absolutely nothing?"

"It is my own conclusion," said Mark.

Justine cast a glance at Clement and another at Aubrey, as though to trace some connection between them.

"Well, little boy, when are you going to show your face?"

Aubrey did not reply that this would be when he found the courage.

"Are you going to cry all day?"

Aubrey saw the awkwardness of the prospect but no means of averting it.

"Tell me what it is, Clement. I can see that you know."

"I told him to hold on to your apron strings and produced this result."

"Poor little boy, he has no others to hold on to. Oh,

that is what it is." Justine held out her arms to her brother as his renewed crying gave her the clue. "You must be more careful. And what a silly thing to say! A child is always in the charge of women. You were yourself not so long ago."

"I told him that we were all boys together," said Aubrey, with tears and mirth. "That is what he did not like. He tries to think he is a man."

"Is anyone hurt?" asked Edgar at the door.

"No, Father, only someone's feelings. And they are already soothed," said Justine, encircling Aubrey's head in a manner which for once he welcomed, as it hid his face. "So we need not worry you with it."

Edgar looked at his eldest and youngest children, as they went together from the room.

"There is a good deal on your sister. I hope you will be a help to her. I will ask you both to do your best. A house like this goes ill without an older woman. It will run for a time of itself as it has been set on its lines. But if any part goes off, the whole must follow. We must support that one of us who may be destined to strive and fail."

"I hope that Uncle will live near to us," said Mark.

"I hope so; I think he will do his best. But a separate household will not keep this one to its course. I trust the lines may run together; I trust they may."

Edgar left the house and walked on the path where he was used to walking with his brother. He held his head upright and his hands behind his back, as if seeking a position to replace the old one. His face was still and set, as though he would not yield to any feelings that would cause a change. He looked at his watch, surprised by its slowness, and at once replaced it and walked on.

Justine, watching from a window, left her place and hastened to her room. Coming downstairs in outdoor clothes, she passed her brothers with a sign.

"Do not ask me where I am going. Do not see me. Do

not remember I have gone. Go on with what you are doing and leave me to do the same."

"Where is she going?" said Mark. "What is the mystery?"

"I suppose to see Aunt Matty. She may be about to make some scene. It is a good thing to be out of it."

"Is Aunt Matty very lonely without Mother?"

"She must miss the concern which it had taken sixty years to work up. I should think it could not have been done in less. It is no good for anyone else to begin it."

"It is a pity that Grandpa is too old for a companion to Father."

"You are less sure of yourself in that character?"

"That aspect of me does not seem to strike him," said Mark, with his easy acceptance of the truth. "And I hesitate to bring it to his notice."

"We shall be a wretched household if Unclc—when Uncle goes. And I shall be obliged to spend more time in it."

"You take your usual simple attitude."

"What would happen to me if I did not?"

"You might devote yourself to doing a mother's part by Aubrey."

"You might have more success in that part yourself than as a wife for Father."

"Successful!" called Justine's voice, as her rapid feet bore her though the hall. "Successful and you need not ask in what way. That is in my own heart and I do not need to reveal it. I am content with my own sense of satisfaction."

Clement paced up and down, silent and as if preoccupied. When Maria came up the drive he glanced through the window, and continued pacing as if unaware of what he had seen.

Three weeks later Aubrey came to the others.

"I saw Father and Miss Sloane saying goodbye."

"Did you?" said his sister. "Well, that was not

much of an event. They must meet and part every day."

"Do people—do men kiss the women their brothers are going to marry?"

"Oh, that is what you saw? So that is what it has come to. Well, I am glad it has. They can carry that off, being the people they are. I don't know whether it is conventional between brothers and sisters-in-law, but that does not matter with these two. No doubt they felt that. They must know themselves as they are."

"Father will miss Miss Sloane when Uncle marries," said Clement.

"And shall we not all miss several people? A great part of our life will be a blank. This is something to be a help to him until the break comes. It is sad that we should think in that way of the consummation of Uncle's life, but we can hardly help it. I question indeed whether I have been wise in throwing Father and Maria so much together. I meant it for the best; God knows I did; but it will be something else to be relinquished. And I have been so glad to see him brighter and hear the old spring in his step. Well, we will not anticipate trouble. It will be on us soon enough."

"He must be better for being helped through the first stage. When that is over, he will have himself in hand and can look to his future. He must be used to his loss, before he is master of his own life."

"And people get used to anything," said Mark. "Even if he never gets over it, he must get used to it."

"He will get over it," said Justine. "To be honest, we know he will. His feeling for Mother was sound and true, but it was not that, not the kind to live by itself when its object was gone. You do not misunderstand me?"

They did not, and she stroked Aubrey's hand to help him over this initiation into the truth of life.

"We are all leaving our loss behind," said Clement. "And it is the better for us and for other people, the sooner it is done."

"I hope it does not mean that our little mother is drifting away," said Justine, frowning as she tried to think of another meaning. "But what dear, good boys you are in these days! You will not leave your sister alone at the helm. It is only Father whose future troubles me. He does seem to be separated by a wide gulf. Mark and I hoped that we could bridge it, but we found our mistake. That is why I am glad if Maria can get even a little way towards the self which is hidden. Somehow he seems to want to keep it so. Somehow I feel that there is a higher barrier between us than there was. There is something which I can't put into words about it."

"Does Father like Miss Sloane better than Mother?" said Aubrey.

"Now, little boy, you know better than to ask such questions. It is not worth while to answer them. But Father's life is not my affair, if he does not wish it to be. I was presumptuous to feel that I could in any way take Mother's place. I am content that Maria should do so to any extent that she can. The trouble is that it cannot be for long."

"Then Father likes Miss Sloane better than you, Justine."

"Oh, come, I am Father's only daughter, since Mother died the only woman in his family. You will know better when you are older, what that means. He may not want to mix up other relations with it. He has a right to have it by itself, simple and intact, if he wishes."

"Uncle is coming back to-morrow," said Clement.

"And Father's life will be full for the time. And we will not look further."

"Uncle has written to Miss Sloane every day," said Aubrey. "I saw the pile of letters on Aunt Matty's desk."

"Really, little boy, I don't know what to say to that. I hope they remained in a pile; I am sure they did; but even then I don't know what has become of my training."

"I don't think she writes to him as often," said Mark. "I took their letters to the post one day, and there was not one from her to him."

"My dear boys, what has come to you? I suppose you must have your little curiosities, but this goes too far. People must have their private lives and you must leave them. In some ways convention is a good thing. Mark, you are too old not to be quite certain about it."

"It is a wonder that the young are not worse than they are, when everything is condoned in them," said Clement. "We do all we can to prevent their improvement."

"Do you think Clement is softened lately, Justine?" said Aubrey.

"He has been more at home," said Mark. "I hoped, Justine, that our combined influence might do something for him. And I am not wholly disappointed."

"Don't talk nonsense. It will only end in a quarrel. And one thing I want to say. When Uncle comes back and meets Miss Sloane, don't all stand round in a circle, gaping at them. Let them have their moment."

"I do not remember grouping ourselves in that manner or with that self-indulgence. It was not a conscious effect."

"Well, you know what I mean. Anyhow you all seem to know a good deal. Talk about the curiosity of women! I seem to have much the least. Keep away and allow them their first hour. I expect even Father will do that. And it will be more to him, a foretaste of the time when he will be deserted. For that is what I fear he will feel in spite of his children. Dear, dear, I hardly dare to look at the future."

Edgar did not do as his daughter foretold. He met his brother, standing at Maria's side, and shook hands with his eyes on his face, as if he felt it was his duty to meet his eyes. Dudley took a step towards them, but stopped short, warned by some instinct that things were not as they had been. He drew back and waited for them to speak, feeling with his natural swiftness that this imposed on them the most demand and gave him the fullest chance. Maria's letters came to him, and he saw in a flash that this was not how she wrote. He waited to hear that she wanted release and had enlisted his brother's support. What he heard was always to return to his mind, each word sharp and heavy with all its meaning.

"Dudley, I must say what I must. Everything comes from me. You must hear it from my lips. Maria wishes to be released from you and has consented to marry me. We would not continue in a lie to you for a day. I cannot ask you to wish us happiness, but I can hardly believe, with my knowledge of you, that you will not wish it. And I can say that I wished it to you, when it seemed that things were to be with me as they are with you."

Dudley looked at his brother with motionless eyes, and in an instant recovered himself and met the moment, seeming to himself to act a part over unrealised feeling.

"So I am to be a hero. Well, it will suit me better than it would most people, much better than you, Edgar. I see how unheroic you are. And I return to my life of living for others. I don't think that they have really liked my doing anything else. And I see that it is nicer for them. And I shall keep you both instead of giving up one for the other. I expect that is what you have been saying. It sounds an improvement, but I shall not let you think it is. I must have some revenge for being put in this position. I shall look so foolish, standing aside in simple renunciation."

"You will indeed keep us both," said Edgar, in so low a voice that he seemed to feel it unfitting that he should speak.

"I ought to have thought of this myself. It would have come better from me. It does not come at all well from you, Edgar. I wish I could have the credit of suggesting it. I suppose I can't have it? We can't pretend that it did come from me?"

"It did in a way, Dudley. You gave us so full a share of each other."

Dudley recoiled but in a moment went on.

"And you have both taken a larger share than I meant. That is the worst of kindness; people take advantage of it. You really have done so. It will give me a great hold on you both."

His words, and his voice more than his words, laid a spell on his hearers and kept them still. Maria did not speak. She had nothing to say, nothing to add to what Edgar had said. Dudley looked at her, aloof and silent, and over his tumult of feeling continued to speak. He felt that he must get through the minutes, get them behind, that he must meet his brother's children and break the truth, before he went away alone to face the years. He could not face them with anything more upon him.

"I will go and tell Justine and the boys that I am to remain in their home. I suppose you do not wish me to leave it? You don't feel as guilty before me as that. They will betray their pleasure at the news, and I suppose that will be balm to my sore heart. I may be fortunate that I have never needed any balm before. They would rather have me than you, Edgar. I suppose I have really been the only father they have known. It is a good thing that you have not to face this ordeal. You would be quite unequal to it. You have been very awkward in this last scene. I see what people mean when they say that I am the better of the two."

"So do I, Dudley."

Dudley left them with a light step and they still stood apart. But as he paused to get his grasp on himself, he saw them move to each other and lift their eyes. Their ordeal was over: his had begun.

He paused at the door of the upper room and listened to the sound of voices. Justine and Aubrey and Mark were playing a game. Clement was standing on the hearth, as he had stood while the scene went on below. Dudley had not thought to dread this moment as much as he dreaded it. It had seemed that his main feeling must drown any other, and a thought just came that he could not be suffering to the last. He stood just inside the door and said the words which he felt would be his.

"I bring you a piece of good news. You are not going to lose me. I am to remain the light of your home. You thought that my gain was to be your loss, but I am not going to have the gain. It seemed impossible that I should be going to marry, and it is impossible."

"What do you mean, Uncle?" said Justine. "Have you changed your mind?"

"No, I am better than that. I have been rejected in favour of my brother and I have risen above it. I am the same person, better and finer. The last little bit of self has gone. It was rather a large piece at our last interview, but that does not matter, now it has gone."

"Tell us what you mean," said Mark.

"I don't think I can be expected to say plainly that Maria has given me up and is going to marry your father. Surely you can save me from the actual words. I shall soon have said them. Surely you have taken the hint."

"It is really true, Uncle?"

"Yes, you have taken it," said Dudley, sinking into a chair as if in relief.

"We are to accept this as definite and acknowledged? It affects us as well as you."

"It does, doesn't it? I had not thought of that. I am glad that you are to share the embarrassment. A burden is halved if it is shared, though it almost seems that it would be doubled. And you must be very uncomfortable. It is very soon for your father to want to marry."

"But Father can't marry Miss Sloane," said Aubrey. "He is married to Mother."

"No, dear," said Justine, in a low tone. "Mother is dead."

"But she would not like him to have another wife."

"We do not know, dear. Hush. Mother might understand."

"So that is what it has meant," said Mark, "their being so much together."

"Is that what it was," said Aubrey, "when I saw them——"

Justine put her hand on his to enforce his silence.

"Yes," said Dudley, "all of it was that. It is bad enough to bring out the best in me, and it has had to be the very best. And your position is not so good. Your father is losing no time in filling your mother's place. I must make one mean speech; I can't be the only person to suffer discomfiture. But of course you see no reason why I should suffer it, and of course I see that your mother would have wished this to happen, and that your father is simply fulfilling her wish."

"We cannot but rejoice that we are to keep you, Uncle," said Mark.

"Yes, we must feel that for ourselves," said Justine.

Clement and Aubrey did not speak.

"I don't wonder that you are ill at ease. And I must embarrass you further and tell you that you will have your money back again. I want you to feel some awkwardness which is not caused by my being rejected. No doubt you see that I do. But you will have the money after you have proved that you could give it up. It is just the position one would choose. And I have simply proved that I could take it back. My situation would not be chosen in any way. What do you think people will think of me? Will they despise me for being rejected? I do not say jilted. A vulgar word could not pass my lips."

"They will think what they always have of you, Uncle," said Justine.

"That I am second to my brother? Well, they must think that. Do you think a vulgar word could pass their lips?"

"I am sure it could not in connection with you."

"That is a good thing. Perhaps I am a person who can carry off anything. I must be, because that is what I am doing. You will have to support me and not show it. I should not like it to be thought that I needed help from others. And as I am still well off, people won't entirely despise me."

"You are many other things, Uncle."

"They are not the kind of things that people would see. People are so dreadful. I am not like them, after all."

"When will Father marry Miss Sloane?" said Aubrey.

"We do not know, dear. No one knows," said his sister. "Some time will have to pass."

"That seems so unreasonable," said Dudley. "Why should people wait to carry out their wishes? Of course they should not have them. I see that; I like to see it. I am not a man without natural feelings. I could not rise above them if I were without them. And that seems the chief thing that I do."

"Will you be taking up the repairs to the house again?" said Justine, in a practical tone, as if to liberate her uncle from the thrall of speech.

"Your father will think of that. It will be to his advantage. Oh, I must not let myself grow bitter. People are ennobled by suffering and that was not the speech of an ennobled man. And I thought of my advantage when my turn came. That came as a shock to people; I like to remember that it did. I was not a person who could be trusted to think of himself; they actually hardly expected it. If I had not become engaged, my true self would never have emerged. And now I shall never be thought the same of again. But I suppose nobody would be, whose true self had emerged."

"Is Father's self made manifest now?" said Aubrey.

"Yes, it is, and we see that it is even worse than mine."

Justine rose and shook out her skirt with a movement of discarding the traces of some pursuit.

"People's weaker side is not necessarily their truer self," she said, in a tone which ended the talk and enabled her uncle to leave the room.

A silence followed his going.

"Are men allowed to marry someone else as soon as they like after their wives are dead?" said Aubrey.

"How many weeks is it?" said Mark.

"I do not know. We will not say," said his sister. "It can do no good."

"It may have been the emotion of that time which prepared the way for the other."

"It may have been. It may not. We do not know."

"Is it often like that?" said Aubrey.

Justine sat down and drew him to her lap, and as he edged away to save her his weight, suddenly raised her hands to her head and burst into a flood of tears. Her brothers looked on in silence. Aubrey put his knee on the edge of her chair and stared before him.

"Well, that is over," she said, lifting her face. "I have to let myself go at first. If I had not, it would only have been bottled up and broken out at some inopportune time. Witness my passages with Aunt Matty. Well, I have betrayed my feelings once and am in no danger of doing it a second time. I can feel that Uncle will be able to face his life, and that I shall be able to face seeing him do it."

"Shall we all be able to, or must we all cry?" said Aubrey, who was himself taking the latter course.

"Well, women look into the depths more than men. But you need not fear that I shall reveal myself again."

"Shall we all follow Justine's example?" said Aubrey, glancing at his brothers to see if they had done so.

"Uncle did a difficult thing well," said Mark.

"I wondered when he was going to stop doing it," said Clement.

"Clement! Ah well, it is your feeling that makes you say it," said Justine.

"Justine helped him to stop," said Mark. "I wonder what would have happened if she had not."

"He would have managed for himself. I had no real fear. I only wanted to spare him all I could."

"It seems that we have been blind," said Clement.

"Have we?" said his sister. "Did we see anything? Did we foresee it? Shall we ever know?"

"Of course we shall," said Mark. "We know now that we have had a shock."

"It seems that there must have been signs, even that there were. Well, then, so it was."

"I wonder what the scene was like between Uncle and Father," said Clement.

"We need not wonder. We know that it was an exhibition of dignity and openness on the one side and generosity and courage on the other."

"Miss Sloane was there," said Aubrey. "I saw them all go into the library together."

"And what quality did she contribute?" said Mark. "But there was surely no need of any more."

"I wonder which of them one's heart aches for the most," said Justine.

"For Uncle. Mine only aches for him."

"I don't know. If I know Father, he has his share of the suffering."

"I think it is clear that we did not entirely know him. And Uncle is reaping the reward."

"Yes, yes, that in a way," said Justine, putting her hands round her knee and looking before her. "That, indeed. And yet there is something so stimulating in the thought of Uncle's course. It is such a tonic sadness. One wonders if such things are ever not worth while."

"Not for Uncle, I am afraid. The benefit is for other people."

"Do you know, I don't know?" said Justine, beginning again to gaze before her but checking herself. "Well, I must go and pursue the trivial round. Even such things as these bring duties in their wake. Miss Sloane will be staying to dinner, and I suppose Aunt Matty must come to preside at this further involvement of her fortunes with ours."

"Is that the best thing?" said Mark.

"Yes, my dear," said Justine, simply. "It saves Uncle the most. He gets it all over in one fell swoop and has his path clear. Let him go to bed to-night, feeling that his hard time is behind, that he has finished with heroism and has only to look forward in his old way to the happiness of others."

"Finished with heroism!"

"Well, begun it then, begun the real part. Begun to serve his sentence, even if it is for life. That is not so foreign to Uncle. We are not on his level. We can trust him to go further than we could."

"And fare worse, it seems."

"And fare as he may," said Justine with a sigh. "Now we have to take our thoughts from him and think of Father."

"A less elevating subject."

"No, no, Mark. We will not cross our proper bounds. Though Father is changing his life and ours, we are none the less his children."

"Will Aunt Matty be any relation of Father's now?" said Aubrey. "It was because of Mother that he was her brother."

"Oh, what a muddle and mix-up it all is! Well, we must leave the future. We have no right to mould or mar it. Aunt Matty is Mother's sister and has a right in our home. And she is also Miss Sloane's friend. It is strange that I do not feel inclined to say Maria now. But I daresay that is littleness and perhaps, if I knew, self-righteousness. She has brought this happiness into Father's life, and we must not forget it, though we have counted the cost. Let me see bright faces now. It is due to Father and to her, yes, and to Uncle too, that we should show a pleasant front to those who are managing their lives in their own way."

"Certainly not ours," said Mark.

"The whole point is the feeling between Father and

Miss Sloane," said Clement. "It is best for things to happen according to the truth underneath."

"We can't help resenting the truth; that is the trouble," said his sister. "We shall have to hide our feelings, and we shall not be the only people doing that. It is surprising how little we are in control of our minds. I found myself wishing that Mother were here, to help us out of the muddle which has come through her death."

"Well, she is not, and Father has to make his life without her. And he would be a more tragic figure alone than Uncle, if only for the reason that he would be lonely and Uncle will not."

"Not on the surface. We shall all see to that. But there is such a thing as being alone in a crowd. And perhaps we had some feeling that Father ought to be lonely at this time. Well, if we had, we had; I don't know what it says for us. Now will you walk across to Aunt Matty, and break the news cheerfully, gently—oh, how you please, and come back and tell me if she is coming to-night? To see her friend taking her sister's place may be a thing she can face, and it may not. Only she can know. Dear, dear, I don't see how things are to straighten out."

"I believe that you are a contributing cause of all this," said Mark to Clement as they set off. "It was your idea that Uncle should stay away to serve Aunt Matty. That is how things had the chance to turn themselves over. They could hardly have done it otherwise."

"It was a good thing they had it, with all this working underneath. It would not have done for the future to go on without any root in the truth."

"Have you had any base thoughts in your mind?"

"What do you mean?"

"Have you begun to think of having your money?"

"Oh, that. Uncle said something about it."

"He said the one significant thing."

"I suppose I shall come to it: I see you have done so."

"I was wondering if my mind were baser than anyone else's. I see it is baser than yours."

"Oh, all our minds are alike," said Clement. "Everyone is base in a way."

Dudley came across the grass behind them, raising his voice.

"Are you going to see your aunt? Then I will come with you and get the last piece of my ordeal over. I have shown you how a person should bear himself under a reverse, and now I will give the same lesson to Matty. We do seem to feel that she needs lessons, though I begin to see that her failings are not so bad as such things go."

Matty's voice came to their ears, raised and almost strident.

"Of course I should not be treated like this. You seem to be devoid of any knowledge of civilised life. Here have I been sitting alone all day, imagining everything, anxious about everyone, yearning for some word or sign! And here I am left as if I were nothing and nobody, and had nothing to do with the people who are the nearest in my life. I have lost my sister, but her children are my charge, and the woman who is to take her place is my friend. I am deeply involved in all of it and it is torment to be kept apart."

"I only said that they must have had a shock, and may not have thought of sending anyone down."

"Then don't say it; don't dare to say it. Sending anyone down! As if I were some pensioner to be cast a scrap, instead of what I am, the woman who stands to my sister's children in the place of a mother! You have never felt or had any affection, or you could not say such things."

Miss Griffin looked at the window, opening her eyes to prevent any other change in them, and Matty broke off, touched her hair, laid her hands on her flushed cheeks and leaned towards the door.

"Come in, whoever you are, and find a poor, wrought

up woman, tired of knowing nothing, tired of being alone. You have come to put an end to that. I am not quite forgotten. And do I see three dear faces? I am not forgotten indeed. But I have been feeling quite a neglected, sad person, and I am not going to sympathise with anyone. I have used up that feeling on myself. I know how the day was to go; I had my place behind the scenes; and I am just going to congratulate two of you on keeping your uncle. I know that I am striking the right note there."

The three men greeted the women, Mark guessing nothing of the scene, Clement part of it, Dudley the whole.

"Well, so I am to hear what has happened, all of it from the beginning. You tell me, Dudley. You are too interested in the whole panorama of life to be biased by your own little share. You know that I use the word, little, in its relation to your mind, not to mine. So tell me about it, and when it is all to take place, and what you will do with your wealth, now that it has come back into your hands. You won't think there is anything I do not want to hear. I include all human experience in my range. You and I are at one there."

"I think you have got me over my first moment better than anyone," said Dudley, reminded of Blanche by her sister and catching the deeper strain in Matty's nature. "I can really pretend that I feel no embarrassment. We ought not to feel any when we have done nothing wrong, but there are so many wrong things people do without feeling it, and so few they can have done to them. And being rejected in favour of a brother is not one of those. People will say that I am behaving well, but that I shall keep the most for myself by doing so, and how wise I am. They said it thirty-one years ago, and I remember it as if it were yesterday, and now it is happening again to-day. And you just said that my wealth had come back into my hands. And that is one of those words which we carry with us. I have never heard anyone say one of those before."

Matty flashed her eyes over his face and touched the chair at her side.

"Now you and I have to suffer the same sort of thing. I feel that my sister's place will be filled, and that I have not quite the same reason for being here as I had, and not quite the same claim on her family. And people will say the things of me, as you say they will of you."

"Do you really think they will? I like someone else to have things said, but I expect we can depend on people."

"Miss Griffin, suppose you run away and find something to do," said Matty, in such a light and expressionless tone that she might almost not have spoken.

Miss Griffin, whose eyes had been fastened on the scene, withdrew them and went to the door, with her face fallen and a step slow enough to cover her obedience to a command. Matty turned to her nephews.

"Well, you thought that you were to have a new aunt, and you are to have a new—what can we say? Well, we can't say it, can we? You and I can't. So we will just say that you are only to have one aunt after all. We do not want to cloud other people's happiness, and we will not; we shall be able to steer our way; we will keep to the strait and narrow path. But now we have made our resolve, we will get what we can out of it for ourselves. Let us have our gossip. That is much less than other people are getting, and if we do not grudge them their big share, they must not grudge us our little one. So when did you see the first hint of change, the cloud no bigger than a man's hand?"

"We saw no cloud until it broke," said Mark.

"Let me get my word in at once," said Dudley, "or I shall feel more awkward. It is best to take the bull by the horns. That is a good figure: it shows that we are talking of a terrible thing. Well, the cloud fell on me, sudden and complete, and I lifted my head and went forward. I told people myself; I went through my strange task, shirking nothing, and adding my own note with what was surely the most heroic touch of all. I am sure you would not dare to pity me. If you would, I must just face the hardest part."

"Well, you know, I do not feel that about pity. I often feel that I deserve it and do not get my share. People so soon forget to give it."

"That is another kind thing to say. But is pity really better than forgetfulness? Then I have still to suffer the worst indeed."

"Justine wants to know if you will join us at dinner, Aunt Matty," said Mark. "We can send the carriage when you like."

"Mark thinks I am talking too much about myself. Forgetfulness is already coming, and I see how bad it is. And coming so soon too! It is the only thing that could do that."

"What time, Aunt Matty? Justine was firm on the point. She wants an exact answer."

"Dear Justine! A time is always exact, I should have thought. Well, a quarter to seven, if that is not too early, if she can do with me so soon. She is still the regent in the house."

"I suppose Mark wanted to save me from myself. He is afraid that I may run on and not dare to stop, for fear of the silence that may follow. He has noticed that is my tendency. So will someone speak at once?"

"Well, perhaps half past six," said Matty, with immediate and smiling response. "Half past six and brave, bright faces. We have all made up our minds. So goodbye for the moment and good luck to our resolve. And tell Justine exactly half past six."

"You go on and take the message," said Dudley to his nephews. "And I will have a word with Miss Griffin. I find her regard for me very congenial. This trouble has come from someone's being without it."

Miss Griffin was lingering in the hall with almost open purpose.

"Well, you and I have more than ever in common, Miss Griffin. People think too little of both of us. I have been rated below my brother, and I am wondering if it will add to me to accept the view. Everyone feels that that ought to be done for me just now, and keeps trying to do it. And we ought to do what we can for ourselves."

"We don't all think you are below him."

"Most people do, and I expect I shall accept the judgement of the many, though it is known to be a silly thing to do. I am glad you are not so foolish."

"I am not indeed; I mean, I don't accept it."

"Of course I may be inferior to him. It is true that when I inherited money, I thought it put me on a pedestal. And when I gave it away, I thought it was wonderful. To give away money that cost me nothing to gain. But between ourselves I am still inclined to think it was. And I am not sure that he would have done it."

"Anyhow it was unusual."

"So now I am going to give it back, because if you can part with money, you can do something that very few people can do."

"I suppose people could do it if they liked," said Miss Griffin, in sincere thought.

"No, they could not. They are the slaves of money, not its masters."

"It seems funny, doesn't it?"

"I used not to understand it. But when I had money myself, I understood. I had to act quickly in case I became a slave. I nearly became one."

"But you did not quite."

"No, but soon afterwards I did. I feel I must speak so that you can only just hear. I asked for the money back again."

Miss Griffin smiled as if at a child.

"Did you not know that?"

"No."

"Isn't it extraordinary that such news does not spread?

I should like so much to hear that about anyone. I did not know that people were so unimportant. And they are not: everyone is important."

"Of course everyone is."

"Do you feel that you are?"

"Everyone ought to be."

"I am afraid I am thought important because of what I can do. And it may be the same with you."

"I cannot do much for anyone."

"I thought you did everything for Miss Seaton."

Miss Griffin looked aside.

"It is extraordinary how people put things to themselves. I daresay my nephews will take back their money with a sense of doing something to improve my position. And Miss Seaton probably thinks that you lead the same life as she does. And my brother may say to himself that he is saving me from a loveless marriage, when everyone knows that it is wise to found a marriage on other feelings. And Miss Sloane must have those for me now, when everyone makes such a point of it. And I will tell you something that I have told to no one else. I think it is ordinary of her to prefer my brother to me. It already makes me like her less. Our marriage might not have been loveless, but I think our new relation may be. It seems so obvious to choose the eligible brother."

"Is he more eligible? A widower with a family? Everyone would not say so."

"Perhaps he is not. Perhaps she really does prefer him to me. Then that makes me like her less still. I am glad if she is making a bad match. I wonder if people will recognise it. People have such average minds. It is something that I can speak of her in this detached way. I wish she knew that I could. Do you like her?"

"I did very much, until——"

"Until you heard that she had rejected me. So she has lost some of your affection and mine in the last hours. There is no gain without loss. And I shall make the loss as great as I can. That sounds unworthy, but it is natural. We really only want one word for natural and unworthy."

"There is Miss Seaton!" said Miss Griffin.

Matty came towards them with her slow step, her deep eyes fixed on their faces. Dudley caught a footfall on the stairs and looked up to address her father.

"We have been waiting for you to come down, sir. Miss Griffin said it would be soon. Are you going to join us to-night and be a witness of my courage?"

"Your virtues are your own, my boy, and will be no good to me. So I do not look for a chance to enter my daughter's house, and see her husband cheating himself that he can forget two-thirds of his days. Perhaps you will remain a moment and let me hear a human voice. And then you can take my poor Matty to do what she must in the home that was her sister's."

"Isn't it nice that we are all in trouble together?"

"It is better than being in it alone. It is the truth that we find it so. We will remember it of each other."

"We are sure to do that," said Dudley. "I shall not deny myself anything at such a time."

Miss Griffin and Matty had gone to the latter's room in silence. During Matty's toilet they hardly spoke, Miss Griffin fearing to be called to account and Matty uncertain whether to probe the truth. Matty maintained an utter coldness, and feeling for the first time an answering coldness in Miss Griffin, resented it as only someone could who had wreaked her own moods through her life. She left her attendant without a word, appearing unconscious of her presence. As she reached the hall and heard her step moving lightly above, she paused and raised her voice.

"Miss Griffin, will you bring my shawl from the bed? You did not give it to me. I am waiting for it."

Miss Griffin appeared at once on the landing.

"What did you say, Miss Seaton?"

"My shawl from the bed! It was under your eyes. You can run down with it in a minute."

Dudley took less than this to run up for it, and more to receive it from Miss Griffin, and Matty turned and walked to the carriage in silence.

"Oh, my shawl; thank you," she said, taking it as if she hardly saw it.

Dudly took his seat beside her, indifferent to her mood, and she felt a familiar impulse.

"Well, how are things to be to-night? Is it to be an evening of rejoicing or of tactful ignoring of the truth? In a word, are we to consider Edgar's point of view or yours?"

Dudley read her mind and felt too spent to deal with it.

"Well, are we not to have an answer to an innocent question?"

"It was a guilty question and you will have no answer."

"Well, we will try to do better. Let us take some neutral ground. Justine remains safe and solid. How does she feel about yielding up her place? Dear, dear, these are days of relinquishment for so many of us."

"Justine thinks very little about herself."

"Then I know whom she is like," said Matty, laying her hand on Dudley's.

Dudley withdrew his hand, got out of the carriage and assisted Matty to do the same, and, leaving Jellamy to hold the door, went upstairs to his room. Matty passed into the drawing-room, unsure of her own feelings.

Maria was sitting alone by the fire. The others had gone to dress, and it was not worth while for her to go home to do the same. And it seemed to her that any such effort for herself would be out of place.

"Well, Matty, you see the guilty woman."

"I see a poor, tired woman, who could not help her feelings any more than anyone else. I began by liking Edgar the better of the brothers, and Blanche liked him better too; so if you do the same, both she and I ought to understand. And I feel she does understand, somehow and somewhere, my dear, generous Blanche."

Maria looked up at Matty, sensing something of her mood.

"I am not troubled by its being a second marriage. That has its own different chance. Nor about having made a mistake and mended it. But I wonder how things will go, with me at the head, and Edgar's children living under a different hand. It does not seem enough to resolve to do my best."

Matty regarded her friend in silence. So she did not disguise her own conception of the change. Her simplicity came to her aid. She saw and accepted her place.

"Perhaps Justine will take most of it off you. She may remain in effect the head of the house. And things will not go far awry while she is there."

Maria met the open move with an open smile. She knew Matty better since she had lived in her house.

"She will not do that. Her father would not wish it, and she is the last person to feel against him. And I must set her free to enjoy her youth."

"My poor sister! How ready people are to enjoy things without her! But you will not have much freedom for yourself."

"I shall give up my freedom. I have had enough and I have made no use of it."

"It is dead, dear, the old memory?" said Matty, leaning forward and using a very gentle tone.

"It is not dead. But the cause of it is. I ought to have realised that before."

"You knew it at the right moment. Dear, dear, what a choice you had! Your understanding of yourself came in the nick of time."

"That can no longer be said. We must forget that I had a choice, as both of them will forget it."

"Stay there, stay there," said Justine, entering and motioning to Maria to keep her seat. "That is the chair which will be yours. Remain in it and get used to your place. Father will sit opposite, as he always has. There has to be the change and we will take it at a stride. It is best for everyone."

"Yes, you do welcome it, dear," said Matty.

"Now, Aunt Matty!" said Justine, sinking into a chair and letting her hands fall at her sides.

"Now what, dear?"

"Already!" said Justine, raising the hands and dropping them.

"Already what? Already I face the change in the house? But that is what you said yourself. You called out your recommendation from the door."

There was silence.

"Well, it is the replacement of one dear one by another," said Matty.

There was silence.

"It is good that they are both so very dear."

There was still silence. Maria lifted a fan to her face, screening it from the fire and from her friend. A current seemed to pass between her and Justine, and in almost unconscious conspiracy they held to their silence. Matty looked at the fire, adjusted her shawl with a stiff, weak movement, saw that it stirred a memory in her niece, and repeated it and sat in a stooping posture, which she believed to be her sister's in her last hours downstairs.

"No, no, Aunt Matty," said Justine, shaking her head and using a tone which did not only address her aunt. "That is no good. Conscious acting will do nothing."

Matty altered her position, and instantly resumed it, a flush spreading over her face. Justine held her eyes aside as if she would not watch her.

As Edgar's sons entered, Maria rose and went to a bookcase and Justine took her seat.

"What a long day this has seemed!" said Mark, speaking to avoid silence.

"Yes, I expect it has, dear," said his aunt with sympathy

"It has taken you from one chapter of your life into another. We cannot expect that to happen in a moment. It generally takes many days. This has been a long one to me too. I seem to have lived through so much in the hours I have sat alone. And it has not been all my own experience. I have gone with you through every step of your way."

"Yes, we have taken some steps," said Justine, "and in a sense it has been an enlarging experience. I don't think Miss Sloane minds our talking about it. She knows what is in our minds, and that we must get it out before we leave it behind."

"And she knows she is fortunate that it can be left," said Matty.

"It will fall behind of itself," said Maria.

"The first touch of authority!" said Justine. "We bow to it."

"It was not meant to be that. I am here as the guest of you all."

"It was just a little foretaste of the future," said Matty. "And quite a pleasant foretaste, quite a pretty little touch of the sceptre. I think we must hurry things a little; I must be taking counsel with myself. We must not leave that capacity for power lying idle. Now this is the sight I like to see."

Edgar and Dudley entered, at first sight identical figures in their evening clothes, and stood on the hearth with their apparent sameness resolving itself into their difference.

"This is what I used to envy my sister in her daily life, the sight of those two moving about her home, as if they would move together through the crises of their lives. I used to feel it was her high water mark."

"And they have just gone through a crisis and gone through it together," murmured Justine. "Yes, I believe together. Miss Sloane, it must be trying for you to hear this family talk, with my mother always in the background as if she still existed, as of course she must and does exist in all our minds. But if it is not to your mind, put a stop to it. Exert your authority. We have seen that you can do so."

"I should not want to do so, if I had it. I know that I have not been here for the last thirty years. I shall begin my life with you when I begin it. That is to be the future."

"And we will share with you what we can of ours."

"I hope you will. I should like it."

"Is Justine glad that Father is going to marry Miss Sloane?" said Aubrey to Mark.

"She is glad for Father not to be alone. It is wise to make the best of it. We can do nothing for people who are dead."

"It is a good thing that Mother does not know, for all that," said Aubrey, with an odd appeal in his tone.

"Yes, we are glad to be sure of it."

Aubrey turned away with a lighter face.

"Edgar," said Matty in a distinct tone, "I have been thinking that I must be making my plans. Come a little nearer; I cannot shout across that space; and I cannot get up and come to you, can I? The wedding will be my business, as Maria's home is with me. And I think I can make the cottage serve our needs. You will like a simple wedding, with things as they are? And it cannot be for some months?"

"I shall know about such things when I am told."

"I thought we ought to save you that, Aunt Matty," said Justine, sitting on her aunt's chair and speaking into her ear. "It does not seem that it ought to devolve on Mother's sister."

"Why, you are not sparing yourself, dear, and you are her daughter. And that is as close a tie, except that its roots are of later growth. I shall be doing what I have done before for your father. It is fortunate that I am so near. And I think we need not be troubled for your mother.

If we feel like that, this should not be happening. And she will go forward with us in our hearts."

"No," said Edgar, suddenly. "She will not go forward. We shall and she will not."

"Her wishes and her influence will go on."

"They may, but she will not do so. She has had her share, what it has been."

"I can see her in all her children," said Maria. "I shall get to know her better as I get to know them."

"And yet Edgar can say that she does not go on."

"She does not, herself. It will make no difference to her."

"We cannot serve the past," said Mark, "only fancy that we do so."

"Only remember it," said Justine, looking before her.

Maria and Edgar exchanged a smile, telling each other that these days had to be lived. Matty saw it and was silent.

"I shall be best man," said Dudley. "I think that people will look at me more than at Edgar. I shall be a man with a story, and he will be one who is marrying a second time, and the first is much the better thing."

"You need not worry about any of it," said Matty, with apparent reassurance. "People's memories are short. They too will feel that they cannot help what is gone, and they will not waste their interest. You will soon be a man without a story again."

"Do you resent a tendency to look forward?" said Clement.

"No, dear, but it seems to me that people might look back sometimes. Not for the sake of what they can do for the past, of course; just for the sake of loyalty and constancy and other old-fashioned things. My life is as real to me in the past as it is in the present, my sister as much alive as she was in her youth. But all these things are a matter of the individual."

"Aunt Matty," said Justine, in a low tone, bringing her

face near to her aunt's, "this house is moving towards the future. It is perhaps not a place for so much talk of the past."

"They are a matter of age, I think," said Mark. "The young are said to live in the future, the middle-aged in the present, and the old in the past. I think it may be roughly true."

"And I am so old, dear? Your old and lonely aunt? Well, I feel the second but hardly the first as yet. But I shall go downhill quickly now. You won't have to give me so much in the present. I shall be more and more dependent upon the past, and that is dependent upon myself, as things are to be."

"People are known to be proud of odd things," said Dudley, "but I think that going downhill is the oddest of all."

"Yes, you forget about that, don't you?" said Matty, in a sympathetic tone. "About that and the past and everything. It is the easiest way."

"Miss Sloane, what has your life been up till now?" said Justine, in a tone of resolutely changing the subject. "We may as well know that piece of the past. You know our corresponding part of it."

"The man whom I was going to marry died," said Maria, turning to her and speaking in her usual manner. "And I did live in the past. It may not have been the best thing, but it seemed to me the only one."

"Then long live the future!" said Justine, slipping off her aunt's chair and raising her hand. "Long live the future and the present. Let the dead past bury its dead. Yes, I will say it and not flinch. It is better and braver in that way. Mother would feel it so. Aunt Matty, join with us in a toast to the future."

"Aunt Matty raises her hand with a brave, uncertain smile," said Aubrey, as he himself did this.

CHAPTER VIII

"NOW ALL TO the fore," said Justine, "and in a natural way, as if you were thinking of Father and not of yourselves. It is his occasion, not ours, you know. People do not return from a honeymoon every day."

"It is not the first time for Father," said Mark. "And Maria planned it for herself before."

"I wonder if Father will think of last time," said Aubrey.

"Now I should not wonder that sort of thing," said his sister. "Just take it all simply and do what comes your way. The occasion is not without its demand. I do not find myself looking forward with too much confidence."

"Boys, can you look your father straight in the eyes?" said Aubrey.

"Will he want just that?" said Mark. "Will he be able to do it with Uncle?"

"Oh, why should he not?" said Clement. "He need not hang his head for behaving like a natural man."

"That is a thing I never thought to see him do."

"I can still only think of Uncle as he was at the wedding," said Justine. "Easy, self-controlled, courteous! It was a lesson how to do the difficult thing. We have only to think of that example, if we find ourselves at a loss."

"Is Father in love with Maria?" said Aubrey in a casual tone.

"Yes, we must say that he is. The signs are unmistakable. We could not be in doubt."

Aubrey did not ask if the same signs had been seen between his father and mother: he found he could not.

"Come, Mr. Penrose," said Justine, as the latter edged through the group. "If you want to slip away before the arrival, we will not say you nay. We know that it is our occasion and not yours."

Mr. Penrose responded to this reminder by hastening his steps.

"Were you wondering about me?" said Dudley, approaching from the stairs. "The scene would lose its point if I were not here. I shall not try to acquit myself as well as I did at the wedding. There are not enough people here to make it worth while. I hope the memory of me then will remain with them."

"It remains with us, Uncle."

"Justine spoke quietly and simply," said Aubrey.

"That is not what I meant. Does it remain with Mr. Penrose?"

"Yes, indeed, Mr. Dudley. Mrs. Penrose and I found it a most enjoyable occasion. We have several times spoken of it."

"Oh, away with you, Mr. Penrose," said Justine, with a laugh. "Your heart is not in the occasion as ours is. And indeed why should it be?"

Mr. Penrose did not admit that he saw no reason.

"I am most interested, Miss Gaveston."

"Of course you are, most interested; and what a feeling compared with ours! Away with you to the sphere which claims your feeling."

Mr. Penrose obeyed, but with some feeling over for the sphere he left.

"Oughtn't Aunt Matty to be here?" said Mark.

"No," said his sister. "No. I decided against it. You do not suppose that I have not given the matter a thought? We must break the rule that she is to be here on every occasion. We must not hand on such rules to Maria, ready made. Things cannot be quite the same for Aunt Matty here in future. Maria has a debt to her and doubtless will repay it, but the manner and method thereof must be her own. It may not be her choice to be confronted by her husband's sister-in-law on her first home-coming. Aunt

Matty will be with us at dinner, and that is as much as I felt I could take on myself."

"You and I are wasted on this occasion, Justine," said Dudley. "It must be enough for us if we have our own approval. My trouble is that I only care for other people's."

"Uncle, you know you have enough of that."

"Is Maria very old to be a bride?" said Aubrey.

"Not as old as Father to be a bridegroom," said Mark.

"Well, men marry later than women," said Justine.

"Welcome to the bride and bridegroom," said Aubrey, raising his hand.

"Welcome to your father and his wife," said his sister, gravely.

"Welcome to my brother and the woman who preferred him to me," said Dudley. "I am equal to it."

"I should not be, Uncle," said Justine, in a gentle aside. "I should put it out of my mind, once and for all. That is the way to gain your own good opinion and mine. Oh, here are the travellers! I feel we ought to raise a cheer."

Aubrey gave her a glance.

"I should suppress the impulse," said Clement.

"Oh, you know what I mean."

"Well, so would everyone else."

The scene was over in a minute. Maria was simple and ready, kind and natural; Edgar was stilted and sincere; and both were themselves. Dudley shook hands with both as if after an ordinary absence. His natural spareness and the flush of the occasion covered his being worn and pale. Maria kissed her stepchildren as if she had thought of nothing else, and took the head of the tea table without demur. She made some reference to Blanche in the course of supplying her family, and joined in the talk of her which followed. They felt that the situation was safe, and had a sense of permanence and peace. They had begun to talk when a trap drove up to the door.

"Aunt Matty!" said Aubrey.

"That high trap!" said Justine.

"Is she not expected?" said Edgar.

"Not until dinner, Father. I thought it was all arranged. And that fidgety horse! Will she ever get down?"

Dudley and Mark and Jellamy were perceived to be approaching the scene, and Matty was set upon the ground.

"Perhaps she has come to welcome me," said Maria.

"She has come for no other reason," said Clement.

"She comes!" said Aubrey.

Matty came in and went straight up to Maria, her eyes seeking no one else.

"My dear, I was so sorry not to be here to welcome you. The trap I had ordered did not come in time, and Miss Griffin had to go for it. I would not have had you arrive without a familiar face from the old world. You have so many from the new one."

"I have had a very good welcome."

"Yes, they are good children and mean to continue to be so. They are my own nephews and niece. But I feel that I am the bridge between the old life and the new, and I could not let you cross the gulf without it. The gulf is so much the widest for you."

"I am safely on the other side, with the help of them all."

"So you are, dear, and I will sit down and see it. I will have a chair, if I may. Thank you, Dudley; thank you, Mark; thank you, my little nephew. You are all ready and willing; you only want a little reminder. I will sit near to Maria, as it is she who is glad of my presence. Do not let me displace you, Edgar; that is not what I meant. We will sit on either side of her and share her between us. We are used to that sort of relation. I want to feel that this second time that I give you your life companion, is as much of a success between us as the first." Matty gave Edgar a swift, bright look and settled her dress.

There was a pause.

"We did not know you were coming," said Justine, "or we would have sent for you."

"You asked me to come, dear. I should have done so, of course, but you did remember the formality. But it was for dinner that you said. I did not know that they were expected so early. I only found it out by accident."

"We did not mean to give a wrong impression."

"No, dear? But you said for dinner, I think."

"I did not know you expected—that you would want to be here for their arrival. We thought they would have a rest, and that you would see them later."

"Have a rest, dear?" said Matty, with a glance round and a twitch of her lips.

"Well, stay with us for a little while, and then go upstairs by themselves and meet everyone at dinner."

"Maria never rests in the day, even after a journey," said Matty, in the casual tone of reference to someone completely known to her.

"I am finding all this a rest," said Maria.

Matty looked round again, with her mouth conscientiously controlled, but with a gleam in her eyes.

"Well, can it be true?" said Clement.

"I am finding it a great strain," murmured Aubrey.

"Hush, don't whisper among yourselves," said their sister.

"I think I will have some tea, Justine dear," said Matty. "Or am I to remember that I was only asked to dinner?"

"Really, Aunt Matty, I shall not reply to that."

"I am afraid I am pouring out the tea," said Maria, laughing and taking up the pot.

"Are you, dear? I thought you were having a rest, and that Justine would still be directing things. I have had no directions except from her."

"You could not have them from me until I returned."

"You did not write to me, I thought you would want to arrange your first day yourself."

"I did not think of it. I was content just to come home."

"No, no, Aunt Matty. You will not make bad blood between Maria and me," said Justine, shaking her head.

"Bad blood, dear?" said her aunt, in a low, almost troubled tone. "I did not think there was any question of that. I had put the thought away. I am sure there is none any longer. I am sure that all the little pinpricks and jealousies have faded away."

"Justine does not know what such things are," said Edgar.

"Well, I said they had faded away, and that amounts to the same thing."

"It is on the way to the opposite thing."

"Dear Father, he has come back to his only daughter," said Justine.

"Incontrovertibly," said Aubrey, looking down.

"Well, am I to have any tea?" said Matty.

"When you stop holding everyone rooted to the spot," said Clement. "As long as they are petrified, they cannot give you any."

"Well, I must lift my spell. I did not know it was so potent. Some people have more power than others and must be careful how they wield it. Thank you, Dudley, and a penny for your thoughts."

"I was thinking that I had never made a speech which carried a sting."

"I was wondering when we were going to hear your voice. I have never known you so silent."

"I recognise the sting. I almost think that the gift of speech is too dangerous to use."

"What should we do without your talent in that line?"

"I believe that is a speech without a sting."

"Oh, Aunt Matty, if you would only do it oftener!" said Justine, sighing. "You don't know how far you could go."

"Don't I, dear? I sometimes think I should be left in a backwater. I admit that I sometimes feel driven to apply the goad."

"Aunt Matty, how wrong you are! If only you would realise it!"

"It must be a trying obligation," said Maria.

"If you can manage without it in your ready made family, you are fortunate."

"I see that I am."

"And we all see that we are," said Mark.

"I am sure—I hope we have many happy days before us," said Edgar.

"Rest assured, Father, that we are not poaching on your preserves," said Justine. "Maria is yours, root, barrel and stock. We claim only our reasonable part in her."

Aubrey looked at his sister.

"You don't understand my wholehearted acceptance of our new life, do you, little boy? When you get older you will realise that there is no disloyalty involved."

"It is a rich gift that I have brought you," said Matty, smiling at Edgar. "So do you think I may have it in my own hands for a time, while you and Dudley go and make up your arrears, and the young ones play at whatever is their play of the moment."

The word was obeyed before it was considered. Edgar withdrew with his brother and his children found themselves in the hall.

"If I were Maria," said Clement, "I would not let Aunt Matty order the house."

"She will not do so for long; do not fear," said his sister. "There are signs that she is equal to her charge. I am quite serene. And I was glad to see Father and Uncle go off in their old way. Uncle still has his brother. I don't think anything has touched that."

Edgar and Dudley were sitting in their usual chairs, their usual table between them, the usual box of Dudley's cigars at Edgar's hand.

"The young people have given no trouble?"

"None."

"You have not lavished too much on them?"

"Nothing. They keep to what they have."

"Is there anything to tell about the house?"

"The work goes on. Mark and I have had our eye on it."

"Dudley," said Edgar, keeping his voice to the same level but unable to control its tones, "I have always taken all you had. Always from the beginning. You did not seem to want it. Now, if I have taken something you did want——"

"Oh, I am a great giver. And giving only counts if you want what you give. They say that we should never give away anything that we do not value."

"It is the rarest thing to be."

"Well, I don't wonder at that. It seems to be one of those things which may end anywhere. We see that it has with us. But I had to follow my nature. It may have been my second nature in this case. It would be best to hide a first nature quickly, and I was very quick. I hope people admire me. To be admired is one of the needs of my nature; my first nature that would be. But I should only expect them to admire the second. It would not often be possible to admire first natures. I used to think that you and I only had second ones, but now we have both revealed our first, and it gives us even more in common."

Edgar looked at his brother, uncertain whether to be cheered or troubled by the tangle of his words.

"You find you are able—you can be with Maria and me?"

"Yes. There is not so much of my first nature left as you fear. And I daresay it is best that I should not marry. If a man has to forsake his father and mother, he ought to forsake his brother, and I find I could not do that. I suppose you have forsaken me in your mind? You should have."

Edgar looked up with a smile, missing what lay behind the words, and the cry from his brother's heart went unanswered.

When Edgar's children came down to dinner they found their aunt alone.

"Well, here is the first evening of our new life," said Justine. "I feel easy and not uncheerful."

"Yes, I think so do I, dear," said Matty. "I think I can see my Maria over you all, as I could not see anyone else."

"I already see her taking her place at the table in my mind's eye," said Justine, leaning back and closing her other eyes to give full scope to this one. "Easily and simply, as if she had always had it."

"Well, perhaps not quite like that, dear. That might not be the best way. I think she can do better."

"That would be well enough," said Mark.

"I daresay she will take her place like anyone else," said Clement.

"I think the boys admire their young stepmother, Justine," said Aubrey.

"Well, we are at a difficult point," said Matty. "We are the victims of a conflict of loyalties. We must be patient with each other." She smiled at them with compressed lips, seeming to exercise this feeling.

Maria took her seat at the table as if she were taking it naturally for the first time.

"The place is taken," murmured Aubrey.

"And as I said it would be," said Clement.

"Well, I want a little help in taking my place," said Matty. "I am not able to take it quite like that. Thank you, Edgar."

"I shall so enjoy shelving the household cares to-morrow," said Justine. "No housewife ever parted with her keys with less of a pang."

"You will give what help you can?" said Edgar.

"No, I shall not, Father. I know it sounds perverse, but a house cannot do with more than one head. Nothing can serve two masters. I go free without a qualm."

"I only serve one master," said Aubrey. "Penrose."

"Do you feel you would like a change?" said Maria.

"No, no, don't pander to him, Maria; he will only take advantage. I mean, of course, that that is what I have found. You will form your own conclusions."

"Perhaps I shall find that I have learnt more from Penrose, than many another lad at a great public school."

"I don't know what ground you have for the view," said Mark.

"It was just one of my little speeches. What would the house be without them?"

"It would be better with Uncle and no one to copy him," said Clement.

"Now, Clement, come, there is a real likeness," said Justine.

"Clement is jealous of my genuine touch of Uncle."

"Does Dudley see the likeness?" said Matty, with a faint note of sighing patience with the well worn topic.

"I should think it is the last thing anyone would see, a likeness to himself," said her niece.

"Should you, dear? The opposite of what I say. We are not all like your uncle."

"I make no pretence of lightness and charm. I am a blunt and downright person. People have to take me as I am."

"Yes, we do, dear," said Matty, seeming to use the note of patience in two senses.

"Clement thinks that I try to cultivate them," said Aubrey, "and it makes him jealous."

"You may be wise to save us from taking you as we take Justine," said Clement.

Aubrey gave a swift glance round the table, and sat with an almost startled face.

"Maria, what do you think of our family?" said Justine. "It is full experience for you on your first night."

"It is better not to have it delayed. And I must think of myself as one of you."

"This is the very worst. I can tell you that."

"I have often been prouder of my sister's children," said Matty.

Edgar and Dudley turned towards her.

"I believe the two brothers are so absorbed in being together that no one else exists for them."

There was a pause and Matty was driven further.

"Well, it is a strange chapter that I have lived since I have been here. A strange, swift chapter. Or a succession of strange, swift chapters. If I had known what was to be, might I have been able to face it? And if not, how would it all be with us? How we can think of the might-have-beens!"

"There are no such things," said Edgar.

"We cannot foretell the future," said Mark. "It might make us mould our actions differently."

"And then how would it all be with us?" repeated Matty, in a light, running tone. "Maria not here; Justine not deposed; nothing between your father and uncle; everything so that my sister could come back at any time and find her home as she left it."

"Is it so useful to have things ready for her return?"

"It is hardly a dependable contingency," said Clement.

"No, no," said Justine, with a movement of distaste, "I am not going to join."

"So my little flight of imagination has fallen flat."

"What fate did it deserve?" said Edgar, in a tone which fell with its intended weight.

"Did you expect it to carry us with it?" said Mark.

Matty shrank into herself, drawing her shawl about her and looking at her niece almost with appeal. The latter shook her head.

"No, no, Aunt Matty, you asked for it. I am not going to interfere."

"What do you say to the reception of a few innocent words, Dudley?"

"I have never heard baser ones."

Matty looked at Maria, and meeting no response, drew

the shawl together again and bent forward with a shiver.

"Have you a chill, Matty?" said Dudley.

"I felt a chill then. There seemed to be one in the air. I am not sure whether it was physical or mental. The one may lead to the other. I think that perhaps chills do encircle you and me in these days."

"That is not true of Uncle," said Justine. "He is safely ensconced in the warmth of the feeling about him."

"And I am not? I am a lonely old woman living in the past? I was coming to feel I was that. Perhaps I ought not to have come to-day, sunk as I was in the sadness of this return." Matty ended on a hardly audible note.

"It was certainly not wise to come with no other feeling about it," said Mark.

"No, it was not, because that was how I felt. So perhaps it is not wise to stay. I will make haste to go, and lift the damper of my presence. I feel that I have been a blight, that your first evening would have been better without me. I meant to come and join you in looking forward, and I have stood by myself and looked back. I am glad it has been by myself, that I have not drawn any of you with me." Matty kept her eyes on Mark's, to protect herself from other eyes. "But I have been wrong in not hiding my heart. My father sets me an example in avoiding the effort destined to fail. I thought I could follow your uncle: I meant to take a leaf out of his book. But I can't quite do it to-day. To-day I must go away by myself and be alone with my memories. And I shall not find it being alone. And that is a long speech to end up with, isn't it?"

"Yes, it is rather long."

"Very well, then, go if you must," said Justine.

"What does my hostess say?"

"Oh, of course, I should not have spoken for her," said Justine, with a little laugh.

"Justine has said the only thing that can be said. But the carriage cannot be here at once."

"Well, I will go and sit in the hall. Then I shall have left the feast. There will no longer be the death's head at it. I shall be easier when I am not that. That is the last thing I like to be, a cloud over happy people. We must not underrate happiness because it is not for ourselves. It ought to make us see how good it is, and it does show it indeed."

"Who is going to see Aunt Matty out?" murmured Aubrey.

"Perhaps Dudley will," said Matty, smiling at the latter. "Then he and I can sit for a minute, and perhaps give each other a little strength for the different effort asked of us."

Dudley seemed not to hear and Maria signed to her husband.

"Aunt Matty would have been burned as a witch at one time," said Clement.

"Does Clement's voice betray a yearning for the good old days?" said Aubrey.

"Witches seem always to have been innocent people," said Mark.

"That will do. Let us leave Aunt Matty alone," said Justine. "She may merit no more, but so much is her due."

"What does Maria say?" said Dudley, in an ordinary tone.

"We are all moving forward. And if Matty does not come with us, she will be left behind."

"She may pull herself up and follow," said Justine.

"She will probably lead," said Clement.

"She will not do that," said his father, returning to the room.

"Has Aunt Matty gone already, Father?" said Justine.

"No. She asked me to leave her, and I did as she asked."

After dinner it was the brothers' custom to go to the library. Blanche had had her own way of leaving the room, pausing and talking and retracing her steps, and any custom of waiting for her had died away. Dudley put his arm through Edgar's, as he had done through his life. Edgar threw it off with a movement the more significant that it was hardly conscious, and waited for his wife, giving a smile to his brother. Dudley stood still, felt his niece's hand on his arm, shook it off as Edgar had done his own, and followed the pair to the library. He sat down between them, crossing his knees to show a natural feeling. Edgar looked at him uncertainly. He had meant to be alone with his wife and had assumed that his brother understood him. This withdrawal of Dudley's support troubled him and shook his balance. Something was coming from his brother to himself that he did not know.

"Does Maria mind smoke?" said Dudley, knowing that she did not mind, knowing little of what he said.

"No, not at all. I am used to it."

"I do not smoke; I never have; I get the cigars for Edgar."

"I could not afford them for myself," said Edgar.

"I must give you some as a present," said his wife, feeling at once that the words would have been better unsaid.

Dudley looked at her and met her eyes, and in a moment they seemed to be ranged on opposite sides, contending for Edgar. Edgar sat in a distress he could not name, moving his strong, helpless hands as if seeking some hold.

"They come from some foreign place," said Maria, taking up the box. "We shall have to depend on Dudley for them."

Dudley lifted eyes which looked as if he were springing from his place, but held himself still. The silence held, grew, swelled to some great, nameless thing, which seemed to fill the space between them and press on their hearing and their sight. Edgar rose and showed by his rapid utterance as well as by his words how he was shaken out of himself.

"What is this, Dudley? We cannot go on like this. We should not be able to breathe. What is it between us?

It is not fair to give me everything, and then turn on me as an enemy."

"Not fair to give you everything?" said Dudley, rising to bring his eyes to the level of his brother's. "Do you think it is fair? Does it sound fair as you say it? For one person to do that to another? For the other person to take it? Or do you take it all, as you always have, you who know how to do nothing else? And turn on you as an enemy? What have you been to me but that? If you have never thought, think now."

"So it has come to this, Dudley. It has all been this. This has been before us, and so between us, all our lives. You have given me nothing. You wanted to have me in your hands in return. No one can give really, not even you; not even you, Dudley. I shall not think that any more of you. You are not different. Why did you let me think you were? I would not have minded; I could have taken you as you were; I did not want anything from you. And now I have lost my brother, whom I need not have lost if I had known."

Edgar turned his face aside, and the simple movement, which Dudley knew was not acting, pierced him beyond his bearing and flung him forward. His pain and his brother's, the reproach which he suffered in innocence and sacrifice, flooded his mind and blurred its thought.

"You have lost your brother! Then know that you have lost him. Know that you speak the truth. You may be glad to be left with your wife, and I shall be glad to leave you. I shall be glad, Edgar. I have always been alone in your house, always in my heart. You had nothing to give. You have nothing. There is nothing in your nature. You did not care for Blanche. You do not care for your children. You have not cared for me. You have not even cared for yourself, and that has blinded us. May Maria deal with you as you are, and not as I have done."

Maria stood apart, feeling she had nothing to do with the scene, that she must grope for its cause in a depth where different beings moved and breathed in a different air. The present seemed a surface scene, acted over a seething life, which had been calmed but never dead. She saw herself treading with care lest the surface break and release the hidden flood, felt that she learned at that moment how to do it, and would ever afterwards know. She did not turn to her husband, did not move or touch him. The tumult in his soul must die, the life behind him sink back into the depths, before they could meet on the level they were to know. She felt no sorrow that she had not shared that life, only pity that his experience had not found cover as hers had found.

Dudley went alone from his brother's house, taking nothing with him but his purse and covering from the winter cold. He went, consciously empty of hand and of heart, almost triumphant in owning so little in the house that had been his home. As he passed Matty's house, forming in his mind some plan for the night, he heard a sound of crying behind the hedge, which seemed to chime with his mood. He followed the sound, thinking to find some unfortunate who would make some appeal, and willing for the sense of being met as a succourer, and came upon Miss Griffin bent over the bushes in hopeless weeping. She raised her head and came forward at once, spreading her hands in abandonment to the open truth.

"Miss Seaton has turned me out. I have been out here for some time. I haven't anywhere to go, and I can't stay here in the dark and cold. And I can't go back." She looked round with eyes of fear, and something showed that it was Matty in relenting mood, with an offer of shelter, that she feared.

Dudley put his arm about her and walked on, leading her with him. She went without a word, taking her only course and trusting to his aid. Her short, quick, unequal steps, the steps of someone used to being on her feet, but not to walking out of doors, made no attempt to keep time or pace, and he saw with a pang how she might try the nerves of anyone in daily contact. The pang seemed to drive him forward as if in defiance of its warning.

"You and I are both alone. People have not done well by us, and we have done too well by them. We should know how to treat each other. We will keep together and forget them. We had better be married, and then we need never part. We have both been cast out by those who should have served us better. We will see what we can do for ourselves."

"Oh, no, no," said Miss Griffin, in an almost ordinary tone, as if she hardly gave Dudley's words their meaning. "Of course not. What a thing it would be! We could not alter it when it was done, and of course you would want to." Her voice was sympathetic, as if her words hardly concerned herself. "And what would people think? You can help me without that." The words stumbled for the first time. "If you want to help me, that is, of course."

"I was trying to serve myself," said Dudley, too lost in his own emotions to feel rebuff or relief. "I must serve you in some better way. You can think of one yourself. And now we must hurry on and get you under a roof."

He walked to Sarah Middleton's house, seeing his companion's thinly covered feet and uncovered head, and the scanty shawl snatched from somewhere when she was driven into the cold. On the steps of the house she looked up to explain the truth, that he might know it and express it for her.

"She came back from the house very early and very upset. I could hardly speak to her. Nothing I said was right. And she did not like it if I did not speak. It was no good to try to do anything. Nothing could have made any difference. Mr. Seaton had gone to bed and we were alone. At last she flew into a rage and turned me out of doors. She said it drove her mad to see my face." Miss Griffin's voice did not falter. She had felt to her limit and could not go beyond.

Dudley asked to see Sarah and told her the truth. She

heard him in silence, with expressions of shock, eagerness, consternation, delight and pity succeeding each other on her face. When at last she raised her hands, he knew that his task was done. He saw her hasten into the hall and bring the hands down on Miss Griffin's shoulders. Her husband rose and put a chair for the guest, keeping his face to the exact expression for the action.

"You will be safe, my dear; we will see that you are safe," said Sarah, showing that Miss Griffin was not the only person in her mind.

Miss Griffin parted from Dudley with eager thanks, and he saw her go in to food and fire with greater eagerness.

He left the house, feeling soothed and saner, and found himself imagining Sarah's experience, if she had known his own solution for her guest. He went to the inn to get a bed for the night, indifferent to surprise or question, finding a sort of comfort in the familiar welcome. He slept as he had not slept since his brother's engagement, the sense of suspense and waiting leaving him at last. He found that his mind and emotions were cleared, and that his feeling for Edgar had taken its own place. He had been lost in the tumult of his own life, and the hour passed in another's had done its work. Edgar stood in his heart above any other. The knowledge brought the relief of simplified emotion, but fed his anger with his brother, and confirmed his resolution to remain out of his life.

He went to Miss Griffin in the morning in almost convalescent calm, prepared to live his life without hope or eagerness. She came into the hall to meet him, wishing to see him without Sarah, as her sympathy with curiosity did not lessen the trial of response.

"Oh, it was everything to be warm and safe. I shall never forget that waiting in the cold. I don't know what would have happened if you had not come."

"What would you like to do now? And in the future?"

"I should like to get away from Miss Seaton," said Miss Griffin, meeting his eyes in simple acceptance of his knowledge. "It seems a dreadful thing to say after all these years, but every year seems to make things worse. I should like to have some peace and some ordinary life like other people, before I get old." Her voice broke and her eyes filled, both actions so simple that she did not heed or disguise them. "I don't feel I want to have had nothing: it doesn't seem right that anyone should go through life like that. You only get your life once. Of course, if people were fond of you, that would be enough; but Miss Seaton seems to hate me now, and I don't know what to do to make it different. I only want to be peaceful somewhere, and not always driven and afraid, and to be able to do something for someone else sometimes." Her eyes went round the hall as if its narrow comfort satisfied her soul.

"You would like a cottage of your own, and a little income to manage it on, and perhaps a friend to live with you, who needed a home."

"Oh, I know two or three people," said Miss Griffin, in gladness greater than her surprise. "I could have them in turn, to make a change for me and for them. Oh, I should like it. But I don't know why you should do as much for me as that." Her voice fell more than her face. She depended on Dudley's powers, and would have liked so much to do this for someone, that she hardly conceived of his not feeling the same.

"I shall like to do it, and I can do it easily. I shall be the fortunate person. We will arrange for the money to come to you for your life. I shall not be living here, but that will make no difference."

Miss Griffin hardly heard the last words. She stood with a face of simple joy. She believed that Dudley would not miss the money, would have been surprised by the idea of his doing so, and saw her life open out before her, enclosed, firelit, full of gossip and peace.

"What will Miss Seaton say?" she said, in a tone which was nervous, guilty, triumphant and compassionate. "Well, she will soon get used to it and settle with someone else." A spasm crossed her face but did not stay. She had been tried to the end of her endurance, and knew that she could not continue to endure. "Perhaps you could come and tell Mrs. Middleton. Then I need not talk about it, and other people will hear."

Sarah was startled, incredulous, rejoiced, desirous that Miss Griffin should have enough for her ease, anxious that she should remain a much poorer person than herself, relieved when it was apparent that she would; and betrayed her feelings partially to Dudley and completely to Miss Griffin, without surprising or estranging either. Miss Griffin's thought followed hers. She did not want a whit more than she needed, felt that the money would have more significance if every coin had its use, looked for the pleasures of contrivance, and allowed for a touch of laxness in herself, which Matty had combated with bitterness, with an open self-knowledge which to Sarah was sensible, and to Dudley comic and touching. She did not stress her gratitude, almost betrayed a faint sense of envy of anyone who could give so much without sacrifice. If she had not forgotten the offer of marriage, she behaved as if she had, and he saw that in effect they would both forget it, that she saw it simply as an impulsive offer of rescue. If she divined that it had some root in his own life, she saw the life as too far removed from her own to be approached.

Dudley left her with the natural sense of elation, and as it fell away, walked on with the single intention of going further from his brother, thinking and caring for nothing beyond.

CHAPTER IX

EDGAR AND HIS wife were left looking at each other. Maria was the first to speak.

"We must go on as if nothing had happened. We could not help it. I do not think we could. We might have seen it had to come. But I thought it would not come, with Dudley. Did you think that?"

"I thought it," said Edgar, hardly parting his lips. He was summoning up his brother's experience, grasping at its meaning as his brother had lived it. He had taken from him the thing he had asked, taken and held it for himself, and let him move aside to walk alone, but near him that he might give his support. The demand was exposed, and he felt that he could not believe in the sight. Maria saw that it was useless to be with him, that each was alone.

By common consent they remained apart that night. When they met in the morning they felt it was a new meeting, that it came after a sudden separation and brought them to a new future. It almost made a fresh bond between them, giving them a common knowledge out of all they knew.

"Well, this is a sobering morning," said a voice, which seemed to be neither Aubrey's nor Justine's, but was really the former used in imitation of the latter. "But we shall be stimulated by it. We must live in Father's life and not allow ourselves to cross the bound. I will take it all at one fell swoop and lead the way into the room."

"You both look tired after your long day," said Mark.

His father felt that his words should cover that part of the day he did not know.

"Maria is tired," he said.

"She will soon be rested in her own home," said Justine. "I already enjoy a personal sense of relief. I am a mere unimportant child of the house again."

"Will you wait breakfast for Mr. Dudley, ma'am?" said Jellamy.

"No. He is not coming back so early."

"Where has he gone?" said Clement.

"Away for a time, I am afraid," said Edgar. "He felt he wanted a change. I fear that he found the sight of the two of us together too much."

"Well, I think it is a thoroughly good idea," said Justine at once. "Uncle has been attempting altogether too much of late. He can't go on being superhuman. Even he is subject to the rules of mortal life. I wanted to suggest his having a break, and would have done so if I had dared."

"He has done his duty in giving you a welcome, and feels he is free," said Mark, realising the false impression he gave.

"He has taken no luggage, ma'am," said Jellamy.

"And does that prevent your bringing in the breakfast?" said Edgar.

"He will be sending for what he wants, I expect," said Maria. "He had to get away at once. Yes, bring in the breakfast."

"I thought it might imply that he would be back this morning, ma'am."

"You heard that he was not coming back," said Edgar.

"Bring in the breakfast, Jellamy, and make no more ado," said Justine. "You will forgive me, Maria; the words slipped out. I can't keep my tongue from leaping out at that man sometimes."

"I feel with Jellamy," said Mark to Clement, as they followed the others to the table. "He wants to know why Uncle has suddenly gone, and so do I. And the luggage is a point. Either he is coming back at once or he has left in storm and stress."

"Don't whisper, boys," said Justine, turning and lowering her own voice. "Things are difficult and we must do our part. Pull yourselves together and remember that we are mere pawns in the game of skill and chance which is being played."

"Are we as essential to the game as that? I feel a mere spectator. And it is really a simpler game."

"Well, don't look as if we were making some mystery."

"We could hardly contrive to do so. It is clear on what lines the break came, if break there has been."

"Shall I remove Mr. Dudley's place, ma'am?"

"No," said Edgar, as he saw the traces of his brother about to be obliterated. "Leave it as it is. It is likely—it is possible that he may come back."

"We will all take our own places," said Justine. "Then Uncle can return and find his place ready for him, and the others occupied round him, as will be right and meet."

"Not a gap in the circle," said Aubrey, flushing as he realised his words.

"No one can be expected to show himself in Uncle's place," said Mark.

"Yes, to take it would be even less easy—would be almost as difficult," said Justine—"oh, what a time this is for innocent and inapposite speeches!"

"No one tries to take anyone's place," said Maria. "Empty places remain and new people make their own."

"Of course. Why cannot I put things as you do?"

"If you knew the reason," said Clement, "I am sure you would deal with the matter."

"Well, that comes well from you. We don't see much sign in you of a gift for words."

"Should we have said that silence was golden, if we had only known Clement?" said Aubrey.

Maria laughed, and Edgar looked up and smiled more at the sound than at his son's words.

"Yes, cheer up, Father," said Justine. "You have not lost everything with Uncle. And he will come back and everything will be as it has always been—everything will be straight and well."

"Silence is golden," murmured Aubrey.

"Oh, I don't know. I believe I would give all the silence in the world for a little healthy, natural speech."

"Well, you have always done so," said Clement.

"And I do not regret my choice."

"Clement raises his brows," said Aubrey.

"Aubrey is readier with his words than you will ever be, Clement."

Aubrey looked at the window.

"Can you see through the curtain?" said his brother. "If you can, it is still dusk outside."

"I can see the wide, wintry expanse with my mind's eye."

Edgar looked up, with his mind following his son's, and meeting the picture of his brother with no refuge before him or behind. He turned to his wife and knew that she saw the same.

"Did Uncle say anything?" said Justine. "Did he—oh, I will take the bull by the horns, as he does. Has he any plans? Did he leave any address?"

"He had none to leave. He went suddenly," said her father. "He may—it will be possible for him to send one later."

"We know all," murmured Mark to Clement.

"You know all we can tell you," said Edgar.

"A flush mantles Mark's cheek," said Aubrey.

Maria was again amused, and her stepson showed his nonchalance by rising and walking to the window and pulling the curtain aside.

"Aunt Matty! Coming across the snow!"

"Across the snow? Aunt Matty?" said Justine.

"She must be coming across the snow if she is coming," said Mark.

"Did you know she was coming, little boy? Why did you go to the window?"

Aubrey did not give his reason.

"Boys, get your coats and go to meet her. Perhaps she has some news of Uncle."

Edgar rose.

"I hardly think so," said Maria. "She would not be coming herself."

Matty was approaching with her halting step, holding a wrap across her breast, holding something to her head in the wind, pressing forward with a sort of dogged resignation to her slow advance. She gave a faint smile to her nephews as she suffered them to lead her in.

"You have come alone, Aunt Matty?"

"Yes, I have come alone, my dears. I had to do that. I shall be alone now. My dear father has left me, and left me, as you say, alone." Matty sank into a chair and covered her face. "I must be content alone. I must learn another hard lesson after so many."

She kept her hand to her brow and sat without moving, as the family gathered about her.

"Yes, I have had a life of deep and strange experiences. It seems that I ought to be used to them, that I ought to have that sad protection."

There was silence.

"Losing her father when she is over sixty herself is not a startling one," said Clement.

"Is Grandpa dead?" said Aubrey.

"That is a better way of putting it," said Mark.

"Well, his life was over," said Justine. "It was not hard to see that."

Matty was continuing to Edgar and his wife.

"He had gone to bed early as he was very tired. And I sent up something, hoping that he would eat before he slept. And it was found that he was already sleeping, and that he would not wake again."

"We cannot improve on that," said Mark.

"Yes, it was a good way to go," said Matty, misinterpreting his words. "He was full of years. His harvest was gathered, his sheaves were bound. For him we need not weep. But I must grieve for myself, and you will grieve for me a little."

"Dear Aunt Matty, we do indeed," said Justine. "And Mother would have suffered equally with you."

"Yes, dear. That is my saddest thought, that I have no one to do that. But I will be glad that yours is the lighter part. I had thought that my sister and I would sorrow together in this natural loss. But so much was not to be for me."

Maria took the seat by Matty, and Matty gave her her hand, putting the other over her eyes, but in a moment laid both hands on her friend's and looked about with a smile. "Well, I must not fail in resolution. I must be myself. I must be what I always was to my father. I must not be lonely when I am not. I will not be."

"Look round and see the reason," said her niece.

"Yes, I see all my reasons," said Matty, looking about as if to discover the truth. "All the dear reasons I have for clinging to life, the dear faces which I have seen growing into themselves, the dear ones whose link I am now with one side of their past. Well, it should forge the link strongly. We shall go forward closely bound."

"How was dear Grandpa found? Did Miss Griffin go in to him?"

"No, dear, the maid went in and found him as I say. As she thought at first, sleeping; really in his last sleep."

"Poor Emma, it must have been a shock for her. Was she very much upset?"

"Well, dear, I was the more upset, of course. She was troubled in her measure. And I was sorry for her, and glad that she only had her natural share of the shock. Your grandfather had been always good to her. But she is not a young woman. There was nothing unsuitable in her being the one to find him. One of us had to do so, and I am not in the habit of going up and down stairs, as you know."

"And now Miss Griffin is managing everything?"

"No, dear; Dr. Marlowe is seeing that everything is done for me. He is a good friend, as you have found. There would not have been much for Miss Griffin to do."

"She will feel it very deeply. I daresay she is too upset to be of much use. It is a long relation to break."

"Yes, well, now I must tell you," said Matty, sitting up and using an open tone. "You will think that I have had a stranger life than you thought, that I seem to be marked out for untoward experience. Well, I was sitting in my little room alone, waiting for the shadows to close in upon me. It seems now that I must have had some presentiment; I had been so wrought up all day; you must have had your glimpse of it. And it was found that Miss Griffin had left me, that my old friend with whom I had shared my life for thirty years, had vanished and left me alone in my grief. Well, what do you think of that for an accumulation of trouble, for what the Greeks would have called a woe on woe? I seem to be a person born for trial by flame. I hope I may emerge unscathed."

There was silence.

"When did Miss Griffin go?" said Justine. "Did anyone know when she went? Did she suddenly disappear?"

"Well, I must try to answer all those questions at once. But I only know what I have told you. I was sitting alone in the parlour, as you call it, finding the time rather drag as it moved on towards my trouble. I see that the boys are smiling, and I should not have wished to hasten it, if I had known. And I seemed to need the sound of a human voice, and I opened the door of the house—Miss Griffin had run into the garden on some pretext that I had sent her out, or something. You know I left you rather out of sorts; things here had upset me—and I found——Well, you find my tale amusing? I am making a mountain out of a molehill? It is a trifle that I am exaggerating because I am personally involved? Well, we have all done that. You will not find it hard to understand."

"Then Miss Griffin did not leave you after Grandpa died? She had gone before? Yes, I know you implied that she had. But you said that you were alone in your grief. I did not quite follow."

"I meant my grief for your mother, dear. I happened to be remembering. But it was not the time for you to do so, as I had found. Well, I will get on with my story. So I found that was how it was, that my old friend had left me—well, we won't say alone in my grief—alone in a dark hour. And what do you say to that for a sudden revelation? I won't say that I have nourished a viper in my bosom; I won't say that of Miss Griffin, who has been with me through so many vicissitudes, and whom I have spared to you in yours. I will just say—well, I will say nothing; that is best."

"I don't think we can say anything either. We must find out where she has gone unless she returns very soon. But in the meantime tell us how you are yourself, and if you are staying here for the time."

"Well, it is to Maria that I must answer that question," said Matty, turning to her friend. "Answer it as a matter of form, because I must remain with you. I cannot go back to that house alone. So the formal question is answered, and I can settle down in as much content as I can, in as much as will prevent my being a damper on other people."

"Would you like anything fetched from your house?" said Maria.

"No, dear, no; Justine can lend me things of her mother's. I need not trouble you for anything."

"I hope you will trouble anyone for anything you need."

"Yes, dear, I know it would not be a trouble," said Matty, with a faint note of correcting the term. "But I am a person of few wants, or have learned to be. Now shall we leave me as a subject and go on to all of you? Or would you like to hear more of the old friend, or old aunt, or old responsibility, or whatever you call me to yourselves?"

"We should like to know all we can. Have you given any thought to the future? You clearly have not had time. But will you settle down in your house or will you be too much alone? Did you mean to stay there after your father died?"

"One moment, Maria. One thing, Aunt Matty," said Justine, leaning forward with a hand on Maria's arm. "Is Emma alone in that house? Let us get that point behind."

"No, dear, she has a sister with her. You have not reached the stage of arranging such things for other people as a matter of course. And that being so, it was a natural anxiety. Well, what was Maria saying? Yes, I was to stay here after my father died. He meant me to, and so did my sister. And I shall follow what I can of their wish. It will seem to bind me to them closer, to carry out our common plan. So I shall be too much alone: I must answer 'yes' to that question. But I shall not be too proud to accept any alleviation of my solitude." Matty smiled at the faces about her. "I have no false notions about what exalts people. I have my own ideas of what constitutes quality."

"We will do all we can for the sake of the past, for your sake," said Edgar. "Maria will do it with us, as she will do everything."

"Thank you. So we shall all have helped each other. We have done our best with Blanche's place in filling it and finding that we cannot fill it." Matty turned the smile on Maria. "And now we must do what we can with another, and I know you will do your part. We are used to striving together to meet a common loss."

"I read Aunt Matty like a book," murmured Aubrey. "I wonder if it is suitable for Justine's little boy."

"And we hope that Miss Griffin will come back and be with you, Aunt Matty," said Justine. "I cannot imagine the two of you apart."

"It is a relief not to have to think of them together,"

said Aubrey, turning to meet his brothers' eyes. "Yes, I am sure that is what Uncle would have said. You can see that I am trying to prevent your missing him."

"Cannot you, dear?" said Matty to her niece. "I have had to go a little further. You see I am having the experience. But shall we leave my prospects to the future, as we cannot in the present say much for them? I am holding you up in your breakfast. I will sit down and try to go on with it with you. I must make as little difference as I can."

"Here is a place all ready for you."

"Is there? How does that come to be? Had any news reached you? No, you were unprepared. Did you expect me to stay last night and order a place for the morning? Well, I must be glad that I went home to my father. Something seems to guide us in such things."

"The something took a clumsy way of doing its work," said Mark.

"So it was to be my place?" said Matty, seeming pleased by the thought. "Perhaps you hoped that the truant guest would return and expiate her sins?"

"It is Dudley's place," said Maria, knowing that the truth must emerge. "We thought that you would not be here. But he has followed Miss Griffin's example and left us for the time."

"Has he? Dudley? Has he run away and left you? Do we all manage to make ourselves impossible to those near and dear to us?" said Matty, her voice rising with her words. "Is it a family trait? Well, we can all assure each other that our bark has quite wrongly been taken for a bite."

"Barking may be enough in itself," said Mark. "It may not encourage people to wait for the next stage."

"Our Dudley? Has he found things too much? Well, I can feel with him; I find things so sometimes. But running away is not the best way out of them. They will not get the better of him, not of Dudley. I should have been glad to get a sight of him, and borrow a little of his spirit. It seems that people who show the most have the most to spare. Theirs must be the largest stock. Well, I must have recourse to my own, and I have not yet found it fail. It is not your time to need it, but you may look back and remember your aunt and feel that you took something from her."

"Why had Aunt Matty not enough spirit to give some to Miss Griffin?" said Aubrey.

"She gave her a good deal, or she got it from somewhere," said Mark.

"Yes, it is Miss Griffin, is it?" said Matty, with a different voice and smile. "Miss Griffin who takes the thought and takes the interest? That is how it would be. The person who has suffered less makes less demand. And we who suffer more must learn it. Well, we must not make a boast of spirit and then not show it."

There was silence.

"I think we ought to find out where Miss Griffin has gone," said Justine. "I do really think so, Aunt Matty."

"Yes, dear, I said she would be in your minds. And I think as you do. I shall be so glad to know where she is, when you can tell me."

"I suppose we have no clue at all?"

"That I do not know, dear; I have none."

"You have no idea where she may have gone?"

"None as she has not come here. I had a hope that she might have. I am so used to finding the house a refuge myself"—Matty gave her niece another smile—"that I did not think of her being perhaps struck by it differently. Especially as she has spent her time in it in another way."

"We are all very grateful to her. I am very hurt that she has not come here."

"Yes, dear? She has hurt us all."

"Has she any home?" said Mark.

"Her home has been with me. I know of no other."

"She has no relations she could go to?"

"She has relations, no doubt. But, you see, to them she would be, as you say, a relation. It is to you that she is the person outside the family."

"She has no friends in the neighbourhood?"

"She has those to whom you may have introduced her. She can have no others."

"Aunt Matty, I know that you think we might have introduced you to more people," said Justine. "But the truth is that when the house was running at full pressure, with all of us at home and you and Grandpa coming in, Mother could manage no more. It worked out that your coming here to meet our friends meant that you could not meet them. It implied nothing more and I am sure you know it, and Maria may manage better; but as concerns the past that is the truth. It seemed to be a rankling spot, and so I have let in a little fresh air upon it."

"No, dear, that is not the line on which my thoughts were running," said Matty, lifting her eyes and resting them in gentle appraisement on her niece. "They were on the death of my father, as they hardly could not be. And friends and houses and Miss Griffin all came second to it. Indeed only Miss Griffin came in at all."

"We have no clue either to my brother's whereabouts," said Edgar, taking the chance of opening his mind. "It is a strange fashion, this silent disappearance. We must try to get on the tracks of them both. Was Miss Griffin prepared for going? It is very cold."

"As far as I know, she went out of the garden without hat or coat or anything. The action was sudden and unpremeditated and she will probably be back at any time. She may be back now, in which case my father's death will have been a great shock to her."

"Did she wander in the garden without hat or coat in this weather?" said Clement.

"Take care; Aunt Matty must have driven her out," said Mark. "And she did not wait to be called back, but went on her own way. And if she freezes or starves or dies of exposure, and it seems that she must do all those things, she will be better off than she has been."

"Had she money, Aunt Matty?" said Justine.

"I do not know—yes, dear, more than I have at the moment."

"And had she it with her?"

"I can only know that, when you find out and tell me. That thought has been in my own mind from the first."

"She cannot have gone far," said Maria, who had listened in silence. "We could send someone to drive about the country and look for her. We had better do it at once."

"May I interpose, ma'am?" said Jellamy.

"Yes, if you have anything to tell us."

"Mr. Dudley and Miss Griffin were perceived to be walking together last night, ma'am."

"Oh, they were together. That is a good thing. How did you hear?"

"The information came through, ma'am."

"You are quite sure?"

"The authority is reliable, ma'am."

"Well, that is the worst off our minds about both," said Justine. "We need not worry about anyone who is in Uncle's charge, or about anyone in Miss Griffin's. Each is safe with the other. They both have someone to think of before themselves, and that will suit both of them."

"It is a mercy that their paths crossed," said Mark. "What would have happened to Miss Griffin if they had not?"

"She would have gone home, dear," said Matty, with a change in her eyes.

"Well, they did cross, so we need not think about it," said Justine.

"We can hardly help doing that," said Maria. "It was the purest chance that your uncle passed at the time."

"There are inns and other shelters," said Edgar, glancing at the window.

"For people who have money with them. She seems to have gone out quite unprepared."

"I told you that the action was unpremeditated," said Matty. "But they would have trusted her as she is known to live with me."

"People might not trust a person who was leaving the house where she was employed."

"Maria, it is a great feat of courage," whispered Justine, "and I honour you for it. But is it wise? And is it not an occasion when indulgence must be extended?"

"Your aunt had not lost her father when she turned Miss Griffin out of doors."

"Oh, you have your own touch of severity," said Justine, taking a step backwards and using a voice that could be heard. "We shall have to beware. It may be a salutary threat hanging over us."

"Well, what of Dudley?" said Matty. "Are we to hear any more about him, now that Miss Griffin is disposed of? Have you any room for him in your minds? Do you take as much interest in his comings and goings? Did he go out prepared for the weather? Had he any money? Did you have notice of his going? Tell me it all, as I have told you. We must not deal differently with each other."

"We will tell you, Aunt Matty. We admit that he went suddenly," said Justine. "And that we do not know the manner or the wherefore of his going."

"Mr. Dudley was sufficiently equipped for the weather, ma'am," said Jellamy. "Miss Griffin was perceived to be wearing his coat when they were observed together."

"Was she? Then he was no longer in that happy state," said Matty, going into laughter rather as if at Jellamy and his interruption than at Dudley's plight. "We can keep our anxiety to him. Miss Griffin no longer requires it. What about scattering some coats and hats about the road, for people to pick up who have fared forth without them? It is really a funny story. Somebody from the large house and somebody from the small, running away into the weather without a word or a look behind! Well, people must strike their own little attitudes; I suppose we are none of us above it; but I cannot imagine myself choosing to posture quite like that. And if I had had to pick out two people to scamper off into the snow with one coat and hat between them, I should not have pitched on Dudley and Miss Griffin." Matty bent her head and seemed to try to control her mirth. "It was a good thing that the coat belonged to Dudley, if they were to wear it in turn. He could not have got into hers."

No one joined in the laughter, and Matty wiped her eyes and continued it alone, and then stopped short and adjusted her skirt as if suddenly struck by something amiss.

"I have heard better jokes," said Mark. "The weather is icy cold and one coat is not enough for two."

"I wonder who was wearing the hat," said his aunt in a high voice which seemed to herald further laughter.

"Miss Griffin was perceived to be wearing a shawl about her head, ma'am."

"Oh, what a picture! It sounds like a gipsy tableau. I wonder if they intended it like that. I wonder if they had a caravan hidden away somewhere. I know that Miss Griffin has plenty of hats in her cupboard. Some of them I have given her myself. What can be the reason of this sudden masquerade?"

"Perhaps she had none in the garden," said Clement.

"We know they have not a caravan," said Mark. "And it is hard to see how they are to manage without one."

"There is the inn," said his father, in a sharp tone.

"Of course there is, Edgar," said Matty in a different manner. "They all seem to think that the scene is staged on a desert island. But the scene itself! I can't help thinking of it. I shall have many a little private laugh over it."

"But no more public ones, I hope," muttered Mark.

Maria rose from the table, and Justine, as if perceiving her purpose, instantly did the same. Matty followed them slowly, using her lameness as a pretext for lingering in

Edgar's presence. She came to the drawing-room fire in a preoccupied manner, as if the cares of her own life had returned.

"Well, you are well in advance of me. I came in a poor third."

"We know you like to follow at your own pace," said Justine.

"I do not know that I like it, dear. My pace is a thing which I have not been able to help for many years."

"Well, we know you prefer people not to wait for you. Though Father and the boys have waited. I suppose they saw that as unavoidable."

"Yes, I expect they did, dear. I don't think we can alter that custom."

"No, naturally we cannot and we have not done so. But poor Aunt Matty, of course you are not yourself."

"No, dear, of course I am not," said Matty, with full corroboration. "And it has been silly of me to be surprised at seeing all of you so much yourselves. This morning is so different from other mornings to me, that it has been strange to find it so much the same to other people. You have not had days of this kind yet. Or you have put them behind you. Sorrow is not for the young, and so you have set it out of sight. And you have filled your empty place so wisely and well, that I am happy and easy in having helped you to do it. Any little shock and doubt and misgiving has melted away. But my father's place will be always empty for me, and so I must remain a little out of sympathy—no, I will not say that—a little aloof from the happiness about me. But I am glad to see it all the same. I must not expect to find people of my own kind everywhere. They may not be so common."

"I should think they are not," said Clement.

"You mean you hope not, naughty boy?" said Matty, shaking her finger at him in acceptance of his point of view. "You do not want to think they are."

"I only found myself noticing that they were not."

"We might—perhaps we might see ourselves in other people more than we do," said Edgar.

"We all have our depths and corners," said Justine.

"And we all think that no one else has them," said Mark.

"Dear, dear, what a band of philosophers!" said Matty. "I did not know I had quite this kind of audience."

"Do you see yourself in us more than you thought?" said Clement.

"No, dear, but I see a good many of you at once. I did not know you were quite such a number on a line. I had thought of you all as more separate somehow."

"And now you only see yourself in that way?"

"Well, dear, we agreed that I was a little apart."

"I don't think we did," said Mark. "You implied it, but I don't remember that you had so much support."

"I am going to end the talk," said Maria, rising. "Your aunt is more tired than she knows and must go and rest. And when I come down your father and I will go to the library, and you can have a time without us."

"How tactless we have been!" said Justine. "We might have thought that they would like an hour by themselves. But what were we to do while Aunt Matty was here?"

"What we did," said Mark. "No one could have thought that the scene was to our taste."

"I do admire Maria when she gives a little spurt of authority."

"She did not like to think of Miss Griffin wandering by herself in the snow," said Aubrey, bringing this picture into the light to free his own mind.

"Little tender-heart!" said Justine, simply evincing comprehension.

"Without a coat or hat, and I suppose without gloves or tippet or shawl," said her brother, completing the picture with ruthlessness rather than with any other quality.

"It is odd that we feel so little about Grandpa's death."

"Aunt Matty's life puts it into the shade," said Mark.

"Well, he was old and tired and past his interests, and we really knew him very little. It would be idle to pretend to any real grief. It is only Aunt Matty who can feel it."

"And it does not seem to drown her other feelings."

"Perhaps that is how sorrow sometimes improves people," said Aubrey.

"No, no, little boy. No touch of Uncle at this moment. It is too much."

"We might all be better if our feelings were destroyed," continued Aubrey, showing that his sister had administered no check.

"Poor Aunt Matty! One can feel so sorry for her when she is not here."

"You do betray other feelings when she is," said Mark.

"I suppose I do. We might have remembered her trouble. Even Father and Maria seemed to forget it."

"Well, so did she herself."

"She will be very much alone in future. I don't see how we are to prevent it."

"Will grief be her only companion?" said Aubrey.

"Well, she has driven away her official one," said Mark.

"She will be confined to rage and bitterness and malice," said Clement.

"So she will be alone amongst many," said Aubrey.

"No, no, I don't think malice," said Justine. "I don't think it has ever been that. I wonder what Miss Griffin and Uncle are doing. But their being together disposes of any real problem. I think Uncle may safely be left to arrange the future for them both."

"Uncle has been left to do too much for people's futures," said Mark. "And not so safely. We can only imagine what happened last night."

"You are fortunate," said Clement. "I cannot."

"Or unfortunate," said Aubrey, who could.

"I have been keeping my thoughts away from it," said Justine.

"They have had enough to occupy them," said Mark "But they will return. Grandpa's death, Miss Griffin's flight, even Aunt Matty's visit will all be as nothing. We may as well imagine the scene."

"No, my mind baulks at it."

"Mine does worse. It constructs it."

"Maria was there," said Aubrey.

"Yes, poor Maria!" said Justine. "What a home-coming! It never rains but it pours."

"I think it nearly always rains. We only notice it when it pours."

"Yes, it is Uncle. Clear, natural and incontrovertible," said Justine, with a sigh, as if this fact altered no other. "Well, you may be clever boys, but you have a depressed sister to-day."

"How would it all have been if Maria had kept to Uncle?" said Aubrey.

"That is not Uncle," said Clement.

"Little boy, what a way of putting it!"

"Miss Griffin would still have run away; Grandpa would still have died; Aunt Matty would still have paid her visits," said Mark. "Only it might have been Father instead of Uncle who met Miss Griffin. And that might not have worked so well. He would have been more awkward in offering her his coat. So perhaps it is all for the best. That is always said when things are particularly bad, so there could hardly be a better occasion for saying it."

"Look," said Justine, going to the door and holding it ajar. "Look at those two figures passing through the hall, as two others used to pass. What an arresting and almost solemn sight! Do we let our hearts rejoice or be wrung by it?"

"We will take the first course if we have the choice."

"Which is better, the sight of two beautiful men or of a beautiful man and a beautiful woman? I do not know; I will not try to say."

"I am letting my heart be wrung," said Aubrey, grinning and speaking the truth.

"Will they ever be three again? Ought we to wish it? Or ought we just to hesitate to rush in where angels fear to tread?"

"We might be imagining them four," said Aubrey, in a light tone.

"How I remember Mother's slender figure moving in and out between the two taller ones! That is a different line of thought, but the picture somehow came. And it brings its own train. Mother would have wished things to come right between them. And it may be that they will do so, and the three tall figures move together through life. But I fear it cannot be yet. Uncle was heading for trouble, and at the crucial moment it came. He could not go on too long, keyed up to that pitch. The strain of the last months can only be imagined. None of us can know what it was."

"Is Justine transfigured?" said Aubrey.

"Well, I am affected by the spectacle of intense human drama. I do not deny it."

"It were idle to do so," said Clement.

"It would have been better to go away at once," said Mark, "and not attempt the impossible."

"I don't know," said his sister, gazing before her. "It was a great failure. Surely one of those that are greater than success."

"I never quite know what those are. I suppose you mean other kinds of success. The same kind involves the same effort and has a better end."

"And a much more convenient one," said Clement.

"Yes, yes, more convenient," said Justine. "But what we have seen was surely something more than that."

"Something quite different indeed," said Mark.

"Surely it was worth it."

"Well, in the sense that all human effort must achieve something essential, even if not apparent."

"Well, now the human drama goes on in the snow," said Aubrey.

"Oh, surely they have got under shelter by now," said Justine, laughing as she ended. "Oh, what intolerable bathos! You horrid little boy, pulling me down from my heights!"

"You could not have gone on too long any more than Uncle."

"I don't know. I felt I was somehow in my element."

"That may have been what Uncle thought. I believe it was," said Mark.

"A greater than Uncle is here," said Aubrey.

"And they are different heights," said Clement.

"I think Clement is making an effort to conquer his taciturnity, Justine."

"Oh, don't let us joke about it. Do let us turn serious eyes on a serious human situation."

"Miss Griffin and Uncle walking through the snow, with Miss Griffin wearing Uncle's coat and hat!" murmured Aubrey.

"She was not wearing his hat. She—she—" said Justine, going into further laughter—"had a shawl round her head. Oh, why are we laughing? Why cannot we take a serious view of what is serious and even tragic in itself? Miss Griffin's long relation with Aunt Matty broken! Because I suppose it is the break. And her life at sixes and sevens, because that must be the truth. And we cannot see it without being diverted by silly, little, surface things which in themselves have their tragic side, just because they touch our superficial sense of humour." Justine's voice quavered away as this again happened to her. "I suppose we are half hysterical; that is what it is."

"That is the usual explanation of unseemly mirth," said Mark.

"Well, happiness is a good thing," said Edgar, smiling in the door, his voice as he said Matty's frequent words, illustrating the difference between them. "Maria and I are going to walk outside—that is, we are going for a walk before Mark and I begin to work. Your aunt is resting upstairs."

"Oh, Father, it seems that we ought not to be in spirits on the day of Grandpa's death and Aunt Matty's desolation, and all of it," said Justine, taking hold of his coat. "But we are in a simple, silly mood. We have agreed that we must be hysterical."

"Your grandfather's death can only seem to you the natural thing it is. He has not been much in your life and he has had his own." Edgar's voice was calm and almost empty, as if his feelings on one thing left him none for any other.

"But Aunt Matty's loneliness and all that has happened," said Justine, standing with her face close to the coat and bringing the lapels together. "You do feel that you have an anchor in your children?"

Edgar turned and walked away.

"Oh, I suppose I have said the wrong thing as usual. I might have known it was hopeless to attempt to do anything for him. In my heart I did know."

"It is good to follow the dictates of the heart," said Clement.

"Yes, you can be supercilious. But what did you attempt after all? I did try to show Father that he had something to depend on in his home."

"And he showed you that he could not take your view."

"I suppose Maria has taken my place with him. Well, it would be small to mind it. I have never done much to earn the place. And it is better than her taking another. She does not feel she has taken that. We can think of that little place as open and empty, free for Mother's little shadow."

Aubrey turned and slouched out of the room, kicking up his feet. He came upon Maria, who had been to fetch a cloak and was following her husband.

"Are you going upstairs?" she said. "What is the matter? Come back a minute and tell me."

Aubrey threw back his head, thrust his hands into his pockets and turned and sauntered back.

"Odd days these."

"Yes, they are strange and disturbed. But they will pass."

"Days have a way of doing that. It is the one thing to be said for them."

"Too much happened yesterday indeed."

"Indeed."

"Your grandfather had had his full share of everything. And there is no greater good fortune than sudden death."

"No," said Aubrey, his face changing in a manner which told Maria her mistake.

"And he knows nothing now," she said, "not even that he is dead. And that can be said of all dead people."

There was a pause.

"You have had your share of things," said Aubrey, with terse and equal understanding.

"We have all had that and found it enough."

"Too much for me. Quickly up and quickly down at my age. But if I am thought callous one minute, I am thought sensitive the next."

"We need not mind being thought callous sometimes," said Maria, seeing the aspect preferred.

"No. The heart knoweth," said her stepson, turning away.

CHAPTER X

"SHALL I SAY what I can see?" said Mark. "Or does it go without saying?"

"Let us not go to meet her," said Clement. "Let us begin differently and hope so to go on."

"Your aunt is already in the hall or we should meet her," said Edgar with a vision of his brother going swiftly to such a scene.

Matty came forward without exhibition of her lameness or of anything about herself.

"Now I am afraid you must see me as the bearer of ill tidings. And I may deserve to have to bring them. I have made myself the harbinger of sadness and now I am not to come without it. But you will make my hard task easy. You will know that the tidings are sad for me as well as for you."

"What is it?" said Edgar at once. "Is it my brother?"

"Yes, you have helped me. And now I can help myself and tell you that it is not the worst, that all is not lost. There is still hope. He is lying ill at a farmhouse twenty miles away. He walked for days when he left this house, and got wet and got weary, and ate and slept where he could; and came at last to this farm one night, hardly able to say who he was or whence he came." Matty dramatised what she had to tell, but spoke without actual thought of herself. "And the next day they fetched Miss Griffin to nurse him, and a message came from her to me this morning, to say that there is trouble on the lungs and that she does not dare to hide the truth. She has a doctor and a nurse, and the woman at the farm is good. So all we have to do is to go to him at once. All that you have to do. What I have to do is to stay here and keep the house until your return. And if it seems to me the harder part, I will still do it to the best that is in me. I will do what serves you most and what saves you anything."

Edgar had already gone, followed by his wife. Matty suggested some things which might be of use, and before they were ready he had set off on horseback by himself.

"Someone should go with Father," said Justine. "But it is too late."

"Is Uncle a strong man?" said Mark.

"He has seemed to be in his own way. But the troubles must have lowered his resistance, and the wet and cold have done the rest."

"He saved Miss Griffin," said Aubrey; "himself he could not save."

"My dear, think what you are saying. What makes you talk like that?"

"Excess of feeling and a wish to disguise it," said Aubrey, but not aloud.

"Where has Miss Griffin been?" said Mark.

"At the Middletons' house, where your uncle took her on the day when your grandfather died," said Matty, stating the fact without expression. "I know no more."

"We must go. Goodbye, Aunt Matty," said Justine. "Maria is in the hall. Keep Aubrey with Mr. Penrose, and the house to its course. We can't say yet just what we may require of you."

"Command me, dear, to any service," said Matty, with a hint of dryness in her tone.

"You can send me word," said Aubrey, "and I will command my aunt."

Edgar was in advance of his family and was the first to enter his brother's room. Miss Griffin met him at the door, and the way she spoke of Dudley, as if he could not hear, warned him of his state.

"He is very ill. He must have been ill for days. He will have me with him; he will not be left to the nurse."

She stood, stooping forward, with her eyes bright and fixed from want of sleep. "He is like Mrs. Gaveston in that. The doctor says that his heart is holding out and that he may get well."

Dudley was raised a little in his bed, the limpness of his body showing his lack of strength to support himself, his breathing audible to Edgar at the door. His eyes were still and seemed not to see, but as his brother came they saw.

"What is the time?" he said in a faint, rapid voice between his breaths. "They do not tell it to me right."

"It is about twelve o'clock."

"No, it is the afternoon," said Dudley, with a cry in his tone. "I have been asleep for hours."

"Yes, you have had a sleep," said Miss Griffin, in a cheerful, ordinary voice, which she changed and lowered as she turned to Edgar. "It was only for a few minutes. He never sleeps for more."

"It will soon be night," said Dudley.

"Not just yet, but it is getting nearer."

Dudley lay silent, his expression showing his hopeless facing of the hours of the day.

"Does the time seem very long to him?" said Edgar.

"Yes, it is so with very sick people. It is as if he were living in a dream. A minute may seem like hours."

Dudley fell into a fit of coughing and lay helplessly shaken, and under cover of the sound Miss Griffin's voice became quicker and more confidential.

"Oh, I am glad I could come to him; I am glad that he sent for me. It was a good thing that I was not with Miss Seaton. She might not have let me come. She said she would never let me nurse anyone but her again. But I don't expect she would have kept to that."

"I am sure she would not," said Edgar. "Is there anything my brother would like?"

"If only it would stop!" said Dudley, looking at Edgar as he heard the word of himself.

Edgar turned to him with so much pain in his face, that he saw it and in the desperation of his suffering tried to push it further.

"If only it would stop for a second! So that I could get a moment's sleep. Just a moment."

"He is not like himself," said Edgar. "It seems—it reminds me of when my wife was ill."

There were the sounds of the carriage below and Miss Griffin spoke with appeal.

"Is anyone coming who can help? I have been with him all day and all night. He cannot bear to be with strangers, and he should not be nursed by anyone who is too tired."

"My wife and daughter are here," said Edgar, the word of his second wife bringing the thought that he could not replace his brother. "And any help can come from the house at once. In the meantime my sons and I have hands and ordinary sense, and can be put to any service."

Maria came into the room and Dudley saw her.

"It is the afternoon," he said, as if she would allow it to be so.

"Not yet," she said, coming up to the bed. "You did not send for us, Dudley. That was wrong."

"I sent for Miss Griffin."

"Yes, but you should have sent for Edgar and me."

"I only want to have someone here. I don't think you are different from other people," said Dudley, in a rapid, empty tone, which did not seem to refer to what she said, looking at her with eyes which recognised her and did no more. "It doesn't matter if we are not married. I like Edgar best."

"Of course you do. I knew it all the time. And he feels the same for you."

"If I could get to sleep, the day would soon be gone. And this is the longest day."

Maria turned to speak to her husband and Dudley's

eyes followed her, and the moment of attention steadied him and he fell asleep.

Justine entered and kept her eyes from the bed, as if she would fulfil her duty before she followed her will.

"I have come to take Miss Griffin to rest, and then to wait upon anyone. The boys have gone on some messages. Father, the doctor is here and can see you."

Dudley was awake and lay coughing and looking about as if afraid.

"Is it another day? Shall I get well?"

"Of course you will," said the nurse. "It is the same day. You only slept for a little while. But to sleep at all is a good sign."

"People are here, are they? Not only you?"

"Justine and I are here," said Maria.

"Why are you both here?"

"We both like to be with you."

"Is it the afternoon?"

"It will be soon. Would you like me to read to you?"

"Will you put in any feeling?"

"No, none at all."

"Who is that person who puts in feeling? Matty would, wouldn't she? And Justine?" Dudley gave a smile.

"What book will you have?"

"Not any book. Something about——"

"About what?" said Maria, bending over him.

"You know, you know!" said Dudley in a frightened voice, throwing up his arms.

The movement brought a fit of coughing, and as it abated he lay trembling, with a sound of crying in the cough. Edgar and the doctor entered and seeing them broke his mood, though he did not seem to know them.

"Well, I haven't much to live for," he said to himself. "I am really almost alone. It isn't much to leave behind." He tried to raise himself and spoke almost with a scream. "If I die, Miss Griffin must have some money! You will give her some? You won't keep it all?"

"Yes, yes, of course we will. She shall have enough," said Edgar. "But you will not die."

Something in the voice came through to Dudley, and he lay looking at his brother with a sort of appraisement.

"You don't like me to be ill," he said, in a shrewd, almost knowing tone. "Then you should not make me ill. It is your fault."

"He does not know what he is saying," said the nurse.

"I do," said Dudley, nodding his head. "Oh, I know."

"How long will it go on?" said Edgar to the doctor.

"It cannot be quick. He is as ill as he can be, and any change must be slow. And the crisis has yet to come."

The crisis came, and Dudley sank to the point of death, and just did not pass it. Then as he lived through the endless days, each one doubled by the night, he seemed to return to this first stage, and this time drained and shattered by the contest waged within him. Blanche's frailer body, which had broken easily, seemed to have stood her in better stead. But the days which passed and showed no change, did deeper work, and the sudden advance towards health had had its foundation surely laid. The morning came when he looked at his brother with his own eyes.

"You have had a long time with me."

"We have, Dudley, and more than that."

"Do they know that I shall get better?"

"Yes, you are quite out of danger."

"Did you think I should get well?"

"We were not always sure."

Dudley saw what was behind the words, but was too weak to pursue it.

"Shall I be the same as before?"

"Yes. There will be no ill results."

Dudley turned away his head in weakness and self-pity.

"You can go away if you like. There is nothing you can do. Where is Miss Griffin?"

Miss Griffin was there, as she always was at this time.

The lighter nursing of this stage was within her powers. Dudley reached out his hands and smiled into her eyes, and Edgar watched and went away.

These moments came more often and at last marked another stage. Then the change was swift, and further stages lay behind. Dudley was to be taken to his brother's house to lie in his own bed, but before the day came even this stage had passed. The change was more rapid in his mind than in his body. In himself he seemed to be suddenly a whole man. The threat of death, with its lesson of what he had to lose, had shown him that life as he had lived it was enough. He asked no more than he had, chose to have only this. His own personality, free of the strain and effort of the last months, was as full and natural as it had been in his youth.

His return to the house as an essential member of it was too much a matter of course to be discussed. It was observed with celebration, Dudley both expecting and enjoying it. Maria went home in advance to get order in the house and Edgar and Miss Griffin were to manage the move and follow.

Matty had been an efficient steward, but the servants did not bend to her simply autocratic rule, and Jellamy was open in his welcome. She seemed to be oppressed by her time of solitude, and kept to the background more than was her habit, seeming to acknowledge herself as bound less closely to the house. She knew that Maria realised her effect on its life, and was trying to establish a different intercourse, welcoming her as a family connection and her own friend, but keeping the relation to this ground.

The family waited in the door for the carriage to appear.

"Well, what a moment!" said Justine. "To think that our normal life is to be restored! It seems almost too much. It shows us what rich people we are."

"That has hardly been true of us of late," said Mark.

"Yes, it is partly the force of contrast. The sharp edge of our appreciation will blunt. So we will make the most of it."

"I deprecate the method of enhancing our feeling."

"Our worst chapter is behind, our very worst. And I mean what I say; I use the words advisedly. You need not all look at me. You see, our grief for Mother was unsullied. This would have had its alloy."

"Relief from anxiety gives the impression of happiness," said Clement.

"Then let us have that impression," said his brother.

"Here they come! We must set our faces to disguise our emotion," said Aubrey, doing as he said.

"I don't want to disguise it," said his sister, wiping her eyes. "I do not care how much of it is seen by Uncle or anyone else. I should not like to go away and nearly die, and come back to unmoved faces."

"Neither should I," said Dudley's voice. "I could not bear it. I do not like people not to show their feelings. If they do not, they are no good to anyone but themselves, and they don't enjoy them nearly so much as the people who cause them. And it is better to have proof of everything, anyhow of feelings."

"Oh," said Justine, with a deep sigh, "the old touch!"

"I must pay great attention," said Aubrey. "I have been a long time without an example."

"Stay," said his sister, thrusting a hand behind her as she strode forward. "I am going to help Uncle out. I am going to use my feminine privilege in an unusual way."

"She looks equal to it," said Matty, smiling at Maria.

"Oh, someone else is to come out first," said Justine, turning and ruefully raising her brows. "Oh, it is Miss Griffin. Uncle does not forget to be himself. Well, it will give me great pleasure to help them both."

"How do you do, Miss Seaton?" said Miss Griffin, as she set foot upon the ground, embarking on her ordeal at once.

"How do you do, my dear?" said Matty, shaking hands

with cordial affection. "We owe a great deal to you."

"What a good thing it is that I am spared!" said Dudley, descending on his niece's arm. "It is generally the valuable lives that are cut off, but I can feel that a real attempt was made on mine."

"You helped yourself a great deal," said Miss Griffin.

"And heaven helps those who do that. But I really don't remember any help but yours."

"Now up to your room. No more talking," said Justine, bringing her hands together. "Not another moment in this chilly hall. Maria, you do not mind my taking matters into my own hands. You see, Uncle has been bound up with the whole of my life."

"It is well that Maria feels as you say," said Clement.

Justine's words brought a sense of what was behind, and Edgar cleared a way through the hall. Dudley was assisted by his nephews to his room. He would have been able to walk with Edgar's help, but the brothers shrank from following their natural ways, as yet unsure of their footing. The uncertainty had come with Dudley's return to health.

"Well, what are we to do to celebrate the occasion?" said Matty, with something of her old tense touch.

"Go into the drawing-room and sit quietly down," said Justine, in a rather loud tone, "and give ourselves to thankfulness."

"Yes, dear, that is what we feel inclined to do. So we are to indulge ourselves," said Matty, putting her niece's inclinations on their right level, and taking her seat by the fire in silence.

"Uncle will come and join us for an hour when he is rested."

"Well, I will wait for that, if Maria will let me."

"You will wait for it, of course, with all of us," said Maria.

Mark and Clement returned.

"Uncle is resting in his own room and Miss Griffin in another."

"Not in the same room?" said Aubrey.

"Now, little boy, no foolishness on this occasion."

"Those two great, clumsy lads carried Uncle up with hands as gentle as a woman's," said Aubrey, blinking his eyes.

"Poor Miss Griffin, I am shocked by her appearance," said Justine. "She looks more worn than Uncle."

"Yes, dear, I am troubled too," said Matty. "It seems sad that her connection with us should bring her to this. I have never seen her looking in this way before."

"You must have, Aunt Matty, at the times of your own illnesses."

Matty gave a smile and a sigh, as if it were no use to make statements doomed to rejection.

"This was arduous nursing," said Maria. "It could not be helped."

"Of course not, dear. If it could have been it would have. That is the thing that makes us sorry."

"The nursing has not been much for some time," said Edgar. "Miss Griffin is looking fairly well. She was upset by the motion of the carriage."

"And Father behaved with simple chivalry," said Aubrey. "Well, it would have been no good for Clement to be a witness."

"Oh, I believe she always is!" said Justine, sitting up straight.

Matty gave a laugh.

"That sort of thing does make people look ill for the moment," said Maria.

"And Miss Griffin is not used to driving," said Justine.

Matty put back her head in mirth.

"Did you know, Aunt Matty, that she was to have a little house of her own?" said Justine, driven to the sudden announcement. "Uncle is to make it possible."

"No, dear," said Matty, with her eyes dilating. "I did not know. How could I when I was not told? When was that arranged?"

"When they met after—before Uncle was ill."

"Well, I am glad, dear; glad that our long relation is ending like this; glad that I brought her to a family who were to do this for her. It is good that our friendship should have this culmination."

"It was not the one which Aunt Matty planned when she turned her out of doors," said Mark to his brothers. "There was no question of any alternative roof."

"I am sure you are glad, Aunt Matty," said Justine.

"Are you, dear? So you accept something that I say."

"And I am sure it will be the beginning of a new relation with Miss Griffin."

Matty gave a little trill of laughter.

"Now, Aunt Matty, what exactly amuses you?"

"My relation with her, when you have all used her as a sick nurse and nothing else!" said Matty, bending her head and speaking in an impeded voice.

"Maria, would you advise me to move out of hearing of my aunt?"

Matty sat up and looked from her niece to her friend.

"If you think there would be anything gained," said Maria.

Justine rose and went to a distant seat, and her aunt looked after her with open mockery.

"So I am too dangerous a tinder for my niece's flint and steel. Or is it the other way round?"

"Either account will serve," said Clement.

"Well, well, then we must try not to come against each other. Perhaps we are too much alike."

"No, I don't think that is it, Aunt Matty," called Justine. "Oh, what is the good of my moving to a distance if I must communicate from it?"

"No good," said her brother.

"I should move back again, dear," said Matty, easily. "I don't think it does achieve anything."

Justine returned and sat down even nearer to her aunt, raising her shoulders.

Matty looked at her for a moment and turned to Maria.

"You have the whole of your family at home?" she said, stooping as if unconsciously to free her dress from contact with her niece.

"They are all at home as a usual thing. Clement is away for the term, but he gives us a good deal of time."

"He hasn't the house of his own yet?"

"I don't want it yet; I am putting it off," said Clement, in a quick, harsh tone. "I am thinking about it. I shall have it before long."

"I have rather an uncompromising nephew and niece."

"Well, we say what we mean, Aunt Matty," began Justine. "Oh, it is not worth while to waste a thought on us. Here is the person who matters! We might be twice as good or twice as bad and still be as nothing. And Father in attendance, after hovering about upstairs until he should wake! So that is why he crept away. I need not have wondered."

"Can we all quite agree that we are as nothing?" said Matty in a low, arch, rapid tone, looking up at Dudley as he passed. "I have never felt it of myself, or had it felt of me, if I can judge by the signs. So I must hold myself apart from that generalisation, though it is not a thing that matters on this occasion."

"This is the occasion in question," said Clement.

"I have not had any sleep," said Dudley. "I could not lose myself. I may be better down here amongst you all. If you see me dropping off, you could all steal quietly away. Perhaps your talk will lull me to sleep unawares."

Edgar followed his brother, looking as if he had no connection with him and holding his face to prevent an encounter of their eyes. Dudley sat down by the fire and signed for a cushion. His niece was at his side in an instant, settling the cushion behind him and thrusting a rug down on either side of his knees.

"I think Justine is a little more than nothing," said Matty, with a smile.

"I am Uncle's willing slave. That is all I ask to be."

"Well, I would ask nothing better, if I were permitted such a character. But, as I have said, it has not been the one assigned to me."

"Well, you have been an invalid," said Justine, making a sally towards the rug where it was working up.

"Justine explains it," said Aubrey.

"Not always, dear. Not when I was your age, for instance."

"I don't think this talk will lull me to sleep," said Dudley.

"Well, I may not be a slave," said Matty, holding up a piece of needlework for his eyes, "but I have been willing in your service. A little bit of something made by a friend means more, I hope, than the same thing bought out of an ample purse."

"Is every stitch in it worked by loving hands?"

In an instant Justine had the work out of her aunt's hands and before Dudley's eyes.

"Gently, dear, the stitches will unravel," said Matty, leaning forward.

"Barely an inch or two. Nothing compared to the satisfaction of proving to Uncle that the work is all your own."

"He would have taken Aunt Matty's word," said Mark.

Matty retrieved the work and placing it on her knee, set herself to remedy the damage.

"Not much harm done, is there?" said her niece.

"A piece to be worked again, dear. It does not matter. I have all the time to do it, as no doubt you thought."

"Let me do it, just the piece that came undone. Then you will have worked the whole of it once."

"I only want loving thoughts stitched into it," said Dudley.

"You shall have them," said Matty, in a full tone. "Every thought shall be loving and every stitch mine, some of them doubly done."

"Oh, we forgot to ask, Aunt Matty, how you have been managing without Miss Griffin," said Justine, recalled by her aunt's industry to the fact that she was used to aid.

"Forgot to ask!" said Mark to Aubrey. "I would have died rather than do so."

"I think I shall die, now it is done. If I don't, I don't know how to manage."

"Don't talk about dying in that light way," said Dudley. "You have no right. You have no idea of what it is to hover between life and death."

"No experience of the valley of the shadow," said Aubrey.

"None at all. I suppose there will be something in my face now that there is not in yours."

"Don't let us talk about that time," said Justine, with a shudder. "Let us only remember it enough to be thankful that it is past."

"And to feel the value of my presence in your home."

The words recalled the other way in which Dudley might have been lost to them. Justine moved to her uncle and stood stroking his hair, and her father's eyes followed her hand.

"Father might like to help Justine to smooth Uncle's hair," murmured Aubrey, "to help his only daughter."

"Well, Aunt Matty, what have you to tell us about yourself?" said Justine, putting more energy into her hand. "We have been too lost in our own troubles to give a thought to things outside."

"Your aunt has been in similar case," said Edgar.

"Now there is a nice, understanding word," said Matty. "And it is indeed a true one, even though in my case the things were not outside myself."

"Aunt Matty threw Father a grateful glance," said Aubrey.

"So I did, dear. I do not get too much understanding since Mother died, and Grandpa," said Matty, adapting her words to her nephew. "So much of it went with them. I do not mean that I expect more than I have. It would be idle indeed to do so. But I am the more grateful when it comes."

"Well, let us all emerge from that stage and take more interest in each other," said Justine. "You tell us of your plans and we will hear them."

"Well, dear, I have none as yet, as your father would know. Plans need thought and attention, and they have not been forthcoming."

"Try to do what you can about them at the moment," said Maria.

"Shall I, dear? I have been wondering when I should hear your voice. All these loquacious young relatives of mine seem to overwhelm you."

"I have never been a talkative person. Perhaps I have not much to say."

"Don't be afraid, Aunt Matty; Maria can hold her own," said Justine.

"Well, now, I have been asked for my plans. So I must make them and make them at once, so as not to keep people waiting. Well, as Miss Griffin is no longer to depend on me for a home, I must look for someone else who will find it a help to do so. For I cannot rely upon a maid-servant for the greater part of my companionship."

"Indeed no," said Justine, "though it would not be the greater part. You are wise to fill Miss Griffin's place, in so far as you can do so."

"Yes, dear, we all have to deal like that with places, or we all do. And, you know"—Matty gave her niece a different smile—"I do not make a sorrow of a friend's good fortune."

"Ought the next person who is to depend on Aunt Matty for a home," said Aubrey, "to be told that it may be in the garden?"

"I have heard that snow is a warm covering," said Mark. "I don't know if Aunt Matty had."

"Uncle had not, or he need not have given Miss Griffin his coat."

"Depend does not seem a word to use of Miss Griffin," said Justine. "She earned her independence, if anyone did."

"It is clear what your aunt means," said Edgar.

"Father, I believe you are jealous of me for my proximity to Uncle," said Justine, hastening away from Dudley with no idea that her words had any real truth.

Edgar, who only knew it at the moment, put a chair for his daughter and smiled at her as she took it.

"Dear Father, with his one ewe lamb!"

"Suppose Father had more than one," said Aubrey.

"Well, Miss Griffin has certainly earned her independence in these last weeks," said Matty. "And she is to have it. That is so good to hear."

"Uncle had arranged to give it to her before he was ill," said Justine.

"Had he, dear? Well, that does not make it any less good. And if she had not earned it then, she has now. Or if she had earned it then, she has now earned it doubly. Let us put it like that. So she has a right to it. And I shall like so much to see her in her own home, as she has always seen me in mine."

"I really believe you will, Aunt Matty."

Matty appeared once more to strive with her laughter.

"Where is Miss Griffin?" she said, looking round as she overcame it. "Does she not want to be with you all? Or is she afraid of so many of us?"

"She is afraid of one of us," said Mark. "And so am I."

"Where has Clement gone?" said Edgar.

"I expect to his room," said Aubrey. "He is always slinking away by himself."

"Well, he has seen me," said Dudley, "and satisfied himself that I am on the mend."

"And to do him justice, Uncle, he did not go until he had done that," said Justine. "And he has his work.

And we shall have someone else disappearing to-morrow. These holidays are at an end and they come too often. Maria and I are agreed."

"Aubrey could not work while he was gnawed by anxiety."

"Well, the relief will be a tonic now."

"I may wish to give myself to thankfulness for a time," said Aubrey.

"We all feel inclined for that, but the world has to go on."

"I suppose it would have gone on if I had died," said Dudley. "That is what we hear about the world. I think the world is worse than anything. Even Aubrey's lessons stopped."

"They are about to begin again," said Justine, with resolute descent to daily life. "There are many things in Clement which he might emulate."

"And Clement might take many lessons from his quiet little brother," said Aubrey, looking to see his stepmother smile and inconsistently looking away as she did so.

"I suppose you will all understand each other better now," said Dudley. "People do that after anxiety. I can feel that I have not been ill in vain."

"It seems that there cught to be more understanding," said Matty, with a faint sigh.

"Oh, people are not often as ill as I was."

"How does it feel to be so ill that you might die?" said Aubrey, with a desire to know.

"I can hardly say. Perhaps I was ready. I really don't understand about people who are not. When you are delirious and do not recognise people, it is hard to see how you can feel remorse for a lifetime and prepare yourself for eternity. I cannot help thinking that even people who die, are not as ill as I was. I think they are sometimes surprisingly well, even perhaps at their best."

"It is the few lucid moments at the last," said Justine.

"Well, I did not have those, of course. It is odd to think

that we are all to have them. It does make me respect everyone. But long conversations and meetings after years of estrangement must be so difficult when you cannot recognise people. And it hardly seems worth while for a few moments, even though they are lucid. And I see that they must be. When people's lives are hanging by a thread, it seems enough to break the thread. And I think it must do so sometimes, if people die when they are equal to so much, more perhaps than they have ever been before."

Justine looked at Dudley uncertainly, and Matty with a smile.

"Have you been reading the books in the farmhouse, Uncle?" said Mark.

"Yes, I read them while I was getting well. And if I had known I was to be so ill, I would have read them at first."

"I love to hear him talk like his old self," said Matty, glancing at her niece.

"Don't you notice that a new note has crept in? Perhaps it marks me as a person who has looked at death. I think that Justine has noticed it."

"Yes, I have, Uncle," said his niece quietly. "It is the weakness of convalescence."

"Convalescence seems to be a little like the lucid moments at the last. I may not have got quite far enough away from them."

"You will soon forget it."

"I shall not. You will. I see you are doing so."

"I know what you mean," said Matty, keeping her eyes on Dudley's face. "I too sometimes feel rather apart, as I live in my memories and find that other people have lost them. But I would not have them oppressed by what I can carry alone."

"I would; I had no idea that I should have to do that."

"I thought that people would always be as they were at my sickbed. They were so nice then; I thought a great change had come over them, and it had. They must have been expecting the lucid moments and getting themselves up to their level. And now they have returned to their old selves, as you were saying of me. But they have really done it."

"Are you joking, Uncle, or not?" said Justine.

"I am joking, but with something else underneath, something which may return to you later. If it does, remember that it is only convalescence. And now I will go and have another rest. Being here with you has not lulled me to sleep."

"Mark had better go up with you," said Maria. "You are not quite steady on your feet."

Dudley crossed the room, touching something as he passed and letting Mark take his arm at the door. His brother rose the next moment, adjusted something on the chimney piece, went to the door and swung it in his hand and followed.

"Father cannot keep away from Uncle and I cannot either," said Justine. "I am going to follow at a respectful distance, more to feast my eyes on him than to be of any use. I am not going to grasp at the privilege of waiting on him. I bow to Father's claim."

"I will bring up the rear," said Aubrey, "and feast my eyes on Justine."

"And Maria and Aunt Matty can have the hour together for which I suspect Aunt Matty has been pining."

"I shall enjoy it, dear, but so I hope will Maria. It is a thing which depends on us both."

"Yes, have it your own way. Enjoy it together. Forget us; agree that we are in the crude and callow stage; anything; I am quite beyond caring. Oh, I am so happy that I could clap my hands; I could leap into the air." Justine proved her powers. "I am in such a mood that it would be idle to attempt to contain myself."

Aubrey gave a grin towards his stepmother, and opening the door for his sister, followed her with his head erect.

"Quite a finished little man," said Matty. "You should not have much trouble with him. In what order do they come in your affections? They are already there, I can see."

"I hardly know the order. There will be one, of course. I think perhaps Mark comes first; then Justine; then Aubrey and then Clement. I hardly feel that I know Clement yet."

"I think I would put them in the same order," said Matty, who had lost her tenseness. "Except that perhaps I would put Mark after Justine. Yes, I think that my niece comes first, even though we try to quarrel with each other. We never succeed and that says a great deal."

"Why do you make the effort? It seems to be a rather constant one."

"Ah, you are catching the note of my nephews! You are to be a true Gaveston after all. You are not going to be left behind." Matty broke off as a noise came from the stairs.

Dudley had mounted the first flight, and coming to the second, had shaken off his nephew's hand and gone on alone. His limbs gave under him and he fell forward. Edgar sprang after him; Justine gave a cry; Mark turned back and raised his voice; Aubrey ran up the last stairs; Clement broke from his room and hurried to the scene. Dudley was helped to his nephew's bed, hardly the worse. Edgar stood by him, looking as if his defence had broken before this last onset. Clement made a movement to cover something on his desk, stumbled and made a clutch at the desk and sent a mass of gold coins in a stream to the floor.

Justine started and glanced at them; Aubrey paused for a longer moment and stared at his brother; Mark left the bed as he saw that no harm was done, and stood looking from the floor to the desk. Clement touched the coins with his foot, kicked a cloth towards them and thrust his hands into his pockets.

"How nice you all looked!" said Dudley, who had seen what they all saw. "Just as you did when I was ill."

"And we felt like it for a minute," said Justine, turning from her uncle as she spoke.

Edgar sat down and looked at his son, as if he ought to have some feeling over for him.

"Father looks paler than Uncle," said Mark.

"But anyone can see that I am the one who has been ill," said Dudley.

Maria appeared at the door with Jellamy behind, and Clement had the eyes of the household turned on the secret corner of his life.

"Is Dudley hurt?" said Maria. "Was it Dudley who fell?"

"Yes, it was me. It was a silly thing to do. You will get quite tired of all my disturbances and think less of them. It never does to wear out people's feelings."

"Is that money, Clement?" said Justine.

"If it is not, I will leave you to guess what it is."

"Have you been saving?"

"I have been putting by something to spend on my house. You know that I am going to have one, and that I do not spend what I have."

"Why do you keep it in that form?"

"It is like that at the moment. Or some of it is. I have to have some in hand for various things. And I don't care about having interest up to the last moment."

"Clement is a miser," said Aubrey, who accepted this account and did not know how the words struck other ears.

"Well, are you going to leave me?" said his brother, who was strolling up and down, enabled by the smallness of the space to turn round often and hide his face. "Or are you going to settle in my room? Perhaps you forget that it is mine."

"You can allow Uncle time to recover," said Mark.

"He does not need to do so, as you know."

"And the rest of us to get our breath."

"I admit that I took that away from you," said Clement, with a laugh.

"Clement, that is no good," said Justine. "It is not a pretty thing that we have seen, and you will not make it better by showing us anything else that is ugly."

"I have no wish to show you anything. I don't know why you think so. It is your own idea to pry about in my room. I don't know what you keep in yours." Clement turned to Aubrey, who was touching things on the table. "Stop fingering what is not your own and get out of the room. Or I will throw you out."

"Don't do that," said Dudley. "If anyone else has a fall, I shall not be the centre of all eyes. And if you won't share things with Aubrey, why should I?"

"Is anyone of any use to Uncle? And ought not Maria to be in the drawing-room, giving tea to Aunt Matty?"

> " 'The king is in his counting house, counting out his money;
> The queen is in the parlour, eating bread and honey,' "

quoted Aubrey in the door.

Clement took one step to the door and kicked it to its latch, indifferent to what he kicked with it. It opened smoothly in a moment.

"Miss Seaton wished to be told if any harm was done, ma'am," said Jellamy.

"None is done in here," said Mark. "I don't know about outside."

"Master Aubrey has knocked his head, sir."

"Oh, I had better go," said Justine.

"We will come with you," said Maria. "Clement did not ask us in here."

Edgar followed his wife, and Dudley got off the bed and strolled to the desk.

"I am glad that you value your money, Clement. I

like you to take care of what I gave you. And it shows how well you behaved when I asked for it back. I can't think of that moment without a sense of discomfort. We all have a little of the feeling at times. To know all is to forgive all, but we can't let people know all, of course. Does it give you a sense of satisfaction to have money in that form?"

"I don't know. Some of it happened to be like that."

"I wish you would tell me. Because, if it does, I will have some of mine in it."

"I suppose some people sent it in that form, and I put it all together. It will not remain so for long."

"Of course I am not asking for your confidence."

"I hope you have not killed Aubrey, Clement," said Mark.

"Justine would have come back and said so if I had. She would think it worthy of mention."

"I should not like Aubrey to die," said Dudley. "I only nearly died, and it would give him the immediate advantage."

"You must come to your room, Uncle," said Mark.

"It was my duty to see you there."

"I am not going there," said Dudley on the landing. "I am going downstairs again. I have lost my desire for rest. I can't be shut away from family life; it offers too much. To think that I have lived it for so long without even suspecting its nature! I have been quite satisfied by it too; I have had no yearning after anything further. Matty is going and the gossip can have its way. It will be a beautiful family talk, mean and worried and full of sorrow and spite and excitement. I cannot be asked to miss it in my weak state. I should only fret."

"You won't find it too much?"

"I feel it will be exactly what I need somehow."

Matty waved her hand to Dudley and continued her way through the hall, as if taking no advantage of his return.

"Now I feel really at ease for the first time," he said as he entered the drawing room. "I do not mind having fled from my home in a jealous rage, now that Clement is a miser. It was a great help when Matty turned her old friend out into the snow, but not quite enough. Now I am really not any worse than other people. Not any more ridiculous; I don't mind if I am worse."

"You know you are better," said Justine, "and so do we. Now, little boy, sit down and keep quiet. You will be all right in an hour."

"You need not change the subject. I really am at ease. I don't need Aubrey to take the thoughts off me. I don't even like him to."

"Clement believed that I had attained his size before I had," said Aubrey, assuming that thoughts were as his uncle did not prefer them.

"Well, are we to talk about it or are we not?" said Justine.

"Of course we are," said Dudley. "You know I have already mentioned it. "I hope you do not think that it would have been fairer to Clement if I had not. If you do, I shall never forgive myself, or you either. But of course you would forgive me anything to-day; and what is the good of that, if there is nothing to forgive?"

"It is fairer to Clement to talk of it openly, reasonably and without exaggeration."

"Justine speaks with decision," said Aubrey.

"It may be better still just to forget it," said Maria. "We came upon it by accident and against his will. And it may not mean so much. We all do some odd things in private."

"Do we?" said Dudley. "I had no idea of it. I never do any. As soon as I did an odd thing, I did it in public. I am so glad that life was not taken from me before I even guessed what it was."

"How much money was there in gold?" said Aubrey.

"Now, little boy, that is not at all on the point."

"If Clement is to have a house, it will take all he has," said Edgar.

"A less simple speech than it sounds," said Justine. "There is the solution, swift, simple and complete."

"Perhaps he will starve behind his doors," said Aubrey, "and put his gold into piles at night."

"Someone deserved to have his head broken," said Edgar.

"He may suffer from reaction and be driven into extravagance," said Dudley. "We shall all mind that much more. It must be difficult for young people to strike the mean."

"The golden mean," murmured Aubrey. "Clement may like to strike that."

"He will have a good many expenses," said Mark. "A housekeeper and other things."

"We already detect signs of extravagance," said Dudley.

His nephew strolled into the room.

"Well, am I to flatter myself that I am your subject? I am glad that you can take me in a light spirit. I was fearing that you could not."

"We were wondering if you could afford to run a house," said Maria.

Clement stopped and looked into her eyes.

"Well, I shall have to be careful. But I think I can manage with the sum I have saved. I am keeping part of it in money for the first expenses. They are always the trouble."

"Do you think of having the house at once?" said his father.

"Well, very soon now. I shall be going to Cambridge to see about it. I have enough put by for the initial outlay."

Clement went to the window and stood looking out, and then pushed it open and disappeared.

"Is it wise for a young man to spend all he has?" said Mark. "Let us now transfer our anxiety."

"So it is over," said Dudley. "Clement is a victim of the rashness of youth. I hope he will not waste his allowance."

"And all our thought and talk about it are over too," said Justine, rising. "We are not saying another word. Come, Aubrey; come, Mark. Come, Maria, if I may say it; we are really following your lead. We know you want us to leave Father and Uncle alone."

Edgar looked at the door as it closed, and spoke at once.

"The boy has hardly had a father."

"No, you have failed in one of the deepest relations of life. And you are faced by one of the results. Because there is more in this than we admit. I am not going to get so little out of it. I am sure people got more out of my running away from home."

"I hope he will go along now. This may be the result of too little to spare all his life. Your help may be a god-send in more than one sense."

"It seems to have been the cause of the trouble. You can't be a miser with no money."

"You can be with very little, when it is scarce."

"I rather liked Clement to be a miser; I felt flattered by it. It was taking what I gave him, so seriously."

"We may be making too much of the matter."

"Maria would not let us make enough. I will not give up the real, sinister fact. Why should I not cling to the truth?"

"Maria will be a help to us with all of them."

"To us! You knew the word that would go straight to my heart. But you ought to be a success as a brother, when as a father you are such a failure. What can you expect but that the tender shoots should warp and grow astray? They had no hand to prune or guide them. I don't believe you even realised that Clement was a shoot. And he was so tender that he warped almost at once. I think you are very fortunate that he was the only one."

"How much has happened in the last fourteen months!"

"Yes. Matty came to live here. I inherited a fortune. I was engaged to Maria. Blanche fell ill and died. You became engaged in my place. You and Maria were married. Matty's father died. Matty drove her old friend out into the snow. I ran away from my home. I am not quite sure of the order of the last three, but they were all on the same night, and it was really hard on Matty that it happened to be snowing. On a mild night she would not have been blamed half so much. I rescued Miss Griffin and took her into my charge. It was hard on us that it happened to be snowing too. I decided to provide for her for her life. It seemed the only thing in view of the climate. At any time it might snow. I was sick almost to death, and was given back to you all. In more than one sense; I must not forget that. Oh, and Clement was gradually becoming a miser all the time. You would have thought he had enough to distract him."

There was a pause.

"Dudley, I can ask you a question, as I know the answer. Maria does not mean to you what she did?"

"No, not even as much as you would like her to. I cannot see her with your eyes. I have returned to the stage of seeing her with my own. I nearly said that to me she would always be second to Blanche, but it would be no good to echo your own mind. And of course to both of us she is only just second to her. But I think that you married her too soon after Blanche died, and that you may never live it down. You can see that I am speaking the truth, that I feel it to be my duty. I know that Blanche had a good husband, but it would never be anyone's duty to say that."

"I was carried away. I had not been much with women. And I think that emotion of one kind—I think it may predispose the mind to others."

"Why do some people say that we are not alike? We seem to be almost the same. But grief for a wife is a better emotion than excitement over money. Your second feelings had a nobler foundation and deserved success. But no wonder there are no secrets between us. I only have one secret left. But it shows me what it was for Clement, when his only secret was exposed."

"Are you going to tell me?"

"Yes, I am, because it is proof that I have lost my feeling for Maria. I have already proposed to someone else."

"What?" said Edgar, the fear in his tone bringing final content to his brother. "You have not had time. You were ill a few days after you left this house."

"Well, I proposed to her a few minutes after. You see that I lost my feeling for Maria very soon. And she refused me. Women do not seem to want me as the companion of their lives."

"Miss Griffin?" said Edgar, with incredulity and perception.

"How affection sharpens your wits! But you should have said: 'I want you, Dudley.'"

"I think—I see that the sun is coming out."

"So we can go out and walk as we have all our lives. The only difference will be that I must lean on your arm. I have had to say it for you. Saying it in your own way does not count. I said it in anyone's way. I am the better of the two."

"I think you might for twenty minutes, for a quarter of an hour."

The pair went out and walked on the path outside the house, and Justine, catching the sight from a window, rose with a cry and ran to fetch her brothers.

MORE ABOUT PENGUINS AND PELICANS

For further information about books available from Penguins please write to Dept EP, Penguin Books Ltd, Harmondsworth, Middlesex UB7 0DA.

In the U.S.A.: For a complete list of books available from Penguins in the United States write to Dept CS, Penguin Books, 625 Madison Avenue, New York, New York 10022.

In Canada: For a complete list of books available from Penguins in Canada write to Penguin Books Canada Ltd, 2801 John Street, Markham, Ontario, L3R 1B4.

In Australia: For a complete list of books available from Penguins in Australia write to the Marketing Department, Penguin Books Australia Ltd, P.O. Box 257, Ringwood, Victoria 3134.

In New Zealand: For a complete list of books available from Penguins in New Zealand write to the Marketing Department, Penguin Books (N.Z.) Ltd, P.O. Box 4019, Auckland 10.

A HOUSE AND ITS HEAD

Ivy Compton-Burnett

In 1935 a reviewer wrote of *A House and its Head*, 'It is as if one's next door neighbour leaned over the garden wall, and remarked, in the same breath and chatty tone, that he had mown the lawn in the morning and thrust his wife's head in the gas-oven after lunch.' Here, through stark dialogue and a finely integrated plot, Ivy Compton-Burnett writes about an upper class Victorian family, piercing the façade of conventionality to reveal the human capacity for evil . . .

'No writer did more to illumine the springs of human cruelty, suffering and bravery' – Angus Wilson

STORY OF THE EYE

Georges Bataille

Widely regarded as the greatest sexual/pornographic novel of this century, *Story of the Eye* was first published in 1928, and in it Bataille explores his own sexual obsessions.

This edition also includes Susan Sontag's essay, 'The Pornographic Imagination', which discusses this and other erotic classics, together with Roland Barthes's essay on *Story of the Eye*.

A LIFE

Italo Svevo

First published in 1893, *Una Vita* and its author remained in obscurity for over thirty years until James Joyce hailed Svevo as a major literary discovery. As in all his works, Svevo is concerned here with the bourgeois soul, and its inability to will or act. His heroes are typically men of business, but with cultural pretentions, and he depicts them in their free time when they are not working. It is less important to Svevo whether they have spare money or not: the important thing is that they always have time to spare. How they lose it, use it or kill it forms his major theme – worked with all the quixotic genius of which he was capable.

ROSAMOND LEHMANN

DUSTY ANSWER

Enormous acclaim, 'hysterically good reviews' and thousands of letters, including ones from Galsworthy and Compton Mackenzie, greeted the publication of this novel.

The *Sunday Times* wrote: 'This is a remarkable book. It is not often that one can say with confidence of a first novel by a young writer that it reveals new possibilities for literature.'

Dusty Answer is Judith Earle's story – her solitary childhood spent dreaming in her enchanted house by the river, her awkward, intense experiences at Cambridge rounded with passion and disillusionment, and her travels abroad with her elegant, sophisticated mother. Above all, the novel is about Judith's consuming relationship with a family of cousins whose inroads into the dreams and preoccupations of her young womanhood make *Dusty Answer* so uniquely and tenderly subtle and true.

THE ECHOING GROVE

In a novel that is as subtle as it is extraordinarily imaginative Rosamond Lehmann explores the human heart. Her story concerns three characters – Rickie Masters, his wife Madeleine and her sister Dinah, and their fatally interrelated lives are unfolded through their eyes and through their experience. In showing us the rivalry which divides the two sisters and the love which unites Rickie to them, Rosamond Lehmann reveals in her beautifully structured novel a deep and sensitive understanding of both the sublimity, and the pain, of personal relationships.

'No English writer has told of the pains of women in love more truly or more movingly than Rosamond Lehmann' – Marghanita Laski

'She uses words with the enjoyment and mastery with which Renoir used paint' – Rebecca West in the *Sunday Times*

ELIZABETH BOWEN

A selection

EVA TROUT

Few writers can match the brilliance of Elizabeth Bowen's prose. And here the formal grace of her style, her flair for mischievous social comedy and the subtlety of her dialogue go into creating one of her most formidable – and moving – heroines.

'Resonant, beautiful and often very funny . . . Eva is triumphantly real, a creation of great imaginative tenderness . . . Elizabeth Bowen is a splendid artist, intelligent, generous and acutely aware, who has been telling her readers for many years that love is a necessity, and that its loss or absence is the greatest tragedy man knows' – Julian Webb in the *Financial Times*

'Rarely have I come across a novel in which sexual frustration (and sexuality) have been so richly and powerfully conveyed' – Roger Baker in *Books and Bookmen*

THE LITTLE GIRLS

In 1914 they had been eleven years old, three little girls at St Agatha's, a day school on the South Coast. Fifty years later, Dinah, beautiful as ever, advertises in the national newspapers to find the other two – Clare, now established with a successful business, and Sheila, a married woman, glossy, chic and correct.

In this brilliantly orchestrated novel, as subtle and compelling as a mystery story, Elizabeth Bowen asks: can friendship be taken up where it left off? What are the revelations – and the dangers – in summoning up childhood?

'There is that recurring shiver of delight . . . for this story is poetic in its awareness, its stimulus, its beauty of writing; and as full of clues, hints and half-revealed secrets as any thriller' – *Scotsman*

King Penguin
A selection

ASH ON A YOUNG MAN'S SLEEVE

Dannie Abse

Sharp, sad and romantic, Dannie Abse's reminiscences weave the private fortunes of a Jewish family in Cardiff into the troubled tapestry of the times. Unemployment, the rise of Hitler and Mussolini, the Spanish Civil War, the fate of the European Jews; all these themes are the more real for being seen through the angry, irreverent eyes of youth.

'Acutely remembered, admirably told . . . a clever, moving evocation' – Angus Wilson in the *Observer*

BLACK LIST, SECTION H

Francis Stuart

In 'an imaginative fiction in which only real people appear', Francis Stuart looms like a Dostoyevskian figure: married to Maud Gonne's daughter, IRA gunrunner and prisoner in the Civil War, living with whores in Paris, farming, roaming Europe and writing novels. Gambler, rebel, mystic, delinquent – in 1940 he arrives in Hitler's Germany to join the black list of the guilty and damned.

'The strangest book of a strange career . . . Stuart is of Rimbaud's damned and illumined company' – Robert Nye

'A preposterous, dissimulating, macho-machiavellian novelist, but he has a rare streak of genius' – Alan Ross in the *London Magazine*

BIRTHSTONE

D. M. Thomas

Specially revised for this King Penguin edition, this novel explores the magical effects of the birthstone Men-an-Tol on three people – Jo, Hector and Lola – as they settle into a holiday cottage on the Cornish coast. With his characteristic brilliance and wit, the author of *The White Hotel* gives us 'fantasy as Freud envisaged it, powerful enough to counter reality, working like free association and allowing the unconscious to take over' – *London Review of Books*

FALLING IN PLACE

Ann Beattie

It's a hot, sullen summer on America's East Coast. As John and Louise Knapp bicker at their weekend marriage; as twelve-year-old Parker makes another trip to the shrink in New York; as Cynthia the English teacher clings to her freaky lover Spangle – Ann Beattie invades Updike and Cheever territory to give us a cinematic, brilliantly comic view of America's affluent hell.

'Wonderfully funny' – *The Times*

MOTHER'S HELPER

Maureen Freely

The Pyle-Carpenter household comes complete with three children who can do what they like as long as they have Thought It Through, an intercom that never turns off, with Weekly Family Councils and with the television padlocked into a bag. Like Kay Carpenter herself, it was a totally liberated, principled, caring, warm, nurturing nucleus . . . And at first, Laura was completely fooled.

'A novel to weep over or laugh with. Whichever will stop you going mad' – *Literary Review*

THE FATE OF MARY ROSE

Caroline Blackwood

Raped and horribly murdered, the body of ten-year-old Maureen Sutton is eventually discovered in woods near a sleepy commuter village in Kent. With nerve, inspiration and deadpan brilliance Caroline Blackwood draws us into the village to witness the macabre and devastating effects of this story on a local family: the historian Rowan Anderson, his wife Cressida and their sickly daughter, Mary Rose.

'A winner . . . guaranteed to disturb' – Victoria Glendinning in the *Sunday Times*